She tilted her head,

over the edge of her jaw. A spark of...exactly

couldn't guess, gleamed in his dark eyes. One side of his lips quirked into the little smirk she'd come to recognize. She knew he intended it to be ugly, but it still jolted her heart off-kilter.

"You bastard!"

"So, the wildcat shows her true face at last," he drawled.

She'd show him wildcat. She opened her mouth to scream.

He jerked her forward, crushing her breasts against his chest. Shock raced through her and sucked away her breath. She tried to pull back, only to have him swoop in and plant his mouth on hers.

Her intent—thoughts of screaming, escape, hurting him—all shattered into sparkling fragments and scattered on the wind. The entire universe suddenly narrowed to one focus: his lips grinding against hers.

At first, he just held her like that, in a bruising crush meant to smother her cries. Then it changed. His mouth opened over hers, hungry and commanding. She felt the knotted tension in his body, the rapid-fire bursts of his breath against her cheek.

She had wished for this.

What people are saying about Devon Matthews...

"Angel in the Rain by Devon Matthews has a tortured, hunky hero and a feisty heroine with combustible chemistry. This is one book you won't want to miss!" ~ Paty Jager, author

Angel In The Rain

by

Devon Matthews

To Susi,

My friend, I hope you enjoy. Best wishes + happy reading.

All my love + many hugs!

Devon Matthews

Angel In The Rain

Contact Information: info@thewildrosepress.com

Cover Art by *RJMorris*

The Wild Rose Press
PO Box 706
Adams Basin, NY 14410-0706
Visit us at www.thewildrosepress.com

Publishing History
First Cactus Rose Edition, March 2007
ISBN 1-60154-045-0

Published in the United States of America

Dedication

For Darrell. You're my hero, every day of my life.

Chapter One

West Texas—Spring, 1880

The moment she stepped from the stagecoach, cold chills skittered over Evangeline's skin. She saw nothing out of the ordinary. Nothing that should have made her uneasy in the least. So, why did she feel as though someone had just stepped on her grave?

The Agave Flats relay station looked much the same as a dozen others she'd seen since leaving the train three days ago—a crude blend of rough-hewn wood and adobe, flanked by knotty-poled corrals, standing in the middle of an empty landscape.

"Thirty minutes, ma'am, if you want to stretch your legs," the stage driver called.

She forced an answering smile. If she "stretched her legs" much more, she wouldn't be able to fit them inside the coach. With each interminable stop, she found it harder to tamp down a growing feeling of unease. She needed to be home.

A station attendant led away the horses, amid a swirl of dust. Evangeline looked down and slapped at the grit clinging to her fine, fawn wool traveling suit. Aunt Nelda would have a conniption if she could see her standing there without gloves or even a parasol to protect her ladylike pallor from the harsh southwestern sun. She heaved a breath and turned her back to the warm, grit-laden wind.

That's when she saw him.

Nerve endings jolted when she spotted the dark figure nearly blending into the shadows of the relay station. The man stood with a shoulder braced against the outside wall, his thumbs hooked on the edge of a low-slung cartridge belt. One booted ankle anchored over the other. His relaxed pose stretched dark trousers taut over a long, muscled thigh. The black hat riding low on his forehead hid all but his chin and sardonically quirked mouth. His very posture exuded arrogance and something more. Something so darkly compelling it bordered sinister.

She knew he was staring at her. Right through her, in fact. Though the hat brim concealed his eyes, his gaze raked her with the impact of a physical touch.

Being stared at by men was nothing new to Evangeline Clayton. A woman traveling alone was a magnet for every roué along the pike, and she'd received her share of suggestive winks and leers during the train ride west.

Somehow, this man's veiled inspection affected her more, probed deeper, as if he knew her very thoughts. She sensed a coiled energy behind his indifference, like a cat poised to pounce. And she had an eerie feeling that she was his prey.

"Miss Clayton?"

The driver's voice tugged at her. With reluctance, she turned her back on the enigmatic stranger.

"Yes?"

"Just wanted to tell you, there's coffee inside, if you want to step in out of the wind while we change the horses."

"Thank you, Mr. Stewart. I just might do that."

Evangeline watched the driver walk away and worried the inside of her bottom lip between her teeth. Tiny tingles continued to chase up and down her back.

Abruptly, the sensation vanished. She turned, knowing she would find the man in the shadows gone.

****

The monotony of the desolate scenery outside the coach window mesmerized Evangeline. Nothing but sand and an occasional wind-mangled scrap of brush or prickly pear, as far as the eye could see.

The stage had departed Fort Worth with a full complement of passengers. But, one by one, they had faded into the Texas landscape at various stops along the route. Now, after three days, only she remained to traverse the barren lands southeast of the *Llano* plateau.

After spending two years living in the city, where the

multi-storied buildings butted up against each other, the solitude seeped into her soul. Going home should have given her a sense of relief. Instead, each passing mile brought more feelings of disquiet.

The tone of her father's letter, summoning her home, had unsettled her. He'd spoken of his affairs like a dying man. The Roy Clayton she knew had never even hinted at his own mortality. He was a doer. A survivor.

Now, evidently, he was in trouble. Only she had no idea where to focus her concern. Stubborn old coot! Why hadn't he confided in her instead of leaving her to wonder and worry during the entire fifteen hundred mile journey?

Evangeline sighed and thrust a manicured nail between her teeth, then immediately withdrew it and clutched her hands together in her lap. She'd been gone from New York scarcely two weeks and bad habits had already begun to surface. Nail chewing, no gloves, and no escort. Had she spent the past two years attending Miss Marvel's Academy for Young Ladies, all for nothing?

She sat up straighter and lifted her chin. No, of course not. She *had* changed, transformed from an unruly, pants-wearing hellion into the woman of refinement her mother had wanted her to be. She'd learned her classroom lessons well, passed all the tests. When she looked in the mirror, she saw a new, polished miss.

So why did she feel like such a faker?

"You may acquire all the polish in the world, but underneath you're still your father's daughter," Aunt Nelda had told her.

In the deepest corner of her heart, Evangeline knew it was true. Two years of constant classes aimed at teaching her ladylike deportment hadn't altered her thinking one whit. She still harbored the same rebellious inclinations. While she now walked in a composed, sedate manner, at times she wished she could lift her skirts and run with wild abandon.

Warring emotions nagged at her. Being alone inside the coach gave her entirely too much time to think.

A hard jerk of the stage tossed Evangeline against the backrest. Blinking, she coughed and batted at the gritty cloud of dust mushrooming from the worn upholstery.

Beyond the open window, the blurry landscape confirmed the dangerous speed the coach traveled. Several more hard jolts forced her to clutch at the edge of the seat.

Tension gripped her stomach. What did the fool driver think he was doing? Had he fallen asleep and dropped the reins?

A muted pop, like a firecracker exploding inside an empty barrel, jerked her attention back to the window. Was that a gunshot?

From nowhere, two men appeared, pistols in hand, riding lathered horses.

Evangeline ducked back against the seat when one of the riders veered toward the coach. His blurred face loomed nearer as he attempted to peer through the window.

Wheeling away, the rider goaded his horse and moved ahead. Above the grinding clatter of wheels and the thunder of galloping hooves, she dimly heard, "Stop this stage!" More gunshots punctuated the order.

As the coach rolled and bounced to a standstill, Evangeline's heart throbbed painfully against her ribs. She knew the stage carried nothing of value, and she was the only passenger. Surely, not even ruffians would risk being shot merely for the contents of her purse. What were they after?

The man she'd seen through the window stepped into view and shoved a still-smoking pistol beneath the waistband of his dirt-slick pants. A shiver crawled along her spine when he turned and started in her direction.

He jerked the door open and held it wide. "Climb on down outta there!"

Up close, the man looked repulsive. His face was smoke-filthy, the pores of his bulbous nose so clogged with hardened grease, it resembled an overripe strawberry bursting with seed. Beyond his sloping shoulder, she saw his partner aiming a pistol at the old stage driver.

"Hurry up! I ain't got all day."

Summoning the shreds of her courage, she squared back her shoulders. "Just tell me what you want."

His fleshy lips curled in a lecherous smirk. "Come on

out here, sweet thing, an' I'll show you."

Evangeline's skin crawled as if a snake had slithered beneath her petticoat. The interior of the coach offered an illusion of security. But if she stepped outside...

Escape seemed impossible. She had to try. Drawing a deep breath, she leaned, as if to follow his order, then launched herself at the door on the opposite side of the coach.

She was wrenching desperately at the door handle when thorny hands clamped around her waist. She screamed, clawing for purchase as he hauled her backward.

Being tossed down like a sack of grain on the hard ground abruptly ended her scream. Through the still-settling dust, she watched his retreating steps as he moved toward the front of the coach.

"Get this damn stage outta here," he ordered the driver. "Go on. Git!" He pulled his pistol once more and aimed it at the hooves of the skittish horses.

Two shots in quick succession jolted Evangeline. Next to her, a big iron-rimmed wheel lurched. The coach rolled forward, picking up speed, taking all her possessions and her only means of flight.

Evangeline struggled to draw breath into her lungs. Through a haze of stark terror, she saw the big man turn and start toward her once more. Her thoughts whirled madly. They hadn't kept the stage horses. They hadn't demanded her purse. They hadn't even bothered to rifle the baggage.

She yelped when the ugly brute reached down and yanked her upright. The big man's partner moved in behind her and wrenched her arms behind her back, until her elbows butted together. Hot daggers of pain burrowed into her shoulder sockets. The agonizing pressure immobilized her. She gritted her teeth to keep from crying out.

"I got her, Jed."

Evangeline tried to recoil when the brute, Jed, crowded close. With a grubby paw, he fingered the tiny buttons closing the front of her fitted jacket. She bit the inside of her lower lip to stop a whimper when he moved up to the collar of lace at her throat and brushed against sensitive skin. The smells of sour sweat and fetid, unwashed bodies wafting from the two men were enough to make her stomach heave.

Using her weight as leverage, she tried to break the man's hold on her arms, but he didn't give an inch. "Take your filthy hands off me! Let me go! Get...off!" She lashed out with the only part of her still unfettered—her tiny sharp-toed boots.

Surprised anger flashed across Jed's face when she struck his shin. He drew back his hand and slapped her.

The blow snapped Evangeline's head aside and instantly stopped her frantic squirming. A sting shot through her left cheek and jaw. Numbness quickly followed. She tasted blood. She opened her eyes wide, willing back hot tears. These bastards would *not* make her cry.

"I'll see you both hang for this!"

The brute grinned. He shoved his face near hers, putting his rank breath directly beneath her flaring nostrils. "I doubt that, little lady. Now, let's see what we got here."

The weasel snickered.

Threats would have no effect on these scavengers. Their minds seemed set on one thing only.

Jed snatched the natty bonnet from her head and crushed it in his fist, taking hairpins and a great deal of roots along with them. Her long, blond tresses fell free, cascading nearly to her waist.

He dropped the ruined hat into the dirt then reached in with both hands and ripped open her jacket. Twenty-six tiny faux pearl buttons popped like a row of shelled kernels from an ear of corn. When he tore at her thin linen shirtwaist, panic poured through Evangeline.

She twisted and kicked out, landing enough blows to back Jed off a couple of steps.

"Enough of this," he growled. "Get her down and hold her."

Her heart faltered a beat. "No!" With the desperation of a trapped animal, she flung herself forward. The man's grasp at her back slipped a bit. She struggled harder.

Moving in close again, Jed gripped her face in his big hand and applied pressure, trying to still her movements.

Instinctively, she opened her mouth and bit.

He howled.

Doggedly, she sank her teeth deeper. The taste of blood sent her stomach into revolt. Though her throat worked convulsively, she ignored the rising nausea and held on.

Still bellowing, Jed grabbed a handful of her hair and jerked his bleeding hand from her clamped jaws. With a growl of rage, he grabbed for her throat and curled cruel talons around her windpipe. A knife, blinding with the sun's reflected brilliance, flashed in front of her eyes.

He leaned in closer and hissed, "I always give back better than I get."

Evangeline's ragged breath caught. She closed her eyes, steeling herself for the worst—the bite of the knife into her flesh. At least this way, death might come quickly. And death seemed preferable to what these animals had in mind.

She waited, the silence of her empty surroundings so complete, she heard her own labored heart pounding in her ears. Just when she thought her lungs would burst, a gunshot shattered the stillness and rolled like thunder across the empty land.

The vise-like pressure at her throat vanished. Blessedly, she released her held breath and sank to the ground as her knees gave out.

The taste of Jed's blood roiled her stomach. Fighting the urge to vomit, she spat on the sand. She scrubbed a sleeve across her lips and left a rusty smear on the fawn-colored wool.

Evangeline had no illusions about her chances of rescue. They were deep in the badlands—the middle of nowhere. Whoever had fired that shot was probably just a late arrival. Scavengers such as these tended to travel in packs. Once he joined them, she feared all three would pick up where the first two had left off.

Fighting faintness, she lifted her head and drew in deep, fortifying breaths. For the moment, it looked as though her tormentors had forgotten her. Both of them stood, as still as statues, squinting toward the southwest.

Following their direction, Evangeline shaded her eyes against the sun's glare. In the distance, the silhouette of a lone horseman rode the wavering heat trails. Rimmed in fire from the sun at his back, he might well have ascended from the pits of hell.

The apprehensive looks on the faces of Jed and his weasel partner told her the newcomer was unexpected. A tide of desperate hope surged through her.

The mysterious horseman rode nearer. With each step of his galloping black horse, Evangeline's heart constricted more.

It was the dark stranger from the relay.

He reined up a short distance away. Everything grew so quiet, she heard saddle leather creak when he shifted. Around his hips, he wore a Peacemaker in a worn holster, secured to his right thigh with slender leather strings.

Above all, his eyes claimed her attention. They were as opaque as twin chunks of coal. Empty, soulless. She'd never seen such dull, lifeless eyes that weren't set above the deadly fangs of a rattler.

Her dread mounted.

He seemed completely unaffected by the scene he'd stumbled across. Only a knot riding the ridge of his jawline betrayed any emotion.

Slowly, he shook his head. "This is a sorry sight."

His voice—low, dulcet, and somehow too calm—sent a tingle slithering down Evangeline's spine. Who was this man?

Still favoring the hand she'd bitten, Jed's fleshy lips curved in an insolent sneer. "What the hell do you want, Rainman?"

Rainman? It sounded like the moniker of some traveling preacher claiming mystical power over the weather.

"I've come for the woman," the stranger replied with the same unnerving calm. "She's mine now, so walk away from her."

"Like hell!" Jed spat. "We found her first. What makes you think you can just waltz in—"

She never saw him move, yet the sun flashed from the nickel-plated barrel of the Colt as it materialized in the stranger's hand.

Jed's mouth clapped shut around the words he'd intended to speak.

The stranger thumbed back the hammer; the ominous clicks of a well-oiled cylinder cut through the silence. He arched one dark, insolent brow. "Now that I have your attention, I advise you to walk away—while you still can."

Jed huffed a noisy breath, then dropped his chin to his chest, as if conceding defeat. Evangeline saw that he still held the wicked Arkansas toothpick in his hand.

The thought had barely registered when the flashing blade rose in a blur of speed. In the same instant, the stranger's gun exploded.

It happened so fast, she barely had time to flinch.

Jed looked down at the crimson ribbon threading the front of his shirt. His eyes rolled upward in their sockets, and he gave one convulsive twitch. Like a tower of cards, his body buckled and he dropped face-first on the ground.

Still with the smoking gun in his hand, the stranger pinned Jed's gaunt companion with a lethal glare. "What about you?"

His Adam's apple lurching, the weasel lifted his hands from his sides in a gesture of surrender and turned toward his horse. As he vaulted into the saddle and kicked the animal into action, he grabbed the reins of Jed's riderless mount. The horses raced over the vacant landscape with a small sandstorm rolling behind them.

The stranger no longer even watched.

The hammer clicked as he released it and slipped his gun back into the holster. Fresh panic jolted through her when she realized his attention now centered on her.

His dead eyes appeared to snap, like a flash of heat lightning, until they fairly blazed. Her faint hope of salvation withered completely under that searing gaze.

Moving the reins over the horse's head, he dismounted with fluid grace and started toward her with the slow, lithe gait of a stalking predator.

Evangeline's erratic pulse leaped. The man exuded danger on every level.

She sprang to her feet. With each step he took, she retreated, keeping a safe distance between them.

She's mine, he'd said... but not if she could help it.

Slowly, Rane approached the woman. After the ordeal she'd just endured, he feared she'd collapse. The last thing he needed was a hysterical female on his hands.

Earlier, at the relay station, he'd thought her a striking beauty. He hadn't expected a vision to step from the stage. If that old driver hadn't called to her, he might have let her get right by him, uncertain of her identity.

Now, as the wind wildly stirred her pale hair about her face, the wary lowering of her lashes too closely resembled seduction. The mounds of ample, creamy breasts swelled at the top of her corset with each heaving breath.

Maldito! She was the devil's own temptation.

When she backed away, her eyes held the frantic look of a cornered animal. He wasn't surprised when she whirled and bolted.

In five running steps, he reached out and snagged the flapping tail of her jacket. Without slowing, the little minx allowed him to pull it right off her back. He flung the thin scrap of wool to the ground and continued chasing her.

He could hear her breathing, harsh and labored, and his own heartbeat pounding in his ears. He aimed for her skirt, ballooning behind her. It was almost in his grasp when she fell.

He was so close, her sudden plunge sent him tripping down after her. He locked his arms to break his fall, saving her from the full crush of his weight. The jolting impact rattled his teeth.

He blinked against the grit and sputtered as the dust settled over them. She lay facedown on the ground beneath him, and she wasn't moving. Had he knocked her unconscious?

Rane levered himself off her and lay on his side. Still, she didn't move.

"*Señorita* Clayton? Can you hear me?"

Nothing.

He laid his hand over the point of her shoulder and rolled her to her back...and she came up fighting.

Hissing like a cornered cat, she lashed at him with fists and legs.

After several attempts, he caught her flailing hands and straddled her hips. Leaning forward, he pinned her wrists against the sand.

She wouldn't give up. With surprising strength, she lunged straight up and tried to buck him off.

The ride she gave him didn't dislodge him, but it *did* have a disconcerting effect. The repeated thrust of her pelvis and the sight of all that luscious exposed flesh sent jolts of arousal straight to his groin.

"Stop it!" he commanded.

She didn't. But she was tiring. He saw the strain on her taut features each time she bore his weight upward.

"*Sangre de Cristo!* If you don't stop that right now..."

Didn't the fool woman realize what she was doing? The mere sight of her would stimulate any red-blooded man. Not to mention what she was doing with the lower half of her body.

If she wouldn't listen to reason...

She thrust, and he parried, meeting her halfway. It was almost his undoing, but the contact got her attention. He saw her startled eyes go even wider. And then she went still beneath him.

Their gazes locked—midnight and blue sky—while awareness crackled between them like static before an August storm.

Her full lips parted, her breath coming even harder now.

His own breath had grown ragged and harsh, but not from the exertion.

A tense moment passed.

"I'm not going to hurt you."

"Prove it," she said. "Get off me."

Chapter Two

The feel of the stranger's body didn't repulse Evangeline. She'd seen him kill Jed without twitching a hair. Contact with him should have left her cold—cold as the death he so easily dealt. But she wasn't repulsed. Far from it. Heat invaded her. He radiated warmth, vitality, and all the places where he touched her tingled with awareness.

He hovered so close his breath fanned her flaming cheeks. His smell enveloped her, leather, dust, sunshine, and a hint of some musky spice. All potently male.

Banked fire from his heavy-lidded, dark eyes bore into her. His thighs pressed each side of her hips. The heat of his body penetrated even her skirts and undergarments.

She drew in a shaky breath and slowly relaxed her fisted fingers, trapped beneath his grip against the sand. Would he go back on his word?

No. He released her and rose so abruptly she flinched. She sat up and stared at him in mute surprise.

The stranger walked toward his horse. For a heart-stopping instant she wondered if he intended to leave her there.

No such luck.

Reaching the horse's side, he pulled a canteen strap from the horn of his saddle. Without sparing her a glance, he uncapped the top and put it to his lips.

Evangeline swallowed hard, suddenly reminded of the cottony dryness clogging her throat. A curious mixture of hatred and longing seeped from her every pore while she watched him drink his fill.

After a moment, he lowered the canteen and swiped the back of his hand beneath his chin. Under a black Stetson, hair as dusky as a moonless night lay over the collar of his shirt. The stark, cruel beauty of his face hinted of something almost exotic—high, chiseled cheekbones and rich sun-bronzed skin. His stance and the proud tilt of his head were those of a man who stepped aside for no one. She had seen his kind before. The dark, predatory looks. A loner. Obviously of mixed blood. No doubt, he would be regarded as something of a pariah among Texas Anglos.

Could he be reasoned with? Or was she dealing with a man who had nothing to lose?

When he started toward her, she stayed put, though her pounding heart belied her outward calm. He hunkered down before her, so close she again picked up his strangely enticing scent. He offered the canteen.

Without hesitation, she took it. A musty smell drifted from the open cap, but the wetness coating her lips and sliding down her parched throat was a taste of Heaven itself.

After a long drink, she sucked in a gasp and lowered the canteen.

He stared at her with a frown knitting the tanned skin between his inky brows. She licked her lips. An open cut stung when her tongue came into contact.

When he reached to examine her injury, she jerked her head aside, avoiding his touch.

For the space of several heartbeats, his hand hovered there, not quite touching her. Then, slowly, he withdrew it.

"From the way you were fighting me a moment ago, I gather you're not hurt too badly."

Holding his gaze steady, she spat on the sand with all the venom she possessed. There! That should show him exactly what she thought of him and his concern.

His eyes narrowed, reminding her of the compelling darkness she'd sensed in him from the first. "Don't drink too much." Reproach rang through the mildly spoken words. He pushed to his feet and started to walk away again.

Evangeline rose on wobbly legs and took a step to follow. She was tired of being tossed about like the object in a keep-away game. "What do you intend to do with me?"

He halted and turned, a small quirk flirting with an

outer corner of his sinfully sensual mouth.

That she would notice such irrelevant details at a time like this completely unnerved her. How could she possibly find anything attractive about the man?

"Are you very sure you want to know, Angel?"

Her stomach clenched so hard, the water she'd just swallowed attempted to slide back up her throat. Not good, not good at all. He'd called her "Angel." Her father had given her that pet name when she was a child. Only those closest to her referred to her so intimately.

Evangeline's heart thudded harder. He'd been listening, she remembered. He'd stood in the shadows of the relay, watching her when the old driver had called to her by name.

He'd also been waiting there for her. What other conclusion could she draw? He knew who she was, even down to her nickname. If she had any gumption at all, she'd walk right up to him and slap his face. But she didn't dare. He'd probably slap her back. Or worse.

Her insides turned a quick somersault. "Yes, I want to know. I hate surprises." And, so far, the day had held nothing but.

"Your father's involved in a range war."

Several seconds elapsed before his words penetrated. Her jaw dropped, and she realized she was gaping at him like an utter fool.

"A range war! With whom?" So, this was the trouble she'd read between the lines of her father's letter.

"Horace Lundy."

"Horace Lundy!" She was beginning to sound like a shrill parrot. She planted her hands on her hips. "My father and Horace Lundy have been neighbors for thirty years. There's never been any trouble between them."

"Until your father put up a fence."

This just kept getting more incredible. "Pa doesn't believe in fences."

"Things change," he said.

"What things? And what does this have to do with me?"

"Horace Lundy's got a bounty on you. By now, every hardcase along the border is out looking."

"A bounty! For me! Why? What does he want with

me?"

"I imagine he plans to use you as leverage."

Her thoughts whirled in confusion. None of it made any sense.

"This is ridiculous," she uttered at last. "I don't believe it. Horace would never do something this despicable. He's known me all my life. Do you really expect me to believe he's got men out hunting for me because of a stupid fence?"

He waved a hand toward the dark, still form lying some distance away. "Someone should have told that to Jed Wiley."

With maddening nonchalance, the stranger turned and started walking again.

Growing fury burned at her temples. Evangeline stared at the man's proud, erect back. "So...what? Are you telling me you intend to deliver me to Lundy and collect the bounty?"

Once more, he paused and stared at the ground a long moment before swinging around to look at her. "Oh, I intend to take you to Lundy, all right. But not for the money."

"If not money, then why?"

His obsidian gaze narrowed as cold resolve hardened across his features. "You're now *my* leverage. Horace Lundy has something that belongs to me. Now, I have something he wants. I intend to make a trade."

****

Evangeline was so exhausted, she could barely hold to the saddle horn.

"Easy, boy."

She blinked as the stranger's voice yanked her to awareness. Her mind had wandered. For how long, she didn't know. Her eyes felt gritty, as if she'd been on the verge of sleep. But that was ridiculous. Under the circumstances, she wouldn't dream of falling asleep. She pulled in a deep breath and immediately regretted it.

At the stranger's insistence, she wore the filthy, salt-ringed hat that had belonged to the dead man, Jed. She hadn't wanted to touch it, much less put it on her head. But he'd left her no choice. Now, the hat was tipped over the side of her face, shielding her against the lowering sun's rays. And the smell...

The other side of her face pressed against something warm, solid, and infinitely more pleasant where masculine scents were concerned. How had she ended up getting comfortable with the stranger's hard-muscled chest? Last she remembered, she'd been sitting sideways on the saddle in front of him, trying to maintain some distance.

A sinewy arm curved around her back, supporting her. She stalled, letting him think she'd fallen asleep while she grappled with self-disgust. The very last things she should be feeling were cozy and protected.

This man threatened to destroy everything she'd worked to accomplish in the past two years. Even if she managed to escape, should anyone in Clayton Station learn she was out here alone with him, her name would be blackened beyond anything time and a finishing school could repair. The gossips would rip her to shreds.

They stopped moving. Too curious to play coy any longer, she pulled away from him and sat up.

Her head reeled when she realized the stranger had brought them to a dead standstill at the very edge of a bluff. A movement of the horse's hooves sent small stones skittering down the incline. She held the saddle horn in a death grip.

A blinding sun hovered just above the faraway horizon. Directly below, nearly hidden amid a tangle of brush and collapsed slipstone, stood the relic of a long-abandoned dwelling. The roof was gone and only four crumbling adobe walls remained.

She wondered if they'd reached their destination, but didn't bother asking. During the ride, her abductor had proven to be a man of few words. In fact, he had been a man of no words at all.

Except for the low keening of the wind in the surrounding cliffs, an eerie stillness sat over the land. Beneath her, the stranger's corded thighs tensed. A movement of his arm brushed her shoulder as he laid the reins against the horse's neck. The signal sent the horse onto a path angling down the face of the cliff.

Tension coiled tighter through Evangeline. As they neared the bottom of the drop, another worry replaced her fear of falling. In the distance, the sun slipped below the horizon by quick degrees. Dread of the approaching night tied her insides into knots.

****

Rane moved through the darkness outside the adobe walls and paused to sling his saddlebags atop the chest-high barrier. Now that he'd finally stopped for the night, exhaustion crept over him. Thoughts of getting to Angel Clayton ahead of the bounty hunters had kept him moving much of the previous night. His eyes burned from lack of sleep, and a dousing with cold water hadn't helped one bit.

The smell of simmering beans teased his nostrils. He'd spent the entire day riding, not even stopping long enough to eat. Hunger gnawed at him.

But as he watched the woman seated near the small fire within the ruins, a different kind of hunger seeped into his blood.

Earlier, against all odds, she'd relaxed against him while they rode. He suspected she'd even drifted off to sleep. The warm, feminine feel of her body still clung to him.

He watched as, pulling in a long breath, she drew her knees up beneath her skirt and wrapped her arms around them. Then she glanced down and tugged at the gaping fabric of her torn shirtwaist. No matter how she rearranged the bodice, a generous portion of cleavage remained exposed above her corset. More than enough to make his mouth water and lure his thoughts down a carnal path.

Firelight shimmered over her tumbled hair, turning it into threads of silver and molten gold. He already knew its softness, so fine it barely registered against the toughened pads of his fingers. The memory did nothing to turn his thoughts from touching her.

A tiny worry frown marred the space between her pale brows. Delicate, finely sculpted. How many women would sell their souls to possess such a face? Her lush lips captured his attention. More temptation. More forbidden fruit.

Angel Clayton.

Her exploits were legend along the river. He'd heard

the stories of the skinny tomboy who rode alongside the rankest cowboys. She'd piled up quite a reputation, until her father took the situation in hand and sent her back east.

She was all grown up now. And underneath her eastern spit and polish lay more heart than most men possessed. He'd seen it earlier in the way she handled herself. But he expected no less. She was the daughter of Roy Clayton, a hard-boiled old cattleman with enough guts to fill a washtub.

Rane marveled at the hand Providence had played in their lives that day. If the timing had been different, if he had happened along just minutes later....

Purple bruises marred the sides of her pale throat. The sight angered him all over again. He felt no remorse about sending that filthy bastard straight to hell. He only wished he'd been given an excuse to dispatch his weasel partner as well.

She thinks you're no different.

The voice of his conscience nagged at him. Kidnapping women wasn't his style. He didn't use others to get what he wanted. But Horace Lundy had no such qualms, and he wanted Angel Clayton. The wheels had already been set in motion. Rane had merely seized an opportunity.

He'd done her a favor. That was one way of looking at it. Left to the mercies of men like Jed, she'd probably end up dead before Lundy ever got the chance to bargain with her father. At least she'd wish she were dead.

If she only knew.

Perhaps she did. If not, he had no plans to reassure her. As long as she remained fearful of him, she wasn't likely to attempt escape. He'd keep her safe, or die trying. But if she knew the thoughts tumbling through his mind each time he looked at her, she'd be fighting tooth and nail to get away from him.

Her pale beauty disturbed him. Challenged everything in him he'd tried so hard to civilize. He liked to think he was above the animal depravity of men like Jed Wiley. But she tempted his baser instincts, and that was one aspect of this venture he hadn't figured on.

Sitting on the ground, soaking up the warmth given

off by a small, nearly smokeless fire, Angel smothered a yawn. A continuous flow of adrenaline had kept her from feeling the punishment dealt her body that day. Until now.

Every sore, aching muscle screamed for rest.

But she couldn't rest, not completely. Not while she still distrusted the stranger's intentions. Not while he stood just on the other side of the wall, watching her every movement.

All her senses were attuned with an edgy awareness of him. Who was this brazen man? The searing intensity of his dark eyes sent curious chills racing up and down her body. The very air around him seemed charged with danger.

I'm not going to hurt you.

Each time she recalled his words, her resolve faltered. She wanted to believe him. This misery would be so much easier to bear if she knew she wasn't in imminent danger every moment. But that would require some measure of trust on her part. Trusting him would be a mistake.

She wanted to ask him more about this range war between her father and Horace Lundy. Range war. The very words tightened her stomach. Were bullets flying at that very moment? If anything happened to her father...

She had to get home!

Again, she tugged at the torn edge of her shirtwaist. Her clothing was ruined, no longer fit to preserve modesty. She felt the stranger's eyes follow the movement, and her heart stuttered.

Deliberately, she lifted her head and looked at him. "Excuse me. Señor Rainman? I have a request, if you're not too busy." She hoped he wasn't too dense to recognize sarcasm.

"That's not my name."

Angel's ears perked up. Did she hear a defensive note in his voice? Had she finally struck a nerve? And here she was beginning to think the man didn't possess any that weren't made of cold steel.

He skirted the crumbling wall, joining her inside the perimeter of the ruins. A deep, pale sickle scar angled through the blue-black shadow on the curve of his chin.

Up close, his eyes—so dark and piercing—unsettled her even more.

She tried to conceal her gut reaction and met his steady gaze head-on. "What did you say?"

"I said, that's not my name."

"Then what should I call you?"

Abruptly, he lowered to one knee on the opposite side of the fire. Even that movement hinted of an inherent grace. After testing the heat with two quick touches of his fingertip against the handle, he pulled the pan of beans from the flames. "Rane," he said. "Call me Rane."

She watched, fascinated despite herself, as his exquisitely curved lips formed an O and blew against his fingertips.

"Rane," she repeated. "Unusual name. And it doesn't sound very..."

"Mexican?" he supplied. An amused glint sparkled in his dark eyes. The flames leaped, illuminating the upward curve of his disturbing lips. "You were expecting something like Juan or José?"

"Not necessarily."

"Ránaldo Rafael de Mantorres," he said, rolling the "R's" to perfection. His smile slowly faded. "That's my given name. But, like you, I've been stuck with a diminutive."

She held silent. He was mocking her for some reason. Or himself. She couldn't figure which. That the man even knew a word like "diminutive" stunned her speechless. She ran it over in her mind. Rane Mantorres. Easy to see where he'd gotten the "Rainman" moniker.

He returned his attention to the pan of beans. "What is this request?"

"Clothes. In case you haven't noticed, mine are ruined."

One inky brow peaked. "I noticed."

Though he commented no further, she read a million meanings into his momentary pause. Self-consciousness added to the heat the fire put in her cheeks. Damn his hide.

She wet her suddenly dry lips. "All I need is the loan of a shirt."

He produced a spoon and stuck it in the pan, then

stood and offered it to her.

Angel shook her head. "I'm not hungry."

She expected an argument. That's not what she got. He sat the pan on the ground and walked to his saddlebags, slung over the top of the wall.

When he turned around, he held a pair of pants and a shirt in his hands. He tossed them to the ground beside her.

"Put those on."

She picked up the shirt and clutched it against her too-exposed bosom. Under his watchful eyes, she stood and took a step toward the outer wall. "I—I'll just step behind the wall and change."

"Take the pants, too," he said.

His edict stopped her dead. She felt as though he'd slammed a fist into her chest. Surely, only crushed ribs could prick her heart so painfully. The man had no idea what he asked her to do. If she put on those pants, the past two years would have been for nothing. She'd be right back where she was. Before New York. Before those torturous sessions at Miss Marvel's Ladies Academy...before her father sent her away for being too unladylike.

At last, she sucked in a deep breath and stiffened her spine. "I don't want to wear the pants."

"There's two hundred miles of rough country between here and Clayton Station. Put on the pants."

Her chin tipped upward a notch. "If I refuse?"

"You'll still wear them. One way or another."

An image popped into her head of him stripping her down to her drawers and forcing the trousers up her legs. She had no doubt he'd do it.

A very unladylike grunt escaped her lips. Treating him to her most quelling glare—to which he seemed immune—she bent and snatched up the pants.

Angel stepped outside the enclosure, behind the concealment of the shoulder-high wall. Frustration ate at her. Separated from the fire, cold air washed over her, raising goosebumps. She chafed her arms and shivered. At this time of year, the temperature dipped drastically after sundown. Something to remember when she enacted her escape. Which, she vowed, would be *soon*.

After thinking about it, it only made sense. When she *did* escape, she would have to move quickly. It would be much easier in men's clothing.

A faint ghost of a smug smile briefly touched her lips. Oh, yes. She would put on the pants—for now.

Sparing them one final look of disgust for good measure, she draped the wrinkled garments—brown trousers and a colorless muslin shirt—over the wall in front of her and started stripping.

The pants fit over her hips like a glove. She knew they would leave little to the imagination, but at least now she could ride astride.

On the other side of the wall, her captor had taken the pan of beans and moved away from the fire. Leisurely, he spooned them into his mouth. Though he didn't look at her directly, she knew he watched her from the corner of his eye.

After a moment, he sat the pan on the ground and added more fuel to the fire. Sticks he'd gathered from the brush just before dark. A hiss and pop accompanied a shower of sparks shooting skyward.

She took a breath and asked the question that had been eating at her all evening. "How did you know I'd be on that stage?"

"You sent your father a message, telling him to expect your arrival."

Evangeline clenched her jaw. If it was the last thing she did, she'd see to it that some loose-lipped telegrapher lost his job.

"How did this feud between my father and Horace get started?"

He tossed the last twig, the one he'd been using as a poker, into the flames and sat there a long moment, as if debating his answer.

"Lundy's cattle were diseased. He ignored it. He just stood by and watched while they dropped. Your father put up the fence to keep Lundy's cattle away from his herd."

"How could Horace find fault with that?"

"He claims the fence kept his cattle from pasturing, that they starved. He wants payment for the entire herd."

"That's ridiculous." She slipped the shirt on. "And this plan to hold me for ransom, or whatever he has in mind. How does he think he'll be able to show his face after this? He'll be done for in this country."

"He's done for anyway." Rane sat back on his heels. "I think he plans to use the money to cut and run. His place is mortgaged to the hilt."

The news that Horace Lundy was strapped financially came as no surprise. He and his wife had always spent money as though they dipped it up from the creek in buckets.

Along the border, the Lundys had been an enigma. When she was a child, Angel viewed them as some kind of displaced royalty. Especially Horace's wife, Francine. The woman had conducted herself like a queen.

Rather than raising cattle, the Lundys held court at the Hacienda. The outrageous house they'd built squarely in the middle of a barren wasteland where only longhorns and rattlers thrived.

The Hacienda, itself, was about the only thing remaining of those glory days. In it had gone the finest furnishings and fixtures money could buy, all freighted in from the East Coast and even as far away as Europe. It was well known that Francine came from Boston's upper crust and refused to live in anything but the style to which she'd always been accustomed.

After Francine's short illness and subsequent death, the guests had stopped coming and the money had ceased to flow. About that time, Horace had started looking at his cattle venture in a more serious light. Naturally, everyone concluded that the Lundy affluence had been funneled in by Francine's family back in Boston. When she died, the remittance was cut off.

Now, Horace had aimed his sights on a new source of revenue—her father. The very idea made her so mad she no longer noticed the cold air against her skin.

Clad in skin-tight pants and a loose shirt, Angel felt she'd taken a step backward in time. Guilt washed over her. She quickly forced it to the back of her mind. This was merely a detour. Once she was home again, she'd slip back into the fashionable dresses and new air of refinement with no problem. She hoped.

Angel walked back and forth along the wall several times, nearly jaunty with the freedom of being uncorseted.

"Finished yet?"

His question intruded like a dash of cold water. He expected her to return to the fire. She hesitated, feeling self-conscious, before stepping away from the concealment of the wall.

He merely watched her in silence with an unreadable expression in his dark gaze while she crossed the short distance and rejoined him.

The flames writhed before Angel's eyes in a hypnotic dance. She smothered another yawn. She was exhausted, yet how could she even think of falling asleep? She ventured a glance at the bleary-eyed man reclining an arm's length away. His eyes appeared closed.

"I never sleep," he said, as if he'd read her thoughts. "Remember that." But his voice had grown gravelly since the last time he'd spoken.

Without moving, he reached out an arm and latched onto the bedroll he'd taken from the horse along with his saddlebags. He pitched it next to her.

Tomorrow, she promised herself. After she rested, she'd tackle the problem of escaping.

Chapter Three

Rane pried open his resistant eyes. Within those first seconds, panic flared inside him. He'd been asleep, *deeply* asleep, and something was wrong.

Though his body felt strangely lethargic, his heart slammed hard and fast, jolting him to full awareness.

His arms were full of clinging woman.

Angel lay twined in his embrace like a well-sated lover. Her ample breasts expanded against his chest with each breath she took. Softness and heat penetrated to his skin right through the layers of their shirts and the silken remnant of the chemise she wore.

One slender knee was drawn up and wedged tightly between his thighs. Pressed against his trouser buttons, her hands moved with her restless sleep as she tried to burrow deeper into his warmth.

He sucked in a long, shuddering breath and released it into the chill darkness. ¡*Mierda*! Her fumbling had turned him hard as stone.

How had she ended up in his arms? And why had her first touch not alerted him?

He lay still, reluctant to move. If he shifted, she might awaken or turn away. And he didn't want that. Not just yet.

Damn fool, whispered a weak voice of reason.

Her blond head lay cradled against his shoulder, so close her tangled strands of hair nearly brushed his nose. A subtle, flowery smell still lingered. The purely female scent wafted through his senses like wisps of smoke. A siren call. He filled his lungs with her and wet his lips. If he pressed his mouth to her pale flesh, would she taste as sweet?

He glanced down and homed in on the lushness of her mouth. If he moved his arm, her head would tilt just so and bring her lips in line with his. So tempting.

He squeezed his eyes closed. Without the distraction of sight, his other senses heightened, making him acutely aware of every square inch where her body melded with his. Each breath she took trailed warm, moist fingers of sensation along his throat. He swallowed as a shiver raced over his skin.

Her breathing broke with a soft catch, and she murmured in her sleep. Had she felt his heart's wild rhythm?

He held his breath. She would move now, or wake up.

Instead, she snuggled closer and pillowed her face against the hollow of his throat. Her hands delved deeper between them, exerting even more pressure against his straining fly. He gritted his teeth and clenched his stomach until it neared pain to keep from flexing to her touch.

His own hands twitched with the instinctive need to move and stroke the supple curves pressed against him like an invitation. He ached to arch against her. To surrender himself to the stroking she was giving him through his pants. *¡Maldito!* He burned with lust for a woman who wasn't even aware of what she did.

He knew he played with fire. One so hot and consuming it threatened to burn to cinders the very heart of his resolve. His only salvation was to put some distance between them, the sooner the better.

Rane held his breath as, inch by inch, he lifted her head from his shoulder. Still, she didn't awaken. He pulled the blanket higher and eased away.

Parted from her warmth, he shivered like a fever victim and sat back, staring at her in the darkness. His good sense told him she had no idea what she had done. But every nerve in his body still screamed with arousal.

Shaken, he rammed fingers back through his hair and expelled a quick breath. What the hell had he gotten himself into?

****

Angel clung to sleep, resisting the nudge against her shoulder. As long as she remained in that misty state between dreams and wakefulness, she could pretend she was still safe and comfortable, still lying in a crisp linen covered bed at her aunt's townhouse in New York.

Although she whimpered in protest, the nudge persisted until she could no longer ignore it.

She opened her eyes to the flicker of low flames casting dancing shadows over Mantorres' face hovering above her. She lay stone still, until he moved away. She sat up, pulling the blanket with her and clutched it tightly around her huddled shoulders.

The moon had already set. The night sky resembled an oversized jeweler's display, rich black velvet sprinkled with glittering diamonds.

Mantorres hunkered near the fire, pouring dark liquid from the pan—the same one he'd used to heat beans—into a battered tin mug.

Coffee. The bracing aroma teased Angel's nose.

He shifted and extended the mug, handle first. "Morning," he said. His voice sounded raspy, telling her he hadn't been awake long himself.

Was he trying to be pleasant?

She looped a finger through the handle and took it from him, but said nothing. She wasn't about to return his "morning" as though they were friendly campers looking forward to the day's adventures. Though he hadn't actually said "*good* morning," it was implied. As far as she was concerned, there was nothing "good" about it. She was still his prisoner, still being taken somewhere she didn't want to go.

Angel held the dented cup and savored the warmth stealing through her chilled fingers. After a moment, she chanced a sip. The grainy brew was bitter, stout enough to float a rock, and dropped straight to the pit of her empty stomach where it churned like black acid.

"We'll be leaving as soon as it's daylight."

"Fine," she said. "The sooner this is over with, the better."

Setting the cup aside, she struggled to her feet. Soreness from the rough treatment she'd suffered the previous day had settled into her muscles. And sleeping in the open, with nothing but a thin blanket between her and the ground hadn't helped matters. She hobbled to the opening in the adobe wall and continued walking toward the concealment of the thick brush beyond. He let her go, and she was relieved not to have to explain her need for privacy.

Nearly an hour later, Angel leaned a hip against a rotting timber that had once framed a doorway in the adobe and watched the sun slide up at the edge of the horizon. Brilliance flooded the desert floor, turning each plant and rock into impossibly long shadow figures reaching across the sand. She lifted a hand and shielded her eyes. Not a cloud in sight.

And neither was her captor.

Minutes earlier, he'd picked up camp and then made himself scarce.

Despite the strange dreams that had plagued her sleep, Angel felt rested, but her relaxed pose was a lie. Nerves raw and taut, her pulse increased with each passing moment.

At the edge of the thicket a short distance away Mantorres' horse stood ready, packed with his bedroll and saddlebags. His rifle scabbard was conspicuously absent. She silently cursed her rotten luck. She would need some type of weapon.

The stallion appeared restive. All power and sleek grace, just like its owner. Could she manage such a fearsome looking animal?

It had been two years since she'd "forked" a horse and rode hellbent for leather over risky terrain. Her hands had since grown soft, and she no longer possessed the athletic, muscled limbs of her youth. Saturday jaunts in Central Park with her companions from the Ladies Academy, mounted on an English sidesaddle and a sedate nag, had left her ill prepared for the task before her.

No matter. She knew she'd probably never have a better chance.

Pulling in a deep breath, she released it quickly and sprinted across the sand. Approaching from the near side, Angel yanked loose the slipknot tied to a branch and flipped the reins back over the horse's head. The big stallion tossed his head, nostrils flaring, and shied away.

"Whoa. Eeeasy, boy," she soothed. Her heartbeat raced to war drum cadence. The horse sidestepped, and she moved with it, grappling for a firm enough grip on the saddle to lift her foot into the stirrup.

Already clammy from exertion, trickles of sweat

broke from behind her ears and the cleft between her breasts. She practically tasted victory. With a white-knuckled grip around the horn, she pulled upward.

From nowhere, Rane's arm banded the front of her waist. She squealed from pure instinct and thrashed out her frustration. He jerked her backward, dislodging her foot from the stirrup, yanking away her wild, desperate hope of escape.

The jarring collision with his solidly muscled chest stopped her mid-scream. She sucked in a gasp. Determined to fight, she gathered strength and swung wildly, flailing at him. "Let go of me! Let...go!"

With one arm still anchored around her waist, he hoisted her off her feet. Her head reeled at the unexpected lift. Off balance, she clutched his arm with both hands and drove her heels backward, striking blindly. His grip around her midsection tightened like a steel cinch.

Too quickly, the strength drained from her limbs, and she began to tire. A sharp ache settled in her legs. Damn his black heart. All he did was stand there and let her wear herself out. At last, near choking on defeat and lack of adequate breath, she went limp against him.

Slowly, he lowered her and loosened his arm, but didn't release her completely.

Angel wheezed for air and locked her trembling knees. Against her back, his chest expanded, his rapid gusts matching her own. Grim satisfaction filled her. She hadn't beaten him, but at least she'd left him winded.

She stared straight ahead, conscious of his arm wedged against the undersides of her heaving breasts. He shifted, and the beard stubble on his face caught against her hair. He'd put his face right next to hers. Without moving, she glimpsed a blurred outline of his bronzed profile from the corner of her eye. She turned her gaze forward once more and tried to calm her breathing. And waited to see what he would do.

His breath raked her cheek and curled like liquid heat against the side of her throat. Helpless to stop it, a shiver started at the back of her neck and quickly crawled down both arms. Beneath her borrowed shirt, her breasts tightened. Mortified, she could only stand there, helpless, while her nipples expanded beneath the thin cotton.

Was he looking down? *Oh, God.* She dared not look to find out. Instead she clenched her teeth and tried to will away her instinctive reaction.

A feathery brush against her jaw sent new tingles slithering down her neck. His moist breath invaded her ear. She squeezed her eyes closed and tensed.

"Where did you think you were going?"

The question was spoken softly, nearly a whisper, but subtle warning underscored each word. He'd used the same tone on Jed and the weasel.

Just before he killed one of them.

Angel opened her eyes and barely dared to breathe. She'd seen him kill. Yet, he'd made no move to harm her. The only time he'd laid hands on her was to stop her from running away. If he meant to hurt her, surely he would have done so before now.

She gasped when he dropped his arm from her waist and spun her to face him. Cool air rushed to the moist, heated places where he'd held her, leaving her chilled.

Suddenly confronted with the dark slits of his eyes, she imagined she saw fiery pinpoints blazing within their depths.

"I said, where did you think you were going?"

"You figure it out," she said.

For an eternal moment, he simply stared at her. Then he huffed a breath, lifted his hand, and let it fall against his thigh with a slap. "There's nothing out there. How far do you think you could get? Alone? Lundy's men would be on you before you went twenty miles. If my horse didn't kill you first."

A thin ribbon of sweat seeped through the dust on his cheek. He lifted an arm and swiped at it with his shirtsleeve. "Don't be stupid. And don't try to steal my horse again."

With that, he stepped past her, heading for the skittish stallion. The missing rifle scabbard was slung behind one shoulder.

Angel watched him go, then ducked her head and released a short, relieved breath. She curled her trembling hands into fists to stop their shaking. Damn it. The man had come at her from nowhere. How did he do that?

Her train of thought ended abruptly when Jed Wiley's smelly hat landed on the sand in front of her. She looked up and found Rane standing beside the horse, waiting.

"Time to ride," he said.

****

The man was relentless. For several hours, he dragged them through territory any sensible person would have avoided. She knew he was keeping off the established trails. They covered way too much of the distance on foot, in her estimation, even though she knew he was sparing the horse their double weight.

For a man who'd ridden nearly two hundred miles to kidnap her, he hadn't planned very well.

Angel's feet ached, her ankles wobbled, and her legs threatened to give out beneath her with each step. Her wretched little boots had been designed for paved city walkways, not the uneven, rock-strewn terrain of the Texas badlands.

In late afternoon, he led them into a dry gully choked by boulders and sapling willows. After nearly an hour of tromping through bogging sand, a shimmering pool appeared around a bend in the wash.

Angel sank to the sand at the water's edge and fought tears of relief and utter exhaustion. They'd made little progress that day, and she knew she'd never make it to their destination. Not at the pace they were going.

Except for the dark sweat rings circling his shirt, Mantorres appeared no worse for wear than he had that morning. While his horse sucked up its fill of water, her kidnapper hunkered beside the beast and drank from his cupped hands.

The rippling water beckoned. She licked her parched lips, then eased into a kneeling position and followed his example. The water didn't taste like the cold sweetness she'd been hoping for, but at least it was wet and there was plenty of it.

After drinking her fill, she sat back on the sand. Weariness pulled at her. She felt herself drift, the surroundings blur, but couldn't seem to keep her eyelids open.

"You just going to sit there?"

Angel's head popped up. Pain ripped through the back of her stiff neck. She'd fallen asleep sitting up.

The shadows had shifted and lengthened across the gully. The horse was nowhere in sight.

Mantorres stood at the water's edge, looking at her with a frown sketched over his forehead. Was he surprised to find her exhausted after walking half the day over rock and sand? What did he expect?

"I refuse to take another step today," she informed him.

His frown faded, only to be replaced by something even more disturbing. The corners of his mouth quirked upward, revealing a brief flash of white teeth.

His smile devastated her far worse than his anger and strong-arm tactics.

Angel averted her gaze, flustered by her reaction. He'd simply surprised her. That's all. There was no way she could find anything about the man attractive. He was the antithesis of everything she found admirable.

Liar, the wind seemed to whisper.

Under normal circumstances, their paths would never have crossed. She could think of no valid reason why she would ever have occasion to even speak to such a man. Nothing good could come of this. It made no difference now if he turned her over to Lundy, or if he didn't. He'd already sealed his fate. He was a dead man, and her father would be his executioner.

The soft melody of *Cielito Lindo* drifted to her ears. She looked up, surprised once more. Scoundrels weren't supposed to whistle pleasant, familiar tunes. Seemingly oblivious, he tugged the shirttail from his trousers. Her eyes widened when he raked the garment up his body, revealing a tight network of corrugated muscle overlaying his flat stomach.

Angel's breath snagged in her throat.

She realized she was already far too familiar with the feel of Rane's body and the woodsy spice scent that clung to his skin. Throughout the day, while she'd sat atop his bedroll wedged behind the cantle of his saddle, her hands had strayed often to his strong back for support. She knew his intense heat, the way his shirt clung when he stretched his arms forward to guide the horse over a particularly rough patch of ground, and the firm, steady feel of his flesh beneath her hands.

Feeling was one thing. Seeing was another.

Higher up his chest, a small patch of crisp looking, coal colored hair dusted the skin beneath his collarbone and the center of his breast. Though small, it tapered and continued in a straight line downward, disappearing beneath the band of his pants. He pulled the shirt over his head and tossed it onto a boulder.

"Wha—what are you doing?" Did her tremulous voice betray her thoughts?

"Taking a bath."

He said the words matter-of-factly. But there was nothing casual about Angel's reaction. The last remnants of exhaustion fell away. Like a rabbit, caught in the path of a marauding longhorn, not knowing which way to run, she tensed. Should she turn away while she still had the chance? She fully expected him to drop his trousers next.

He didn't. Disrobing completely would mean disarming himself. She should've known he wouldn't leave his gunbelt lying on the bank where she could get her hands on it.

What would she have done if he had?

Dropping to his knees at the pool's edge, he leaned forward and slid his arms below the surface. Cupping handfuls, he worked the water beneath his armpits and through his hair.

Supple muscles rippled under smooth skin just a shade shy of burnt sienna. Angel released a long, erratic breath. After squeezing the excess water from his hair, he hung there for several moments and allowed himself to drip. When he stood, he reached for his shirt and turned his back to her while he slipped it over his head.

Just beneath his left shoulder blade, Angel noticed a scar. Her stomach lurched. She'd seen her share of wounds. His was old, white against his tanned skin and long since healed. A bullet hole at the point of entry. He'd been shot in the back.

He turned, as though he sensed where her attention had strayed. His dark gaze pinned her while he worked the shirt back down his torso.

"I'm going to find us something to eat," he said. "Go

ahead and wash, if you want."

He walked away, jabbing his shirt beneath the band of his pants. The horse was nowhere in sight. Had he hidden it from her?

Probably. Her attempted escape that morning had put him more on guard. Grim thought.

She sighed and turned to stare across the shimmering water. Wash, he'd said. Did he expect her to strip, too? She wasn't about to take off her clothes while he lurked somewhere back in the bushes. But she did intend to soak her aching feet. Even if they swelled twice their size, she was determined to remove those torturous boots.

Angel eased her bare feet into the water and groaned with pure pleasure. Just for a moment, she wished she could push away the worrisome thoughts that had nagged at her all day. Thoughts of her father. She wondered if he'd yet received the news of her abduction. Was he, even now, riding eastward to look for her? And what would happen when he found her?

She remembered the disturbing image of the scar on Rane's back and went still. Her breath ran shallow. She had to get away. Her father would expect her to do whatever it took to save herself and try to salvage what was left of her reputation.

Angel sighed once more and leaned forward, wrapping her arms around her bent knees. She wriggled her toes through the silt at the bottom of the pool and watched the rising swirls of mud cover her feet. Leggy insects skittered across the surface of the water. Idly, she wondered if they ever sank.

Gathering the stray hair dangling at each side of her face, she brushed it back, straightened...and froze in horror. She couldn't breathe, couldn't force the scream she wanted to send howling between the walls of the gully.

A trio of Indians stood silently on the other side of the pool, and all three of them stared straight at her.

Chapter Four

Angel sat on the sand, her breath frozen. Her heart slammed against her ribs with telltale jerks.

Fear of the Comanche had been ingrained since her earliest memories. She'd heard all the horror stories, the accounts of gruesome tortures practiced on white captives.

The three half-naked men standing on the opposite side of the pool looked as wild and bloodthirsty as starving wolves. Greasy black paint streaked their dusky-skinned faces. Barechested, they wore only buckskin leggings draped with breechclouts and plain moccasins on their feet.

Angel tried to draw a normal breath, but it wouldn't come. She kept her head ducked, not daring to make eye contact, and watched the savages from under her lashes.

While the other two knelt beside the pool and drank, the third man calmly studied her with his arms crossed over his broad chest. Was he imagining her long, pale hair strung for a trophy on the end of his lance? He seemed unusually tall for an Indian. And his eyes... Even across the distance, she felt his gaze bore into her like pale shards of ice.

Dread intensified with each passing second. Why didn't they race around the pool and attack? Were they playing cat and mouse, letting her fear build? She'd heard they derived pleasure from their victim's cries of terror and pain.

Oh, God!

Where was Mantorres with his lightning Colt?

She opened her mouth to scream for her abductor when the tall Indian uncrossed his arms and lifted his right hand.

It was an odd gesture, almost like a wave. Angel jerked her feet from the water and stood.

What kind of trick was this?

As if on signal, the other Indians stood and all three started around the pool.

Angel's heart sped to a dead gallop, sparking bright pinpoints of light before her eyes. Prepared to run, she turned and slammed into a solid wall of male chest.

Rane's arm slid across her back and anchored her closer, melding her with the front of his body. "Don't be afraid," he said.

Swamped with relief, she sagged against him. Never had a voice sounded so beautiful. Never had another's touch filled her with such a sense of refuge as his did at that moment.

She realized she was trembling, her breath nearly sobbed against his strong shoulder. And her hands had twisted into the bunched fabric at his waist as she clung to him like a terrified child.

"Don't be afraid," he repeated. "Turn around and look."

She felt his arm against her back loosen, felt it fall away. The sudden emptiness sent a cold chill streaking down her spine. She didn't want to turn around, but having one of her worst horrors slipping up behind her was far worse.

She turned and found the Indians almost upon them. Yet Rane's very calmness allayed her initial terror. He stepped past her and continued walking, until he stood face to face with the tall Indian at the side of the pool.

"Wolf."

"*Hermano*," the Indian replied.

Angel's ears perked up. The Indian had just called her captor "brother" with easy familiarity.

"I brought a horse."

Though clipped, the Indian's words were not the guttural English spoken by the "blanket" Indians who crowded the train depots at every stop, selling their wares of blankets, pottery, and beaded jewelry to disembarking passengers.

"Good." Rane nodded. "I was beginning to think I might have to ride double all the way to the border."

Wolf's gaze swept past Rane and raked her from top to bottom, lingering on the snug trousers molded to her legs. "Why would you complain?"

Heat poured into her cheeks. Then, for one brief instant, she found herself looking directly into the Indian's strange blue eyes. And his name was Wolf. How fitting.

Blue eyes, even paler than hers. No wonder his stare had seemed so cold. The unusually tall Indian was a half-breed. The knowledge made him no less fearsome. Up close, she realized the two with him were barely more than youngsters, still in their teens.

"Where's the horse?' Rane asked.

Even to Angel, his voice sounded suddenly tense.

Slowly, Wolf returned his attention to Rane. A coy grin curved one side of his lips. "I left the horse tied with yours. If I had wanted to, I could have slipped in behind you and slit your throat. If I had been one of Lundy's men, you would be dead now."

"How much you willing to bet on that?"

Rane's voice was so low, Angel barely heard him. A long pause followed the challenge, and she sensed undercurrents that chilled her blood. Something outside her understanding passed between the two men. And yet the smile never left Wolf's face and neither of them appeared truly angry.

Wolf crossed his arms over his bare chest and tipped up his chin. "I saw you drop some rabbits back in the brush. You plan on asking us to stay for supper, or not?"

****

At dusk, the two young Indians led the horses near the newly established camp and secured them to a picket line strung through the willows. While Rane skinned the rabbits with a wicked looking knife he pulled from inside the haft of his boot, Wolf scooped a shallow pit into the sand and started a fire.

Angel sat huddled next to a boulder and tried to make herself as inconspicuous as possible. The fire's warmth beckoned, but she dared not go nearer. She wondered how two scrawny jackrabbits would feed five people, until the two nameless youngsters appeared with an armload of blankets and knapsacks filled with provisions. She tried not to think about where they might have gotten them.

Seated on his haunches, Wolf pulled one of the

knapsacks toward him and upended it on the sand. An assortment of cans rolled out, along with a cigar box and a cheesecloth bound parcel that contained three flattened loaves of bread.

Wolf took one of the loaves and pushed to his feet. When Angel realized he was headed toward her, she huddled lower and wrapped her arms around her drawn-up knees.

He stopped directly in front of her and extended the loaf.

Hesitant at first, Angel unclasped a hand and accepted his offering. The yeasty smell made her mouth water. "Thank you," she said lowly.

A flash of white teeth appeared in the half-breed's swarthy face. She glanced up and saw that the friendly expression reached all the way to his unusual eyes. Earlier, he and his companions had bathed in the pool and washed the hellish black streaks from their faces. Except for the dull raven's wing hair reaching below his shoulders, he looked more like a normal human man now. Less threatening. Still, though manners dictated that she give the proper response to his kind gesture, she didn't return his smile.

"You're welcome," he said. He turned and went back to the fire.

Rane spitted the rabbits and positioned them over the low flames. Just the smell of mesquite smoke had Angel's stomach gnawing on itself. She pinched off a bite of bread and thrust it into her mouth. Refusing the beans he'd offered her last night had been a mistake. She was starving.

There was no telling what ordeals lay ahead. She had to keep her strength up. It would be hard to manage an escape with her head reeling from hunger.

She nibbled on the bread. Though the Indians fascinated her, Rane captured her attention more.

He hunkered near the fire and accepted the slender cigar Wolf offered. The leaping flames cast the right side of his sinfully handsome face into sharp relief, turning his chiseled features to gleaming bronze. Damp tendrils of hair as dusky as midnight clung to his skin. Angel realized he was younger than her first impression had led her to believe. Dark stubble nearly disguised the smooth, unlined face of a man doubtless still shy of thirty.

A couple of times he reached up and clawed at the blue-black shadow on his jaw as though it itched something fierce. How would he look clean-shaven?

As though he sensed her attention, he turned and looked directly at her.

For the space of several seconds, his fathomless gaze held her captive far more efficiently than any bindings or threats and triggered an unfurling sensation in the pit of her stomach.

Just as quickly, he turned his attention to the empty canvas knapsack lying on the ground and examined the flap, and the initials sewn into it. "Where did you get these supplies?"

Wolf picked up a burning twig and held it against the end of the cigar thrust between his teeth. He inhaled deeply, then blew a column of smoke skyward into the night. "A patent medicine drummer."

Rane's brows took a pronounced dip. "You stole them?"

His words were loaded with disapproval. Strange that a man, who had no qualms whatsoever about kidnapping a defenseless woman, would object to a few stolen canned goods.

Wolf shrugged. "That drummer had a wagon full and wouldn't miss it if we had taken more. Desperate times, *hermano*." He hooked a thumb toward the two youngsters, who reclined against the pile of blankets. "My cousins ran away to find me. On the reservation, they're not allowed to be Comanche. They wanted to raid on the white eyes *tejanos* before they go back."

"So that's why you were wearing the paint. You were playing war party."

A lopsided grin appeared on Wolf's face. "No one got hurt. We waited until he drank a bottle of his opium remedy and fell asleep."

Rane shook his head. "Still a bad idea."

Wolf sat back once more. "Hey. I got a good horse for you."

"They hang horse thieves. If that drummer picks up your sign, he'll have the army on your trail."

"He won't."

Rane pulled an ember from the fire and lit his cigar. The two men sat in silence for several moments.

Finally, Wolf said, "You're not going to ask for my help, are you." It was more statement than question.

"No," Rane replied. "This is something I have to do alone."

Wolf edged closer. "You're loco. Lundy's bounty boys are out there waiting. Most of them have paired off. They're squatting on every waterhole between here and Clayton Station."

Rane visibly unclenched the knot along his jaw and pulled a long drag from his cigar. "I expected no less."

"Want me to go kill a few for you? Lower the odds? They'll never see it coming."

"No. No killing. Take your cousins back to the reservation before they end up getting into real trouble."

Wolf lowered his head, then lifted it and stared into the darkness. "You're mule-stubborn, Rane. It won't go well if you get yourself killed."

Rane huffed an incredulous laugh. "A little late for concern."

"Maybe. But you've never tried to shoot your way through an entire army of hired guns before."

"And I don't intend to now."

The Indian's expression brightened. "You have a plan?"

Rane's lips curved in a bittersweet smile. "As you said. Desperate times."

Maybe a little too desperate, the cost too high.

Rane had a plan all right. He planned to dangle Angel Clayton under Lundy's nose and force the bastard to give in to his demands. The only problem was in getting to the destination. For that, he had no plan. But he wasn't about to tell Wolf the truth about the hole he'd dug for himself. What he was attempting was probably nothing short of suicide, and he didn't want to drag Wolf into the middle of it.

The moment he'd heard Lundy was spreading the word—reward money for the Clayton girl—he'd seen his chance and dashed off to get ahead of the pack. It was only a stroke of luck that his trail had crossed Wolf's, who agreed to find a spare horse and deliver it at some point along the return route. Unfortunately, Jed Wiley and his skinny partner had blundered onto the woman before him. How, he didn't know, but it never should have happened.

Rane looked beyond the fire to where Angel sat huddled against a boulder, nearly outside the circle of light. She refused to sit any closer. Wolf had made an effort to show her he intended no harm. Yet, she still looked as if she might bolt at any second. Rane knew she was hanging on their every word. Time to end the conversation, before she heard too much.

Tremors racked her shoulders at regular intervals. At least he could remedy that.

"Enough talk," he said. He stubbed his cigar in the sand and stood. He circled the fire and snatched his bedroll from the ground. Taking the thin blanket, he approached the shivering woman.

She didn't look at him, nor did she move when he draped the woolen cover across her upper back and hunkered down in front of her. He tugged the ends together over her drawn-up knees, forming a sheltering cocoon.

"Angel, if you're cold—"

Her head lifted, revealing the blaze of emotion in her blue eyes. Against her pale skin, her darkened pupils made them appear enormous, filled with accusation.

"Let me go," she said.

The note of desperation in her plea chipped at his conscience. "I can't. Even if I wanted to."

"Why not? You've got an extra horse now. Just let me get on it and ride away."

The very thought of her out there, alone... "I don't think you understand."

"Then why don't you explain it to me."

"You need me now, even more than I need you."

Her eyes widened, but then immediately narrowed with suspicion. He waited. Either she would laugh in his face, or begin to nurture the first grains of uncertainty he hoped he'd planted.

A moment passed. "That's ridiculous," she said. He didn't realize that his hands had come to rest against her knees, or that he still held the edges of the blanket, until she jerked it from his grasp. "I don't need you. I can take care of myself."

"Like yesterday? Like you took care of Jed Wiley?"

The unpleasant reminder doused some of the heat from her anger.

"Like it or not," he continued, "I'm the only thing standing between you and Lundy's hired guns. Some of those hombres make Jed look like a saint."

He meant to frighten her, to scare the unholy hell out of her if possible. Anything to make her think twice before trying to run away again. And he didn't even have to lie to accomplish it. He'd told her nothing but the truth.

She stared at him with the firelight behind him dancing in her eyes. He expected more anger. He knew how to deal with that. But he wasn't prepared to see her defenses slip, revealing the yielding, unsure woman within.

In that brief unguarded instant, something tender invaded him. The fragile spark of emotion caught him by surprise. For many years, the forces that drove him had all been tied to basic needs. Hunger, thirst, lust, and most importantly the quest for revenge.

She recovered quickly and firmed her jaw, and then clutched the blanket tighter around her shoulders and shivered.

It was too late to block the fleeting glimpse into her soul. He'd seen it. He wanted to reach for her. Wanted to wrap his arms around her and warm her with his body, assure her he would keep her safe. The urge was so strong, he curled his hands into fists and stood in one abrupt motion.

There was no place in his life for this kind of weakness. Not now. Maybe never again.

"I'm taking a walk," he said for Wolf's benefit.

"Want company?"

"No."

Rane stalked into the darkness, trying hard to ignore Wolf's knowing chuckle. The sound burned against his ears with prickly heat. He was starting to act like a damned fool.

The night opened welcoming arms, cloaking him in

blessed darkness while he battled the opposing forces inside him.

Angel was nothing more to him than a pawn in a very dangerous, complicated game. Still, her mere presence distracted him and lured his senses down paths where he had no business treading. Worst of all, she triggered feelings of guilt that had him starting to wonder if he was doing the right thing.

Part of his problem was that he was beginning to admire her.

She'd been through hell already. Yet not once had she whined or complained. Under the circumstances, she'd borne the entire ordeal with a fair amount of poise and dignity.

She wasn't at all what he had expected.

He'd heard talk about her. Gossip that painted her as a hard-riding, rough talking hellion with the morals of a cat. He shook his head. After spending the past twenty-four hours with her, he saw that the reputation didn't fit the woman. Perhaps the rumors were nothing more than vicious lies.

Then again, why had her father suddenly whisked her out of Texas and sent her to an eastern finishing school at the advanced age of eighteen? Most young women were already married by then. Had it been a drastic effort to try and "clean" her tarnished name?

Rane stopped walking and expelled a long breath.

Not that it mattered. He didn't give a damn if she was a firebrand hiding behind a lady's guise. She'd just spent the past two years learning to be a lady. Evidently, she'd mastered deportment classes and learned to speak with a civil tongue.

****

Angel snuggled deeper inside the uncomfortable bedroll and willed herself to sleep. Her eyes flew open at every pop and crack of the dying embers inside the fire pit. How would she ever fall asleep with three Indians lying just on the other side of camp?

Other night sounds intruded. Crickets in the brush kept up an incessant chirp. Up on the gully rim, a coyote howled low and mournfully.

Most disturbing of all was the sight of Rane seated

alone by the dying fire.

I'm the only thing standing between you and Lundy's hired guns.

Surely, by now, her father had received word of her abduction. If so, he would have men out looking for her as well. She clung to the thought like a lifeline. If they were out there, she could find them. But first, she had to get away from this man who threw her heart into such turmoil.

Get away. Yes, she would escape and go home to her father. He'd be pleased with her now, with her proper speech and pretty finery. At last she'd show him she could be the kind of lady her mother had been...

Angel's thoughts drifted. Drowsiness closed around her with a warm haze, until a draft of cold air hit her back. Something nudged her bottom. Then the cold air was replaced by warmth radiating from a solid male body.

Someone had crawled into bed with her!

She sprang upright and twisted around. In the murky darkness, she made out Rane's face against the thin padding. He lay with one arm curled beneath his head, facing her.

"What do you think you're doing!" Her voice came out shrill, a whispered scream of outrage.

"Going to sleep." He sounded drowsy.

Panic pulled her sleep-dulled senses to sharp focus. Was her gallant abductor beginning to show his true colors?

"You can't sleep here!"

"Why not? You didn't seem bothered by it before."

She blinked several times while her thoughts tumbled with confusion. "What the devil are you talking about?"

"Last night. I woke and found you curled around me like a warm kitten."

"That's a lie!"

His unencumbered shoulder lifted with indifference.

Angel's heart galloped. Last night. Those strange dreams. Dreams of feeling safe and warm, of feeling sensations she'd never before experienced. She had dreamed of being held in Rane's arms and pressing shamelessly against him. Was it possible she hadn't dreamed it at all?

Heat engulfed her. Half a minute passed, but it seemed like an eternity.

"Lie down, Angel. It's cold and you're pulling off the blanket."

She sat there fuming. A real lady would never stand for this kind of treatment. The man was compromising her in the worst way. She tried to summon the courage to flounce up and stomp away in a huff of righteous indignation, like a real lady would.

"Lie down!"

His sleepy growl intruded on her inner struggle. She blew out a breath. If she did get up, the brute would doubtless come after her.

After playing tug-of-war with her conscience for another minute, she finally admitted defeat. Slowly, she lowered to her side and scooted to the very edge of the bedding, facing away from him. She tried hard not to touch him and had to brace with her hand to keep from falling onto her face.

The breath left her body in a surprised rush when his hand slid across her hip. He wrapped his arm around her waist and pulled her against him.

She wedged her hands against his rock-solid arm and shoved. "Let go of me."

"No. We need to get some sleep and that won't happen with you falling out of bed all night." His voice, coming from just behind her ear, had grown husky. "Besides, after what you tried to do this morning, I'm keeping you right next to me."

She remained as rigid as a board beneath his arm. The seconds ticked by with agonizing slowness. She found it impossible to draw a normal breath. His nearness threw her heart into an erratic rhythm.

After several moments, sheer fatigue forced her to relax. He had molded his body to the back of hers. His legs and groin cupped her legs and bottom with more familiarity than she'd ever shared with another human. His heat penetrated her clothing and sent pleasant tingles racing over her limbs. He felt better—oh, so much better—than the flannel-wrapped warming pan Aunt Nelda's maid had slipped beneath her bedcovers on cold

New York nights. Her traitorous instincts urged her to snuggle closer, but she willed herself not to move a muscle.

Strangely, the longer she lay there the more acute her senses grew. She felt his breath, hot and moist in her hair. His heart pounded against her, so hard, as if he'd been running. Between them, trapped heat permeated her clothing until it almost felt as if there was no barrier at all separating her feverish skin from his.

Against her waist, his hand moved and he flattened his hot palm against her quivering stomach. The sensation traveled downward and settled deep, igniting a sweet ache in the intimate spot between her thighs. For a breath-stealing moment, she wondered if—and almost hoped—he would dare to do more.

The quickly expanding ridge of male flesh pressed against one side of her buttocks told her that he was no more immune to this disturbing intimacy than she was.

He was just as aware of her. And just as affected.

Was she losing her mind? Or just all sense of right and wrong? Despite the fact that this man continued to drag her across Texas against her will, or the knowledge that he had marked himself for death, her fascination with him seemed to grow by the hour.

Her initial assessment of him had been dead on. He was dangerous. Not only had he taken away her freedom and all but sabotaged her chances of arriving in Clayton Station with her newfound reputation intact. Now he posed an even more serious threat—to her heart, to her very soul.

And worst of all, if she didn't get away from him before long, God help her, she had a feeling she would soon no longer care.

Chapter Five

The descent into the lower desert basin was like riding into the first level of hell. Barren sand reflected furnace heat. Angel's uneasiness edged up a notch when the scrubby trees disappeared and even the prolific clumps of prickly pear grew scarce.

On the wide, level terrain, Rane pushed the horses to a mile-eating lope. Angel rode a length behind and to his left, dodging the worst of his dust. Anticipation soared as the paint mare beneath her gamely kept pace with his big stallion. Just being in a saddle again—even a stolen one—with her feet planted firmly in the stirrups empowered her. She now had the means to escape. All she needed was an opportunity.

Scanning the faraway horizon, Angel searched for some sign of other riders. Every mile they traveled carried them closer to Clayton Station. And her father. Surely, he had men out looking for her by now.

But other than Rane, she'd seen no living soul since the Indians had departed camp at dawn.

The sun inched toward its zenith and the little mare showed signs of flagging. Rane slowed the pace, and Angel became even more aware of the intense heat beating down from above.

She drooped and swayed in the saddle. The constant jarring settled into her bones. The ache in her legs had long ago faded into numbness. But the excruciating stitch in her side persisted and stabbed into her with each bounce. Those sedate Saturday jaunts in Central Park hadn't kept her saddle-ready. Like any green rider, her bottom ached, and the inner sides of her thighs had chafed against the leather until they felt raw.

Around them, the land slowly changed. Outcrops of multi-hued stratum thrust upward from the desert floor, breaking the monotony. Angel no longer watched the horizon—she could no longer see it.

When the sun had climbed straight overhead, Rane halted his horse in the scant shade at the base of a low bluff.

Angel almost wept with relief. Grimacing, she eased from the saddle. Her knees threatened to buckle when she dropped to the ground. She stood there a moment on wobbly legs, braced against the stinging sensation shooting through her limbs.

"You'll get used to it."

She looked up. Rane watched her from a few feet away.

"Maybe tomorrow it'll be better," he said.

Tomorrow. It was only midday. She doubted he planned to camp here at the base of this bluff. After a short rest, they'd move on, try to make up some of the time they'd lost while walking yesterday. How would she stand more endless hours in the saddle?

"I'm fine," she said, unwilling to admit weakness.

An amused spark appeared in the dark depths of his eyes, just before he turned away.

Angel blew out a breath. A fine layer of ashen dust covered her from head to toe. She uncurled her stiff fingers and looked at her hand. Even without peeling back the edge of the shirtsleeve, she could tell the sun had darkened her exposed skin. A mere two days in the Texas badlands had undone two years of Aunt Nelda's night poultices meant to preserve her creamy, pale complexion.

It's not your fault.

No matter how loudly that inner voice spoke, guilt still dogged her. She'd worked so hard and had gotten within two hundred miles of home, only to have her dream of arriving in Clayton Station dressed to the nines, combed and manicured, of seeing the gleam of pride in her father's eyes snatched away. If her father appeared at that very moment, he'd find her dressed like a man, her hair snarled and sweaty beneath a dead man's filthy hat and her skin quickly turning as brown as a nut. He'd find she hadn't changed much at all in the past two years.

Swallowing her frustration, it went down hard with the grit clogging her throat. She reached for the canteen hanging from her saddle horn and uncapped it. The first mouthful tempted her to swish and spit, but she didn't. Wasting even one drop of precious water in this climate was pure folly.

"How much do you have left?"

"Nearly half," she replied, "and I'm considering pouring it over my head."

"Save it. There's water ahead, but..."

"But what?"

"We may have a hard time getting any of it."

Lundy's bounty boys are squatting on every water hole between here and Clayton Station. Wolf's warning from the previous night echoed through her head. New dread stepped up her heart's rhythm.

Rane uncapped his canteen and put it to his mouth. He tilted his head and swallowed, his Adam's apple sliding beneath the skin of his tanned throat. When he lowered the canteen, his dark gaze came level with hers.

A tiny flutter settled low in her stomach.

White, even teeth scraped across his bottom lip when he turned it inward and caught a stray drop of wetness. She followed the movement. How would it feel to have those wickedly sensual lips kiss her?

Quickly, Angel turned away. Scorching heat, beyond anything the sun had inflicted, burned her cheeks. What was wrong with her? Was she now openly lusting after him?

She had to stop. *Now*. By his own admission, they could soon be riding into trouble. She had to harden her heart. It was the only way she would survive this ordeal unscathed.

Rane Mantorres was a dead man. Either by her father's hand, or one of Lundy's hired killers, he was now marked. She had known it from the beginning.

So why did she find it harder to accept?

****

The climb up the steep rockslide had taxed Angel's muscles until lifting one foot in front of the other turned into pure agony. Now, lying belly-down at the top of a barren ridge, sweat seeped from every pore in her body. She swiped a sleeve over her face and it came away wet. Her breath heaved, hot and dry, making her mouth feel like the only part of her that wasn't clammy. She licked her parched lips and tasted salt.

Nearly a hundred feet below, no farther than a stone toss in the distance, lay a brackish looking pool of water. Tall reeds surrounded the edges, trampled into the mud in places, patches of deep beautiful green against the ochre colored earth.

She squeezed her eyes closed. So close. Yet the pool might as well have been miles away. Between them and the water stood a pair of horses, saddled and outfitted with bedrolls and packs. The riders were nowhere in sight.

Minutes dragged by, stretching Angel's nerves as taut as a fat lady's corset strings. Why didn't the men below show themselves? Rane had warned her to expect more bounty hunters the likes of Jed and the weasel. But until she knew who they were, hope of finding some of her father's men refused to die.

Right next to her, Rane lay stomach-down, braced on his forearms. He removed his hat and put it aside. His cheek nearly brushed against hers when he leaned over and peered through the gap in the rocks where they hid.

From the corner of her eye, she watched him. There was an occasional twitch of his inky lashes while he made a slow, searching sweep of the terrain below. She suspected no stone went unnoticed. Up close, his skin looked smooth and fine textured beneath the blue-black whiskers. Such a handsome face, a near perfect face, except for the telltale white scar that sliced across the bottom of his chin.

She looked away. The earth right under her nose smelled scorched. Mixed in were the scents of sweat and horse, and she knew not all of it belonged to Rane. She'd never felt so dirty and foul smelling in her life. She refocused her attention on the beckoning water below.

An eternity passed. A dull ache began to throb at her temple. Beneath the thin muslin shirt, her back broiled and a crick settled into her neck. She rested her head on the curve of her arm, and found herself looking straight up at Rane's stoic profile.

His dark gaze flickered down at her for a brief instant. Otherwise, he hadn't moved a muscle. How could he hold himself so still? He didn't appear bothered, neither by the heat or the ticklish sweat seeping from his hairline. She watched as one gleaming drop broke free and streaked to the base of his jaw. It hung there for a long, glittering instant before it dropped to his shirtsleeve.

Quick and silent, he pulled away and turned to his back.

Alerted, Angel lifted her head and ventured a peek below. At first, she saw nothing. After a moment, an odd sight snagged her attention. A tan colored hat, the wide-brimmed variety favored by drovers, floated at the water's edge. Seconds later, a man stepped into view from directly beneath them. Walking away from the base of the ridge, he reached down and adjusted the tied-down holster snugged low against his right thigh.

No, not an ordinary cowhand after all. But who was he, and what brought him here?

Pausing beside one of the horses, he yanked at a loose cinch strap. Then he continued to a low-growing clump of prickly pear and stood with his back turned to the ridge.

Seconds later, a yellow stream spattered against one of the flat cactus pads. Despite the distance, Angel heard his low, relieved moan. She looked away quickly.

Rane cradled his Colt in his hand and slowly, methodically turned the cylinder. The metallic clicks sounded loud in the utter stillness. Angel counted five bullets. Then he reached down, pulled a sixth bullet from the cartridge belt around his hips and inserted it into the empty "safety" chamber. After easing the loading gate back into position, he again turned to his stomach. Grim determination now honed his chiseled features.

Her heart drummed harder. What was he planning to do?

Want me to go kill a few for you? They'll never see it coming.

Wolf's offhanded offer from the previous night echoed ominously through her frantic thoughts.

Ambush.

She swiveled toward the opening in the rocks, her hands curling into fists in the dirt beneath her. Below, the man had finished his business and was walking toward the pool. In mid-stride he stopped and cocked his head, listening.

She ducked lower and held her breath.

The man lifted his head and raked back his unruly mane of dirty blond hair with both hands. For several seconds, full sunlight fell across his mule-homely features.

Buck Sweeney.

Angel sucked in a breath. She shoved her hands beneath her, preparing to leap up and reveal herself. An arm snaked across her back and flattened her to the ground. Before she could open her mouth to scream, Rane's hand clamped hard across the lower half of her face.

The next seconds passed in a frenzied blur. She started to reach up and pull his hand from her mouth, only to have him band her arms against her body and jerk her back against his chest. A hard muscled leg came around her, trapping both of hers. No matter how she wiggled and tried to thrash free, he held fast. Pressed back to front, he had her wrapped up like a yearling calf at a branding fire.

Tears of fury and frustration blurred Angel's sight. She wanted to bite him. But the pressure he exerted beneath her chin made it impossible to even open her mouth. She struggled. Her chest heaved. She couldn't draw enough air through her nostrils. The smothering sensation brought her to the very edge of panic. Couldn't he see he was suffocating her!

She stopped fighting and went limp. He didn't relax his crushing hold one inch. *The bastard.*

Long seconds passed. She breathed easier, though he still kept his hand clamped over the lower half of her face.

He removed his arm from around her middle long enough to brush the wild tangle of hair off one side of her face. Then his lips grazed her ear and he whispered, "Don't fight me. Don't make one sound, or you'll regret it."

Angel squeezed her eyes closed. A weighty pressure that neared pain fisted her heart. How foolish she'd been. With sudden clarity, she realized she'd never truly feared him.

Until now.

Beguiling devil. He'd given her hope with his promise

not to hurt her and his decent, calm manner of speaking. He'd lulled her with small comforts. A cup of coffee, a pleasant whistled tune, a much-needed blanket. Even the warmth and protection of his own body. Worst of all, she'd deceived herself with the notion that such a handsome countenance had to house *some* good.

Pretty is as pretty does. Why the worn out adage occurred to her at that precise moment, she didn't know. Nor did she have time to think about it before he moved again and started dragging her away from the top of the ridge.

When they were well below the skyline he stood and pulled her to her feet. The rest of the descent down the rocky grade was a jerky, awkward undertaking. It would have been much easier if he'd taken his hand from her mouth, but he didn't.

By the time they reached level ground, Angel felt lightheaded and bright pinpoints flared before her eyes. When he pulled her back against his chest, she didn't resist and leaned into him for support.

With his hand still pressed over her face, he settled the back of her head against the hollow of his shoulder and again brought his mouth to her ear.

"We're going to talk," he said breathlessly. "You need to hear me out. I will take my hand away if you give me your word you won't scream."

Her eyes narrowed. Was he out of his mind? Sure, she'd give her word. She was even curious to hear what he had to say. But after that, all deals were off.

She inclined her head as far as she could.

The palm pressed hard across her lips slackened, then fell away.

She stepped away and turned to confront him. "What were you planning to do back there? Shoot them like fish in a barrel?"

He shook his head. "No."

"Ha!" she scoffed. "And did you expect me to just sit by and watch?" She flung out her hand. "I know that man."

"How?"

"He's a Flying C hand. He works for my father."

"No. Not anymore. I know Buck Sweeney, too. He's a

drifter, a man who will hire his gun for the price of a meal, or a bottle of cheap whiskey."

She crossed her arms and planted them stubbornly beneath her breasts. "I don't believe you."

He edged closer and cocked one hip, casual-like. But the intensity in his dark eyes as he stared down at her was anything but relaxed. "Believe this," he said. "It's been less than forty eight hours since you were taken from the stage. How long after that do you think your father got the word? Twelve hours? Twenty-four? Are you good at subtraction, Angel? If the wire's down, he still may not know."

His words battered against the iron wall of Angel's certainty.

"Let's assume he does know," he continued. "How soon would he have dispatched a search party? Taking into account the distance, do you think anyone riding from Clayton Station could have reached this waterhole ahead of us?"

Oh, God. What he said made sense. Logical, indisputable sense. Her father couldn't have sent those men at the waterhole. She wavered a moment, wanting to deny, while hope died a slow, whimpering death inside her.

"I don't shoot men in cold blood."

She lifted her head and looked at him, finding a focus for her anger and frustration. "But you *do* shoot them, don't you?"

"They can leave. I'll give them the choice."

A choice. He would give them a choice. Meanwhile, he gave her no choice whatsoever. She shook her head at the irony. She remained his unwilling captive, subject to his whim and command. And just moments ago he'd proven he wouldn't hesitate to manhandle and threaten to keep her under his control.

Well, by God, she wasn't going to stand for it anymore.

Dropping her arms to her sides, she marched toward him. Rage, fiery as the sun overhead, burned to cinders her last shred of caution.

She recognized the calculated, measuring gleam in his eyes. He doubtless expected her to let fly at him with a tongue-lashing.

She had something much more satisfying in mind.

When she was two feet away from him, she halted, clenched her teeth, and swung at his smug face.

Swift as a striking snake, he caught her wrist only inches from his cheek.

His lightning reflex stunned her. She hesitated a heartbeat before she lashed out with her other hand, only to have it captured like the first in his unyielding grip.

She struggled and jerked against his hold, too furious to give in. He held her easily and that angered her even more. Her wrists burned in his relentless grasp by the time she finally settled, breathing hard and seething with pent-up violence that begged for release.

Mere inches separated them. She tilted her head, and his ragged breath cascaded over the edge of her jaw. A spark of...exactly what, she couldn't guess, gleamed in his dark eyes. One side of his lips quirked into the little smirk she'd come to recognize. She knew he intended it to be ugly, but it still jolted her heart off-kilter.

"You bastard!"

"So, the wildcat shows her true face at last," he drawled.

She'd show him wildcat. She opened her mouth to scream.

He jerked her forward, crushing her breasts against his chest. Shock raced through her and sucked away her breath. She tried to pull back, only to have him swoop in and plant his mouth on hers.

Her intent—thoughts of screaming, escape, hurting him—all shattered into sparkling fragments and scattered on the wind. The entire universe suddenly narrowed to one focus: his lips grinding against hers.

At first, he just held her like that, in a bruising crush meant to smother her cries. Then it changed. His mouth opened over hers, hungry and commanding. She felt the knotted tension in his body, the rapid-fire bursts of his breath against her cheek.

She had wished for this.

Only a few times in her life had she been kissed, and never with such unrestrained, savage urgency.

Her fevered blood responded. She opened her mouth

to him, and he swirled inside with a low moan trapped in his throat. Unable to resist, her tongue joined with his in a slow, sinuous dance. Tension gripped her body and sent her straining toward him, seeking his male hardness as though pulled by a magnet.

Her clinging hands smoothed over the corrugated planes of his ribs. She didn't know when or how it happened, but he had released her wrists at some point. His arms were now wrapped around her, one hand spread against the small of her back, holding her so close only the fabric of their clothing separated them.

But, not close enough. The wondrous thrust and glide of his tongue, the slow stroke of his hands, the hard pressure of his thigh crowded between her legs demanded even more. A sweet, achy sensation tightened her breasts and pooled low in her belly.

The newly turned out Miss Evangeline Clayton, lately of New York, where she'd spent two grueling years learning to deport herself like a lady and the proper way to deter a gentleman's unwanted advances was helpless to defend herself against the disreputable gunfighter's scandalous assault on her senses.

Worst of all, she wished he'd never stop.

"Well, now. Ain't this damn cozy!"

The gruff voice intruded like the buzz of an annoying gnat.

For Rane, it must have sounded more like a giant bee. He jerked away from her as if stung and spun around.

The sudden emptiness staggered Angel. Unsteady, she turned.

On the rockslide behind them stood Buck Sweeney, grinning down at them like they were the sweetest sight he'd seen in a while. A few feet away stood another man. Evidently, the owner of the second horse they'd seen over by the waterhole.

Buck took another step down the talus slope. The motion sent sunlight skipping along the barrel of the pistol in his hand. Angel darted a glance at his companion. With sinking dread, she saw that both men had their weapons pointed straight at Rane.

Chapter Six

Angel froze, afraid to move, afraid to even breathe too deeply.

Buck Sweeney held his cocked pistol at waist level and shifted to a hipshot stance. The oily smile on his face beamed confidence. "Make one move toward that Peacemaker, greaser, and you'll be makin' yer peace with the big *jefe* up yonder."

From the corner of her eye, she saw Rane slowly lift his hands and hold them palms outward.

"Just don't get spooked, *gringo*." Rane's accent had grown thicker. He gave the "r" an extra tumble before he rolled the insulting word off his tongue.

Buck flashed a mouthful of teeth as discolored and sturdy as a mule's, the beast Angel had always associated with him. "Afternoon, Miz 'Vangeline." He didn't take his eyes off Rane for an instant.

Angel swallowed and drew in a shaky breath. "What are you doing here, Buck?"

"Why, lookin' for you, naturally." To Rane, he added, "Right handy of you to bring her to us."

"Yeah, you made it almost too easy," Buck's companion said. "The two of you was makin' enough noise over here to wake the dead. Too bad for you, your brains fell in your pecker, boy." The man threw back his head and cackled like a hen that had just dropped an egg.

"Shut up, Arch," Buck ordered.

They intended to kill Rane. The reality exploded in Angel's mind with a blinding, white flash. It churned like sickness in her stomach and nearly buckled her knees. Her heart kicked in so hard she felt the vibration clear to her boots.

She no longer cared who Buck and his partner worked for. Somehow, she had to stop them.

Buck flitted a glance in her direction. "Walk over

there and get his gun," he said, waggling the business end of his six-shooter in Rane's direction. "Bring it here to me."

Angel didn't move. "What do you intend to do with him?"

Buck bridled, as if the question surprised him. "Well, what would you *like* fer me to do?"

"Let him go."

Buck plastered a frown on his unpleasant mug. "That might not be too healthy."

Arch cackled again.

"Shut the hell up!" Buck snapped. He gnashed his big teeth. "I swear to God, Arch, that laugh of yourn would peel the hide off a wooden Injun." He motioned with the pistol once more. "Go on. Get his gun."

Moving with deliberate slowness, Angel turned and stepped directly between Rane and the two pistols aimed at his chest. She doubted Buck and his crony would risk a shot while she stood in the line of fire. After all, she wouldn't be worth much to them dead.

Even so, knowing where their guns now aimed, her back muscles knotted with tension.

The transformation she saw in Rane sent icy shivers racing up and down her spine. The wind played with a sable strand of hair that had fallen across his forehead. The elflock gently lifted, moved, a soft contrast against his features that now looked as though they had been sculpted from cold stone.

The absence of expression in his eyes ran her blood cold. They had gone flat and black, until no spark of warmth or emotion remained. The eyes of a deadly predator. Just as they had looked the first time she'd seen him.

Beneath his bronzed skin, a blue vein pulsed at his temple. She looked closely at his uplifted hands, trying to detect if they trembled, if the angry pounding of his blood set up a vibration.

They were as steady as a dead man's.

He had the ability to mask his anger and control it. She'd never known anyone with such iron discipline. Would it give him the needed edge?

She halted before him, mere inches away. "I don't

know what to do," she whispered. "Tell me what to do."

"What's the holdup?" Buck demanded.

Rane didn't move so much as an eyelash. Looking beyond her shoulder, he kept watching the two men behind her. "Don't touch my gun," he said softly.

"What should I do?"

"Start walking. Walk away from me, but don't get behind me. If this goes badly, take the horses and make a run for it. Ride straight south, you'll find the stage road."

"No more talkin' over there," Buck yelled. "Get his gun and get the hell over here!"

"I have a score to settle first," Angel called over her shoulder.

With that, she reached up and clutched the front of his shirt, wrapping it in her fist until it threatened to rip. Rane dared a fleeting glance at her face and found her blue eyes luminous with unshed tears. She was trembling, frightened, her breath heaving in and out of her chest in quick pants. Then she seemed to draw herself up and said, "Damn you! Don't you dare let them kill you!"

"Go," he ordered.

She released him and stepped aside. Rane listened to the sound of her footsteps, retreating, slow at first, then faster and faster, crunching on the gravelly sand.

"Hey, what the hell! Come back here!" Buck yelled.

Both men watched her, puzzled, and looked like they might run after her at any second. And it was just the distraction Rane had hoped for. He held his breath and waited for their reaction. He was gambling with her life that the bastards wouldn't shoot her. They wanted her for the bounty. But if he was wrong...

He dropped his hands. "Buck!"

Buck turned, bringing his gun in line for the shot. His face twisted, bracing for the repercussion.

Rane snaked the Colt from his holster and fired.

A dark spot appeared on Buck's forehead, snapping his head back. He dropped straight down on the rockslide like a hewn tree.

Arch was backing up the slope, slipping, shooting wild as he went.

A slap against Rane's shoulder nearly spun him off balance. Hot wetness spurted across the left side of his face. He righted quickly and fired a second shot and a third with sixteen inches of flame igniting from the end of his gun barrel.

Arch clapped a hand over his chest and dropped to his knees. He hung there for seconds, reeling, then fell to his side on the rocky slide.

Echoes of gunshots rolled across the land like reverberating thunder. Then, there was silence and all that remained was the acrid stench of burnt powder. Rane had fired three shots, all in a space of five seconds.

"You all right?" He called out the question to Angel without taking his eyes from Arch's prone body.

"Yes."

She was safe. Still on guard, he approached Arch, walking right past Buck without a glance. The man had a bullet hole in his forehead and posed no further threat.

Crouching at Arch's side, he pulled the man's hand from his chest. A plate-sized splotch of blood had bloomed on the front of his shirt. Rane placed his fingers against his throat, feeling for a pulse, and found none.

He stood, resigned, and shoved the Peacemaker down into his holster.

Angel waited in the distance, clutching her arms against her stomach. He motioned her forward and stepped out to meet her halfway. Only then did he allow himself to let down his guard, to feel again.

He ran his tongue across his lower lip and tasted the coppery taint of blood. His blood. White-hot talons dug into his shoulder with each movement. He clamped his teeth, fighting nausea. He'd been shot.

****

Angel knelt in the cool mud at the edge of the waterhole and dipped up handfuls, splashing her feverish face with the blessed wetness. She hung there a moment and stared at her rippled reflection, at the image of a woman who seemed a stranger, and clenched her trembling hands into fists against her thighs.

God, help me. I can't do this.

Behind her, Rane rummaged through the saddle packs slung across the backs of the horses that had belonged to Buck and Arch. Using his right hand, while his left hung useless at his side, he discarded one item after another, as if he searched for something in particular.

"¡Salud!"

Evidently, he'd found it. Angel looked over her shoulder. A whiskey bottle dangled from his hand. He moved away from the horses, found a spot next to a fallen slab of stone and eased to a sitting position on the ground.

Angel sat back, away from the lapping water, and picked up the white petticoat she'd worn on the stage. He'd kept it. For the past two days it had been stuffed inside his saddlebag. She ran her hand over the fine linen, wrinkled now, and remembered the day she'd stepped onto the train platform in New York. An educated society belle. It seemed long ago. Tears welled in her eyes as she gripped the garment between her hands and ripped.

Gunfighter. The epithet repeated, over and over, in her mind. Except for the wound on his body, the events of less than an hour ago—the fact that he'd killed two men—had left no outward mark.

He's used to it. It has no meaning to him.

She still marveled at the feat she'd witnessed on the far side of the ridge. His blurring speed and deadly aim. The daring deeds of quick-draw artists such as Billy the Kid and Wild Bill Hickok had gained popularity in the dime novels back east in recent months. Out of curiosity, she'd read a few of them. The books all made the gunplay sound very noble and romantic. But she'd just seen the harsh reality.

The memory of his caress plagued her. How could the touch of his hands thrill her so when they were capable of ending a life with such dispassion?

"You ready?" he called.

Angel swiped at the tears brimming on her eyelashes and gathered the torn strips of linen in her arms. She stood and turned, and nearly stumbled back into the pool. He had removed his shirt and tossed it over the stone he used as a backrest. Dark blood smeared his chest and oozed bright red from the wound high on his left side.

She swallowed the bile rising in her throat.

His dark, pain-filled eyes bored into her. "You're a strong woman, Angel. Don't go soft on me now."

No, she wouldn't go soft. She was still a long way

from home. And God only knew what she might have to endure before she got there. Shoving aside her instinctive revulsion, she crossed the distance and knelt beside him on the sand.

"I'm ready," she said.

He closed his eyes. An ashen pallor lay like gray dust on his tanned skin. Lifting his hand, he scrubbed away the beads of sweat dotting his forehead. Then, he nodded. "Go ahead."

Angel pulled in a breath, held it, and very slowly lifted her hand and inserted the tip of her index finger between the blackened edges of the bullet hole beneath his collarbone.

He hissed through his teeth.

She stopped.

"Go on," he said.

She pressed deeper, sinking her finger in his pulsing flesh nearly to her knuckle, until she touched the flattened lead fragment that had done the damage.

Rane lifted the bottle of whiskey nested in the sand between his sprawled legs and poured a copious drink down his throat. He swallowed and sucked in a harsh breath. "Can you feel it?"

"Yes."

"Try to move it."

A new rush of sweat erupted on Angel's skin. She closed her eyes for a moment, willing back the returning wave of sickness that rolled through her stomach.

She backed off by scant fractions, until her fingernail scraped lead. Bearing down, she tried to loosen the embedded slug. It didn't budge.

She pulled away from him and sat back on her heels. "I think it's lodged in the bone."

For several beats of silence, he stared into space, his jaw bunching and unclenching. Rivulets of sweat seeped down his naked torso, mixing with the blood that continued to leak from his wound. Her probing had started a fresh flow.

She folded a strip of petticoat and attempted to staunch the bleeding.

He flinched away. "Don't waste good cloth. We're not finished yet."

Dread sped Angel's heart. "What do you mean?"

In answer, he leaned forward, hitched up his trouser leg and slipped his hand inside the haft of his boot. Secreted within, a slender sheath sewn into the leather held the knife she'd seen him use on occasion. He pulled it free and sat back. Deftly, he flipped the knife and caught the flat edge of the blade. He extended the handle to her. "I want you to dig it out."

Angel stared at the lethally honed steel gleaming in the sunlight. She recoiled and shook her head. "No. I won't do it."

"There's no one else," he said evenly.

Then she made the mistake of looking into his eyes. Into the dark, fathomless depths that always threatened to draw her in with promises beyond her understanding.

For one fleeting instant, he allowed her a glimpse of his pain. A sympathetic ache gripped her. He was entrusting her with his life.

With her heart rising like a wild, fluttering bird in her throat, Angel took the knife from his hand. She looked at the blade. It was much too wide. She would have to cut him more to get to the bullet.

"I'm not a doctor, Rane. What if I cut an artery? You'll bleed to death."

"Bleeding to death would be easy compared to what will happen if the slug doesn't come out." He gave her a wan smile. "You may have inherited your mother's beauty, Angel, but I know for a fact you have your father's nerve." He handed her the bottle of whiskey. "Here. Douse the blade and just get it over with."

While she worked, Angel tried not to look at him. Tried not to notice that his hand curled into a white-knuckled fist bearing down on the sand. Tried not to see the corded tendons standing out in his neck or the way his flat stomach caved and jerked each time she applied pressure with the knife. But through it all, he didn't utter a sound.

Fresh blood streamed down his breast. It oozed over the knife blade and dripped from her hands, which had grown slick with it. The raw smell filled her nostrils until she could almost taste it. At last, the flattened lead loosened and slid down the blade on a red tide and dropped to the sand.

Angel withdrew the knife and sat back, breathing hard. Blessedly, all the tension had drained from Rane's body. With a wobbly hand, he lifted the bottle to his lips and took a fortifying swallow. "*Gracias, mi ángel.*"

She padded the wound with linen and bound it as best she could to stop the bleeding. But it was an awkward binding since the bullet had struck midway between his neck and arm, just under the collarbone.

Then she washed him with cool water from the pool, trying to ignore his small moans of pleasure. A glance at the half-empty whiskey bottle confirmed her suspicion that he was a little drunk.

His shirt was ruined, but there was no help for it. It was all they had. She helped him slip his arms into the sleeves and buttoned it for him. As quietly as possible, she sneaked away, into the concealment of the rocks. Away from his sight, she fell to her hands and knees and retched.

****

Rane sat propped in the shade, feeling whiskey-mellow, with his hat tipped low over his forehead. Watching Angel as she stood beside the waterhole, finger-combing her long, silver-blond hair almost made him forget about the dull throb that radiated from shoulder to fingertips with each beat of his heart.

Though her movements were quick and efficient, she looked relaxed. Her brow had smoothed from the constant worry furrow she had worn earlier. She lifted her arms and gathered the hair at the crown of her head, fashioning a braid, stretching the shirt taut against the graceful arch of her back.

Through the dingy muslin, the glaring sunlight behind her clearly defined the size and shape of her breasts. He slowly balled and unclenched his fingers. Pure imagination nestled her silken flesh within his palms. He pulled in a long, deliberate breath and held it, prolonging the muzzy warmth slowly seeping through his veins.

She shifted, and his attention lowered to her slender, curving hips. To her rounded little bottom straining against the seat of the trousers he'd forced her to wear.

He smiled and settled lower against the rock,

shuttering his gaze until her image blurred. In his mind's eye, she turned and looked at him, curving her full lips in a seductive simper. With slow, tantalizing steps, she crossed the space that separated them and straddled his lap with her long legs. Leaning forward, she pressed her palms against the front of his trousers. He held his breath and waited. With deft, practiced fingers she flipped open his first button.

Rane heard himself groan and opened his eyes. Beside the pool, Angel squatted on her heels as she filled a canteen. And she watched him.

"Are you all right?"

¡Mierda! He must have actually groaned aloud. And how did he answer? No, he was not all right. He was in pain. Not only did his shoulder hurt like a sonofabitch, his little fantasy had turned him so hard, he was afraid he would shatter if he moved.

"I'm fine," he croaked.

She went back to filling the canteen.

Arch had been right. He'd let his brains fall down in his pecker.

Earlier, on the other side of the ridge he'd lost focus. Her passionate response to him had ignited something so powerful and all consuming he'd let Buck and Arch walk right up and get the drop on him. Lack of control had never been a problem before. Never. So, why now?

He wanted her, that's why. He wanted her so badly, he was growing accustomed to the perpetual ache in his balls.

And he could have had her, right there on the side of the ridge—if Buck and Arch hadn't intruded. Problem was, the thought of taking her in the heat of anger didn't sit well.

Angel was one hell of a woman. Today, his admiration for her had made the leap up to respect.

He wanted her, with a slow, sizzling burn that had been robbing his sleep at night. But he wanted her willing.

Each time their eyes met or they touched, flames ignited in his groin. He knew the lure of forbidden fruit and figured one hot, sweaty bout of sex would cure what ailed him. But he would never force her.

Keeping her with him against her will was another matter. There was no going back now. He was still her only hope of reaching Clayton Station safe and whole. She was still his best bet for wringing what he wanted out of Lundy. But each time he thought about turning her over to that bastard, his conscience gnawed at him like a starving dog on a marrowy bone.

Too late for regrets. The devil himself had dealt this hand. Rane didn't have the option of tossing in his cards. He had to play it through.

He braced his back against the rock and put his feet under him. A wave of dizziness staggered him back a step. He sat on the rock and waited while the scenery around him, which had turned out of kilter, righted again.

No more whiskey. Dull, sluggish reflexes were the last things he needed. "Time to go," he said.

Angel's head snapped up, surprise on her face. "Now?" She looked at the horizon. "There's not much daylight left."

"This waterhole's not safe."

The furrow was back in her brow. She stood, suddenly tense. The apprehension he saw in her face was more like it. After what happened earlier, maybe she wouldn't be so eager to call out the next time they crossed paths with strangers. Maybe she was beginning to realize he truly was the lesser of two evils.

Angel plundered the dead men's packs, but found little more than starvation rations. A few strips of dried meat, canned tomatoes, and yet another bottle of whiskey.

While she filled canteens, Rane pulled loose cinch straps and bridles. The exertion had fresh sweat popping out on his body. Each jar sent new shocks of pain shooting through his shoulder. Dizziness rolled over him in waves. He set the extra pair of horses free. Besides having water, dried looking clumps of grama grass dotted the area. The horses would survive until someone found them.

Rane only wished he could feel as certain about the fate that awaited him and Angel. By the time he climbed into his own saddle, fighting to stay upright and oriented was all he could manage.

This physical weakness worried him because he knew there were more two-bit guns, like Buck and Arch, out there watching and waiting to make their play to take Angel away from him.

When the next challenge came, would he be ready?

****

The narrow stream running through the center of the gully gleamed like a silver snake in the moonlight. Angel waited while Rane angled his horse down the side of the steep cutbank and attained the level, sandy bottom. Then she followed, trusting the horse to find its way down the crumbling earthen bank. Looping her reins, she slid wearily from the saddle and allowed her horse to amble to the water.

The moon rode high in the sky, casting every rock and cactus into sharp relief. All evening they had ridden due west, toward a line of low-lying hills in the distance.

How far were they from the border? Though they had ridden straight at them all evening, the distant hills didn't appear any closer. The fact that Rane had steered them west, rather than southwest, since leaving the ill-fated waterhole bothered her. She figured he was trying to avoid any chance meetings, but the course he'd set didn't take her any closer to home.

All evening she'd followed behind him, conscious of the droop and sway of his broad shoulders. He sat his saddle like a boneless heap, a drastic change from the masterful rider he'd been earlier that day. Blood loss had weakened him, and she could only imagine how excruciating the jarring ride must have been.

His knees dipped when he touched solid ground. Unsteady, he held onto the saddle.

The clothes on Angel's body still felt damp with sweat. Chill night air sent a shiver trickling over her skin.

"Do we camp here?" she asked.

"Yes. We'll move on in the morning."

His voice sounded weak and breathy. She doubted he would be able to go any farther, not until he rested and healed a bit. Would a few hours sleep be enough?

The brown and white paint horse still sucked up water from the stream. Angel unlashed the saddlebags and bedroll and tossed them onto the sandbank, away from the water. Her arms felt weighted. She wanted nothing more than to stretch out between the thin covers and close her eyes.

"What about the horses?" Under normal circumstances, she would never leave a horse saddled for such a long period. To do so was nothing short of cruel. But these weren't normal circumstances. "Should I pull off the saddles?"

He didn't answer.

Angel turned. The big black stood several yards away and Rane no longer clung to the saddle. A quick glance showed her he wasn't hunkered beside the stream. She skirted the stallion's hindquarters, taking care to stay out of hoof-striking range, until she reached the off side. She nearly stumbled right over Rane's prone body, lying facedown on the sand.

Chapter Seven

Rane lay in the deep shadows nearly beneath the stallion's hoofs. The sight halted Angel so quickly she nearly tripped on her own momentum. For each second he didn't move her pulse accelerated a frantic beat.

The black shifted nervously. She'd always heard a horse would avoid stepping on a fallen rider, but this was no time to test the theory.

Moving quickly, she wrapped her hand around the horse's cheek strap. The big brute tossed his head and tried to shy away from her. "Whoa, boy. Easy. You know me," she crooned.

With a firm grip, she led him to a scrubby bush growing from the side of the gully and secured his reins to a branch.

Hurrying back to Rane, Angel dropped to her knees. He lay so still. Was he unconscious, or was he... Her heart rioted. No, he couldn't be dead.

Breath rasped from his parted lips.

A relieved whimper lodged in her throat. She laid her hand against his back. Heat scalded her palm right through his shirt. Fever. He was burning up with it.

Dread swirled through her mind like a black fog. She wrapped both hands around his uninjured shoulder and turned him to his back.

"Rane. Can you hear me?"

His inky lashes fluttered. He curled in on himself and clutched his arms against his chest. "C-cold." His teeth chattered so that she barely understood him.

Infection. One dire reality conjured others: gangrene, blood poisoning, amputation. Death. She had to help him. But she wasn't sure how to go about it. Bed. Quilts. A hot warming pan. Those were the usual treatments for chills. She and Rane were far from those comforts. Could she make do with what they had?

She left him lying on the damp sand near the water's edge and gathered both their bedrolls. One pad and blanket she spread right against the base of the gully wall. The other she laid aside to cover him. She chose a spot where a thick cluster of creosote bushes grew from the top of the bank and leaned inward, forming a living canopy. It would help keep off the falling dew. She only hoped a snake or some other creature didn't choose the leaning brush as an access down into the ravine.

When she returned to him, Rane still lay with his arms clutched against his chest. She leaned down and placed cool fingers against his feverish cheek.

"Rane. Listen to me. You have to stand."

His lashes flickered again, and she found herself looking into his glazed, moon-silvered eyes. If he saw her, he gave no sign.

"Can you stand up?"

His lids drifted closed again. Still, he didn't respond. Seconds passed, and she started to shake him when he rallied. Dropping his arms from his chest, he levered himself halfway up on his elbows. She slipped her arm across his back and braced him.

Angel's breath labored as she struggled to pull Rane upright. For a man who was always so agile on his feet, he'd suddenly turned into a load of dead weight.

She propped him up with her hands to steady him, then wrapped her arm around his waist and steered him to the waiting pallet.

His chest rose and fell in a faster cadence by the time he lay flat on his back on the bedding. Skimming down his length, Angel's attention caught on the bulky gunbelt strapped around his hips. According to the dime novels, men such as he often "doctored" their weapons by filing the firing mechanism to a hair trigger. If he rolled onto the gun in his sleep, would it discharge?

Why risk it? She knelt beside him and worked loose the knot in the slender leather string tied just above his knee. The heavy buckle lay snug against his trousers, nestled just above the rounded bulge that betrayed his manhood. She reached for it, and his hand clamped over hers with surprising strength.

"No."

Her gaze jumped to his face. Through the narrowed slits of his eyes, he watched her.

"I just want to move it. How can you rest with a gun wedged under your hip?"

"Much better than I could without it."

She sat back on her heels. "Fine. Keep it."

Slowly, his long fingers relaxed and fell away from hers. He looked like he'd fallen asleep. She waited another moment, then pulled the cover to his chin and stood.

While she settled the horses for the night, a plan began to take shape in her mind. Here was the opportunity she'd waited for. All she had to do was get on the mare and ride away.

They must be close to the border. If she continued due west, she'd find the Rio Grande. Once she made it to the river, she felt certain she could elude capture. The many cutbanks and more abundant vegetation would provide cover to hide her. All she had to do was follow the river south, until she reached Clayton Station and home.

It was a sound plan. But each time she glanced at Rane's still form lying beneath the bedroll padding, pressure gathered in a tighter grip around her heart.

How could she leave him? He was defenseless, maybe even dying.

For several long minutes, Angel stood perfectly still beneath the moonlight. She closed her eyes, drawing in deep, cleansing breaths and listened to the horses' soft snuffles, the constant chirp of crickets in the surrounding brush. A few feet away, the whispered rush of the stream. The loneliness of this wild, remote place bore down on her like tangible grief carried in the low moan of the wind.

With purpose, she turned and walked to the saddlebags slung behind the saddle on the stallion's back, speaking softly all the while so the rank creature wouldn't spook. She knew exactly what she was looking for. Lifting the flap on the right hand bag, she dipped inside and pulled out Buck Sweeney's six-shooter.

When she lifted it free, the sheer weight of the weapon dropped her hand to hip level. It had been a long time since she'd held a gun but, like riding, the knowledge had been ingrained during her youth. Her fingers trembled against the cold metal when she opened the loading gate and checked the cylinder. Four bullets and one spent cartridge. It would do.

Rane lay as she'd left him, still shivering beneath the cover. Angel sat on the sand and placed the revolver next to her, prepared to keep a vigil through the long night.

After only a few minutes of inactivity, the chill air penetrated her thin shirt. She wrapped her arms around her drawn-up knees and hugged them to her chest. A fire would have been welcome, but the flames and smoke would serve as a beacon to anyone out there. Better to shiver in the dark.

Once more, she reached over and laid fingertips against Rane's exposed cheek. The fever still raged. He gave off more heat than a pot-bellied stove.

She stared at his dark head and bit her lip. She'd never known anyone like him. Was he brave, or simply too arrogant to believe in his own mortality?

He was a hard man, sometimes deadly. This was the image he cultivated. Still, at times she'd seen glimpses of...what? Softness? No. Goodness? Perhaps. He'd become a mass of contradictions. Brutality and gentleness. Ugliness and beauty. Inconsistencies that threw her into turmoil.

For reasons she didn't fully understand, he'd chosen to stand between her and an army of money-hungry ruffians. He claimed to have his own purpose. But what could possibly be worth such a price?

Finally, giving in to the lure of the man and his heat, Angel lifted the cover and slipped in next to him.

Lying there shivering, he seemed so harmless. She wrapped her arms around him and pulled him closer. Like a child in need of comfort, his dark head came to rest against her chest. He moaned softly and slid his arm across her waist. She snuggled closer, pulled the thin blankets over his shoulder, and tucked them against his back. For several moments, he continued to tremble at regular intervals, chilling from the fever raging through his blood.

After a while, he stilled and Angel knew he'd fallen into a deeper sleep.

His face, completely relaxed and pillowed against her

breast, fascinated her. So perfect and yet so overwhelmingly male. His too-hot breath saturated the front of her shirt, scalding and moist against her skin.

Since Rane had imposed himself on her life, she seemed to grow more sentient with each passing day. Her senses had never been so keen. Had she ever before experienced such stormy and tearing emotions? Had her heart ever beat so wildly?

Impulsively, she pulled her hand from beneath the covers and lifted it to his face. Gently, she raked the hair back from his temple, letting her fingers glide into the silken mass. The tendrils at the nape of his neck felt thicker, coarser. Like the man, a blending of textures that enticed her to explore and savor.

Resting her cheek against his head, she continued to hold him and felt a strange sense of contentment. Of rightness.

Exhaustion pulled her to the blurry edges of sleep, to that place where dreams merge with reality. She saw her father, right down to the worry etched into his weathered face. "Oh, Pa. I did what you wanted. Look at me! I look like Mama now."

Instead of giving her a smile or greeting, he shook his head. "You're still driving me to drink," he said. Then he turned from her, pulling away, farther and farther.

A sob lodged in Angel's throat, choking off her denial. She'd done what he wanted, turned herself into a lady.

Then the dream faded and the gauzy light grew harsh. It glared, nearly blinding, and she completely lost sight of her father. She looked down and saw instead the grit and blood smeared on the manly trousers she wore.

****

Rane floated somewhere between heaven and hell.

Hammers pounded at his temples from the inside. For a moment he thought the pain ripping through him resulted from a belly full of bad whiskey. Had he spent the night drinking and carousing? To further the notion, a female body lay pressed so close not even air penetrated between them. How had they ended up like this? He sure as hell couldn't remember.

Stifling heat drenched him in sweat. By slow degrees, he registered the fact that he was fully dressed, right down to his holstered Colt, and several layers of blankets covered him. He started to move and throw off the suffocating load of wool, until a stab lanced through his shoulder. The pain stopped him dead and sucked away his breath.

For several minutes he lay still, drawing in careful breaths, until the agony eased. He forced his eyes open. A rumble rolled through the empty pit of his stomach. He raked his tongue over his teeth and wished he had a drink to wash the stale dryness from his mouth.

Slowly, awareness leached through his senses. He realized he lay on the ground, not in a bed. The first gray light of morning was seeping into a ravine rather than a bedroom.

Right against him, Angel slept with her tempting little butt spooned to the front of his body. They fit together perfectly. Maybe a little too perfectly. Evidently, he was growing accustomed to sleeping next to her, to having her body cupped so intimately to his.

His arm rested atop the side of her trim waist and curved possessively across her stomach. Wedged beneath her, his hand had gone numb. He tried to move it, then changed his mind.

Her breast overflowed his splayed fingers. He sucked in a ragged breath and held it. Closing his eyes, he tried willing the sensation back into his rogue digits.

Deliberately, he slid his hand upward. The cotton shirt separating her skin from his touch frustrated him. Gently, he savored the firm, yet pliant feel of her flesh through the cloth. His strokes grew bolder as he applied soft friction to her sensitive tip. He was rewarded when her nipple hardened and thrust into the center of his palm.

Instinct, he knew. But her reaction gave him a measure of satisfaction and deepened his breathing.

She stirred slightly, and he stilled. Arching her back, she pressed herself more fully into him and moaned. The soft sound reminded him of a cat's contented purr. He wanted to moan right with her.

No slack remained in the front of his trousers. Her sweet, firm buttocks, his own body, and the heavy gunbelt buckle trapped his expanding bulge on every side. All combined, the exquisite pressure was nearly more than he could bear.

He gritted his teeth.

Lifting his head scant inches, he used his chin to rake aside her heavy braid and expose her pale throat. Even in the gray, muddied light, he could see the steady throb of her pulse. He lowered his lips to the spot and covered her with his mouth.

The heavy rhythm of her heart trembled against the sensitive inner sides of his lips. Her taste filled his mouth. Salt and sweetness. The texture of warm velvet. No trace remained of the floral fragrance she had worn. Nothing but pure female bombarded his senses. The primal male within him reared his head and roared to life. The savage urge to claim her had him strung so tightly, he thought his skin would burst.

Another kittenish moan ended on a sigh. Hot anticipation surged through him like a heady slug of hundred proof liquor.

He lifted his head higher and ventured a peek at her face. Disappointment washed over him. The damned woman was still sound asleep!

Heaving a frustrated breath, he stopped stroking her. Willpower. Where was it when he needed it? Summoning his last shreds, he removed his arm and carefully rolled to his back.

A chill crept over his exposed skin and the white fog of his breath surprised him. Hell, he was burning up. He shoved fingers into the rumpled hair over his forehead and sucked in a long, cold breath.

"¡Sangre de Cristo!" he muttered. "I should have been a priest!"

****

Angel carefully peeled the scrap of linen away from Rane's wound. The skin looked puckered and red, but there was no trace of the infection she'd drained several times during the past two days. The depth of her relief, which made her want to cry and shout at the same time, surprised her.

She sat back on her heels. "Your wound is healing."

"About time," he mumbled.

He'd acted surly all morning and even refused the

meager breakfast of canned tomatoes she'd offered. There was little else left in their packs.

"You might be a little happier about it," she said.

His dark head snapped up. "Happy? The moment we cross the border, then I'll be happy."

So, he planned to take her into Mexico. She tucked the information away. Not that it mattered any longer.

He relaxed against the bedrolls stacked behind his back, lifted the nearly empty bottle of whiskey in his hand and poured a swallow into his mouth. She'd gotten used to the sight of him drinking. He'd nearly worked his way through the second bottle.

Breathing hard, he swiped the back of a hand over the stiff blue-black whiskers on his chin. One thing she regretted. She'd never get the opportunity to see him clean-shaven.

"Anyway," she said, "I'm glad the infection is gone. For a while, I thought you were a goner."

Though his chest continued to rise and fall, she sensed a stillness settle over him. He turned his head and looked directly at her for the first time since she'd sat next to his makeshift bed. Grazing over her lips, his dark gaze narrowed, then lifted to her eyes and locked.

"Would you have cared?"

The low, husky tone of his voice sent a warning hum along her nerve endings. It was a loaded question, or so it seemed to her. How could she answer? *Of course, I would have cared.* Flippant. Off-handed. Nothing more than common human decency, the same as she would feel toward any poor suffering soul.

No, that was a lie. If it had been Jed Wiley lying there burning with fever, she would have ridden away with barely a backward glance. Her feelings for Rane ran far deeper than common kindness. She *did* care. Too much. And each time she found herself thinking about him, her purpose grew hopelessly tangled with other intangible desires.

Especially when she remembered the things she'd already experienced because of him. With him. During idle moments when her mind wandered, she couldn't seem to stop herself from reliving certain events, over and over. Like the passionate kiss they'd shared on the side of the ridge. Lying next to him each night, holding him safe. And other things. Dreams, mostly, of an erotic nature that went beyond anything she'd ever imagined.

Was this his plan? To seduce her to the point of willingness? To prey on her sympathy and basic feminine instincts until she followed him without a fight? Raw heat jolted through her. Well, she'd be damned if she'd give him that satisfaction!

She'd already formed her decision during the night. Clenching her jaw, she shoved to her feet and glared down at him. "Don't flatter yourself," she said with all the coldness she could muster.

Without bothering to wait for his reaction, she snatched up a pair of canteens and stalked to the stream. With each step, she nurtured her anger, fed it. Oh, yes. Anger would make this so much easier. She uncapped the canteens and soused them both beneath the clear water.

"Angel?"

She concentrated on the gurgle of bubbles as the canteens filled and shut out the sound of his voice behind her.

"What are you doing?"

She clamped her lips. No. She wouldn't answer him. She capped the brimming vessels, slung the straps around her shoulder and stood. Without looking at him, she continued along the floor of the ravine.

The paint mare was rested, and she'd made sure both horses had been well fed on the abundant grama grass in the area. She dropped the canteens into the dirt, snatched up a saddle blanket and slung it across the little mare's back.

"Angel!"

She squeezed her eyes closed and refused to turn around. Hefting the saddle in both hands, she lifted it in place and started fastening straps, working as fast as she could. The bridle came last.

Both bedrolls were tucked behind Rane's back. No matter, she'd just have to survive without that small comfort. She wasn't about to walk back there and attempt to take one of them out from under him.

On the ground where the saddle had lain, the gleam of metal winked at her. The revolver she'd taken from his saddlebags their first night in the ravine. She'd almost forgotten that she'd hidden it under the saddle. Now, she had need of the gun again.

She bent down and wrapped her hand around the walnut grip. Boots crunched on the ground behind her. Then, the sound ceased.

Her heart beat so wildly she heard it in the sudden silence. Steeling herself, she straightened and turned.

Rane had walked within ten feet of her and stopped. His dark brows ruched over the bridge of his nose, his expression tacitly questioning. He spread his hands wide and that devilish smirk appeared on his lips. "Was it something I said?"

He dared to mock her! She straightened her spine and lifted her chin. "It's everything you've said, and everything you've done."

He wasn't looking at her face. His attention focused somewhere lower.

Angel glanced down. When she'd turned, she'd lifted the gun in her hand without even realizing. Now, the lethal weapon pointed directly at him. She didn't lower it.

"Where are you going, Angel?"

He spoke softly, as he might to a child who'd accidentally picked up a loaded gun.

"Home," she replied with conviction. "I'm going home, Rane."

His gaze lifted, and the hard as flint expression she had come to recognize settled in his eyes. "I can't let you do that."

Angel tried hard to mask the dread surging through her. "You can't stop me this time."

Again, his dark eyes flickered over the Colt in her hand. "Do you intend to shoot me? If so, it might be easier if you cock the gun."

Was he daring her? Or trying to distract her? Perhaps both. Her pounding heart sped even more and echoed in her ears. Did she dare call his bluff?

Deliberately, she lifted her other trembling hand to the wooden butt to steady it. She moved her thumb over the hammer and slowly levered it back. One click. Two. It seemed a long way, but it only brought the gun to half cock.

Ticklish sweat seeped between her breasts. Her hands felt wet, slippery. She exerted more pressure, hoping, praying her thumb didn't slip off the oily mechanism and let it discharge.

Another sickening double click and the gun was fully cocked.

Call and raise, Rane.

With grim satisfaction, she watched him, gauging his reaction. The maddening smirk was still on his lips. He took a step forward.

Rather than retreat, she lifted the gun higher and locked her elbows. "Stay back or, I swear, I'll shoot."

He shook his head as he dared another step. "No. I don't think you will. If you wanted me dead, I wouldn't be standing here now."

"I started to leave you that first night."

"Then why didn't you?"

Because she was afraid he *would* die. Because she couldn't bear the thought of him lying there, suffering and alone. Because she simply couldn't bring herself to leave him...

"I stayed with you. Took care of you. You owe it to me to let me go."

He canted his head, as if considering her words. "I thought you understood. There are men out there looking for you. Hard men. Men without conscience, who simply take what they want. You're asking me to throw you to the wolves."

"I can make it through."

"No. When we leave here, we go together."

He moved toward her again, another slow, measured step. She whimpered, knowing he wouldn't stop. He would never stop, not until he accomplished what he'd set out to do. Or until he was dead.

Her finger twitched against the trigger. The instinctive reaction frightened her so badly sick panic flooded her stomach. She wanted to drop the gun, but couldn't force herself to release her death grip on the accursed thing.

He stood right in front of her, so close the end of the gun barrel prodded the center of his chest. She stared at the blackened hole and the long-dried blood on his soiled shirt. The thought of inflicting yet another, even more serious, wound on his beautiful body nearly buckled her knees.

"Please," she whispered. Only now she didn't know which she pleaded for, him to let her go, or for him to stop scaring her to death with his own mad disregard for the weapon in her hands.

The hardness still glittered in his eyes. "It's your play, Angel. Either give over, or shoot. I'm not stepping aside."

He meant it. Defeat drained the rigid tension from her body. She suddenly felt like a pure fool, trying to beat him at his own game. Who was she trying to kid?

His hand lifted and wrapped around the gun barrel. She allowed him to pull it from her hands.

"I should turn you over my knee," he said.

That brought her hackles back up. "You might try."

He tilted the gun skyward and levered the hammer down to its normal position in one precise motion. "Never point a gun unless you're willing to pull the trigger."

"Now you're beginning to sound like my father."

"Perhaps you should have listened to him."

"Perhaps in future I shall." She stalked past him and headed back to camp, wondering if she'd made a mistake after all in not pulling the trigger.

Chapter Eight

True to his statement, when they crossed the Rio Grande, Rane's foul mood dissipated. With good reason. Though Mexico differed little from West Texas, Angel knew no one looked for her here.

He had outmaneuvered them all. Lundy's guns for hire. Even any men her father may have dispatched to find her.

After crossing the river, they continued due west for several hours. Then he headed south and paralleled the border, yet stayed well away from it. Several times she spotted a village in the distance, but he avoided even those primitive havens.

He no longer wanted or needed her help. His wound had closed and the debilitating fever that had laid him low had left him along with the infection. Though the injury continued to limit movement in his left arm, the stubborn, relentless man kept to the trail as though nothing at all had happened.

After two days of steady riding, Angel knew they were nearing the end of their journey. Even though the territory was unfamiliar, she felt each mile taking them ever closer to Clayton Station. Evidently, Rane intended to slip in through the back door with no one the wiser.

Her anxiety escalated when he veered west once more and struck a faint trail, long unused and nearly overgrown with seedling *piñon* pine and juniper. The region abounded in prickly pear and thorny clumps of black looking creosote bushes. Yucca and agave choked the rocky hillsides. Brilliant splashes of scarlet Indian paintbrush and vivid yellow mustard bordered the trail. Where was he taking her?

In the distance, hazy mountain peaks hid the lowering sun. The trail led them into a shallow basin where a line of willows marked a stream. Next to the stream, nearly hidden in a small grove of cottonwoods, stood a solitary thatch-roofed adobe. A thin, white column of smoke curled upward from the chimney. When they neared the dwelling, he halted and waited until she rode up beside him.

A gaunt Mexican sat with his head on his knees, sound asleep in the adobe's open doorway.

Rane pinned a critical gaze on the man and dropped quietly to the ground. "Stay put," he ordered.

Angel remained in the saddle while Rane slipped up to the man on cat's feet.

"Benito, *alerta!*"

The man's head popped up from his knees, hitting the door facing in the process. His eyes rounded when he saw Rane standing over him. "Señor Mantorres!" Awkwardly, he propped a crutch under his right arm and scrambled to his feet.

"Where is Carmella?"

Benito's expression went blank.

"I am here, Señor."

Rane turned. Angel shifted on the saddle to follow the movement.

A woman emerged from the willows near the stream, carrying a brimming bucket of water.

Who were these people?

The smile of welcome the woman bestowed on Rane sent burning resentment crawling over Angel's skin. This Carmella was a mature beauty with dark, flashing eyes and glossy raven hair swinging freely about her shoulders. Her scant peasant garb accentuated a stunning figure.

Angel grew uncomfortably conscious of her own wretched state. Constant wind had whipped her hair into a tangled mess, and she was covered in dried horse lather, blood, sweat, and gritty dust. The manly garb she'd worn for the past eight days and nights showed off more than she liked of her figure, but did nothing to enhance her femininity.

The woman stopped walking and lowered her bucket to the ground when Rane neared her. They fell into animated conversation. The occasional word Angel overheard was spoken in Spanish. She gathered more from their body language.

Carmella appeared distressed about the gunshot wound Rane had suffered. From the frequent glances darted in her direction, Angel concluded that she was their main topic.

When the two finally broke apart, Rane headed for the adobe with the water bucket in hand. The woman turned and approached Angel with quick steps.

"Please, come in, Señorita Clayton. I will try to make you comfortable after your long journey."

Comfort. Did it still exist? She dismounted wearily and stood facing the woman over the seat of the saddle. They looked to be very nearly the same height.

The woman smiled at her reassuringly. "I am Carmella Reyes." She gestured toward the little man still standing outside the door. "That is Benito, my husband."

Married. The knowledge filled Angel with a vague sense of relief. "I don't suppose there's any need to introduce myself," she said. "You already know who I am."

"*Sí.*" The woman beamed. "We have been expecting you for days."

Angel dropped her reins to the ground and followed Carmella to the tiny dwelling. The adobe's interior consisted of one long room. Neat, but crude. The floor was hard-packed dirt. A table and two backless benches standing before an open fire pit took up half the space. The other half had been relegated to sleeping quarters and storage. The entire abode was smaller than the parlor in the big, white house on the Flying C where Angel had grown up.

A modest fire blazed on the hearth and a delicious aroma wafted from a big, blackened pot stationed on iron feet within the flames. Angel's mouth watered at the prospect of a real meal.

While Carmella opened a leather trunk stationed at the foot of a bed that was nothing more than a few boards nailed together to form a frame, her husband continued to hover in the doorway. Rane stood before the hearth with one hand braced against the thick mantle and stared into the fire, as though deep in thought.

Angel leaned against the cool earthen wall with nothing but questions parading through her mind. Who were these people? What were they to Rane? More importantly, how did they figure into his plans?

Carmella bustled across the room with her gaily-colored skirts swishing about her legs, her arms laden with a stack of clothing. She deposited the garments on the table and moved on, into the kitchen work area.

Angel's attention snagged on the clothing. A man's brown shirt and a pair of soft buckskin breeches. The wheat colored cloth she saw peeking from between, she suspected, was a pair of drawers. The clothing looked like things that Rane would wear. She certainly couldn't picture Carmella's gaunt husband, whose garments hung on him like loose feed sacks, wearing those breeches.

Carmella returned with a razor and strop and laid them on the table as well. "Benito, why are you still standing there?" She lifted both hands and waved them in a shooing motion. *"¡Vámonos! Atender los caballos!"*

Angel glanced at Benito in time to see his eyes narrow with unmistakable resentment, all aimed at the back of Rane's head. Jealousy or out-and-out hatred? Probably a little of both. A troubling picture began to take shape in her mind.

Rane dropped his hand from the mantle and turned. "I'll help with the horses," he said. He picked up the clothes and razor and followed Benito outside.

Carmella watched them, then turned to Angel, planted her hands at her hips, and expelled a relieved breath. Then, she smiled and seemed to take in Angel's measure with knowing dark eyes. "I would guess that you would very much like a bath. *Sí?*"

"Oh, *sí*," Angel replied without hesitation.

****

Despite having to pull her knees nearly to her chest in order to fit in the wooden tub, warm water and soap felt better than Angel could ever remember them feeling. Her hair was thoroughly clean again and scented with some wonderful homemade wildflower extract Carmella had added to the rinse water.

The atmosphere inside the adobe felt close and warm. Carmella had strung blankets from a rope stretched across the room, dividing the sleeping area from the kitchen to provide some privacy.

Except for her cramped position, if she closed her eyes, Angel could almost imagine she was still in her aunt's New York townhouse, being attended by her maid. While she soaked, Carmella sat on a stool behind her and worked a comb through her tangled hair.

"It's very nice of you to do this," Angel said. "*Gracias.* I appreciate you making me welcome in your home."

Carmella chuckled softly. "Is nothing. It is my job."

Angel winced at a hard tug against her scalp as Carmella applied the comb. "Your job?"

"*Sí*. Señor Rane is my *patrón*. This is his home."

Angel had thought there was nothing more she might learn about him that would surprise her. She'd been wrong.

"I only take care of it for him," Carmella continued. "And sometimes, I take care of him."

Angel didn't much care for the sound of that. What kind of care would a man like Rane require?

The comb slowed. "He does not come here much. It is a sad place for him. But sometimes, he is tired, he needs to rest. So he comes here to be alone."

Carmella's soft voice betrayed a note of melancholy. A sad place, she'd said. Angel took in the surrounding adobe walls, barren, stark and colorless. She looked at the coarse bed and imagined Rane lying upon it, staring up at the darkened rafters, alone and hiding out from the world. Humble lodgings for a man who rode a magnificent stallion and had the bearing of a lord. Yet, he said the money Lundy offered for her capture was not what he sought.

"What is he trying to get from Lundy?" Angel asked.

The comb's movement stopped completely. "This, I cannot say."

"But you do know?"

"*Sí*."

"And you also know what he plans on doing with me?"

"*Sí*."

"Do you think it's right?"

"It is not for me to judge. He is my *patrón*."

"So, you won't help me."

"No. He warned me you would ask."

She should have known Rane's own people weren't likely to help her get away from him. But hearing the words loosed an unexpected rush of anger—at him.

Carmella started in briskly with the comb once more. "You have beautiful hair."

The tugs against her scalp, while gentle enough, betrayed impatience. Angel figured the compliment signaled a change of subject. Perhaps Carmella was fearful of divulging too much. Therefore, Angel was surprised when the woman leaned forward and whispered, "Do not be afraid, Señorita. I know Señor Rane. He will not let anyone harm you."

****

Angel sat on the side of the bed, clean, groomed, and dressed in the clothes Carmella had given her. A deep blue skirt and white camisole blouse with a drawstring closure at the front that left the neckline scooped well below her collarbones. Underneath, she wore a pair of plain cotton drawers and nothing else, which made her feel strangely unfettered, but more exposed than Rane's trousers ever had.

It was the outfit of a Mexican peasant. Judging by the intricate floral embroidery sewn into the front of the blouse, Angel suspected Carmella had given her the best she owned.

She still hadn't eaten and the savory aroma that filled the air from the other side of the room had her clutching her stomach to quiet its rumbling. She knew she should stand up and go join the others at the table. But the hushed conversation taking place just beyond the hanging blankets stopped her.

Though she only caught an occasional word, she heard Lundy's name mentioned. She also heard the words "two days" spoken several times. Was that when Rane planned to make his trade—her for whatever he hoped to get from Lundy? Her heart sank lower. How could he? How could he intend to carry through with his scheme after all they'd been through?

The sounds from the other side of the room changed. Evidently, the discussion had ended. Angel pricked her ears, but heard nothing other than the soft shuffle of footsteps and a dull thump, as if something had been dropped.

Carmella's face appeared between the blankets. She no longer smiled. "Remember what I tell you, Señorita. *Vaya con Dios.*" Then the edge of the blanket fell back into place, and she was gone.

Curiosity brought Angel from her seat on the bed. She walked to the blankets and parted them.

Rane stood alone at the open doorway, looking out with one hip cocked in a relaxed pose. The buckskin breeches hugged his long rider's legs and accentuated the pleasing shape of his tightly muscled buttocks. One arm was lifted above his head, his forearm braced against the door facing. Around him, the day's last rays of light spilled onto the earthen floor and illuminated half the table behind him.

"Where have they gone?"

Leisurely, he lowered his arm and turned. Her breath lodged in her chest. She'd finally gotten her wish. He'd shaved his whiskers. Now, a beguiling stranger faced her.

She stared at him. She couldn't help it. The bewhiskered scoundrel she'd grown accustomed to had disappeared and in his place stood a devastatingly rakish devil. Swept back from his face, his long, freshly washed hair gleamed like wet, black coal. The pale, off-center scar in his chin was evident once more, an intriguing fault in an otherwise flawless countenance. She couldn't take her eyes off him.

His dark gaze narrowed. "Something wrong?"

She didn't know whether to smile at him, or burst out laughing like a lunatic at the absurd joke fate had played on her. "I was just thinking. It's amazing what a little soap and water can accomplish."

"Yes." The word hissed between his perfect, white teeth. "Amazing."

The dark heat in his eyes seemed to scorch her. Now that she was dressed in feminine clothing, his brazen inspection of her person filled her with self-consciousness. She clenched her hands at her sides to keep from crossing her arms over her chest, from turning away, from ordering him to stop looking at her as though he'd never seen her before.

She swallowed the thickness that gathered in her

throat and pulled in a deep breath. "I asked you. Where have Carmella and her husband gone?"

"I sent them on an errand," he replied.

"And would that errand be to deliver a message to Horace Lundy?"

A muscle ticked in his bronzed jaw. "Yes."

She stared at him a long moment with disappointment and anger welling like caustic poison. Deep down, she'd known he wouldn't relent. He'd already proven that. He'd told her what he planned from the very beginning.

"I don't know what it is you hope to gain by all this. I'm sure you won't tell me, any more than Carmella would. I just hope whatever it is, it's worth ruining my life for."

"I haven't ruined your life. I've saved it."

"No. It started out that way, but you've proven you're no different from Jed Wiley. Or Buck Sweeney. You're using me, just the same as they would have."

He shook his head. "Not the same."

"My father won't see it any differently, Rane. To him, you'll be the man who kidnapped his daughter and turned her over to his enemy. It doesn't have to be that way. You could take me to my father instead."

"No, no, *no!*" He glared at her. "Stop talking! Nothing you say will change my mind."

She clamped her lips and glared right back at him. Oh, God, how she wanted to hate him. But, she couldn't, damn it! No matter what he said or did, she couldn't bring herself to hate him.

Strangely enough, during all the time they'd been together, she'd never seen him come so close to losing his temper and raising his voice as he had now.

He must have realized it, too, for he dragged in a long breath and released it slowly. In his usual calm tone, he said, "Sit down and eat."

She didn't move.

"Sit!" he ordered.

Moving as slowly as possible, Angel pulled out a bench and seated herself at the table.

Rane crossed the room in four long strides, took a bowl from a shelf and thumped it down in front of her. He ladled stew from the big pot standing in the center of the table. Angel's mouth watered. A pan of cornbread was shoved in her direction. He tossed down a spoon, and then sat down heavily on the opposite bench.

Angel stared into his stormy eyes. He stared back.

She broke off a chunk of cornbread, picked up her spoon and started eating.

He lifted a slender cigar from the breast pocket sewn into his shirt and thrust it between his teeth. Raking a Lucifer along the table edge, he cupped the flame as though they sat in a high gale and puffed the cigar to life.

A flick of his wrist sent the match flying into the hearth. She observed each movement, fascinated by his natural, fluid grace. Then he planted his elbows on the table and continued watching her in silence.

She didn't care. They'd shared too many meals together on the trail for her to feel awkward about eating in front of him.

"Carmella's a good cook," she remarked in hopes of drawing him into normal conversation again.

One dark brow twitched, but he said nothing.

"She's also very pretty," Angel continued. "Has her husband always been crippled?"

A thoughtful frown drew Rane's brows together. "No," he said after a moment. "Benito was not always a cripple. Once he was head *vaquero* at a *rancho* just outside the City of Mexico."

The way he pronounced "Meh-hee-co" forced a smile to Angel's lips. "What happened?"

"A horse fell on him."

"That's too bad," she said. "How did they end up here with you?"

He shrugged. "We were friends. I hired them to stay here. When I'm here, Carmella cooks, sees that I have decent clothes to wear."

An unfamiliar sensation wiggled into the pit of Angel's stomach. "She seems very devoted to you."

"She's grateful." His cigar had gone out. He gave it a look of disgust and tossed it into the fireplace. "I hired her to keep her from working in the fields or being forced into service in a bordello. What else could she do? She has to earn money for both of them now. Benito will no longer even try."

Rane picked a breadcrumb from the pan and thrust it into his mouth. "One day, she will leave him," he predicted.

Angel's heart lurched. He sounded so sure. Why would he want Carmella to leave her husband? Only one reason she could think of.

"You have feelings for her?" Her voice sounded barely above a whisper.

"I told you, she's a friend. A good woman. She deserves better than Benito. She works while he does nothing but eat and sleep. And he steals her money to buy whiskey."

Angel glanced down at the pretty, embroidered camisa and suffered a pang of guilt. Carmella, evidently, had very little, yet she'd freely offered her best to make Angel feel comfortable. She made a mental note. If, or rather when, she made it home again, she'd see to it that Carmella Reyes was amply repaid for her act of kindness.

"She pities him," Rane continued, "and he doesn't deserve her sympathy."

"Have you never considered that she might stay with him because she loves him?" Angel asked softly.

His brows beetled as if the idea was a novel one. "How could she still love him?"

Angel stared into her nearly empty bowl and raked the tip of the spoon through the gravy congealing on the bottom. She blew out a breath. "Well. From what I've seen, when it comes to matters of the heart, I don't think we have much choice about who we love or don't love."

He sat very still for a moment, and then huffed a short breath that plainly showed he mocked her theory.

"We all choose," he said. "Each step we take. Each thing we do. We choose. The weak make easy choices, and that's what separates them from the strong. You and I must have had different experiences, Angel, because from what I've seen, *that's* the lesson I've learned."

He stood and returned to the open doorway, staring out at the gathering darkness with his hands thrust down in his pants pockets.

Watching him, Angel's heart ached. She'd been lonely her entire life. But she couldn't imagine the depths of loneliness he must have endured that had turned him into such a cynic.

****

Rane dropped his bedroll just inside the door. On the only bed, Angel was already asleep. Damned woman. Their "dinner" conversation still rankled. How could she champion Benito when she knew nothing about him?

The accident that had affected Benito's legs had also shriveled his soul. The injury had not only changed his body, it seemed to have touched his mind as well. There was darkness in him now that peeked out at times. It manifested in lies and petty thievery. In cruel words to the woman who took care of him when no other would have bothered.

No, Benito had gone beyond pity. Rane felt only contempt for him now because he spat on and defiled the one thing he had left that made his life worth living. His wife.

Rane straddled the bench before the hearth and sighed heavily in the stillness. After pulling off his long-shanked boots, he dropped them in a heap on the floor.

As though drawn, he shifted on the bench. The lamp glow reached across the room and shimmered softly down the length of a long strand of Angel's silver-blond hair spread across the dark blanket.

Angel. Strong, defiant, and fiery. Admirable qualities. But he knew another side of her as well. The gentle, caring side. The tender, feminine side that made him want to burrow in with her and never come out. Dangerous thoughts, but impossible to push aside completely.

She had accused him of ruining her life. Her words kept plucking at his already ragged conscience. Soon she would know the truth. He had no intention of turning her over to Lundy now, but he still meant to use her to entice the man to meet him face to face.

He still meant to use her...

¡Christo! Maybe she was right. Maybe he wasn't all that different from Jed Wiley or Buck Sweeney. He shook his head, rejecting the notion. No, not the same thing, and soon she would see this for herself.

All he wanted from Lundy was the truth, to hear the

bastard speak the words, even if he had to choke them from him with his own hands. This, she would never understand.

On the other side of the room, she murmured softly and turned beneath the blanket. Rane didn't realize he'd curled his hands into fists, until he glanced down and saw them pressed against the tabletop. The urge to walk across the room and slip into bed beside her put a hard knot in his stomach. If he did, she probably wouldn't notice. He knew from experience she could sleep through... well, *almost* anything.

Chapter Nine

The black stallion raced through the night, so smooth and swift it must have sprouted wings on its hooves. Angel clung with desperation to the flailing mane of the great beast. The wind keened in her ears like all the tortured souls of hell. Voices taunted her with soft mocking laughter, and then faded to tormented moans. The sounds washed over her on the breath of the unnatural wind, burning her nostrils with smoke and sulfur, warning her, "Go back...."

Fear rode in tandem with her, pulling at her, whispering promises of horrors that sped her heart to near bursting. She couldn't go back. Rane was here somewhere, lost in the hellish abyss of unending night. She had to find him. Save him from the unholy, burning wind and darkness.

A burst of gunfire and the grand horse faltered. She dug in her heels and goaded him onward, riding blindly toward the new peril. Before her arose a swirling white mist. She hauled back on the horse's mane and his motion ceased. She waited, trembling and breathless. Moonlight sliced through the blackness, parting the mist. On the ground in front of her, caressed by the light, Rane lay as still as death. A ribbon of blood gleamed like liquid rubies down the center of his chest.

A deafening explosion brought Angel straight up on the bed with her heart lurching. She gasped for breath, unable to draw enough air past the tightness pressing in on her chest. Her mind seized the only explanation. A gunshot!

Throwing back the blanket, she scrambled from the bed.

The oil lamp on the table still glowed softly, but Rane no longer sat on the bench. Near the door, his bedroll leaned against the wall, unopened. His boots lay in front of the hearth, telling her he'd left in a hurry.

She couldn't shake the nightmare. Her heart pounded harder as she envisioned Rane lying somewhere in the darkness with a bullet in his chest—just like her dream. An achy sob wrenched from her throat. She rushed to the door and swung it open. Heedless of any threat, fearing one of Lundy's men had finally gotten to him, she ran from the adobe.

Outside, her surroundings mimicked her dreadful dream. A thick blanket of darkness shrouded the land. No moon. No stars winking in the sky. The wind had picked up, wrapping her skirt about her legs. Strands of her long hair lifted eerily and whipped at her face with stinging lashes. Panic pounded harder in her breast.

"Rane!"

The strange wind, thick and oppressive, swallowed the sound of her voice.

In the distance, a low vibration set in and grew in strength until it boomed like cannon fire and shook the ground beneath her bare feet. It was only thunder. Just thunder, she assured herself.

She turned in a complete circle and tried to penetrate the blinding darkness. "*Rane!*"

As though his name conjured it, the heavens opened and the rain poured down in wind-driven sheets, drenching her in the space of two heartbeats.

A brilliant flash illuminated the surrounding landscape. Silvered tree trunks flickered like specters before her eyes. Another flash. She instinctively cringed, her terrified shriek lost in the deafening stuttered crackling that tore across the sky.

She saw Rane, dashing between the trees with his head bent against the slashing downpour. For a moment, the cold, blowing rain and even the deadly bolts of lightning ceased to exist. He was alive.

She lifted the sodden hem of her skirt and rushed to meet him. With a muffled cry on her lips, she threw her arms around his neck and clung to him. Cold rain soaked them both, but it couldn't douse the warmth and vigor emanating from him.

Too soon, he wrapped his hands around her upper

arms and pushed her away. His dark hair was plastered to his scalp and rainwater steadily streamed from the tip of his nose. "What are you doing out here?" His shouted words competed with the storm.

"I thought I heard a shot."

"Lightning struck a tree. I went to check the horses."

"Are they all right?"

"Yes, but we need to get inside."

Grabbing her hand, he pulled her toward the adobe. The flame in the oil lamp guttered when they burst into the room. Rane closed the door and lowered the bar across it to shut out the storm's fury.

Thick clay walls muted the sounds of thunder and driving rain. If only Angel could as easily shut out the tumult raging in her breast. She stood there, dripping onto the earthen floor. A deep shiver ran through her, but it had nothing to do with the cold, wet clothes on her back.

Rane crossed the room, as barefoot and wet as she. Muttering, he pulled down the toweling she'd used earlier from the strung rope. Without looking at her, he thrust the towel into her hands. "Here. Dry yourself."

Why didn't he look at her?

Only ash-covered embers remained in the grate. He gathered several small sticks from the wood basket, then knelt on the hearth and stirred the coals. The dry twigs crackled and burst into flame. He reached for bigger pieces of wood and fed them into the growing blaze.

Angel continued to watch him, unmoving and suddenly unsure. Something had changed between them, at least for her.

Outside, she'd thrown herself into his arms. The sight of him stepping from the darkness, alive, had filled her with such wild joy she'd simply reacted.

Never had she wanted a man to touch her, but Rane's touch had become like water and air. An elemental need, vital and necessary.

Dear God! I'm afraid I'll lose him.

How can you lose something you've never possessed, challenged her voice of reason.

For fleeting snatches of time during those hours and nights when she'd held him as helpless as a babe against her breast, he'd seemed like hers alone.

Now, those innocent interludes weren't enough. She wanted and needed more. She needed him with a desperation she'd never known. She wanted his heat and passion. And damn the consequences.

Rane stood and pried open the buttons closing his shirt. Turning his back to her, he peeled the clinging wet garment from his body and hung it on a nail at the end of the mantle.

His movement sent firelight playing over his damp bronze skin. She saw the bullet scar high on his left side in passing now—expected it. Warmth seeped through Angel's blood. She stepped behind him and lifted the towel in her hands to his back, unable to stop herself any more than she could calm the storm raging outside the door.

At her touch, his muscles flinched and rippled. He stiffened as though she'd scorched him.

"What are you doing, Angel?"

The question probed deeper, implied more than why she stroked his back with the cloth. She had no answer, at least not one she wanted to admit. She asked him a question instead.

"What does it look like I'm doing?" His long hair had separated into sodden ropes lying against the nape of his neck and leaked in steady streams down his back. She moved the towel up, gathered his hair into it and squeezed.

He chuckled, low and dubious. "If I didn't know better, I'd swear you're trying to seduce me."

White-hot, clammy heat crawled over her skin. She closed her eyes. What if he laughed at her? Rebuffed her? No, surely he wouldn't. She remembered the hunger in his kiss that day on the ridge. He'd wanted her then. Of that, she felt certain.

She said nothing, afraid, yet hopeful, that her very silence answered him in spades.

Rane waited, expecting her to tell him he was dreaming, or to go to hell. Instead, she said nothing. Faint, desperate hope sped his heart.

The breath he'd been holding ran out. He turned, slow and careful. He didn't want to make any sudden movements that might spook her and send her away from him.

Now that he faced her, she continued to dab at his chest with the towel, even though his bared skin had grown quite dry and warm from exposure to the fire.

She, on the other hand, looked like a drowned kitten. The camisole clung to every contour of her upper body—molded to her breasts—and moisture had rendered it all but transparent. He'd avoided looking at her. Why look when he couldn't touch? The need to touch her was so strong he could no longer deny it.

"Your turn." He pulled the towel from her hands and draped it around her hair, squeezing the long tresses with the cloth to soak up the wetness, as she'd done for him. She stood before him with her head slightly bowed—and he knew her to be anything but humble—and allowed him to dry her.

He waited, drawing out the towel strokes, conscious of the sound of each breath, while his thoughts tumbled. If he stopped, would she turn and walk away? If he tossed off the cloth and used his hands instead, would she slap his face, or surrender to his touch? Her submissive silence gave no clue.

Though the smell of wood smoke pervaded the room, he caught the essence of wildflowers drifting from her hair. He wanted to bury his nose in the silver-blond mass and breathe her in to his heart's content.

Still, she wouldn't look at him. Evidently, she'd found a fascinating spot on his neck, since that's where her attention seemed focused. Or, perhaps, modesty had gotten the better of her. Impatience gnawed at him. He gave her hair a final brisk swipe, then tossed the towel onto the table behind her.

"Look at me, Angel."

For a moment, the snap of burning wood was the only sound in the room. Then she pulled in a breath, expanding her chest until her wet camisa was as strained as his self-possession. She tipped up her chin and looked at him.

The misty softness in her eyes sent a ticklish thrill rippling through the pit of his stomach. Longing. An invitation. He knew that look. He'd seen it many times in the eyes of other women, but he never dared to dream he'd see it in hers.

Was this the same woman who just three days ago had held a gun to his gut and threatened to shoot him? Her lips parted, her breath coming a little too hard.

"Angel?"

"Yes, Rane?"

She arched one brow at him quizzically. That, coupled with the way she practically purred his name, snapped his restraint like a brittle twig beneath the hooves of a stampeding longhorn.

"Come here," he growled.

Reaching out, he slipped his arm around her waist and hauled her against him. He sucked in his stomach and a sharp breath, recoiling from the shock of her cold, wet clothing touching his skin. But he didn't let her go. No, he couldn't let her go. Even if her clothes had caught fire, he would have stood there and burned. He looped his other arm around her and anchored her to him.

She leaned back and braced her hands against his chest, a puzzled frown knitted across her forehead. "What's the matter?"

"Your clothes are wet. And cold. You should take them off."

"But, I don't have anything else to wear."

He plastered on his best wolf's grin. "Then we'll just have to think of some other way to keep you warm."

Before she could reply, he captured her mouth with his, hot with need, fierce with desire. The rumble of her whimper vibrated through him, as though it had come from his own throat. He swallowed the sound and plunged his tongue inside her mouth, swirling through her soft recesses, coaxing her response. Demanding it.

Slow down, an inner voice warned him.

He tried, but his hands traveled in restless strokes over her back, slipped to the sides of her waist, then returned to the space at the base of her spine to meld her closer. Her breasts pressed hard against his chest and he felt her nipples, already spiked to stiff peaks from the wet camisole. Oh, how he itched to rip the damned clothes from her body.

After a moment, she leaned fully into him, slid her

hands over his shoulders and locked them together at the back of his neck. He felt her surrender as she joined her tongue with his in long, languorous strokes.

During their time together, he'd often fantasized about making love to her. About driving her slowly crazy, until she squirmed beneath his touch and begged him to take her. Ha! Another chimera shot to hell. He'd barely started kissing her and, already, the buttons on his breeches were ready to rip.

So much for going slow.

Following his lead and guided by instinct, Angel responded to the ravishment of Rane's kiss, stroke for maddening stroke. On the surface, he was torrid heat and solidly muscled male. Within the depths of his mouth however, she drowned in soft liquid velvet. Molten honey seeped, pooled, tingled in all the places that defined her as a woman.

That this was wrong no longer mattered. She shouldn't want him, shouldn't allow him to do this. He was her captor, she his prisoner, as much as if she wore shackles around her wrists and ankles. She wanted him regardless, with a desperation that was both frightening and exhilarating beyond anything she'd ever imagined.

His hands skimmed the sides of her waist and met at the center of her stomach. She shifted, allowing him access. Long fingers molded each rib as he moved upward. Yes, she wanted him to touch her there. She ached for him to touch her there.

Instead of moving over her breasts, he reached between them and pulled loose the limp bow closing her camisole. Still holding her in thrall with that drugging kiss, he loosened the gathered neckline and eased it from her shoulders.

She gasped a soft, surprised sound into his mouth when her bare skin met his. She thought she knew the feel of him, smooth, warm, but nothing had prepared her for the sensation when her damp-cool breasts fused with his solid heat.

His mouth left hers and settled near her ear. "Do you want me, Angel?"

She knew what he was asking. "Yes," she whispered, breathy and without hesitation.

Shifting his hold, he picked her up and started across the room.

The unexpected lift had her clinging even harder around his neck. "Rane! Your shoulder!"

"What shoulder?"

As though she weighed nothing, he carried her to the bed and lowered her to the lumpy mattress. An instant of panic shadowed her bliss when he loomed over her.

How could this be wrong when it felt so right?

With trembling hands, she helped him strip away her clammy skirt and coarse drawers. Near darkness emboldened her, softened the sight of her naked body lying next to him.

His lips trailed over her cheek and settled, hot and tingly, against the side of her throat. She strained against him as her body quickened into an aching bundle of need.

He moved lower, dragging his tongue into the valley between her breasts with slow torture. Her nipples hardened, begging for him. When he finally scaled one pale peak and settled the moist, scalding heat of his mouth over her, she gasped and nearly came off the bed. She hadn't known. Nothing had prepared her. She moaned and tangled her fingers into the damp, silken hair at the back of his head, holding him. When he applied suction and drew her deep into his mouth, an echo of sensation throbbed between her thighs. Raw pleasure rippled through her belly and lapped downward.

His heart pounded against the side of her ribs. Harsh breaths competed with the sounds of the rain pelting the shuttered window and door. After a lingering kiss on her swollen nipple, he moved to her other breast and bent his leg so that his buckskin-clad thigh came between hers.

The same hand she knew capable of absolute violence settled atop her stomach with utter gentleness, inflicting warmth and curious little thrills that burrowed deep into her core. He stroked downward, moving against the inside of her thigh, brushing against the moist heat centered between her legs with just enough insistence to send her following his movement with her body.

She arched her back and curled her fingers trapped in his hair, digging into his scalp. Instinctively, her legs tightened around his hard-muscled thigh.

He lifted his head. Breath heaved between his parted lips. Heavy-lidded with passion, his dark eyes seemed to glitter in the semi-darkness. "*Mí Dios, mí ángela.* I want to be inside you."

To be inside you... The words, their intent, sank in on Angel. She swallowed thickly, but offered no objection. She couldn't. She wanted him, too.

Bracing himself on one forearm, he moved the hand that had been stroking her, unfastened his trouser buttons, and shoved the buckskins down his long legs with jerky movements. When he pressed against her once more, his erection came to rest atop her leg with scorching heat and a weighty presence she found surprising. Even this felt right. Oh, so right.

With a low groan rumbling in his chest, he levered himself onto his knees and hovered over her, his heat centered between her legs. She felt the leashed tension vibrating through his rigidly held muscles, humming almost, as a too-tightly strung run of barbed wire.

Rane couldn't hold back any longer. A shiver trickled down his spine, and pushed him ever closer to losing the miniscule control he had left. He squeezed his eyes closed and pulled in a long breath, fighting for it. No woman had ever had this devastating effect on him. Until Angel.

Why resist any longer? She was as wet and swollen as he was.

Grasping her hips, he arched and drove into her in one, long shattering stroke. Her body's tightness squeezed him almost painfully. He registered the slickness bursting around him, heard her small cry, felt her nails scoring the flesh on his upper arms where she held him in a death grip.

His mind stumbled over the implications. He froze, as an improbable thought took precedence over his body's demands.

Against the dark blankets, she looked pale, her face drawn with the pain she tried valiantly to hide.

"Angel? Is this...the first time?"

She nodded, and that simple motion sent an icy chill spearing through his heart. He started to pull back.

"No!" In a move he could only attribute to instinct, she wrapped both legs around his waist and held him. "I want you to do this."

Just that quickly, her action halted his body's retreat. "I don't want to hurt you."

She offered a brave smile. "I knew what to expect."

The damage had been done, common sense argued, and no power under the sun could restore her virtue. He didn't want to disappoint her, any more than he wanted to deny himself the satisfaction of finishing what they'd started. Silently, he cursed himself for a weak fool.

Still firmly embedded inside her, he braced on his hands and locked his elbows to hold his weight off her. God above, she was a vision. Just looking at her, her tight little body gripping him, he felt himself growing even harder. Her eyes widened.

"Angel, I don't want to hurt you. I want to give you pleasure."

Laying her hands around his wrists, she stroked upward to his shoulders and smiled. "I trust you're capable of doing just that."

If she meant to simper at him seductively, her expression reminded him more of a shy miss flirting with her first beau.

"It would be better if you relax," he suggested.

"I thought I was relaxed."

"Trust me, you're not relaxed. Try squeezing me."

Her brows pulled together. "How?"

He pried his right hand from the bed and splayed his fingers across her lower abdomen. "Here. Try it."

She caught on quickly. He sucked in his breath as her strong little muscles closed around him even tighter. "Now, relax and try it again."

After the second time, he started to move within her when she relaxed her inner muscles. They played at this give and take until he thought he would explode. But he felt her opening to him, accepting, stroking him back. Making love to him with her body.

Rane's heart stampeded. A primal pulse slogged heavily in the place where his body joined to hers. He couldn't hold back much longer. Reaching between them, he found her secreted bud and worked a little magic with a moistened fingertip.

She sucked in an audible breath and arched up

beneath him, convulsing around him in the throes of release. He let go then and tumbled with her. Spiraling into that white, blinding flash of intense pleasure, he drove deep one final time and held there, adrift in a sea of pure sensation. And somewhere, in the midst of it, he heard her cry out his name. The sound echoed through the long-sealed chamber of emptiness he kept buried deep in his heart.

Rane lifted his head, still panting for breath, his heart tripping in double-time. Beneath him, Angel's pale body glistened with a fine sheen of moisture. He thought he saw tears seeping from the corners of her eyes, but a dreamy smile of contentment curved her lips. She looked like a sleek kitten that had just lapped up an entire bowl of thick cream.

His arms trembled from the prolonged strain of holding his weight above her. She had sapped him, drained him of his seed and his strength as no one ever had.

He levered himself over and collapsed in a loose-limbed sprawl beside her. When he lifted his arm and laid the back of a wrist across his eyes, she turned to him and slipped her arm around his waist.

"Rane?" Her voice sounded uncertain.

In answer, he curled his arm around her shoulders and pulled her closer, stroking the tangled strands of hair from her face. He kissed her forehead, her cheek, and tasted the salty bite of her tears on his tongue.

"Don't cry, Angel. It's too late for tears."

"I'm not crying."

"Then go to sleep." The words came out sounding harsher than he intended. She snuggled down against him, one long, slender leg draped over his, her arm curved across his stomach. He felt the hard pounding of her heart against his ribs, felt it slowly lessen until her soft breath settled into a slow, even rhythm.

He ventured a glance at her upturned face and saw that her eyes were closed. The innocence of her sleeping, angelic features speared him with guilt.

A virgin! In innocence, she had come to him, and he had taken what she offered with greedy hands.

He muttered a vile curse and damned to hell all the

wagging tongues that had spread lies about her. But most of all, he damned himself for listening, for not trusting what he had felt in his own gut all along. It had been so much easier to believe the lies and think of her as a wanton.

He should have known. In fact, he *had* known, but lust had blinded him.

It was too late for regrets. All he could do now was try to keep his wits about him and stay alive until he finished the job he'd set out to do. But the guilt still nagged at him. He had dared a taste of the forbidden fruit. He couldn't help wondering, somewhere down the road, what price they would both be forced to pay for their one stolen hour of intense sweetness.

Chapter Ten

The shutters on the solitary window stood open and soft, white daylight filled the room. Angel stretched with lazy contentment and ran her hand beneath the rumpled blankets. The space beside her was empty. No Rane. Not even a trace of his warmth remained.

She turned to her side. The movement touched off a dull ache in uncustomary parts of her body. Bunching the cover in her hand, she held it tight against her chest, thinking, remembering. A murmur of sensation bloomed low in her belly when she recalled the intense, soaring pleasure Rane had given her in the darkest hours of the night. Feminine instinct told her, somehow, she had given that same gift back to him. The ultimate mystery revealed. If the worst should happen today, she would have no regrets.

The smell of coffee coaxed her fully awake. She draped the cover around her bare shoulders and sat on the side of the bed. Rane was nowhere in sight.

Streaks of dried blood smeared the insides of her thighs. She stared at it and traced a fingertip over the tender skin. The smudges were all that remained of lost innocence, once preciously guarded, a treasure she had discarded all too easily when it suited her.

Fallen. Soiled goods. The denigrating words reared up like phantom vipers and hissed at her. She shook her head. *No.* She wouldn't listen. She didn't feel the least bit soiled. If anything, she felt reborn. She had given herself to the only man she'd ever wanted... the man she loved.

Angel's hand flew to her mouth. *Dear God in heaven!*

At some point during the past several days, her vision of her future had changed. She no longer saw herself standing in some grand ballroom surrounded by a throng of admiring beaux, the sons of cattle barons. She no longer saw her father standing on the sidelines, beaming with pride. Now, her thoughts of going home all included Rane somewhere in the picture.

How could that be? She'd fallen in love with a man who not only had a disreputable past, he also, almost certainly, had no future. Even if her father didn't shoot him on sight, he'd never accept Rane. He'd disown her before that happened. She'd spent two long, grueling years in New York, learning to behave like a proper lady, only to return to Texas and commit the one act the gossips had always accused her of—being a wanton woman.

Her father would be furious. Devastated. How could she face him? How could she not? If it came to a choice, her father's respect or Rane, which would she choose?

She shook her head. Getting ahead of herself only borrowed grief. Somehow, during the past eight days, she'd lost her heart to Rane Mantorres. That didn't mean he felt the same. To a man such as he, she was probably nothing more than another conquest. A conquest easily won, she realized. She'd practically thrown herself at him.

Her breath hitched as the pressure around her heart increased to a poignant ache. Sitting there on the side of the bed, trying to second-guess him would get her nowhere. There was only one way to find out.

Fortified with strong coffee and dressed in the scant peasant clothes—which Rane had evidently hung to dry on the rope stretched across the room—Angel walked out of the adobe nearly an hour later. With her hair swept up and pinned into a neat coil around the crown of her head, she hoped she more closely resembled the civilized woman who had boarded the train in New York nearly three weeks ago.

Outside, the night's storm had lain to rest the dust and sand. Sunlight streamed through the trees, shifting dappled patches of light and darkness over the ground. The air smelled fresh and sweet. Her little paint mare and Pago, the name she now knew Rane called his big stallion, stood in the corrals, chewing contentedly on rations of grain. The stallion's owner was nowhere in sight.

Footprints showed up plainly in the freshly washed sand. They milled at the corrals, then led toward the creek. Angel followed. With each step, her nerves thrummed. The thought of facing Rane in the bare light of day after the intimacy they'd shared made her want to turn tail and run. But she had to know where she stood.

The narrow stream ran swollen and muddy with floodwater. Following the tracks, Angel paralleled the rushing water southward. Limber willows bordered the banks, dripping moisture from their trailing branches. The tracks led her to another stand of cottonwoods.

In the midst of the trees, a weathered slab of stone marked a solitary grave. Rane stood beside the narrow mound with his hat in his hands, his dark head bowed, solemn and respectful.

Angel halted. Her first impulse urged her to turn around and go back. She felt like an intruder. Yet, curiosity rooted her to the spot. She leaned against a tree trunk, dug her nails into the rough bark, and focused on the name carved into the headstone.

Maria Mantorres.

Angel stared at the name until it blurred before her eyes. An ominous fog crept over her and blotted the cheery sunlight. Had Rane abandoned her in his bed to commune with a dead woman who shared his name? The sorrowful droop of his proud head was unmistakable.

She pulled her stinging fingers away from the tree and pressed her back to it instead. Jealousy washed over her in sickening waves. She squeezed her eyes closed for a brief instant and tried to will it away. When she opened them again and looked at him, he settled the hat over his head and started toward her.

He'd seen her.

Her heart lurched like a wild thing and sent heat racing into her face. A Peeping Tom caught in the act. That's what she felt like. When he neared her, she drew a deep, steadying breath and pushed away from the tree.

"Good morning." He sounded so brusque.

"Morning," she murmured.

His features were etched in granite, as cold and remote as the stone marker in the distance. He had closed himself to her again, allowing her to see nothing. She thought she'd broken through some of his barriers, and now it looked as though he'd put them all solidly back in place. She hadn't known what to expect, but the hard-eyed man before her in no way resembled the warm, passionate lover whose bed she had shared.

"Were you looking for me?"

Again, he sounded so cold. The threat of tears stung her eyes. She sucked in another deep, strengthening breath and stiffened her spine. She would not allow him to see her cry.

"Yes, and I'm sorry I disturbed you," she said, following his example of cold formality. "Had I known you were busy with your devotions, I wouldn't have followed you."

A muscle in his jaw knotted. He continued to glare at her. "Go back to the house, Angel."

She narrowed her eyes. His hostile treatment flew in the face of everything she had hoped for and expected. "I'm not going anywhere until you tell me why you're so angry."

His expression darkened, as if a shadow moved over his features. "How did you expect me to feel," he demanded, "after the fast one you pulled on me last night?"

The question wasn't what she expected. She clutched her arms against her waist. "Wh-what are you talking about? What fast one?"

He leaned nearer and looked directly into her eyes. Flashing anger and cold darkness bored into her. His look both scorched her and chilled her to her very marrow. "Why didn't you tell me you were a virgin?"

That's what he was angry about? "I didn't think it mattered?"

A soft, incredulous laugh burst from his lips. "You didn't think it mattered?" He straightened and laughed again. Shaking his head, he shifted to a hipshot stance, but she knew the relaxed pose was a lie. "It mattered," he said. "I'm not in the habit of seducing *niñas*."

The fine hair covering her arms stood on end as if a frigid wind blew through the trees. After the intimacy they'd shared during the night, how dare he call her a child.

"You think I'm a child?" Her voice trembled, and she hated betraying even that small sign of weakness. She wanted to grab him and shake him, make him look at her with a spark of tender recognition, instead of the indifferent eyes of a stranger. "I'm a grown woman, Rane, and I know my own mind. Besides, that's not the way it happened, and you know it."

"No, that's not the way it happened," he agreed. A sneer curved his lips. "What did you hope to gain, Angel?"

She held his level gaze, seething, while his words pelted her, shredded her heart into a million tiny pieces.

"Did you think I would let you go if you offered up your precious, lily-white virtue to me?"

If he'd drawn his gun and shot her, she wouldn't have been more appalled. Reflex brought her hand up. Without thinking, she slammed it against the rigid plane of his cheek. The resounding crack and the sting in her fingers startled her. She gasped and retreated a hasty step.

She had finally broken his cold restraint. Exposed reaction leapt to his face. He looked... wounded? And if she didn't know better, she would almost swear the haunted look in his eyes resulted from fear. But that was impossible. She had seen him look into the hideous face of death itself and betray no emotion.

With only a flicker from his dark eyes and a hardening of his mouth to warn her, he reached out and captured her arm. Forcing it down to her side, he levered her resistant body closer.

"What do you want from me?"

Your love. Nothing more. Nothing less.

She might as well wish for the moon. Obviously, his actions last night hadn't been motivated by anything beyond his physical needs. She'd been a fool to think otherwise. But she couldn't let him see her devastation. She wouldn't be able to bear that humiliation. Somehow, she had to make him believe her behavior had been just as cold-hearted and calculated as his.

Squaring back her shoulders, she lifted her chin and assumed the guise of the haughty society demoiselle, just as Aunt Nelda had taught her. "Why would I want anything from someone like you?"

The barest twitch of a rigid muscle in his cheek betrayed that she had pricked his defensive armor. "That's not strictly true," she amended. "I did want something from you, and I got it...last night."

With that, she wrenched her arm from his grasp and whirled past him, presenting him with a properly stiff back as she stalked away.

His hand snaked out and wrapped around her arm once more, stopping her dead. He stepped in front of her. When she refused to look at him, he placed his fingers beneath her chin and forced it up.

"Why did you do it, Angel? Why me?" he asked. "Why didn't you save it for your wedding night?"

"I'm twenty years old, Rane. Maybe I got tired of 'saving it'!" She stepped back, distancing herself from the disturbing power of his touch. "If it was such an issue, why didn't you just back off?"

"*¡Cristo!* woman! I'm only human. I've thought of little except getting my hands on you since the first moment I saw you."

So... there it was. Spoken in plain words. He had lusted for her body and nothing more.

Angel turned her back on him and resumed her angry retreat, praying he wouldn't try to stop her again lest he see the scalding tears streaming down her cheeks.

This time he let her go.

Rane watched Angel disappear among the cottonwoods, admiring her more than ever.

She hadn't tried to corner him, hadn't demanded that he return her "favor" tit for tat. No hysterics or accusations. Angel Clayton was some kind of rare woman, which made her words sting even more.

Why would I want anything from someone like you?

Someone like you...

He was a mongrel caught between two races, considered dangerous by the Anglos who, for the most part, resented his very existence. Angel wasn't the first *gringa* who had believed herself superior, then invited him into her bed on the sly. Those other women had used him as much as he had used them. For the thrill of sleeping with someone outside their social status, someone forbidden. The danger seemed to spice up the sex for them. He had been only too happy to feed their fantasies and play the role of the hot Hispanic lover.

This time, he felt no satisfaction with his conquest.

Angel was no world-wise strumpet. She had sacrificed her virginity for him, and he was at a loss to know why, no matter what she claimed. What had happened between them last night went beyond casual sex. The words "making love" flitted through his mind. He resisted the thought. In fact, it scared the hell out of him.

He pulled off his hat and raked back his hair with an unsteady hand. "What the hell have I done?"

****

Angel, chilled and shivering, stood in the open doorway with her arms hugged tightly beneath her breasts. Water streamed from the edge of the thatched roof and spattered on the muddy ground in front of her feet. Fine mist settled over her face and muslin clad arms. Still, she was reluctant to move. The soft hush of the steadily falling rain soothed her, but the new wounds inflicted on her heart still ached.

Outside, the corralled horses had blurred to gray ghosts beneath the new deluge.

Behind her, Rane straddled one of the benches at the table. The smell of gun oil hung heavy in the still, thick air, overpowering even the smoking wood blazing on the hearth.

The inclement weather had forced them both indoors, but the chasm that had opened between them that morning seemed wider than ever.

She signed and braced a shoulder against the wooden door frame.

The day her father sent her away had marked a turning point in her life. She had vowed she would never be hurt that badly again. The two years she'd spent in the east should have matured her, hardened her. But the old pain was still there, as raw as ever.

Rane had assumed he knew all about her that he needed and hadn't even bothered to ask. He'd believed the lies he'd heard. That fact galled her the most. He didn't know the first thing about her. How could he understand the loneliness of growing into a woman, isolated and friendless, except for the company of a bunch of crude cowhands?

She could well imagine the stories he'd heard. The vile gossip and outright lies. Because she'd worn britches and rode with her father's men, vulgar rumors had circulated. Her father had shielded her from the worst of it, but she knew the gossips had assumed she also allowed her father's cowhands the use of her body.

Rane's shocked expression at finding her still untouched flickered through her mind like a recurring vision. She had hoped the past would no longer affect her, that time and distance had laid it to rest, but it hadn't.

In the end, she was still the same lonely girl she'd always been, desperately grasping for love that was forever held beyond her reach. First by her father, and now Rane.

The ultimate irony of that hit her hard. She ached with it, a hollow pain that thrummed from within and settled deep in her heart. The threat of more tears burned her eyes. She turned her face up to the cooling mist, refusing to give in to them again.

"Evil unto him," she murmured, "who thinks evil."

"Did you say something?"

The words were softly spoken, casual. Resolved, she turned and found him with his elbows carelessly propped on the table. In one hand, he held his pistol, broken down for cleaning. In the other dangled a slender metal rod with an oily rag tightly wrapped around the end. When she didn't answer, he lifted his head and looked at her.

"No," she said.

"Oh." He returned his attention to the weapon in his hands. "I thought I heard you say something."

She shrugged, though he didn't see. "Talking to myself, perhaps."

"Bad habit," he said.

He lifted the gun to catch the pale light filtering through the door and squinted down the barrel. Totally absorbed, it seemed. She knew the image would stay with her forever. Weapon in hand, what went through his mind during idle moments such as this? Did he think of himself as a killer, or an avenging angel?

Did it really matter? Watching him manipulate his precious gun was a jolting reminder of who he was. What he was. She'd been the worst kind of fool to imagine he might be something more.

The nerve-racking silence expanded, filled with

nothing but the soft rush of falling rain and the occasional scrape and click of metal sliding against metal. Drawn despite herself, Angel crossed to the table and sat on the bench opposite him. He reassembled the Peacemaker and loaded it. His movements wasted nothing and, as always, his hands fascinated her. His long, beautiful fingers could have belonged to an artist, a healer—or a gentleman. Last night they had stroked her body with the same loving care he now gave to his damned gun.

She hated the comparison. Worst of all, she hated knowing she held no more significance to him than the object in his hand, and still she longed to reach across the table and touch him.

But she didn't. She wouldn't make that mistake again.

His silence frustrated her more now than ever. Pulling in a deep breath, she finally braved the question that had been eating at her all day.

"Who was Maria Mantorres?"

He kept running the oily rag over the surface of the Colt and appeared solely focused on polishing it to a high shine. "My mother," he replied at last.

Hard on the heels of overwhelming relief, shame flooded Angel. Unwelcome heat splashed into her cheeks. She'd been jealous of his mother. "I—I'm sorry."

One corner of his mouth twitched briefly, as if she'd touched a nerve. But she couldn't let it go that easily.

"How long has she been...gone?"

He expelled a heavy breath and deliberately laid the pistol atop the table. "Too long," he said. "Twelve years. I was fourteen when she died."

His hesitation warned her. His mother's death wasn't something he normally talked about. Nor did he wish to now. At least he'd answered her and satisfied her curiosity. In doing so, he'd revealed more about himself within the past nine seconds than he had during the past nine days. Odd to think of him as being only twenty-six years old.

He shifted on the bench and looked at her.

She remembered the first time she'd seen him, and again that day at the base of the rockslide. She'd thought his eyes dull and lifeless. That he was a man who viewed the world from an empty vessel because he'd lost his soul. How wrong she'd been. A whole array of emotions warred within their dark depths. Now, she understood that he held his pain inside, carefully disguised.

"At least you have memories of your mother," she blurted. More than anything she wanted to take his mind from whatever had put that haunted look in his eyes. She ached for him, and she didn't want to. She didn't want to feel anything where he was concerned. "I don't even remember mine. She died when I was just a baby. All I have of her is one photograph. Just one flat, cold image. It stands on the mantle above the fireplace in the parlor."

She fell silent as sharp regret stabbed her. Her mother's photograph. Her beautiful, picture perfect mother posing for the photographer in her striped silk dress of unknown color. Sitting with her stylishly coifed blond head held high, and her black lace gloved hands folded primly in her lap. Her final wish in life had been for Angel's future. She'd wanted her daughter to be a fine lady, like herself.

And Angel had failed. Miserably. Last night had cinched it. But she couldn't think about that now.

"What about your father?" she asked. Anything to keep him talking, to keep herself from thinking about how easily she had succumbed to temptation the first time it crossed her path.

His black gaze narrowed sharply. "What about him?"

"Is he still living?"

"Yes." Rane swung his leg over the bench and stood. Taking the gun from the table, he levered back the hammer and spun the cylinder, listening to the rhythmic sound of the well-oiled clicks. Then he shoved the gun firmly into the holster strapped around his hips and turned to her with that familiar, maddening smirk on his lips. "Maybe one day I'll introduce you to him."

Just that quickly, his mood had shifted. After a final adjustment to his gunbelt, he lifted his hat from the peg near the door, then capped it over his head and tugged it down snug to the tops of his ears. Without another word, he walked out the door and quickly merged into grayness with the steadily falling rain.

****

Rane jerked his head from the hard pillow of his arms crossed atop the table. In his haste to stand, he nearly tripped backward over the bench where he sat. Reflex clapped his right hand over the butt of his Colt, withdrawing and cocking it in one continuous motion as he swung to face the barred door.

The pounding from the other side resumed. “Señor Rane! Open the door!”

Rane eased off the hammer and slipped the gun back into his holster. A quick glance at the bed showed him Angel was already awake. Wide-eyed and upright, she stared at him, clutching the blanket against her like a shield.

“It’s Carmella.”

Angel dropped the blanket and came off the bed. “Something must have happened.”

His thought exactly. He lifted the heavy bar and pulled the door open. Carmella nearly fell into his arms.

He grasped her shoulders and righted her, held her away from him, searching her frantic, fearful eyes. “What’s wrong?”

Anguish aged her beyond her years. “You have to leave,” she said. “Right now! Lundy’s men know you are here.”

“How?”

Sudden tears brimmed her eyes. She no longer looked at him.

Dread hummed through him, drawing each nerve and tendon to straining intensity beneath his suddenly clammy skin. He tightened his hold and shook her slightly. “Look at me, Carmella! What happened?”

She still refused to look at him. “I deliver your message,” she said. “Then when I go back to the village, Benito is gone. I look for him. Finally, I find him, but it is too late. Lundy’s men, they buy him whiskey to get him drunk.” She looked up then, and the heartbreak he saw in her eyes ran his blood cold. “Benito told them you are here with the Clayton girl.”

Chapter Eleven

Angel, riding astride the paint mare, plodded along behind the dark silhouette of Rane's stallion while the eastern horizon turned a slightly paler shade of black. Approaching dawn was both a blessing and a curse. Come daybreak they would be able to see where they were going and make faster time. But daylight would also make them visible to those who hunted them.

Though the rain had stopped, high, dark clouds still skidded like dirty tufts of cotton across the moon and stars. The woolen poncho draped over her shoulders was a sodden weight. Her back ached from the relentless tension that had gripped her body since leaving the adobe and her eyes felt gritty from lack of sleep.

The grueling ride through the black of night seemed as though it would never end until, ahead of her, Rane halted. Wet saddle leather squeaked when he shifted to look back.

"We'll rest here a while," he said.

Gladly following his lead, Angel slid from the saddle and led the mare into a stand of brush at the base of an outcrop. The thick bushes hid the horses and the towering rock formation would provide shade when the sun came up.

After beating the sparse grasses and low bushes within the rock cleft to frighten off any hidden wildlife, Rane stretched out on his back on the packed sand and cradled his head in his hands. He yawned and wriggled his hips to settle them, as though sleeping there was the most natural thing in the world.

Angel scanned the nearby rocks and grass tufts with a wary eye. Even after sleeping on the trail for nearly two weeks, the unfamiliar surroundings assumed frightful shapes in the darkness. Every crooked twig resembled a snake. With reluctance, she sat and scooted as near to

Rane as she dared. Chilled to the bone, the wet poncho had turned to useless, dead weight. She pulled it over her head and tossed it aside, then sat shivering and hugged her drawn-up knees to her chest.

Despite her exhaustion, she couldn't relax. Too much had happened that night, and the danger was still very near. Between the biting air and her tightly stretched nerves, she feared her spine might snap at any second.

She glanced at Rane, but couldn't tell in the dimness whether his eyes were open or closed. "Do you think Carmella made it safely to the village?"

His voice, edged with drowsiness, rumbled up from his chest. "I'd say Carmella is warm and safe and tucked beneath a blanket sound asleep right now."

"I doubt that. She was too upset."

"Try to rest," he said. "I'll wake you when it's time to go."

"What about you?"

"I'll doze. The horses will warn me if anyone comes near."

Angel scanned the surrounding sand again. Nothing moved. Somewhat reassured, she lay down and turned to her side, curling an arm beneath her head. The ground under her felt damp. She couldn't stop shivering. They'd abandoned the adobe in such a hurry, they'd left the bedrolls behind.

After a moment, Rane sat up and scooted nearly against her. He peered down at her for a second, then lay back and opened his arm. Patting his chest, he invited her to use him for a pillow. "Body heat," was all he said.

Given a choice between snuggling with Rane or chattering her teeth out of her head, Angel curled against his side and settled her cheek against his solidly muscled chest. His arm curved around her shoulders, holding her close, and his heat instantly warmed her.

Soft gray light stole into their hiding place while she lay there, unable to close her eyes, unable to fully relax.

Beneath her ear, his heart pounded in a solid, even rhythm. The side of her nose pressed against his muslin shirt. It smelled of him, like him, a mixture of clean, warm male and cool air, and just a hint of the musky spice that must have scented his shaving soap. She lifted her lashes and glanced up. His chin, which sported nearly twenty-four hours worth of stubble again, was only inches from her face.

"Rane?"

"What."

"How did you get that scar on your chin?"

Against her ear, his heart sped an infinitesimal beat. "Knife fight."

She sighed. "I should have known. Have you always lived so close to the edge?"

She felt him stir slightly, not a movement really, but she knew she'd sparked his interest.

"What do you mean? The edge of what?"

"Danger, pain...death. You seem to court them."

"You planning to give me a sermon about the way I live?"

"Would it do any good?"

"None at all."

"Then I'll save my breath."

Bull-headed man. She didn't know why she bothered talking to him. Of course, nothing she said would convince him to change his ways, but she couldn't help wondering about it. If he wanted to, and tried, could he change? What sort of man would he be if he did?

"Angel."

"Hmm?"

He moved without warning, shifted to his side so that she lay on her back and he hovered above her. His arm still cradled her, holding her head above the dank ground.

With his face only a breath away, the troubled furrow marring his brow had her mirroring his expression. Intensity sizzled within his dark-as-death eyes.

"I have something to tell you."

She barely dared to breathe. "What is it?"

His gaze raked her face. Almost absently, he ran the backs of his fingers from just beneath her ear to her throat. The feathery caress unfurled all the way to her toes.

"I'm taking you home to your father."

Elation burst inside her, like a bubble of hope that had been building and expanding until it could contain nothing more.

"Why?" she asked. "Because it's the right thing to do? Or because your plan has gone awry and now there's nothing else you *can* do?"

"Does it really matter?"

Yes, she wanted to scream at him. *It* does *matter. Your reason makes all the difference in the world! To me. It matters to me!*

"Whatever happens," he continued, "I wanted you to know that nothing was meant to hurt you. Before the day is over, you'll be safe in your father's house."

And this will be the last time we spend alone together, she finished for him.

Her heart swelled, trembled, verged on breaking at the thought of him never holding her like this again.

Desperation clawed at her. The threat of tears burned her eyes. Her fingers curled, fisted against his chest. Then, resolved, she slowly relaxed and lifted her hand to his face. He swallowed; the point of his throat glided smoothly beneath his skin. Barely daring to touch him, she flitted a fingertip over his grimly set mouth. His lips parted, bathing her fingers in heat with each shallow breath.

He wrapped her hand in his and trapped it against his chest. "That tickles."

For a moment, she feared he would pull back. His pulse throbbed madly just beneath the tanned surface of his throat. Need carved fine webs at the corners of his eyes that were now clouded with desire. His head dipped with infinite slowness. She held her breath, and he touched his lips to hers.

It's lust. Nothing more, she reminded herself.

His kiss was gentle, unlike his impassioned explorations that stormy night in the adobe. Close-lipped, almost chaste, his mouth softened against hers, and the sensation burrowed deep down. Only this time the feeling dove straight to her heart.

After that too-brief taste of him, he withdrew. She opened her eyes and found him close, watching her. Confusion warred with longing.

"What is it?" she whispered.

"I...I want you, Angel. Right here, right now, even though we don't dare take off a stitch of our clothes."

She swallowed thickly, forcing back her pride and all the recent pain he'd inflicted on her heart. "It's okay," she said. "I want you, too."

"So, we understand each other?" he asked.

A cold, brittle edge formed around her momentary bliss, but she shoved it away, refusing to let it spoil the here and now. If this stolen moment was all she was destined to have of him, then so be it. She would take it and gladly. She would cling to him with both hands and glory in his touch while she could.

"We understand each other," she assured him.

He lowered his mouth to hers again, so tenderly a sweet, new ache gathered around her heart.

Rane.

She lifted her hands and wrapped them around the back of his neck, holding him closer, needing him.

His breathing grew harsher as he closed his free hand over the peak of her breast through the damp camisole. He pressed harder, deepening the kiss, parting her lips until his tongue found hers and mated in a sinuous rhythm designed to drive them both half mad.

He pulled back, stroking, nipping, he licked a hot path over her chin and down to her throat. "I have to touch you." His fingers tugged at the neckline of her blouse, baring her breasts.

The cool air and the dampness ceased to exist. Heat consumed Angel from the inside out, turning her clothing into an obstacle she couldn't shed when his mouth, hot and moist, closed over her and drew her quivering flesh inside his mouth.

She arched, strained against him as sensation flowed, built, pooled until she was whimpering for him.

His voice deepened to a sensual growl. "I've thought of nothing but touching you again." He found the hem of her skirt and slipped his hand underneath.

"I want to touch you, too," she confessed.

Without missing a beat, he captured her wrist and carried it down to the front of his breeches, cupping her fingers around the hard ridge of flesh straining the front of his buckskins. She sucked in a gasp and held it when he arched into her hand. His touch aroused feelings she still didn't fully understand. Suddenly she was avid to feel him, skin to skin. She wanted him in her hand.

As though he knew her thoughts, he whispered, “Unbutton me.”

With an efficiency gained from unfastening countless rows of tedious buttons on her own garments, Angel loosed him from his tight prison and delivered him into her palm. Her last deliberate thought was of slick velvet and unyielding steel and how unlikely that the two should complement each other so perfectly.

Then she thought not at all as she yielded to sensation. For the moment, all worries ceased to exist. There was only Rane, touching her, loving her, branding her soul with a fiery passion she knew she'd never feel again.

****

Rane crouched on all fours at the edge of the brush and studied the rim of the gorge before him. From below, the Rio Bravo sounded different than he remembered, louder, rushing. The unprecedented amount of rain that had fallen during the past twenty-four hours had undoubtedly put it on the rise. Another stroke of bad luck.

A trickle of sweat crept down the center of his chest and dripped from his belly. He lifted a hand and flattened his shirt against his skin, absorbing the ticklish moisture. He'd waited until the sun climbed straight overhead before approaching the river. Better to suffer the heat than the disadvantage of having the glare in his eyes. There was no one in sight.

Rane stood and walked to the edge of the gorge. Below, the river ran swollen and muddy, littered with the debris of tree limbs. The narrow strands of sand that normally lined the base of the gorge had disappeared beneath turbulent water.

Silently, he cursed the untimely storms that had dumped this deluge on them. Crossing now would be a risky undertaking, but they had no choice.

He lifted his arm and waved a signal. Angel, leading their two horses, stepped from a shadowy copse of scrub trees and started toward him. He skimmed down her slender, yet blatantly female curves, clad once more in the brown trousers and coarse shirt she'd worn on the trail. Just after sunup, the sight of her pulling the manly garb from her saddlebags and sliding the trousers over her long, creamy legs was a vision that would forever be emblazoned in his memory.

She led the horses nearer, and her eyes widened when she got her first look at the water. "I don't ever remember the river looking like this." The underlying quaver in her voice echoed his misgivings. "Exactly where are we?"

He pointed downriver. "Do you see that hazy looking patch of sky in the distance?"

She followed his direction. "Yes, I see it."

"Clayton Station is the source of that smoke haze."

Mention of home, being near enough to practically see it, put a smile of pure happiness on her lips. Suddenly, he wished he had done something to make her smile like that.

Again, he pointed downriver. "See that bend?"

She nodded, a frown of concentration growing on her lovely face.

"Just beyond that is the bridge."

Expectation leapt to her eyes.

"But we can't cross there," he quickly added. "It will be guarded." He turned and looked down at the roiling water once more. "We have to cross here. It's the only other way down and out of the gorge for miles that I know of."

Angel pulled in a deep breath and moved closer to the edge of the rim. Her gaze swept the narrow switchback path leading down the steep bank beneath them. Then she looked to the opposite bank, where the path picked up again at the edge of the water and led out of the canyon.

She handed over the stallion's reins.

"You ready?" he asked.

She nodded.

Rane started down the path, taking slow, careful steps. Leading Pago, he watched the plodding hooves of both horses in case one of them should make a wrong step. In only a moment, the shadow of the gorge closed over them. He stopped when the path disappeared beneath the swirling tide of floodwater.

Angel clutched the mare's reins with both hands, staring with frightened eyes at the foaming rills rushing past at dizzying speed.

"Mount up," he told her.

She swallowed. "I have a last minute confession." She blurted out the rest quickly. "I'm not very comfortable around water because I don't know how to swim. So, if I fall off, I'm afraid you'll have to rescue me from drowning."

He chuckled, which he knew she didn't appreciate, judging from the way her brows dipped. "You're not going to drown, and you're not going to fall off. When you get into deep water, just give the mare her head and she'll swim to the other side."

Rane climbed into the saddle and ran a soothing hand along the stallion's thickly muscled neck, and then stepped him down to the hidden strand. The water hurtled past, only inches below his stirrups. He looked back.

Angel sat on her horse just above the water line.

"Come on!"

She hauled in a deep breath, then kneed the horse forward.

Satisfied she would follow, Rane angled the horse's head upstream, aiming for the path ascending the opposite side of the gorge. He urged the stallion into deeper water.

When the icy current reached the tops of Rane's boots and began to fill them, he knew the flood was even worse than he'd anticipated. A foaming eddy shoved against the stallion's broad side, then spewed over Rane's knees. The swirling wetness crept higher still, dousing the sensitive skin between his thighs with a cold shock.

The instant Pago's hooves left the river bottom, Rane knew he had completely underestimated the power of the flood. With the horse afloat, the current pushed them downstream. With each passing second, their escape path receded farther into the distance. They'd missed the mark. His heart sank as he realized he'd led them right into a trap of nature's own making.

As if they weren't in enough difficulty, someone yelled, "Look! There they are!"

Bullets sprayed the water near the stallion's haunches. Seated in the saddle above water line, they presented easy targets. Like clay carnival ducks, lined up for destruction.

Rane twisted to look behind him. The mare was close. Angel clung to the saddle horn with both hands, her eyes round with fear.

"Jump!" he yelled.

"No!" she screamed back at him.

"I said jump!"

She looked frozen. The death grip she had on the saddle horn blanched her knuckles white. She had no intention of letting go.

He had to get her off the horse. But to do that, he had to reach her. Reversing position, he lifted his feet to the saddle beneath him and leap-frogged from the stallion's back.

His off-balance dive landed him against the mare's rump. And he felt himself sliding off. In desperation, he lunged upward, wrapped his arm around Angel's waist, and raked her from her seat and into the water with him.

For brief seconds they hung there, lodged against the mare's flank while Angel thrashed and screamed louder than the roar of the river.

The mare, wild-eyed with terror, plunged and kicked, trying to put some distance between itself and the screaming woman. The rushing torrent captured them immediately and sent them hurtling downriver.

Holding Angel in a tight grip, Rane fought to keep them from being swept under. Each time she opened her mouth in a scream, the muddy water sluiced over their heads and she was reduced to a fit of choking and spitting instead.

Always a strong swimmer, Rane had never attempted to hold onto another thrashing body like now as he tried to keep Angel afloat. Her instinctive fear only worsened matters as she slashed out, trying to keep her head above the water.

Only minutes into the maelstrom, his muscles burned with an intensity that required all his willpower just to hold her. They weren't even halfway across. He anchored her waist with his left arm, with the other he sliced at the water, trying to take them closer to the eastern side of the gorge. Something rammed him from behind, slamming into his back with a sharp pain that quickly faded to numbness. Meanwhile, the overpowering current took them, like two tangled pieces of driftwood, along with the flood.

Rane scanned the bank, trying to get his bearings. The path had disappeared, and with it, all hope of escape. His thoughts turned to survival, for it had come down to that.

The current raced around the bend, taking them with it. Through a muddy haze, Rane saw the bridge looming ahead. He dashed a hand across his eyes. Four men stood at the rail, armed with rifles.

Their only hope was to stay in the water and let it carry them out of harm's way.

A man on the bridge gestured and shouted, "Look! There they are!"

Shots rang out.

The imminent threat sent new strength surging through Rane's limbs. Altering his hold, he clutched Angel to his chest and brought his face level with hers. Her skin had paled, her breath labored, and she held her mouth clamped shut to keep out the noxious water.

"I'm going to take us under," he told her, his breath heaving from his own exertions.

Her eyes on him grew frantic.

"When I tell you, take a deep breath and hold it."

She shook her head and tried to pull away. He held her tighter.

Seconds later, the shadow of the bridge closed over them.

"Now!" he ordered.

He gave her no choice. She sucked in a gasping breath and held it, just before he pulled her into the depths.

Rane's eyes were open, but he saw only darkness, cold and suffocating. Then, they must have passed beyond the bridge, because light streamed through the muddy silt. He paddled, no longer fighting the current. Debris battered at them, sticks resembling ghastly snakes. Repeated sounds pressed in on his ears like muffled detonations of thunder. Something streaked past his arm, inflicting a sting and leaving bubbles in its wake.

The stupid bastards were still shooting at them!

Angel began to struggle again. Rane twisted about until they were nose to nose. Her cheeks were puffed to capacity and her long silver hair floated sideways, undulating with the current. In eerie liquid slow motion, she shook her head, then lifted her hand and pressed it hard over her mouth and nose.

Rane's own lungs burned with the need to expel the air he held. His throat worked convulsively, and he knew it was only a matter of seconds before he would have to give in to the irresistible urge. Hot pain shot up the back of his neck and burrowed into the base of his skull.

He gave a savage kick that sent them shooting upward. Their heads broke the surface at once. He sucked in welcome air. From nowhere, pain slapped the back of his head. Through a dim haze, he felt something graze his shoulder and glide away. He shoved against the large tree branch to keep it from bobbing up and striking him again.

In that split second, the river seized Angel and hurled her away from him.

She kicked and thrashed, trying to stay afloat. He swam, trying desperately to close the gap separating them, until something snaked out and landed beside him on the water.

A rope.

Along the gorge, men swarmed down the rocks like a horde of ants. The one holding the rope stood on a narrow ledge just above the waterline, gathering it in for another cast.

Voices raised in excitement echoed between the canyon walls. Others raced along the rim, hurrying to get ahead of them as they drifted downriver. Several of Horace Lundy's henchmen, equipped with ropes, took up scattered positions along the face of the water-carved wall.

The man on the ledge swung out his loop. Rane held his breath as it whirled higher and faster. Then it flew straight at him. The noose snaked across the water. Rane's heart sank when he saw Angel yanked halfway out of the water. The bastard had snagged her, and he was still too far away to be of any help.

A cheer invaded the gorge.

Rane watched Angel being pulled from the river, helpless to stop it, then sucked in a quick breath and dove once more.

Clinging to the rope like a lifeline, Angel heard someone yell, "Damn it, don't let him get away!"

"We got the woman!"

"Lundy wants Mantorres, too! Either captured or dead. It don't matter which. But he don't want him to get away!"

Her captor dragged Angel from the water and pulled her onto the ledge where he stood. The worst part of it was, she couldn't lift a hand to stop him. All she could do was submit, feeling as though the very life had been sucked from her body by the battering river water.

"You just set still and don't move," the roper told her.

Along the gorge, the others stood silent and watchful. Ropes whistled softly as they swung them round and round, waiting for Rane Mantorres to reappear amid the churning waters.

Heedless of the man's warning, Angel clung to a rock for support and lifted to her knees. Like the others, she scanned the river, waiting, tense and breathless, for Rane's dark head to appear on the surface of the water.

Please, God! Oh, please, please, God! Let him get away.

Suddenly, she saw him, his face low in the water, gasping for air. He'd drifted closer to the bank.

"There he is!"

Three ropes whipped through the air.

Rane upended and dived for it once more. One of the loops snagged his foot as it sliced out of the water. The rope snapped taut and a wild thrashing ensued.

"I got him!" The roper braced himself in the rocks and hauled hand over hand.

Rane's head broke the surface. He grabbed for the rope.

"Don't give him no slack!" her captor shouted.

More ropes were cast. One of them landed over Rane's head and jerked tight around his throat. Instantly, he was yanked back and stretched between the two opposing forces.

Angel clutched at the rock with fear vibrating

through every nerve in her body. They were killing him. If by some miracle they didn't break his neck, then they'd surely choke him to death.

All the men converged on the two who held the ropes and the gorge filled with laugher and shouts of encouragement, as if they were trying to land a great fish.

Frozen with horror, Angel watched them pull him ever closer to the riverbank. His hands were no longer in sight, no longer clinging desperately to the rope around his neck.

"They're killing him!" she sobbed.

"They're just givin' him a Mexican hangin'. So what!" her captor growled. "You're the only one Lundy wants brought back alive."

Through a tearful blur, Angel saw Rane's hand lift from the water. Sunlight flashed from the wicked blade in his hand. He raised it overhead and sliced through the rope shutting off the air from his body. The abrupt release of tension snapped the rope high into the air. Using the impetus of release, he angled forward and severed the snare about his ankle.

The men panicked when their big fish spit out the hook. They scrambled down to the water's edge. A handful of them leaped right into the river.

"Don't let him get away!"

But Rane had already disappeared beneath the surface.

The men drew their guns and fired blindly into the river.

Angel's little paint mare, rolled on its side and caught in a tangle of driftwood, floated past. The bastards had killed her. Farther downstream, Pago still swam southward, the only sign of life remaining in the river. The sight of the magnificent stallion, still alive, wrenched a sob from Angel's aching throat.

Still, she stared at the water, watching for any sign of a dark head to appear. Her eyes grew blurry and unfocused, until she saw nothing at all through the dimness of streaming tears. How long could a man hold his breath and still live?

Silence settled into the canyon, broken only by the rushing torrent below. Angel looked up, surprised to find the sun still shining. She scrubbed at her face with the heels of her hands. The curious faces of strange, rough-looking men crowded the edges of her vision.

Two of them stepped in and wrapped their hands around her arms, lifting her. Once on her feet, she jerked from their grasps and nearly fell. She turned, glaring at them and, as one, they stepped back.

If she looked like a madwoman, so much the better. She snarled. "I hope you all burn in hell for this day's work!"

Chapter Twelve

The back of Rane's nostrils burned as though fiery brands had been thrust into them. The sensation clawed into his brain, distorting his vision. The unstoppable current took him, disoriented him, until he no longer knew which way was up. The raw flames in his chest, filling his lungs, commanded him to cough. He fought his body's own instincts. If he gave in, the river would rush in completely and defeat him. He didn't want to die like this, at the bottom of a river that rarely flooded.

His boots scraped bottom. Above, light streamed through the flow of silt. Daylight. If only he could reach for it. He tried, but his arms and legs had turned to leaden weights commanded by the force of the river.

An image of Angel, pale with fear, flickered through the white-hot agony tearing through him. Lundy had her. The bastard had won.

Angel. Rane had promised to deliver her safely home to her father. Now, he'd failed.

The thought goaded him, pricked the one thing within him that still thrived. His pride.

Gathering his last shreds of strength and willpower, he planted his boots against the river bottom and shoved. The motion propelled him toward the surface.

Radiance struck his blurry eyes. Sun-warmed air washed over his face. He gasped a lifesaving breath deep into his agonized lungs, and they seized with the cough he'd held off, trying to expel the noxious river water he'd ingested.

The gorge had narrowed and the cliffs blurred on either side of him, the river pushing him downstream faster than ever. Working against the numbness of fatigue and cold, Rane righted himself. His labored heart clutched onto a new thread of hope when he saw what was in front of him.

Pago.

The black stallion still swam with unflagging strokes. His sleek, wet hide gleamed like a beacon under the noonday sun. Resembling dead, blackened seaweed, the horse's long tail undulated in and out among the muddy, swollen rills.

A lifeline.

Rane reached for it. His breath heaved harder. After several attempts, he caught a handful of the illusive strands. *Victory!* Quickly, he wrapped his hand, winding the coarse fibers more securely. Then he hung on.

He tried to say, "Take us home, boy," but his voice failed him. Without words to guide him, strength gone, he could only trust the instinct of the faithful horse to carry them both to safety.

****

Hushed voices whispered inside Rane's head. The sounds woke him from fitful dreams of dead horses, hundreds of them. No matter how hard he searched, he couldn't find one still alive to carry him from the carnage.

He opened his eyes a mere crack. Nearby, low orange, blue-tipped flames danced against a background of darkness. The warmth against his face and the smell of wood smoke were familiar comforts.

Dim figures, speaking in low tones, moved around the fire. Rane tried to sit up. His muscles resisted, sore and stiff, as if he'd been beaten. He opened his mouth to speak, but forced nothing more than an alien sounding croak from his throat. The effort cost him. Pain, raw and burning, tore through his throat. Sweat broke out over his body and his breath heaved harder.

"Don't try to speak, *hermano*."

Wolf's face loomed above him. The big half-breed squatted on his heels and dropped down to his knees.

Tears of relief gathered behind Rane's eyes. They lay there, never to be shed, their salty sting adding to his discomfort. Despite the throbbing ache in his shoulder, he lifted a hand to his throat, his eyes on Wolf's face, questioning.

Wolf nodded, understanding. "When I found you, you were wearing a rope. From the looks of your neck, I gather the bastards tried to hang you. You're damn lucky they didn't crush your windpipe."

Rane forced himself to relax against the blankets beneath him. Lucky. Wolf didn't know the half of it.

"I made a poultice to help the swelling," Wolf said. He lifted a strip of cloth containing the remedy and applied it with a gentle touch.

A cool weight settled around Rane's neck. Immediately, the smells of wild onions and animal tallow filled his head. He wrinkled his nose and grimaced.

"Rest now," Wolf commanded. "Heal and grow strong to fight another day."

Another day. But when? In capturing Angel, Lundy now had his bargaining chip. If Roy Clayton gave in to his demands, the bastard would disappear before Rane had the chance to exact the justice he'd planned for so many years. He closed his eyes and prayed to the Holy Virgin to grant him a miracle.

****

Angel clenched her arms beneath her breasts and paced the confines of her elegantly furnished prison. Three days had passed in an agony of waiting since she'd been pulled from the river and taken to the Hacienda. Three days of hellish uncertainty and self-torment. The worst of it stemmed from her inability to go look for Rane. She'd never felt so helpless. By all accounts, he'd perished in the river, but she refused to accept his death. Not without proof.

Oh, Rane.

She ached each time she remembered her last sight of him, disappearing beneath the cold river. That was the last anyone had seen of him. But he couldn't be dead. If he were, she would have known it somehow. Her heart would have felt the loss. But she didn't feel that emptiness. Instinct told her he was still very much alive, and he was out there somewhere.

But in what condition?

After her horrific ride down the flooded river, Angel had discovered an array of bruises ranging over her body. Nothing serious. Meanwhile, Rane had been roped and nearly throttled. Lundy's men had shot at him. Then, he'd stayed underwater longer than seemed humanly possible. She knew he was injured. Not knowing the severity of his injuries held her in a perpetual state of torment.

As yet, she hadn't seen Horace Lundy. He hadn't even bothered to put in an appearance when his minions delivered her to the Hacienda that first day. Was he ashamed to face her? Well, he should be!

Upon her arrival, she'd been handed off to an imposing ape of a man who'd locked her in a bedroom. The only person she'd spoken to since then was the Mexican woman who showed up twice a day to bring her food and tidy the room. A guard, whose face changed with each four-hour shift, was posted outside the bedroom's solitary window.

The first day, Angel had asked the servant to deliver a message. She wanted to speak to Horace Lundy. Nothing had happened. Since then, she'd demanded an audience with Horace at every opportunity. She had finally concluded the servant was either too frightened, or too uncaring, to deliver her plea.

Angel expelled a short breath and turned, kicking aside the cumbersome, too-long hem of the dress she wore. The servant had brought her clothes. Dresses, and undergarments, and even a nightgown. Although fine, the garments smelled of old must, as if they'd been packed away for a long time. They were too long, too big in all respects. She suspected they'd once belonged to Horace's deceased wife, Francine. Given a choice, Angel would rather not wear them. But since her ruined shirt and breeches had disappeared on the occasion of her one and only bath, she didn't have the luxury of refusing.

As day three stretched interminably before her, Angel decided she'd played the docile prisoner long enough. It was time to make some noise and get someone's attention.

She stopped pacing and snatched up a tapestry covered footstool. Driven by anger and frustration, she flung it against the massive wooden door. The stool bounced off and dropped to the floor, splintering one leg. Not enough noise, although destroying Horace's property *did* give her some small measure of release.

She scanned the room for more missiles and backtracked when her gaze raked over an expensive, imported Italian lamp with an etched glass shade that dripped crystal teardrops. Now that just might make some noise. She picked it up with both hands and let it fly at a full-length cheval mirror. The resultant crash of shattering glass startled her and sent her leaping back to dodge the flying shards of debris.

The guard posted outside the window pressed his face against the pane, his eyes rounded with surprise. He lifted a hand and rapped so hard the entire casement rattled. "What the hell you doin'?"

Still primed for violence, Angel snatched up the first thing at hand and flung it at his face. The chamber pot crashed right through the window glass and sent the guard reeling backward to avoid the shower of broken glass.

The bedroom door swung inward with a creak of strained hinges, and she whirled to face it. With a slow sweeping gaze, Lundy's big underling surveyed the damage she'd wrought, and then he lifted his eyes and glared at her.

She tossed back her hair with a defiant flip, planted her hands against her hips and aimed a scowl right back at him.

Without a word, he stalked into the room and picked her up bodily, though she flailed and kicked at him with all her might. He flung her down on the bed with such force, she bounced several times.

She cowered against the bed when he leaned over her, his sour breath blasting in furious gusts against her face.

He lifted a skillet-sized hand and jabbed a condemning finger toward the end of her nose. "Don't move! And don't break nothin' else, or I'll come back and tie you up so's you can't!"

Angel attempted to swallow and found her mouth had suddenly gone dry. Somehow, she forced out, "I demand to see Horace Lundy this instant!"

The guard straightened and stood looking down at her from the side of the bed with his ham-fisted, ape-like arms hanging straight down at his sides. His heavy black caterpillar brows collided over his nose that was flattened and crooked. The incorrectly healed breaks forced him to breathe through his open mouth, which made him look like a slack-jawed dimwit. "I'll pass it on," he said. He turned and walked out the door. Seconds later, the heavy bolt on the outside of the door jammed into locked position with a loud click.

Weariness replaced the tension holding Angel rigid on the bed. She sighed, and then slowly relaxed, sinking back into the linen-covered pillows.

Breaking Horace's expensive possessions—while satisfying—was not the way to fight them. They had her at their mercy. Like the big brute said, if she made too much fuss, they could tie her up. If she screamed, they could even resort to gagging her.

What chance did she have? Not even Rane had been able to prevail against them.

Scalding tears welled and overflowed to streak each side of her face. She didn't bother wiping them away. Despite her conviction that Rane still lived, her heart felt bruised and sore, and she could no more stop the tears than she could escape the four walls imprisoning her.

Angel's eyes had started to drift closed when the bolt outside the door emitted a grinding screech. She sprang upright, instantly wide-eyed and alert.

The door opened and, once more, the big guard walked into the room with no warning.

Angel scooted to the side of the bed and set her feet on the floor. Were they moving her now that she'd done some damage? To a windowless storage room, perhaps, barren of furnishings or even light? The thought gave her a deep-seated shudder.

"You're to come with me," the guard said. "Mr. Lundy's ready to see you now."

Surprise brought her to her feet. She submitted when he clamped strong fingers around her arm and led her out the door.

Out on the portico, the heels of her boots rang hollow on terra-cotta tiles. Once fashionable, the boots were now scuffed and the thin leather worn nearly through from the constant rubbing of stirrups. With her free hand, she held the front hem of the dress off the floor to keep from tripping over it.

The guard led her through an arch and into an open-air courtyard. She lifted her head and inhaled deeply of the first fresh air she'd breathed in three days. It was cooler here and smelled of green algae and damp musty earth. Trained wisteria covered the curved stone arches surrounding the yard. At its center, water poured forth in a steady stream from an upended urn held in the dimpled hands of a chubby-faced cherub and splashed into an irregularly shaped pool. The musical sound echoed with a hollow tinkle between the confining walls. Fronds of ferns and other aquatic flora surrounded the artificial edge of the pool. Just beneath the water's surface, the lazy movements of several large goldfish reflected the noonday sun.

The few times in her life she had visited the Hacienda, the courtyard had enchanted Angel. Now, she only saw it in passing. Once on the other side, the big man dragged her through another portal and, suddenly, she stood before the closed door of Horace Lundy's private office.

The guard raised his hand and rapped three times.

"Come in."

Angel recognized Horace's voice. Her heart skipped to a faster rhythm. Queasiness assailed her stomach. She'd imagined this moment countless times during the past three days. Now that it was at hand, all the words she'd planned flew right out of her head.

The guard released her arm. "Go on in," he said. "And don't try anything. I'll be standing right here."

Angel hesitated long enough to draw in a deep, strengthening breath before she opened the door and stepped inside.

Horace Lundy sat behind his desk with his fingers steepled together and propped against his chin. When he saw her, he gripped the chair's armrests and stood.

Angel closed the door and pressed her back against it, taking in the man before her. He'd always dressed to the teeth. But now, his dark suit looked as if he'd slept in it and more than once. Two years had wrought changes. He'd aged and not very gracefully. His once dark hair had gone almost completely white. His skin looked sallow and heavily lined. Although he belonged to her father's generation, Angel had always thought him handsome and distinguished. Now, he simply looked old and not quite healthy to boot. He'd always seemed so devoted to his wife, Francine. Had the woman's death, and his subsequent financial reversal, brought on this rapid decline?

He looked so harmless, almost fragile. All thoughts of murder evaporated from her mind. After all, this was Horace, a man she'd known all her life. Now that he'd seen her, surely he would relent in his extortion scheme. She found herself wanting to feel sorry for him. But she quickly conquered that impulse. Anyone who employed the methods he'd used to get her there didn't deserve pity.

He offered her a tenuous smile. "Evangeline."

Angel pushed away from the door and strode forward with renewed determination. "Horace, I demand to be released this very minute!"

He sighed airily. "So much for pleasantries."

"Pleasant! You call being shot at and held here against my will pleasant!"

"If you'll take a seat, we'll discuss it."

"I'd rather stand."

"Suit yourself." He lowered himself to his comfortable leather chair and laced his fingers over his chest. "I understand you've thrown quite a tantrum in your room."

"If I could, I would demolish this entire house with my bare hands!"

"I understand," he replied with damnable calm, "but I wish you'd try to control your temper. It looks like you might be here for quite some time."

"I don't think so," she retorted. "Do you think my father's just sitting over at the Flying C twiddling his thumbs?"

Horace shrugged. "He doesn't have enough manpower to take any real initiative against me. This place is a fortress. He's still dragging his feet with the money, which is unfortunate. Either he pays up, or you'll be spending Christmas at the Hacienda."

She knew he wouldn't respond to threats. Maybe if she tried reasoning with him. She inhaled a steadying breath and said in a calmer tone, "Please let me go."

"No."

"If you'll let me go to my father, I'll talk to him. He's a fair man. If you release me of your own volition, I'm sure he'll look on it favorably. He might help you, if I ask him to. I'm sure he doesn't want to see you ruined. Be reasonable, Horace, and he'll help you. I know he will."

The corners of his lips curved in a satiric smile. A memory flirted with the edges of her consciousness, but she couldn't quite grasp it.

"I think you overestimate your influence, my dear. Besides, do you think a little loan is going to help me? It's going to take more than that... much more. Roy Clayton fenced off land that's been public domain for the past thirty years. My cattle died as a consequence. I'll accept nothing less than full payment for them."

Angel clutched her arms against her waist and paced in front of the floor to ceiling bookshelves lining the walls, a veritable library of gilt-edged volumes. She paused at the window and stared through the parting of heavy velvet drapes the color of northern evergreens. Sunlight bleached colorless the stone wall in the near distance that blocked the view of the outside world. Horace was right. The Hacienda had been built like a fort. The stone wall continued around the perimeter of the compound. With two men positioned atop each wall, the place was unapproachable. The outer defense had been built at the same time as the house, during the days when raiding bands of Indians and Mexicans were a constant threat.

"For thirty years, I've watched Roy Clayton shout in his crude way and ride rough-shod over everyone to get what he wanted," the bitter man continued. "Just once before I die, I intend to have the last word."

She stopped and huffed an incredulous breath. "So, is that what this is about? Revenge? I thought you only wanted the money."

Horace fell silent. Angel turned to find him watching her with a critical, assessing gaze. She looked down, trying to see what he saw: the ill fitting clothing on her body, her sun-browned hands. Stark disapproval blazed in his sunken eyes.

He leaned forward and transferred his clasped hands to the top of the desk. "I don't see why you're so anxious to go home. Even I can see, two years back east hasn't smoothed your rough edges. You look so much like Ilsa, and yet you're so very different than she was." Lines of sadness creased his forehead. "You *are* your father's daughter."

The words echoed through her mind, only it was her aunt's voice she heard. *You're still your father's daughter.*

"Ilsa wanted so much more for you. If only she had lived..."

Angel's head snapped up. She ground her teeth. "How dare you drag my mother into this and insult me! Do you dare still call yourself a gentleman? You loosed a horde of bounty hunters on me. Did you tell them they were free to shoot at will? What do you think my mother would have had to say about that!"

He regarded her in silence. It was answer enough.

"Is your idea of a lady one who submits passively to this kind of treatment? If so, that's one thing I'll never be." She gripped the edge of the desk with both hands and leaned, trembling, toward him.

"You'll never get away with this. You're out of your depth. Men have died because of your foolishness."

He cocked an indifferent brow. "Dregs," he said. "This country is better rid of them."

A twisting pain wormed through Angel's heart. "Why did you order your men to kill Rane Mantorres?"

Mention of the *pistolero's* name wrought a change in Lundy's composed mien. His eyes narrowed and took on a faraway look. A long moment passed before he answered. "He asked for what he got. For years, he's been a thorn in my side."

"Why?" Angel demanded.

"Oh, you know these Mexicans. They get something into their heads and they turn it into a crusade. They're all fanatics," he concluded, waving his hand dismissively. "But that's all in the past now. Dead and buried."

With a shudder, he visibly pulled himself away from his dark thoughts and met her level gaze once more. "I hope his death hasn't troubled you overmuch. I know when people are thrown together in difficult circumstances, they sometimes form an attachment."

The man's coldness played like icy fingers along Angel's spine. She had a sudden, overwhelming desire to be elsewhere, anywhere but in that room with him. She went to the door and placed her hand over the knob.

"Will you have dinner with me this evening?" he asked from behind her. "It's been such a long time since I've had a female companion at my table."

Angel shivered with deep-rooted revulsion at the softly uttered request. He sounded as though he'd completely forgotten their conversation of five minutes ago. "I'd sooner break bread with a snake," she replied with more sadness than venom.

"Very well." He didn't bother hiding his disappointment.

Angel opened the door and found the guard barring her way.

"Escort her back to her room," Horace instructed.

The guard wrapped strong fingers around her arm and led her away.

Angel was locked inside the bedroom once more. In her absence, the broken glass had been cleared away, along with every remaining unnecessary object in the room. The shattered window admitted only narrow shafts of light between planks that had been nailed over the opening. She sat on the side of the bed, still and thoughtful. Her meeting with Horace had left her feeling more disturbed than before. The man had lost all reason. It was as if he were dead inside. Under the circumstances, there was no telling what he might do.

She had to escape.

Chapter Thirteen

Rane hunkered on his heels and picked up a handful of powdery dead ash, letting it sift through his fingers to blow away on the fitful wind. The acrid stench of it clogged his nostrils. He clenched his jaw, trying to will away the cold rage that quickened his heart.

Fire had blackened the four thick adobe walls surrounding him. Only they and the fire pit remained.

As he looked around the gutted room, memories assailed him. Angel standing at the door. Angel seated at his table, reviling him for ruining her life. Angel in his bed... All so recent. He squeezed his eyes closed, saddened to realize nothing more had ever occurred within these walls that warranted remembering. Had his life truly been that empty?

Leaves rattling in the restless breeze sounded like rushing water. He opened his eyes and lifted them, seeing open sky where once the thatched roof had been. The new growth on a sheltering cottonwood that had been green only days ago hung limp and black.

Nothing worth salvaging remained here. Lundy's men had done a thorough job. Thank God they hadn't blundered across his mother's grave. Hidden in the grove, her stone had gone undisturbed.

Resigned, Rane stood and brushed the ash from his fingers. He stepped through the opening where the stout door had once hung and walked into the yard beyond. He paused, facing the barren southern terrain, the faint trail leading through the desolate Mexican landscape, straight to Clayton Station. His jaw clenched with determination so fierce a shudder ran through him.

The road to his destiny lay before him; he had only to travel it. Angel was being held prisoner at the Hacienda, and Horace Lundy still prevailed, but not for much longer, he vowed. Lundy thought he was dead, and Rane knew when the man found out otherwise, he would stop at nothing now to kill him.

"An eye for an eye, *viejo*."

Pago waited in the yard and whickered softly at Rane's approach. He took the horse's reins in hand and climbed into the saddle. With a touch against the stallion's neck, they turned southward and eased into a slow lope. While the wind blew warm against his face, cold purpose lay like a heavy weight in Rane's heart.

****

The sun was setting, and Angel's spirits sank right along with it. Each approaching night filled her with dread. During the day, light filtered in through the inch-wide gaps between the boards nailed over the bedroom window. If she sat next to it, she could catch a breath of fresh air. If she peered through the cracks, she could watch the activity around the ranch compound. But when the sun sank below the horizon, complete darkness settled around her, as thick and suffocating as a tomb.

The crystal lamp she'd broken hadn't been replaced. In fact, every breakable object in the room had been removed. Lundy could have given her a silver branch of candles, but he hadn't. Was he afraid she'd set the room ablaze?

As night pressed down on the compound, light flared just on the other side of the boards. She moved closer to the crack she'd been looking through. The guard outside was lighting a cigarette. The smell of sulfur drifted to her when he waved out the flame and tossed the match to the ground.

Angel's lips parted with the urge to speak. She inhaled a short breath and held it, refusing to let the words slip from her tongue. She knew she must be going mad when she was tempted to draw one of her ruffian jailers into conversation.

Pressing her forehead against the rough board, she slowly expelled the air she held. Her throat ached with the tears she stubbornly held at bay. How much longer could she stand being shut away in the darkness like an animal?

Angel woke from a doze with the side of her face braced against the board and the overpowering smell of smoke in her nostrils. Faint voices, raised in panic, drifted from somewhere outside. She lifted her head and blinked several times to clear away the fog of sleep.

An unnatural orange glow spilled through the cracks. Alarm jolted through her nerves endings, bringing her fully awake. She bolted up from the chair and crowded her face against the boards, peering between them.

On the far side of the compound, smoke roiled up in an angry black cloud from an outbuilding. Tree-tall flames licked outward from the billowing column and flickered against the blackness of the sky.

Lundy's men ran back and forth, shouting, the brilliance behind them reducing them to wavering, stick-thin silhouettes.

Angel's thoughts tumbled. If her father had launched an attack on the Hacienda, there would have been gunfire. She'd heard no shots. The hope that had soared within her just as quickly died.

Behind her, the bolt on the bedroom door screeched. She turned her back to the window and watched the door swing inward. The dark figure of a man stood in the opening, rimmed against the smoky haze quickly filling the courtyard behind him.

Angel's heart tripped, and then redoubled its frantic pace.

He took a step toward her. "Angel?"

A wild cry of joy escaped her lips as she snatched up her hem and flew across the room, straight into Rane's embrace.

His arms settled around her, holding her close. Weak-legged with relief, she clung, absorbing the feel of him. "I knew you weren't dead!"

Under her hands, his lean, steely muscles shifted. He gripped her arms and held her away from him. Though his eyes were nothing more than black voids in the dimness, she felt his piercing gaze raking her face.

"Are you all right?"

His voice sounded like gravel had been mixed with the smooth, dark velvet she remembered.

"I'm fine," she assured him. "They didn't hurt me."

"Then let's get out of here."

Taking her hand, he led her through the door. Just

outside, the big brute who had been her jailer lay unmoving, propped against the wall. A sizeable lump above his temple leaked a thin trace of blood down the side of his face.

They stepped around the man's sprawled legs, and then Rane moved quickly to the end of the portico. He ducked into a doorway and led her through a passage connecting the kitchen and laundry. The hallway took them outside, into the compound. A gust of night air washed over Angel's face when she stepped into the open for the first time in many days. Rane motioned her to stay against the outside wall.

The shadow of the house covered them in darkness, but overhead the night sky was lit to near brilliance by the fire in the distance. Rane moved to the corner and peered around it. In seconds, he returned. "We're going to make a run for the wall."

Angel's pulse fluttered in panic. How did he plan to get over the wall and do it without being seen?

"Stay low," he instructed.

She nodded, her heart beating so hard she didn't think her chest would contain it.

Angel hitched up the unwieldy hem of the oversized dress she wore and draped it around her left arm. "I'm ready."

Rane grasped her hand in his once more. "Let's go." He stooped low and set out across the open ground.

Angel bent and ran with him. A mixture of fear and exhilaration surged through her veins. Fear of capture, the promise of freedom, and Rane's hand, warm and strong around hers.

In the distance, a swarm of men scurried back and forth. Some had found buckets and attempted to douse the out-of-control blaze. From the corner of her eye, Angel saw the structure tilt with a groan and screech of failing timbers. The roof collapsed, sending sparks shooting into the darkened heavens to rival a Fourth of July fireworks display.

Rane increased the pace. Angel's breath labored, rasping past her lips in quick bursts. They reached the wall and ducked behind a cluster of bushes. Grateful for the respite, Angel braced against the cool stone and pressed a hand against the stitch in her side, panting for breath, and wondered just how he planned to get them out of there.

The fire lit up the entire compound. With the collapse of the building, the men had given up trying to save it and now stood around watching it burn. If she and Rane stepped from behind the bushes, they would be seen instantly.

"How do we get out of here?" she asked breathlessly.

"The same way I got in. Come on."

She turned, and found him standing below her and thought the unnatural light must be playing tricks with her eyesight.

"Come on," he urged again.

A tunnel! Like some feudal castle from a bygone age, the Hacienda had a bolt hole. Wasting no time, she followed him into the pit. The low, narrow space forced them to crawl on hands and knees. Black as pitch, she might as well have been blind. Angel moved forward by feel, inching along the cool stones on the heels of her hands and with each movement tugging the hateful dress from beneath her trapped knees. The air felt chill and reeked of wet molder. She blundered through puddles of dank water. Slime coated her fingers.

Angel's hands felt raw and her knees had started to ache almost unbearably by the time the passage took an upward slant, signaling its end.

They emerged in the middle of a chinaberry thicket, no more than a hundred feet outside the wall. The light from the distant fire had grown dimmer.

Wasting no time, Rane led her to the black stallion tethered to one of the trees and lifted her onto its back.

****

Seated on the front of the saddle and cradled between Rane's thighs, Angel relaxed against him and let the smooth gait of the horse rock her. Under the dim moonlight, she couldn't see much except the dark profile of his face. For the moment, that was enough. He was alive. She settled her head against his strong shoulder and stared up at him, soaking in the feel of his warmth and virile strength. Though they both now stank of the dank tunnel, they had smelled worse. After having known him for only a few weeks, she had a history with this man, and she was amazed at all they had endured together.

"How did you know about the tunnel?" she asked.

"I found it long ago and quite by accident."

"So, you've been to the Hacienda before."

"It's been a while."

Still cryptic. Still not forthcoming. *Horace Lundy has something that belongs to me.* But what?

"Once you take me home, you'll no longer have any bargaining power. Do you still think you can force Horace to give you what you want?"

His chin dipped. After a moment, he lifted it again and looked at her. "I'm a patient man. It may take longer now, but I can wait."

Again, she was struck by the new rough quality underlying his whiskey potent voice. Was the change permanent? Undoubtedly, the rope around his neck had done some damage.

Lifting her hand, she eased her fingers inside the collar of his shirt. To her surprise, he allowed it. Beneath her fingertips his pulse surged, strong and rhythmic. A welt ringed the base of his throat. He had suffered and risked so much. And tonight, just when she was near to giving up hope, he had carried through on his promise. Again, at great personal risk.

She dropped her hand to her lap. "Where have you been, Rane?"

"Across the border. With Wolf."

"Wolf?"

"Yes, Wolf. I owe him. Again. I would have been here sooner, but he hid my gun and horse so I couldn't leave."

To Angel, that simple statement spoke volumes. She knew, if Wolf had managed to take Rane's gun, it was only because Rane had been in no shape to stop him.

"I sensed a connection between the two of you. And he calls you 'brother.' Why?"

"When we were boys, we cut our wrists and mingled our blood."

"So, you became blood brothers."

"Yes, and to this day, the bond remains strong."

She knew how deeply embedded his sense of loyalty,

or was it merely duty and unfinished business that had sent him to the Hacienda to rescue her?

Only the chirp of crickets and the soft thud of the horse's hooves filled the silence. What would happen now? They were already on the Flying C, her father's land. What would happen to them both when she was finally back home again?

The two-story white house loomed out of the darkness. Home. Angel sat up straight, her nerves suddenly thrumming beneath her skin.

Rane halted the horse. Against her back, she felt the tension humming through him. "Are you ready to do this?" he asked.

"No, not really." She released a shaky breath. "Coming home was all I dreamed of for the past two years. Now that I'm here...well, this isn't at all how I envisioned it."

A solitary guard sat on the wide front steps with his back propped against a newel post. Chin drooped to his chest, he appeared to be asleep.

While the rest of the house was dark, yellow lamplight glowed like a beacon from a front corner window on the first floor. Her father's office. Dare she hope he'd been keeping vigil since she'd gone missing?

Rane circled outside the perimeter of the ranch yard and tied the horse in the deep cover of the wild tangle of underbrush and trees that grew along the northwest corner. Except for the sleeping guard, the place looked deserted.

Hugging the deep shadows, they approached the back of the house. Angel found the secreted key above the facing, just where it had always been, and unlocked the door opening into the kitchen. When she entered the house, familiar smells and textures surrounded her. She felt as though she'd stepped back in time. As though she'd never left. Suddenly, all her old fears and insecurities came rushing back, nearly paralyzing her.

"Where to?"

The deep growl of Rane's voice prodded her. "This way." She led him through the kitchen and into the hallway that divided the house down its center. Light leaked from under the door of the front corner room, and there she stopped. "In here," she whispered.

Rane pulled her aside and took her place before the closed door. When he laid his hand around the knob and eased it open, her heart galloped.

Inside, three wicks burned in the overhead fixture, casting a warm glow over the room. Unlike Horace Lundy's combination office and library, here there were no shelves with floor to ceiling books bound in luxurious leather. The furnishings were spare and rough-hewn. A gun rack loaded with a variety of weapons. Crudely drawn maps of the Flying C and its holdings were the only ornamentation on the walls. The floor was bare planks worn smooth from countless footsteps. Many times in the past, Angel had tried to talk her father into putting down a carpet, but he wouldn't have it. This room was his domain, elementary and scarred. He'd always told her he didn't have time to worry about spilling something or dropping a load of ashes on the floor.

Just as Angel had suspected, her father sat slumped in the chair behind his desk with his fingers intertwined atop his chest, sound asleep. Despite the hour, he was fully dressed in worn denims and a faded cotton shirt, even down to his boots, which were propped on a corner of the desktop and crossed at the ankle. An empty bottle of Cyrus Noble sipping whiskey lay overturned on the blotter.

A smile tugged the corners of her lips. The warmth gathering around her heart sent tears of relief swimming across her vision.

Rane took a step inside the room. When the old man still didn't move, he stomped his boot down on the floor.

Her father blinked, coming awake slowly. Obviously, he'd consumed the entire bottle lying on the desk. Then he looked up, spotted Rane, and registered blank surprise. He sat bolt upright, dropped his boots to the floor with a loud slap, and then sprang to his feet. "What the hell is this!"

Rane took another quick step into the room and lifted the Colt from his holster. "Just stand easy, Clayton, and keep your hands above the desk."

Her father frowned at the gun before lifting his hands out from his sides and glaring a hole through Rane.

"Just who the hell are you?"

Angel stepped into the light, snagging her father's attention for the first time.

Confusion entered his eyes, and then she watched some of the mottled color drain from his face. "Angel?"

"Yes, Pa. It's me. I've come home."

Despite Rane's order, her father came around the desk. An arm's length away from her, he stopped. She fidgeted inwardly as his shrewd eyes raked her from head to toe, taking in her bedraggled state. Her unbound hair had fallen in a tangled mass over one shoulder. The too-roomy dress hung limp and was smeared with drying mud and slimy black-green algae.

Angel tried to still her trembling chin, but with each second that passed, she withered a tiny bit more on the inside.

"What on God's earth happened to you?" her father exclaimed.

Angel's heart sank completely. Had she truly expected a smile, or even a hug? She should have known.

She darted a quick glance at Rane. What must he think of this father and daughter reunion? Though the gun remained in his hand, he now looked at her. Was that compassion she saw in his eyes?

Angel stiffened her spine and planted her hands at the sagging waistline of the dress. "Well, that's a fine greeting. I've been gone two years, I'm kidnapped, imprisoned, and all you have to say to me is 'what happened to you'?"

God help her, nothing at all had changed. Her father was still just as cold and angry as he'd always been, and she was still responding to him in kind.

"I think the real question is, what happened to *you*? What have you been doing all this time, while Horace had me locked up at the Hacienda?" Anger on high burn, she strode past him and then rounded on him again, flinging a hand in Rane's direction. "If it weren't for Rane, I'd still be there."

Just as he always had, her father ignored her anger and turned on Rane. "She said 'Rane'. Rane Mantorres?"

"That's right," Rane replied.

Her father huffed an incredulous breath. "I heard you

were dead."

"Rumor." Rane shot a pointed look in her direction. "I've found it's often wise not to listen to them."

Heat crawled into Angel's cheeks. She knew he was alluding to the rumors he'd heard about *her*.

Her father stepped directly in front of Rane and the pistol in his hand. "Put that damn gun away," he demanded. "I won't talk to a man while he's holdin' a gun on me and in my own damn house!"

The two men stared at each other a long moment. Angel could only wonder what passed between them. Some shared understanding? She had no way of knowing. But when it was over, her father turned his back on Rane and walked away. Rane holstered his Colt, and then crossed his arms over his chest and stood staring down at the floor.

When her father reached the desk, he turned and planted his bony behind atop the corner. "How'd you get her out of there?"

Rane shrugged, as if it had been a simple undertaking. "Sometimes one man can accomplish what an entire army cannot. I set fire to the carriage shed, which lured everyone away from house."

Her father quirked one shaggy brow. "You burned Horace's fancy, custom-made rig?"

"The rig, two wagons, and several crates of assorted china and silver pieces that were hidden there," Rane amended.

Her father snickered like a mischievous youngster. "I'd love to see the look on Horace's face when he finds out Angel's gone."

Rane shook his head. "He's not going to be happy."

Sobering, her father's pale gray gaze settled on the gunfighter, and Angel could tell he was sizing him up. "So, what's your stake in this? I heard you bucked Lundy at his own game. Now, you've brought Angel home. Why? Do you expect me to pay you the bounty Horace was promising?"

"No. This has nothing to do with money. It's an old grudge between Lundy and me. To put it very simply, the reason I helped you is because it hurts him."

The jab penetrated all the way to Angel's heart.

Turning her back on both of them, she hugged her arms beneath her breasts and wandered to the darkened window behind her father's chair.

A wooden leg beneath the desk creaked when her father shifted. "So, what're you sayin'? You wantin' to work for me?"

"No. But you do need help. Where are all your men?"

"There's a guard with a shotgun outside. The rest are patrollin' the deadline between here and the Hacienda and the fence. If anybody from down there tries to get across, my men will stop them."

Rane's chuckle oozed sarcasm. "I hate to tell you, Clayton, but your guard is sleeping on the job. And as for your men… We came from the Hacienda. No one stopped us. You need more men right here, around the house. If Lundy decides to strike back at you, there's no way you'll be able to stop him."

"You reckon he'd do such a thing?"

"After tonight, he'll be more desperate than ever."

Despite the devastation roiling inside her, Angel couldn't hold silent any longer. She turned from the window. "Rane's right, Pa. After talking to Horace, I believe he's capable of anything. He's not himself."

Her father came off the desk. "Well, what the hell am I supposed to do? This ain't no fort, and I ain't hirin' a bunch of lowlife gunnies who'll jump fence at the drop of a hat."

"I can get you all the men you need," Rane said.

Roy spun on him quickly. "What men? You mean villagers who don't even own guns and couldn't hit the broad side of the barn even if they did!"

"You provide the guns, and I promise you they'll hit the barn."

Her father shook his head.

"Your choice," Rane said. He threw a frowning glance toward the window. Angel followed the movement with a sinking sensation. He was thinking about leaving.

He shifted and tugged his hat lower on his forehead. "Think about what I said, Clayton. You have your daughter in the house now. Do you really want to gamble again with her safety?"

"I take care of what's mine," her father retorted.

"Good. Then I leave her in your hands."

Rane backed toward the door. Just before he slipped into the shadowed hallway, his gaze collided with hers for one brief instant. Banked fire smoldered in the depths of his eyes. His lips quirked. "Miss Clayton, it's been a pleasure."

Then he was gone.

Angel clutched her arms against her waist, gripping until her nails bit into her flesh, trying to suppress a wild desire to rush after him. She held her breath, listening for the sound of his retreating footsteps, but heard nothing.

She released her breath, turned...and found her father watching her with speculative, narrowed eyes. "Tell me one good reason why I shouldn't have that greaser hunted down and shot," he said with a calm that unnerved her completely.

"Don't be a fool, Pa. Why would you want to kill someone who's helped you and saved my skin more than once?"

"Did he mistreat you in any way?"

Somehow, she met his steady gaze without faltering. "No."

Her father let out a long breath. She realized he'd been holding it.

"This is an ugly business," he said. "There'll be talk, you know that.

She dropped her head and merely nodded.

"The sooner this damned fence war is put to rest, the sooner it'll all be forgotten."

Forgotten. Maybe the fence war would dim in importance with the passage of days, but Angel knew she'd never forget Rane. Her heart ached with the thought that she might never see him again. It burned like a hot coal in her brain. They'd never really said goodbye.

"I'm glad you're home, Angel."

She lifted her eyes to her father's face as his kindly spoken words took her by surprise.

A sudden grin tilted the drooping gray mustache hiding most of his mouth. "You sound like a Yankee when you talk."

The out-of-the-blue remark coaxed a weak smile to

her lips. "You'll just have to get used to it."

Now that they were alone, he stood back and looked at her again. She knew his sharp old eyes missed nothing.

"I hope that dress didn't fit you when you left New York. You look like you've been starved and staked out in the sun to dry."

Chapter Fourteen

Angel picked up the silverware lying atop the folded, yellowed napkin beside her father's plate. For the third time, she realigned the pieces so they were precisely spaced. The cloth covering the dining table looked dingy, though not quite as bad as the napkin. All the linens in the house needed a good washing, but that was just one chore on a very long list of things she'd found that needed attention.

After awakening to an empty house, she'd spent the entire morning dusting, sweeping, and clearing out what had to be several weeks' worth of accumulated trash. It was a wonder the place wasn't infested with rats.

What had happened to the servants?

Rather than pace the length of the dining room and adjacent parlor again, Angel pulled a chair next to the window and perched on its edge. The sun was going down. Where was her father, or anyone else for that matter? When he didn't show up at the supper hour, she'd worried, then gotten angry. Now worry had settled permanently in the pit of her stomach.

Had he run into trouble with Lundy's men? What if something had happened to him? She squeezed her eyes closed and pressed her hands to her forehead. *Damn you, Pa, where are you?*

Blowing out a breath, she opened her eyes, grabbed the arms of the chair and launched herself out of it. Gray dusk had settled within the parlor. She crossed to the fireplace for matches and lit the wicks of the two lamps stationed at each end of the sturdy mantle. As she reached to replace the box, her attention caught on the photograph displayed at the mantle's center.

Her mother's picture perfect image dredged up a new wave of guilt. Unsmiling, her mother sat ramrod straight with her lace-covered hands folded primly in her lap.

Angel moved closer and pressed her fingertips to the sepia-toned image, then quickly pulled them back.

"Ilsa." She whispered the name almost in dread. If she spoke it too loudly, would her mother's apparition appear to smite her? No. Her mother's spirit had never dwelled within these walls. This had always been her father's domain.

Angel had often wondered why a woman such as her mother, a lady of gentle rearing, had married a man as coarse and tempestuous as Roy Clayton. An unlikely match. A fine blooded mare and a common workhorse. She was the result, neither completely coarse nor fine, but something in between, and both sides pulled at her.

From outside, the hoof beats of an approaching horse grew steadily louder. Her heart leaped. Rushing to a window, she saw her father headed for the barn on a big gray. *Thank God.*

On her way out of the parlor, she snatched the box of matches down from the mantle and hurried into the dining room. Six ivory tapers occupied the candelabrum standing in the center of the table. One by one, she lit them. Pinpoints of light reflected from the silver and the rims of the two ordinary china plates she'd set out. Standing back, she realized the yellowed lighting made even the sullied linens appear almost elegant. Perhaps the day's work wouldn't be a total loss.

Out in the kitchen, the back door whined open, and then closed forcefully, sending a shudder throughout the house.

Expectantly, Angel turned and straightened her spine. Her palms were sweaty. She started to scrub them against the skirt of her dress and thought better of it. Calm and poise, she reminded herself. *A lady is always calm and poised in any situation.* That was the first rule she'd learned at Miss Marvel's Academy.

At the very last instant, she remembered to put a smile on her lips.

Her father stepped through the door and stopped. More accurately, he froze. He'd removed his hat and the flattened hair ringing his head was damp with sweat. Fine dust coated his worn denims and his boots. He looked like an old cowhand who'd wandered into the wrong place, and he stared at her as if he'd seen a ghost.

As the seconds passed, Angel felt the smile slipping from her lips. Despite the possible damage to delicate fabric, she gripped handfuls of rustling silk in her sweaty palms. She glanced down, at the peacock blue dress gleaming in the candlelight. The gown was nothing too elaborate, just something she'd worn on occasion for the evening meal at her aunt's back in New York.

Her father continued to stare at her.

"Pa, is something wrong?"

He blinked, and then seemed to come back to himself. He cleared his throat. "No. Why would anything be wrong?"

In the renewed silenced, the big Regulator in the hallway ticked off several seconds.

Her father lifted his hand and motioned toward her dress. "I see you found your belongings."

The smile returned to her lips. "Yes. Thank you."

"They came in on the stage without you. I had everything put up in your room." He cleared his throat again. "So. I guess you found them."

"Yes," she repeated. She tried to smooth the frown she felt pulling at her brows. Why did he seem so ill at ease?

As if he'd read her mind, he chuckled softly and waved a hand through the air. "You know, when I walked in, for a minute there..."

"What?" she prompted.

"Well, you look just like your mother."

So, he *had* thought he'd seen a ghost. Disconcerted, Angel nervously smoothed the side of her upswept hair. He followed the movement. She dropped her hand quickly, realizing she'd unconsciously imitated the style her mother wore in the photograph.

She forced another smile. "Well, then," she said with a serenity she was far from feeling. "I have supper prepared. If you'll take a seat, I'll serve."

He shifted his feet. "I didn't know you'd be cookin', so I ate some beans and pone with the boys over at the line shack."

He must have seen her disappointment because he swept a quick glance at the table and hastily added, "But since you've gone to so much trouble, I guess I could eat a little more."

Bless his old heart. He was trying to meet her half way. The knowledge warmed her.

She carried a plate of fried ham, a bowl of mashed potatoes, and a basket of biscuits from the kitchen and placed them on the table. Her father sat at the head of it, in his usual spot.

"Looks good." He waited until she'd taken her seat at the opposite end of the table, and then reached for his napkin and unceremoniously dumped his silverware. Angel bit her lip as she watched him stuff one end of the napkin inside the dusty, sweaty collar of his shirt. Plucking up his fork, he stretched forward and speared a thick slice of ham.

Angel picked up her napkin and carefully placed it across her lap. "Everything may be a little...dry," she warned. "It's been sitting in the warmer for quite some time."

He tossed her a grin. "Looks good to me. Sorry I left you alone so long today."

He picked up the potato bowl and spooned a huge lump onto his plate. Just as she'd feared, they'd congealed to a solid mass.

"What happened to the help?' she asked.

"Lit out." He took a biscuit from the top of the pile and bit into it. With a sinking heart, she realized he took a long time chewing it before he swallowed. "When Horace's boys started aimin' bullets across the fence, they were too scared to stick around." He shook his head. "Gutless."

He still appeared to be working some of the biscuit around inside his mouth. She'd forgotten drinks.

"I made coffee," she offered.

He nodded. "That'd be good."

After returning with steaming cups of black coffee and sitting his in front of him, she returned to her seat. "So, what have you been doing all day?"

He eschewed the delicate china handle and wrapped his hand around the body of the cup. After blowing back the steam, he took a long drink. "Been keepin' an eye out for what's goin' on down at the Hacienda."

"What's been going on?"

"Horace's men are pullin' out on him. Been ridin' out of there all day, like rats desertin' a sinkin' ship."

Rats deserting a sinking ship, an apt description. A hopeful sign. Perhaps this senseless fighting would end without more bloodshed. "Do you think it's over?"

Her father shrugged. "Maybe, maybe not. Too soon to tell."

"What do you plan on doing now?" she asked.

"Wait." He expelled a heavy breath. "All we can do now is wait and see what happens."

Waiting was the hardest thing of all. Angel felt as if she'd been waiting for one thing or another for most of her life. Her thoughts veered to Rane. He, too, had been waiting. For the opportunity to get to Lundy. Was that time near at hand? Had he also been out there somewhere today watching Horace's men ride away?

When her father had eaten his fill, Angel carried the dishes to the kitchen. After blowing out the candles on the dining table, she followed him into the parlor.

He stood with his elbows propped atop the well-used makeshift bar he'd built next to the liquor cabinet, holding a half-filled glass of whiskey in his hand. The top of the bar was scarred and water-ringed, like many of the furnishings in the house. The parlor's worn horsehair sofa and a pair of matching armchairs looked downright shabby compared to the things in Aunt Nelda's elegantly furnished home. Standing there in her silk evening dress, Angel felt out of step with her surroundings. Her father fit here perfectly, but she no longer knew exactly where she belonged.

Hugging her arms across her stomach, she wandered to a window with a southern view. Across the darkened yard the faint glow of lamplight revealed someone now occupied the bunkhouse. She strained her ears, but heard no banter of rowdy cowhands. Only eerie silence came back to her. Where were all her father's men? Out there in the darkness somewhere, guarding over the house? Somehow, she didn't think so.

"I've been meaning to ask you something." She turned from the window. "When I spoke to Horace, he said you've fenced off lands that are public domain. Is this true?"

His jaw worked with irritation. "Horace is talkin' about the land that stretches between here and the Hacienda. It used to be open range. Well, it ain't no more. For years, I've been buyin' it, piece by piece. The deeds are in my office, if you want to see them. That land is mine, bought and paid for."

"I believe you, Pa. I don't need to see any proof. But I do have another question."

"What's that?"

"When you learned Horace had me locked up down at the Hacienda, why did you still refuse to give him what he was demanding?"

He blinked several times, and then dropped his gaze to the glass in his hand. Lifting the liquor to his lips, he took a long swallow before facing her again. "Cause I ain't never bowed down nor give in to any sorry, lowdown bastard that's tried to take something away from me. If I had, we'd be standin' out there in the road right now without a pot to piss in nor a window to throw it out of."

Typical Pa. Crude. Stubbornness, pure and simple. He'd allowed her to remain locked away in that darkened room, agonizing about the fate of the two men she loved, because he was simply too stubborn to consider doing anything else.

"I would have gotten you out of there," he continued, "if Mantorres hadn't interfered."

He thought of Rane's intervention as interference. With a sigh, she turned back to the window. "Do you think we're safe here?"

"Don't you worry. I ain't gonna let anything happen to you." His baritone chuckle filled the room. "Times sure have changed. Two years ago, you'd have been sittin' out on the porch with a pistol across your knees, guardin' the place yourself."

"Yes, I probably would have," she agreed. Across the yard, the light inside the bunkhouse dimmed, and then was snuffed altogether. Faced with nothing but darkness and her own dejected reflection in the sullied pane, she turned away and pressed her back against the wall.

"If you don't feel safe," her father continued, "we'll see about gettin' some help around here. I didn't want you back home just so you would work yourself to a frazzle, cookin' and cleanin'."

She started to ask why he *did* want her back with such urgency, but a knock at the front door intruded. Strange. She'd heard no horse outside.

Gauging from his reaction, he'd been expecting it. He thumped his glass down on the bar and hurried into the hall. After a moment, the front door opened and her father's voice boomed, "Well, come on in, Will."

Angel rolled her eyes, then stood up straight and wondered if it was too late to slip into the kitchen and up the back stairs without being seen. At the moment, exchanging polite chit-chat with one of her father's cronies was the last thing she wanted to do.

But it was too late.

Her father breezed into the parlor, followed closely by a man whose head nearly brushed the ornate lintel topping the door.

Not what she had expected.

Her father stepped aside, as if to give her an unobstructed view of the prime specimen of manhood he'd dragged into the house. "Angel, do you remember Will Keegan?"

Oh, yes, she remembered him. Will Keegan, youngest son of Eb Keegan, who owned the K-Bar outfit over on the big bend of the Pecos River. An old and distinguished family, there had been Keegans in Texas since before the Republic.

Since he stood head and shoulders above most men, Will had always been hard to overlook. Though he was tall, there was nothing lanky about him. A cattleman through and through, he had the lean, hard physique of a man who spent long days in the saddle. A man who could rope and wrestle a rank steer to the ground with a minimum of fuss. And he'd always been just as adept with the ladies, or so she'd heard.

Back during the days when she'd roamed the range and been privy to campfire gossip, there had been talk of a scandal involving Will and a squatter's daughter. In cattle country, anyone who attempted to plow the land and grow crops was labeled a squatter. The rumors had been quickly swept under the rug, mainly because the farmer had suddenly pulled up stakes and moved his family, including his wayward daughter, to unknown climes. At the time, Angel had known without being told that the tight-knit Keegan clan had threatened the man off his land.

The Keegans had always taken care of their own, so what the hell was Will doing here?

Remembering her training, Angel forced one foot in front of the other and glided forward. She extended her hand. "Mr. Keegan. How nice to see you again."

His severely combed cap of wavy blond hair took a barely perceptible dip. Then, his ice-pale blue eyes lifted to hers and stayed. "Miss Clayton." His deep baritone sounded stiff and formal. Briefly, his big, callused fingers enveloped her hand. When he released her, she stepped back.

The steady way he looked at her, the unmistakable gleam of curiosity in his eyes made Angel feel like a prize breeder being inspected by a potential buyer. As gracefully as she could, she moved away from him and took a seat on the sofa where she could keep both men under a watchful eye.

The twinkle in her father's eyes as he looked from one to the other of them made her uncomfortable. He looked entirely too pleased with himself, as if he knew a secret.

"Want a drink?" her father asked.

"Yeah," Will replied.

Finally tearing his eyes from her, he tossed the hat he'd been holding against his thigh onto the seat of an armchair and followed her father to the bar.

With his back turned, Angel studied him with interest. Instead of the usual cowboy work clothes of denim and muslin, he wore dark gray serge trousers, creased front and back. His big pointed-toed boots were remarkably dust-free. Had he brushed them off while waiting at the door?

Or had he simply walked across the yard to get here?

She remembered the light in the bunkhouse. It had gone out only minutes before he arrived. An unsettling picture began to form.

Her father lifted another glass from the cabinet and

poured a liberal amount of whiskey. He slid it across the bar and picked up his own glass. "Here's mud in your eye."

"Mud" Will nodded. He picked up his glass and drank the entire contents.

Her father splashed more whiskey into the glass. "Drink up. I reckon we got good reason to celebrate tonight."

Will cast a speculative glance at her over his shoulder. Her father beamed. They both downed a second shot.

"After today, I'm hopeful we'll be able to start roundup close to schedule. What do you think, Will?"

The younger man shrugged. "Dunno. Maybe. Depends on Lundy now."

"Course, while all this fightin's been goin' on, the herd's drifted to hell and gone."

From the easy conversation taking place, Angel got the idea that the two of them had done this before, and probably many times. With the other man's arrival, her father had grown animated and looked almost happy. Will appeared more thoughtful. He wasn't as much of a talker as her father. But some men didn't need to use a lot of words to get what they wanted. Things just naturally gravitated to them without being coaxed.

While they continued to talk cattle, Angel stood and wandered back to the window. Reflected in the mirror-like panes, she saw Will Keegan take another drink of whiskey. Then he laid his forearm on the bar and shifted to face her. While he still appeared to listen to her father, he watched her from heavy lidded eyes. He began at the back of her head and slowly worked his way down her body. Somehow, his roaming eyes made her feel exposed, indecent even.

She turned, meeting his insolent gaze for a brief instant. One corner of his lips twitched. Leisurely, he put both arms down on the bar and faced her father again.

Angel clenched her teeth while her heart kicked to a faster rhythm, pouring heat into her face. She wanted Will Keegan gone.

Rather than gnash her teeth, she aimed a sweet smile at her father. "If it's all the same to you, Pa, I think

I'll go to—retire." At the last instant, she amended what she'd started to say, remembering that a lady never made mention of her bed in the presence of a gentleman.

Stupid, stupid rules!

Evidently, Will Keegan wasn't so dense he couldn't catch a hint. He straightened and sat down his glass, and then walked over and plucked his hat from the chair. "I guess I'll be goin' now, Roy. Thanks for the drink."

"But, you just got here."

"It's late," Will replied, "and I think Miss Clayton is still tired from her...ordeal." He walked to the parlor door, where he stopped and looked back at Angel. "It was a real pleasure seein' you again, Miss Clayton."

She forced a smile.

Seemingly oblivious to the undercurrents wafting around the room at twister velocity, her father hurried from behind the bar. "I'll walk you to the door."

Angel watched the two men leave the parlor, and then she waited. She had no intention of calling it a night until she exchanged a few words with her father and found out what was going on.

The front door opened, and then closed, followed by the metallic snap of a lock. Seconds later, her father reappeared.

"What is Will Keegan doing here?" she blurted.

"He works here."

"I gathered that. What I'm wondering is *why* is he working on the Flying C when his family owns one of the biggest cattle operations in West Texas?"

"They had a fallin' out."

"What about?"

"Well, I don't know. And if a man don't offer to tell me somethin', I figure it ain't my business to ask. But it just stands to reason that with five grown men all tryin' to ramrod the same spread, there's bound to be friction. Will showed up about a year ago and asked for a job. Naturally, I gave it to him. But I figured he'd mend fences with his kin after a little while and go on back home."

"And?"

"And they didn't, and he didn't, and so he's still here, and he's one of the best damn hands I've ever had."

"I see," she said, sounding so much like her haughty

Aunt Nelda it startled her. Shades of her youth ran together like spilled ink and colored her thinking. Her father had always been wont to champion a "good hand," but not her. Never her. She had a sneaking suspicion he saw more in Will Keegan than just a good cowhand and meant to keep him. Permanently. "Is this the reason you summoned me home on such short notice while you were in the middle of a range war?"

He appeared taken back by the question. "What do you mean by 'reason'?"

She crossed her arms in a defensive pose. "Why did you summon me back, Pa?"

"Because, in case you haven't noticed, I'm not gettin' any younger." He stomped to the bar and poured himself another drink. "The way things have been goin' lately...well, I didn't know what might turn out, so I wanted you here in case the worst should happen."

Angel snorted. "If you ask me, the worst *has* happened. I'd have been better off staying in New York."

Her father dropped his head and went thoughtfully silent, staring into his glass. After a moment, he asked quietly, "Do you miss it?"

"New York?"

"Yeah."

She waved a dismissive hand. "No. The whole time I was gone, I thought of nothing but coming back here. I wanted to come home."

"I figured you'd meet somebody."

"I met a lot of people, but no one who made me want to stay."

"I'm glad," he said. "When I'm gone, this place will be yours. It'll take a strong hand to run it. I'd like to see you settled with someone man enough to hang onto it."

"Someone like Will Keegan?" Her voice had chilled to ice, but she didn't care.

"You could do a whole lot worse than Will."

What he didn't say was that she could probably never do any better. Not with her reputation, which now bore an even worse stain than before, since she'd spent nearly two weeks alone with Rane, a man whose reputation made hers seem positively angelic.

Her father's motives were so transparent it was

almost insulting. In Will, he'd found her the perfect candidate for a husband. Even her mother would have approved his lineage. And since his own family had evidently disenfranchised him, he had nothing to lose and everything to gain by marrying her.

"Pa, you can't force me to marry a man of your choosing. I won't marry someone I don't love."

He slugged back the dregs of his drink and plopped the empty glass down on the bar. "I don't intend to force you to do anything. I'm just askin' you to keep an open mind."

She was tempted to ask if he'd already had this same conversation with Will, but she was afraid she already knew the answer. Hardheaded old coot. The plain fact was, he'd summoned her home because he'd found someone he deemed suitable who was willing to marry her.

"I'm turnin' in," he said.

"Yes, I think you should," she murmured. "You've done quite enough meddling for one day."

Chapter Fifteen

Angel's middle finger throbbed. A blistered welt circled the skin just beneath the first knuckle. Grimacing, she bore down with the thimble, forced the needle through the thick denim a final time, and then lifted the repaired pant leg to her mouth and bit off the thread.

With a sigh, she sat back and tossed the pants onto the dining table. Finished. All of it, the entire pile of clothing with rent seams, tears, and missing buttons she'd found cast aside in her father's bedroom. She pulled the thimble from her finger, returned it to its niche in the sewing basket and then closed the top.

Outside the window, darkness had settled. She'd lost track of time. So engrossed in the mending and her thoughts, she hadn't even noticed the last time the Regulator in the hallway chimed the hour. *Busy hands make a happy heart.* If that were true, she'd have gone through the past five days skipping with pure glee.

She'd never realized what a pig her father was, but now she saw him with new eyes. He didn't pick up after himself. He flicked cigar ashes into any receptacle near at hand or simply dropped them to the floor if nothing was within reach. He never carried a soiled dish or cup to the wreck pan in the kitchen. That was servant's work. But since they no longer had any servants, it all now fell to her.

Turning a blind eye, like he did, would have been the wisest course, but she couldn't live like that. Not any more. He'd seen to that by sending her to that high-flown finishing school. Unfortunately, she'd now dug a huge hole for herself by doing his work for him. So long as her father ate regular meals, finding replacements for the cook and housekeeper had fallen low on his list of priorities. Well, she had news for him. She hadn't spent the past two years learning to be a proper lady just to return home and take over the roles of charwoman and cook.

Her rebellious thoughts scattered when her father burst in from the kitchen. He stalked right past her without a word and continued into the parlor. Since sundown, he'd prowled the first floor of the house like a corralled bull.

Had there been a new development with the fence war he hadn't told her about? She stood and followed him, determined to find out.

A knock at the front door halted Angel halfway between the dining room and parlor. The last thing she wanted was to endure another of Will Keegan's nightly visits. To be subjected to his cold, speculative gaze while he and her father indulged in their ritual nightcap and rehash of the day's events.

Thinking about Will tired her. He was a puzzle she had yet to solve. After her homecoming conversation with her father, she knew why Will came to the house every night. Yet, he rarely tried to draw her into the conversation. Not once had he asked her to step onto the porch for a breath of air or take a walk. Rather than making his suit, he seemed more like a man who was biding his time. Was he so certain of her father's favor he felt it unnecessary to even court her?

Tonight she would escape up the back stairs to her bedroom.

She forgot about leaving when the murmured voices moved into the hallway. Not Will Keegan. She held her breath, listening, while tingles raced over her rigid back. Even though the visitor's voice was so low-pitched his words were indistinct, she'd recognize him anywhere.

Rane.

Angel clutched the door facing to keep from charging into the hallway. With her heart tripping, she glanced down and self-consciously brushed scraps of thread from the front of her skirt. She'd stopped dressing in anything other than her common, everyday garments since that disappointing first night when she'd tried to impress her father by wearing a silk gown and setting his table with linen and china. Now, she wished she'd worn something nicer than the drab gray skirt and unadorned cotton shirtwaist. With her hair pinned in a severe chignon, she must look like a no-nonsense schoolmarm.

Her father ushered their visitor into the parlor and frowned when he saw her standing there. Angel lifted an unsteady hand to the base of her throat. Beneath her fingertips, her pulse fluttered.

Hat in hand, Rane stepped into the room and stole her breath with his dark perfection. He was clean-shaven. Lamplight gleamed against his long ebony hair, finger-combed back from his forehead in furrowed waves. Tailored black trousers hugged his legs while the familiar gunbelt rode low against his right hip. Inside the open collar of an immaculate white shirt, a loosely knotted black silk scarf covered his throat.

She drank in the sight of him. Composed, controlled, his stony expression betrayed none of his thoughts.

Why was he here?

Roy stepped behind the bar. The moment her father turned his back, Rane's façade slipped. He winked at her. Pleasure bloomed in Angel's breast, along with spots of heat in her cheeks. She started to smile at him and then caught herself when she recalled his parting words to her father.

"What's your poison?" her father asked.

Angel expelled a long-held breath when Rane shifted toward the bar and laid his hat on the stained wood. He cleared his throat. "Whatever you're having will be fine."

Roy snatched a bottle of his best, aged whiskey from the shelf and palmed two tumblers in his other hand. He righted the glasses on the bar and poured each one half full. Without preamble, he lifted his glass. "Here's mud'n your eye."

Rane reached for the other glass and held it aloft. "*¡Salud!*"

Her father drank half of his whiskey and then swiped a cuff across his mustache. "Angel, I've got some business to discuss with Mantorres."

Her glow instantly died. He was dismissing her, sending her to her room like a child. Stiffening her spine, she pushed away from the doorframe and took a step forward. "If it's all the same to you, I prefer to stay."

Grim distaste settled on Roy's face. He pulled in a

noisy breath. If he ordered her from the room, what then? "Fine. Stay," he said. He lifted the glass to his mouth and quickly downed the rest of his drink.

Her father's grudging permission gave Angel no room to relax.

Rane took another sip of his drink and returned it to the bar, but kept his hand cupped loosely around the glass. "You sent word you wanted to see me."

Angel's attention jumped back to her father. He'd sent for Rane? Alarm churned like a tainted meal in her stomach. Her thoughts splintered. Had she given something away, with a look or an unguarded word, about the true nature of her connection with Rane?

Roy lifted a hand to his neck and scratched. "I've been thinkin' about what you said the other night?"

Rane tilted his glass and appeared to watch the dark contents slosh from one side to the other at the bottom. He looked so detached. Angel only wished she could feel as calm as the front he put forth.

"I said many things that night. Which statement in particular stuck in your mind?"

"The part about not havin' enough men to guard the house."

Rane quirked one brow and slowly nodded. "I see."

"You said you could get me all the men I need."

Rane's glass settled to the bar with a thump. "You said you don't want villagers."

"Right now, I'm not so particular."

Angel held her breath and waited for Rane's reaction to her father's careless words.

If Rane took offense, he kept it carefully disguised. "How many do you need?"

"Half a dozen ought to do it."

"And how much will you pay them?"

"Twenty a month and board."

Rane had been looking at his glass, but now his narrowed gaze lifted to her father's face. "That's little more than half what you pay your regular hands." He shook his head. "It's not enough."

Roy straightened. "Just how much would you consider enough?" His voice held a sharper edge.

"Thirty," Rane replied.

Roy chuckled without an ounce of real mirth. "And you think they're worth it?"

Angel's heart sped another beat when Rane angled his dark gaze in her direction. "Riding shotgun on your daughter is risky business. You can't expect them to stake their lives for anything less than regular wages."

Angel recognized the working of her father's jaw muscles as pure stubbornness rather than anger. It galled him to meet the price Rane demanded. She knew Rane was fearless, but to watch him beard her father this way filled her with a great deal of satisfaction.

Roy exhaled a long breath. "All right," he finally conceded. "Thirty a month. But they supply their own guns."

"Done." As if to seal the bargain, Rane lifted his glass and swallowed the last draught of liquor he'd been toying with.

Roy picked up the bottle and splashed more whiskey into each of their glasses. "How soon can you arrange it?"

"They'll be here before noon tomorrow."

Roy opened his mouth to say more, but the sound of the front door opening eclipsed his words. Ponderous footsteps echoed in the hallway. Angel's heart matched their heavy rhythm. Will Keegan's appearance at the parlor door snapped every nerve in her body as taut as a bowstring.

Roy hurried from behind the bar. "Will!"

Evidently, her father hadn't expected to see his fair-haired boy this evening.

Will said nothing, but raked each of them with an assessing glare. Then his ice pale gaze settled on Rane and bored in with undisguised fury. The man needed to practice his poker face. Even Angel could read his intent.

"You two know each other?" Roy asked.

"Only by reputation," Will said.

Roy mumbled a quick introduction.

Neither man moved to shake hands. Not even by a dip of a head did they acknowledge each other. But, if looks could kill, both Rane and Will would have been lying on the worn carpet, oozing blood. The sudden animosity chilling the room raised goosebumps on Angel's arms.

Rane couldn't have been more unsettled if he'd been

staring down the business end of a loaded gun. Will Keegan looked like a powder keg just waiting for a spark. Rane didn't intend to supply the flint. Evidently, old man Clayton had given this hothead Keegan free run of the Flying C. The house, too, judging from the way the man had come barging in, and that could only mean one thing. Roy Clayton had given Keegan his blessing. In all things. Including his daughter.

Hot anger poured over Rane, and he hoped his skin didn't betray the burn he felt. He had to get out of there. Quick. Before he said or did something stupid. "Guess I'll be going now." He plucked his hat from the bar. "Thanks for the drink."

No one said a word, and that angered him more. Deliberately, he settled his hat on his head and turned for one final look at Angel. "It was good to see you again, Miss Clayton."

High color stained her cheeks, and her wide eyes held the frightened look of a cornered rabbit. Her belated smile looked strained. He realized his parting words were the only ones spoken between them since his arrival, and she still hadn't said anything at all. Not to him, anyway.

When he turned to leave, Will Keegan stepped aside, clearing the way. He'd made it halfway through the parlor door when Keegan said, "I'll see you to the door."

Feeling sucker punched, Rane walked the length of the hall, aware of the big blond man hot on his heels. As badly as he wanted to rip Will Keegan's head from his shoulders, he couldn't stop thinking about Angel. He knew where she stood. They'd made that much plain between them in Mexico. No strings and no promises. He'd said his goodbyes a week ago. That should have been the end of it. But Roy Clayton had sent word, summoning him. And he'd jumped at the chance to see her again.

That tense excuse for a smile she'd given him reminded him of a wild mustang with its head snubbed down so tight it hurt. Fastened down and starchy didn't suit her. She looked out of place. Most of all, she looked unhappy.

The thought brought him to a mental halt. Angel's happiness wasn't his concern, nor would it ever be. Fate had thrown them together for a short while, but that was the end of it. He shouldn't give a damn if Roy Clayton had given Keegan his blessing with his daughter.

Trouble was, the way his nerves popped to the surface back there and the gnawing in his gut mocked his unconcern. Despite all his best-laid intentions, he did give a damn.

Rane opened the door and stepped onto the porch, into cooler air and darkness. The chirp of crickets playing night music sounded from the yard. He kept going, hearing the door latch click behind him as he descended the steps. Keegan was still with him.

Tied to the porch rail in the wan moonlight, Pago stamped a restive hoof. Rane stepped to the horse's side and hooked a stirrup over the saddle horn. He reached down and tugged on a strap. Tension hung like a dark fog in the dry air. Without turning he said, "I'm sure you followed me out here for a reason, Keegan. So, what do you want?"

The creak of the porch boards betrayed movement. "I don't talk to the back of any man's head," Keegan said.

One corner of Rane's lips twitched. *Arrogant bastard.* He made one final adjustment to his saddle, and then took his slow, sweet time turning around.

Keegan stood at the top of the steps, leaning against a support post with his arms crossed over his chest. A shaft of lamplight from the parlor window bathed the left side of his body in pale yellow. But there was nothing soft about the expression he wore as he looked down at him. Pure, hard-edged hatred blazed in his eyes.

Rane expected no less. "You have my attention," he said. "So talk."

Will's harsh breath grated through the stillness. His arms lifted and fell with the agitated movement of his chest. "I want you to stay away from this ranch. Angel's name is mud since you drug her off to Mexico, and folks ain't likely to forget if you keep comin' around. So stay away from her!"

Cold realization sank into Rane's gut. He had accurately gauged the situation. The big blond bastard was staking his claim and betraying a streak of jealousy a mile wide.

With a firm grip on the anger surging through him,

Rane curved his lips in a satiric smile. "It seems you and the old man are at cross purposes. He asked me here tonight."

A muscle in Keegan's cheek twitched. "Why are you tryin' to get on the old man's good side? You did him a favor, but only a fool expects nothin' for his trouble. What're you after?"

Rane shrugged. "I ask for nothing. I expect nothing."

"That's horse shit," Keegan spat.

Never had Rane wanted so badly to knock a man's teeth down his throat. Keegan guessed too closely to the truth. Rane did want something here. Thoughts of returning to the Flying C had gnawed at him since he surrendered Angel to her father. He wanted her, but he couldn't have her. She was now as far beyond his reach as the justice he sought from Horace Lundy. Bitter frustration dogged him like an unwanted companion.

"I have no quarrel with you, Keegan."

"Good. Then we have no problem."

"Only one." Rane paused, aware that his next words would gain him yet another enemy, but he had to say them anyway. "The old man asked me here tonight. If he wants me to stay clear of the Flying C, he'll have to tell me himself. I don't take orders from hired hands."

Will dropped his arms from his chest and glared down at him. "Somebody needs to teach you your place."

"Perhaps," Rane agreed, "but I'm almost certain it won't be you."

Rane forced a benign smile to his face, pulled his reins from the porch rail, and again turned his back on the angry man. He stepped into the saddle and turned the eager horse onto the long lane. Easing up on the leather, he gave the horse his head and sped away from the house. His secreted camp next to the river was a good thirty-minute ride, and he was eager to get there. To be alone, to think, and hopefully to dull the sharp, aching need he felt for Angel. He remembered the bottle of whiskey he'd stashed with his belongings. What better way to dull his senses? But the thought of drinking himself into oblivion, with only a cold, empty bottle to hold onto made him feel emptier than ever.

Chapter Sixteen

As Angel browsed the shelves lining the narrow aisles of Dowling's General Mercantile, a buzz of whispers trailed her. Pretending indifference, she paused next to a table piled high with sewing notions and trimmings and absently ran a fingertip along a length of pale pink ribbon. Several of the store patrons were just rude enough to stop and stare at her before they continued about their business.

Her face burned from more than the stifling heat within the close quarters. She'd been the subject of gossip before. In former days she would have thrust out her chin and told them all to go to hell. Now the rumors stung. She knew some of the things they were saying about her were probably true.

Damn her father anyway for insisting she accompany him into town. He thought it important for her to make an appearance to try and squelch the gossip making the rounds about her and Rane. He'd left her no choice and even ordered her to "gussie up" for the occasion.

Their arrival on Clayton Station's main thoroughfare had been nothing short of a spectacle. Will Keegan had ridden at the head of the procession as stony-faced and menacing as some ancient warrior knight. Three of the six men Rane had sent to the ranch flanked the buggy she and her father occupied. All of them had come armed to the hilt. With bandoleers slung across their chests, they looked more like border bandits than guards. Dressed to the teeth in the latest Paris fashion, Angel had felt like a tarnished trophy on display.

Even her thick-skinned father was not immune to the stir their arrival caused. "I hate what this place has become," he'd said as he ran a critical eye along the crowded walkway. "The primary reason I settled here was because there was nobody around. Now, a man can't even spit without it hittin' somebody."

Roy had continued to speak, but Angel hardly heard him. She knew his story by rote. How he'd been the first white man to settle in the area, and how the mapmakers had eventually penned his name onto the tiny settlement.

"¡Soldados! Soldados!"

The voice snapped Angel back to attention. She looked up. The other store patrons rushed for the door as though the place had caught fire. Alarm leaped across her nerve endings.

Beyond the dust-grimed windows, a dark-skinned boy stood in the street and fairly danced with excitement as he shouted and gestured southward.

Angel dropped the satin ribbon and hurried for the door with the others. Outside on the walk, a growing crush of bodies caught her up in the middle of it. The mood of the crowd seemed infectious, nervous and uneasy, like a herd of milling cattle on the verge of stampeding. Dust clogged her nose, and she could hardly breathe. Cheap perfume and pomade tainted the air around her and did little to rarefy an underlying stink of stale human sweat.

"Looks like they got some renegades," one man said.

The scalp beneath Angel's carefully styled coif prickled as though the devil himself had breathed his ill breath against her nape. Driven by some sixth sense, she elbowed and shoved through the tightly packed bodies to reach the edge of the walk. Once there, she clutched one of the uprights supporting Dowling's narrow awning to keep from being shoved the rest of the way into the street.

The noonday sun glared white-hot. Angel lifted a hand and shielded her eyes. The end of the dusty, dun colored street shimmered beneath heat veils. Mounted U.S. Calvary troops plodded single-file into the settlement. From the looks of their dusty hides and the trail-weary slump of both men and horses, they'd covered some ground.

As the group approached, her gaze swept down the line, until she saw the three Indians who walked at the center of the procession.

The captives staggered, so exhausted their heads drooped to their chests. They wore nothing but dark blue cavalry britches and worn out moccasins. The uniform pants, obviously thrust on them, were covered in dust and filth. Dried blood caked their ankles and gleamed in the harsh light as it seeped from galls rubbed by shackles. Manacles also bound their hands and a connecting chain ensured that none could make a try for freedom without dragging the others with him. From the looks of them, they could barely stand, much less run.

Angel's heart jerked against her ribs in an uneven rhythm. Even though his face was hidden behind his straggling hair, the sight of the tall, well-muscled Indian at the forefront of the trio brought back unsettling memories.

The sergeant at the head of the line called a halt in front of the cantina directly across the street. The soldiers dismounted. Three men took charge of the horses and led them toward the town well, farther up the street.

Clayton Station had no sheriff, marshal, nor anything resembling a jail. Angel had little time to wonder what the soldiers would do with their prisoners before they prodded them toward the hitching rail. After a short-lived scuffle, the Indians ended up shoved to the ground amid flyblown mounds of horse droppings. A soldier removed one cuff from each of the captives and laid the connecting chain over the top of the rail before he again locked them into place. The Indians were left sitting beneath the rail with their hands dangling in mid-air above their heads.

Another soldier, armed with a rifle and a pistol, remained behind to stand guard while the rest of the bluecoats filed into the cool interior of the adobe cantina.

One by one, the people around Angel wandered away, muttering among themselves about the "filthy Injuns" and pronouncing their capture a "good riddance."

Her attention remained riveted on the tall Indian seated at the near end of the hitching rail. As she watched, he lifted his head and shook back his hair, revealing shrewd blue eyes that bore into her with frank directness.

Wolf. Angel's heart galloped harder. She released her held breath. She had known, but how had he picked her out of the crowd so easily? The one time they'd met, she had looked vastly different than she did now. The loaded stare he gave her lasted a mere second before he lowered his gaze to the street.

What did he expect her to do? She aimed a scowl at the cantina's open portal. Sounds of laughter echoed from inside. The soldiers were probably swilling cool beer and gorging on frijoles and tortillas. Even the horses had been taken to water and were on their way to the shed at the end of the street, where buckets of oats surely awaited them. For the lowly half-breed and his cousins, there was nothing. Not even the relief of shade or a sip of water after their long, harrowing walk.

Angel's righteous anger shifted to outrage when a group of barefoot boys from the nearby village appeared from an alley and raced down the middle of the street. As they darted past the captives, they loosed a barrage of dirt balls.

One of the dry clods struck Wolf high on his chest and exploded into dust. The silty powder clung and dissolved into his sweat and formed streaks of mud. Though his expression remained stoic, his muscles tensed. She felt his humiliation as though it were her own, complete now at being set upon by children who saw him as no better than a stray cur.

The guard applauded the boy's cruelty by shouting, "Good shot, chico!"

Angel turned a furious glare on the gang of miscreants, who stopped at the end of the street to arm themselves with more chunks of hardened mud. When they started back for another sally, she ground her teeth. *Oh, no, you don't!* Hurrying into the street, she intercepted them. "*¡Alto!*" She clapped her hands. "*¡Vayase! Vayase!*"

The boys veered off and scampered into the alley.

From the corner of her eye, Angel saw that several people had stopped along the walkway and stared at her. They probably thought she'd been in the sun too long. She no longer cared. Anger had already burned away caution. Thank God her father and Will "had business" on the other side of the settlement.

Forcing a display of composure she no longer felt, she retraced her steps toward the store. At the edge of the walk, her three Mexican guards stood waiting. They looked so ill at ease she almost felt sorry for them. After all, they'd been given orders to stick close and keep her safe. But their instructions hadn't included how to protect her from making a fool of herself.

She breezed right past them and entered the store. Moments later, she again drew curious stares when she walked out the door with a shiny new bucket and dipper in her hands.

"You men stay here," she ordered.

Angel walked into the street, her sights on the public well at the center of town. Once there, she hung the new bucket under the pump and worked the handle until clear, cool water gushed forth.

The weight of the full bucket strained at her arm muscles when she took it from the hook. She turned, and found two cowpokes blocking her path. The sour yeast smell of stale beer wafted from them, and they both had mischief written all over their grinning faces. It seemed trouble always traveled in pairs.

"Want me to carry that for you?" one of them asked.

He reached to take the bucket from her and she jerked it back. The water sloshed, darkening a large area on her brocade skirt. "No, thank you. I can manage quite well by myself."

"What'cha fixin' to do?" the other one piped up. "Give them dirty Injuns a bath?"

Angel turned a withering glare from one man to the other and the grins quickly slipped from both their faces. She crinkled her nose. "Judging from the smell around here, I'd say the two of you should join them."

They both gaped at her.

"Now get the hell out of my way!" She set her jaw and waited.

Wide-eyed and speechless, the two men stepped aside.

She switched the bucket to the opposite hand and stepped past them. Wagging the sloshing water made walking with any dignity impossible. Still, she held her head at a proud angle and continued with a susurrus of whispers from both sides of the street beating against her ears like the drone of angry bees.

When she neared the hitching rail in front of the cantina, the soldier left on guard turned and stepped into the street.

"Hold up there, little lady. You're gettin' a mite too close to these prisoners for comfort's sake. Why don't you just take a step or two back."

Angel halted and wrapped both hands around the wire bale cutting into her sweaty fingers. Her breath heaved, both from the exertion and the embarrassed anger burning through her temples. Determined, she eyed the soldier. "I'd like to give these men a drink."

The soldier's lips curved into a nasty sneer. "Men?" He chortled. "Why these ain't nothin' but Injuns."

"They're human beings, just like you and me."

The soldier's laughter died. He eyed her narrowly, up and down, no doubt taking in the cut and richness of her clothes, and wondering what the hell she was up to.

"All right, then," he said, stepping aside. "Go right ahead. But you just watch yourself."

Angel carried the bucket the final steps and sat it in the dirt in front of Wolf. The smell coming from him and the sight of flies crawling over the open sores on his wrists and ankles sickened her. She scooped water into the dipper and paused a moment, suddenly uncertain. What if he turned away and refused to drink? She lifted her gaze and found hum staring directly into her eyes. She clamped her lips against the urge to speak, and the eloquent look he gave her removed any doubt.

She moved, until she stood less than two feet away, and held the dipper of cool water to his cracked lips. He closed his eyes and swallowed greedily, sucking down all of it before he pulled back and looked at her again. Spilled droplets glistened on his chin. He turned his lips inward to savor the last bits of moisture.

The silent desperation in his eyes drew her closer. She leaned down, on the pretense of refilling the dipper.

"Find Rane," he whispered.

A heavy boot with a ham-like leg behind it slammed against Wolf's jaw.

Before her eyes, Wolf's face contorted as he hurled sideways with a stream of crimson shooting from between his parted lips. His chained hands snapped him to a halt mere inches from the ground.

White-hot panic flared in Angel's brain. She turned on the soldier. "Why did you do that!"

"Maybe this filthy animal will think twice next time he starts to open his mouth and speak to a white woman," he said.

Tremors wracked Angel's body. She felt as though she was coming apart from the inside out from the violent emotions warring within. "You're the animal!" she spat.

The soldier's eyes narrowed with hostility, which he now aimed at her. "You better take yourself on out of here, Missy, before you get in big trouble."

"I'm not leaving until I'm finished!"

"And I say you *are* finished." The gruff voice came from behind her.

Startled, Angel spun around.

Will Keegan stood there with a murderous glare on his face. The cold glint within his pale eyes chilled her heart.

"Stay out of this, Will. It's none of your business."

"Anything that concerns Roy Clayton and the Flying C is my business. Including you."

The soldier, who regained his superior height by stepping onto the walkway, turned his animosity on Will. "Mister, if you got any say-so over this woman, I advise you to get her the hell away from here."

Will held up his hand. "No need to get nasty, Corporal. I'll handle it."

"Good. Handle it," the soldier retorted. "Otherwise, the both of you are liable to find yourselves hauled up on charges of interferin' with the United States Army!" Adding insult to the threat, the soldier spat a stream of tobacco juice into the street, aiming a little too close to Will's boots for comfort.

Angel's eyes widened. Above even the town noise, she heard the squeak of Will's grinding molars. She knew he'd like nothing better than to charge at the fresh-mouthed soldier but, surely, he wasn't that stupid. A physical confrontation would earn him nothing but his own set of manacles and a seat next to the three, now openly curious, Indians at the hitching rail.

Turning on his heel, he latched onto her upper arm

and growled, "Let's go."

His clamp-like hold left her no room to argue. She practically ran to keep up with his long, angry strides, knowing resistance would only land her flat on her face.

Angel was completely winded by the time Will hauled her to a stop next to their parked buggy. Damned corset. She pressed a hand to her stomach and struggled for breath.

Her father sat on the seat, watching her, his leathery face pale and pinched. He looked as if he'd seen a ghost. Again.

"Why did you do it, Angel?" She'd expected anger. She preferred his anger if it would erase the tired, hopeless expression from his face.

She answered him the only way she could, the only *honest* way she dared.

"He was thirsty, Pa."

****

Angel paused on the upstairs landing and listened to the sounds of her father's and Will's receding footsteps as they entered the parlor. Feeling like a disobedient child again, she hunkered at the top of the staircase and pressed her shoulder against the wall, out of sight from the doorway below.

During the ride home, she'd endured her father's studied silence. It reminded her—way too much for comfort—of their last ride together, when he'd taken her to the stage depot and sent her east.

She perked her ears at the clink of glass coming from the parlor and envisioned her father pouring drinks for Will and himself. A long silence followed, and she imagined them savoring their whiskey while each waited for the other to speak first.

Will finally took the leap. "What the hell do you think got into her today?"

"Pity," Roy said. "She always did have a big ol' soft spot for dark horses."

"Then you better see to it she takes up respectable charity work and not go around handin' out dippers of water to a bunch of goddamned savages, in the middle of the street, in front of the goddamned saloon!"

Angel's heart sped with shock at hearing Will speak

with such disrespect to her father. Now, maybe he would put the arrogant bastard in his place.

"Now simmer down, Will."

Angel's head snapped up. That was it? That was all he had to say? She waited, barely daring to breathe, but nothing more than silence followed.

After a moment, Will's deep rumble broke the stillness, but she couldn't make out his words. Then he said clearly, "If you ask me, she needs to be kept on a shorter rein, and I'm just the man to do it."

Heat poured into her cheeks, scalding flames that brought tears to her eyes. *Oh, please, Pa!*

"Nobody never said you weren't," Roy replied. "Leastwise, not me."

Despair sank into Angel's heart. Her father wasn't going to champion her. On the contrary. By giving Will permission to put her on a "tighter rein," she knew he'd just handed her over on a pretty platter to a man she despised.

She no longer cared what they said. Their words no longer mattered. Pulling her feet back so they couldn't be seen from the hallway below, she settled the side of her face against the wall and gave in to heartbreak, the likes of which she hadn't felt since she was a child.

By the time her tears dried, a deeper layer of bitterness had settled around her heart. Drawing on an inner strength, she straightened from the wall and swiped at the salty residue coating her cheeks. They thought they would control her, somehow force or cajole her into marriage with an insufferable tyrant not of her choosing.

Well, she'd just see about that.

Chapter Seventeen

Pewter-bellied clouds slid across the moon, pushed by a freshening wind laden with the smell of rain. Like a thief keeping to the shadows, Angel crept along the alley separating Dowling's Mercantile from the hardware store. Clayton Station had settled for the night. From the cantina on the far side of the street, yellow lamplight spilled through the open door, the only sign of life in the sleeping town.

Angel halted at the end of the alley and pressed closer to the wall as silvered moonlight bathed the open ground. Across the street, Wolf and his two cousins were still handcuffed to the hitching rail. Behind them, a soldier sat on the walkway with his back propped against the cantina's adobe wall and his legs sprawled across the uneven boards. His chin drooped on his chest, as though he'd fallen asleep.

She pulled in a long breath and released it slowly. Now what? If only she'd been able to find Rane. Together, they might have come up with a plan. But she had no idea where to look for him, and alone, she felt useless. Even if she somehow managed to distract the guard, the problem of the iron cuffs binding Wolf and the others to the rail seemed insurmountable.

The sound of the guard's snort carried across the street. He shifted, as if trying to find a more comfortable position. Reflected moonlight winked on metal against the dark blue trousers covering his left hip. Angel stared at the gleaming object while her heart quickened. It was a key.

She pressed the backs of her shoulders against the uneven boards and tried to calm her breathing. What was she thinking? Just being here, alone and in the middle of the night, was foolish, maybe even insane. But hadn't insanity been the driving force in her life since meeting

Rane? Wolf was important to him. They called themselves blood brothers. She couldn't allow him to be taken to the fort and hanged as a horse thief without even attempting to stop it somehow.

She needed a plan.

Still hugging the shadows, she backed down the alley. Beyond the confinement of the buildings, a welcome sage-scented cross breeze bathed her clammy skin. She turned and started to round the back corner of the store when a hand came at her from behind and clamped over her mouth. Before she could lift her hands, an arm snaked across her waist and her back fused with a solid male chest.

"Don't scream," Rane whispered against her ear.

Relief enabled her to breathe again. She reached up and pulled his hand from her mouth. "Where have you been?" she whispered fiercely.

He released her.

Angel turned—and nearly blurted her astonishment. The dressed-to-kill gunfighter had disappeared. Instead of his usual tailored garments, he wore sackcloth, both trousers and shirt, the crude garb favored by Mexican field laborers and nearly half the males in the nearby village. After giving her a look that dared her to comment, he snatched a straw sombrero from the top of an upended barrel—one of many piled haphazardly against the back of the store—and capped it over his head. The spacious brim was broken down in several, strategic places. To disguise his face, no doubt. Despite having transformed himself into a common peon, the mere sight of him sent her heart into a quick flutter.

He kept staring at her with a dark, knowing gaze that lingered on her manly disguise of worn denims and loose, faded shirt. He'd seen her this way before, so why the sudden interest?

"Sweet Jesus, Angel. What are you doing here?"

"The same as you, I would imagine. I want to help Wolf." She spotted her battered felt hat on the ground. It must have fallen off when he grabbed her. She reached down and retrieved it.

"You can't."

His refusal caught her in the act of placing the hat

over her head and tucking in her hair. She stopped and looked at him, as if she hadn't heard correctly.

"What do you mean, I can't? I sneaked out of the house, caught a horse in the pasture with nothing but a halter—which was no easy feat, by the way—and rode all the way over here, bareback, so don't tell me I can't."

"I don't intend to argue," he said.

His dismissal stung her. "Do you at least have a plan?"

"Yes, I have a plan. But it's risky. Your being here only complicates the situation."

"Well, then. Since you have it all figured out, I certainly wouldn't want to get in your way." She turned to leave, and hesitated. The moment stretched into awkward silence. Crickets chirped in the tall grass. Overhead, dark clouds continued their silent march across the face of the moon. Yet Angel stood there, hoping he would say something more.

When he didn't, she started to walk.

"Where did you leave your horse?"

The question stopped her. "In the grove, at the edge of town."

"Will you wait there for me?"

Her pulse sped another tiny beat. "Why? I thought you wanted rid of me."

"Will you wait for me?"

She knew she should tell him to go to hell. How many times did the man have to spell out how little she meant to him before it finally sunk in? Walk away and don't look back, her good sense told her, but her treacherous heart refused to cooperate.

"Yes, I'll wait," she said.

As he watched Angel walk away, Rane's conscience flailed him. She'd risked much in coming here tonight. Yet, he'd dismissed her like an unwelcome nuisance. For her own good, he reminded himself. Still, the urge to go after her remained strong. When she melded into the darkness on the far side of the wagon track, he blew out a breath. She would be safe. He had to think of Wolf and the task at hand, yet thoughts of Angel waiting in the darkness, splintered his concentration.

What had she planned to do? What *would* she have

done if he hadn't been there to stop her?

He couldn't think about that now. He couldn't afford a mistake.

Turning his attention to more immediate concerns, he bent and picked up a thick amber bottle. Using his teeth, he pulled the cork and spat it to the ground. The reek of cheap, rotgut whiskey assaulted his nostrils. He held his breath and poured a liberal dousing down the front of his clothing. Fumes wafted upward, engulfing him. Going for broke, he tilted the bottle to his lips until he had a mouthful. He swished and swallowed. Primed for the taste of it, he repeated the process and swallowed a second drink.

Keeping a tight grip around the neck of the bottle, he crept through the dark alley. At the end, he stopped and studied the scene before him. The sleeping guard. Wolf and his cousins. The exact location of the key attached to the soldier's belt.

The street was still deserted. *¡Gracias a Dios!* He pulled in a long breath and released it, then relaxed his spine and rolled his shoulders forward in a pronounced slump. Allowing no time for second thoughts, he staggered forward into the street and the revealing moonlight. Keeping his head down, he aimed for the walkway on the opposite side.

At the corner of the cantina, he paused a moment to get his bearings. Straight ahead the soldier's legs all but blocked the path. Grating snores sawed from his bulky chest. Rane glanced at Wolf and received a barely perceptible nod. Time to carry on with his little playact.

Raising the bottle to his lips, Rane lumbered forward and caught the toe of his boot under the guard's leg. The soldier roused instantly and tried to leap up. Rane never gave him the chance as he collapsed and fell on the man. The soldier's head connected with a dull thud against the adobe wall and all the starch drained out of him.

Rane snatched the key and snapped the string attaching it to the guard's belt. Shedding all pretense of drunkenness, he scrambled to the edge of the walk and dropped to the ground next to Wolf.

"I'd say this makes us even," he said as he unlocked Wolf's cuffs.

Wolf shrugged. “For now, but who’s keeping count? There’s always tomorrow, *hermano*.”

“No tomorrow,” Rane said. “Take these youngsters and head into Mexico. Don’t show your faces around here again.”

“What about you? You’re not going with us?”

“No. I still have unfinished business. But we’ll meet again one day soon. This I promise.”

****

Angel strained her ears, listening for any sound other than the normal chirp and trill of the insects and small creatures in the trees surrounding her. She was still near enough to town if a fracas broke out at the cantina she would hear it. Thus far, she’d heard nothing. The absence of gunshots and shouting didn’t reassure her. Worry for Rane twisted her stomach into knots.

A branch snapped. Angel clapped a hand over her heart and whirled toward the noise. The limbs of a pine undulated just before the black stallion stepped from the blinding darkness with Rane bent low over its neck. Relief weakened her knees. He no longer wore the broken sombrero and a dark shirt had replaced the crude sackcloth.

She emerged from her hidden bower. “What happened?”

He layered his hands on the saddle horn in front of him and eased forward. “There was a mishap in town a few moments ago. A drunken villager stumbled over the guard stationed in front of the cantina. In the confusion, the handcuff keys went missing.”

Remembering his disguise, she didn’t even have to guess the drunken villager’s identity. “A risky plan, indeed,” she said and smiled in spite herself.

“But it worked. Wolf and his cousins are across the border and headed west.”

“Congratulations,” she murmured. She walked to her horse and pulled herself onto its back. She took up the reins and pointed the mare toward the road.

“Where are you going?” he asked.

“Home.”

“You can’t go that way. When the soldiers discover their prisoners are missing, they’ll start beating the brush looking for them. You'll be seen on the road."

"Then how am I supposed to get home?"

"Follow me."

For the better part of an hour, he led them over obscure game trails. Darkness slowed their progress. Sheltering branches overhead offered only an occasional glimpse of the glowing moon. They rode in silence, the horses' footfalls eerily cushioned by past seasons of rotting leaves.

Rane halted his horse at the edge of a stand of cottonwoods. She urged her mount in next to him. Across the distant, open ground, the two-story white house—her home—stood out like a beacon amid blue-black surroundings.

"This is as far as I go," Rane said softly. "I'll stay here and watch, until you reach the house."

And safety.

Though he didn't say the words, she plainly heard them. She knew she should kick her horse into motion and ride away into the clearing. Yet, she hesitated while the knot in her stomach twisted tighter. As always, so many things remained unspoken between them. Things she longed to tell him, yet dared not put into words for fear they would drive him completely away.

It was insanity. They had no future together. She had nothing more of him than these rare snatches of time. Though she loved him with all her heart, nothing at all had changed. Stolen moments were all she would ever have of him.

"Rane?"

She sensed his hesitation. Had he picked up on her mood? Finally, he pulled his gaze from the open view and looked at her with a fierce scowl on his handsome face. He expected her to go.

Leaving just then was the last thing Angel wanted. Something primal and all consuming had her in its grip. Before she could change her mind, she reached out and softly cupped his unyielding jaw. Not waiting for him to react, she leaned over and brushed her lips against his. One miniscule part of her mind screamed in protest at what she was doing. The rest of her gloried at the tremor of response that ran through his body. She knew she still affected him on some basic level. At least that, too, remained unchanged.

He lifted his hand and enfolded the back of her neck, tilting her head to better fuse his mouth to hers. He took command of the kiss with a groan of hard fought surrender. Pressing deep, he parted her lips and delved inside with a hunger that told her he was just as starved for the taste of her as she was for him. The faint flavor of whiskey still lingered and mingled with his own unique woodsy spice.

He backed off slightly, though he didn't fully relinquish her lips. Still touching, lightly brushing, he asked, "Why?"

"I've missed you..." she murmured against his mouth, "...want you."

He pulled back and searched her face, as if looking for some piece of understanding that still eluded him.

The sidestepping stallion separated them. Rane dismounted and tied his reins to a branch. He moved to the side of her horse and held up his arms. Angel lifted her leg over the mare's back and gladly slid into his embrace.

He pulled her tight against him and bent his head to hers once more. She ran her hands over his strong shoulders, up the back of his neck, clinging, unable to get enough of the feel of him. Then he lifted her and carried her away from the horses, into the cover of the trees. He stood her on her feet while he hastily stripped off his shirt and spread it over the spongy, moldering ground cover.

She sat on his makeshift bed and peeled off her denims while he made fast work of the buttons on her shirt, exposing the whiteness of her breasts to the dappled moonlight. He stroked her with his hands, his mouth hot and urgent, as he laid her back on the cushioned earth.

When they came together, the intensity of their mating—untamed with need—lifted her so high she never again wanted to drift down. The feeling both frightened and exhilarated her.

She had no idea how much time had passed. An hour? Two? The moon had dipped lower through the tree trunks. A breeze ruffled the highest branches and created the mock sound of a rushing stream. Nearby, the stallion whickered softly. Rane's arm lay across her, just beneath her breasts, and with each rising breath, the crisp dark hairs tickled her skin.

She felt content, blissfully peaceful. She turned her head, wondering if he'd fallen asleep. Moonlight shimmered in the darkness of his eyes. She started to speak, "I think it's time—," until he pressed a fingertip to her lips and silenced her.

He lifted to one elbow and replaced the pressure against her lips with his mouth. She closed her eyes and gave herself over to pure sensation again. Surprised that she could feel anything at all so soon after their wild lovemaking.

He primed her with long, languid kisses—her throat, her breasts, then lower to her belly—until she tingled with renewed awareness. His lips were an exquisite, dragging friction. A slight scrape of teeth. The gentle lave of his tongue. When he moved lower and lovingly nuzzled the tender insides of her thighs, she couldn't have stopped him if she'd wanted to.

Like a master of seduction, he unerringly found her swollen bud and quickly lifted her so close to the pinnacle, she strained toward him, panting, moaning. Just when she started to tumble into the blinding heights, he buried himself deep inside her and rode them both over the edge of no return.

Rane held himself rigid above her while wave after wave of shatteringly sweet aftershocks rocked through him. Sex had never been anything more than a pleasant interlude, the twining of two willing bodies, a blinding instant of release. But since the first time with Angel, he'd known it would never again be the same for him.

His heart welled with unaccustomed tenderness when she was near. Fierce possessiveness he couldn't control. And this. This most of all. The giving and sharing of pleasure beyond the scope of anything he'd imagined.

Earlier, when she'd turned to him again, his resolve had shattered at her touch, his beliefs tossed to the winds.

She was meant for Keegan. Even Rane could see the way the wind blew in Roy Clayton's house. Yet here she was, in *his* arms, making love with *him*.

Why?

****

Staying low, Angel slipped from post to post along the fencerow. Each time she stopped, she studied the open ground between the back of the house and surrounding outbuildings. Her guards were nowhere in sight. Nothing at all moved around the compound.

Either everyone had gone, or they were all sound asleep—neither of which she trusted for a moment. The windows in the house were all dark. She prayed her father still slept, unaware of her absence. If she could make it to her room, she was home free.

With her heart throbbing in her throat, she reached the back of the house and stepped onto the wide, roofed porch. Crossing to the kitchen door, she palmed the key from her pocket and started to insert it into the lock.

A board creaked. She froze. Another creak betrayed a heavy footstep. Still holding the key, she enclosed it in her fist and clutched it against her heaving chest. Then she turned around.

Against the backdrop of darkness, the silhouette of a man stood at the edge of the porch. His arms lifted, bringing his hands to the front of his body. The scratch of a match broke the tense stillness and sulfur flared in front of his face. Angel's heart lurched when Will Keegan revealed himself and stepped toward her.

He allowed the match to burn for several seconds before waving it out and tossing it off the edge of the porch. Long enough to show her the hard glint in his pale eyes and the angry slash of his mouth.

"Interestin' outfit you got on, Angel." The words sounded strangely devoid of emotion. And she realized he'd dropped the formality of her surname. "Where you been?"

Her shock at being caught quickly shifted to anger. "None of your business," she said.

When he started toward her again, she suddenly remembered, earlier that very day her father had given this man permission to control her. *Control her*. Her mind rioted. How far would he go to attempt it? She knew she didn't want to find out.

Near blind panic, she threw herself against the door. Before she could unlock it, he caught her hand and wrested the key from her fingers. Furious, she turned on him, which was a mistake.

With no effort at all, he pushed her against the house, then caught her wrists and pinned them to the boards above her head.

"Let go of me!" She jerked her arms, trying to break his hold. When that had no effect, she kicked out at his legs.

With a guttural grunt, he crowded closer and trapped the lower half of her body with his.

Shock raced through her. If he would manhandle her this way, what else was he capable of doing?

His angry breath heaved against the side of her face. He smelled of trail dust and day-old sweat. "You've been with him!" He hissed the accusation into her face.

Goosebumps chased over Angel's skin. "Who?"

"That gunfighter. Mantorres. I can smell him all over you, sweetheart. You reek of greaser, just like any two-bit border whore."

She clamped her teeth against the rage burning through her blood. If she could free her hands, she'd slap him into next week or at least attempt it. "Turn me loose right now, you bastard, or I swear I'll scream my head off."

"What kind of fool do you take me for? You're not gonna scream." A pale streak appeared within the dark contours of his face, and she knew he was smiling. "If you do, you'll have to explain what you're doin' out here runnin' around in the middle of the night dressed like a man."

Angel's heart nearly stopped. He had her right where he wanted her. She tried struggling again, but her actions only made her more aware of him. His groin pegged her hips to the wall, and with each movement, he grew harder against her belly. Did having her under his power excite him? Or was he imagining her with Rane? Either possibility sent her stomach into a sick churn.

"You were supposed to play the little lady when you came back here." His hot breath blasted her face again. "Your Pa's been lookin' forward to gettin' you hitched all nice and proper. How's he s'posed to do that with you playin' loose and easy with that lowdown half-blood?

Huh?"

She refused to respond to his goading.

"Just look at you. Miss High and Mighty doesn't look so high right now. And all this time, you've been lookin' down your nose at me. So, tell me," he gritted through his teeth. "What's that Mex got that I don't have?"

While he spoke, he methodically ground his hips against hers.

Angel knew she should be afraid. Will was out of his mind to accost her this way on her father's very doorstep. But, as usual, fury burned away caution. She *would* have the last word, and the devil take the hindmost.

She lifted her chin and looked directly into the black voids of his eyes. "You ask what he has," she said, "so I'll tell you. He has me, Will. *Me!*"

Anger vibrated through him. So palpable, she flinched despite her bravado. His taut muscles quivered with it. She had pushed too far. She fully expected him to release her wrist and strike her.

He did release her, but only to step back. Angel dropped her arms quickly and stood there, wary and waiting for his next move.

He pulled in several deep breaths through his nostrils, as if striving for calm. "You're wrong." Bitterness had replaced the grit in his voice. "He doesn't have you, and he never will. I'll see him dead first. Remember that, cause I'll be watchin' from now on."

Angel sucked in a startled breath when he reached toward her. He paused there a moment, as if savoring the fact that he inspired fear in her. Then, he completed the motion and dropped the key down the front of her shirt.

"Damn you." His bare whisper resonated menace. "You're supposed to be mine."

For several long minutes after Will crossed the yard and faded through the door of the bunkhouse, Angel stood frozen in place with her back pressed against the wall.

Chapter Eighteen

Gloom enclosed the house. A slow rain had started falling sometime during the pre-dawn hours. Angel had been awake to hear it. She hadn't slept at all, and as she descended the back stairs to the kitchen, she couldn't shake the feeling of dread that plagued her through the wee hours of the night.

In essence, she had confessed her affair with Rane. A stupid move, but Will had pushed her beyond the limits of discretion. Now, she could only wait and wonder what he would do with the information.

She lit a lamp and stood it in the center of the kitchen table. The stove was cold, the ashes inside dead and gray. She rummaged through the corner wood box for pieces of kindling and shoved them into the open portal. The small blaze tried to gutter and was slow to catch. When she was satisfied the flames wouldn't die, she lifted the iron cover into place and adjusted the damper.

Her first attempt at making coffee ended in spilled grinds. She was in the process of wiping them up when the back door opened, letting in the smells of wet wood and musty earth. The last person she wanted to see was Will Keegan, but there he stood, filling the entire doorway.

"Mind if I come in?" he asked.

She straightened and tossed down her cleaning rag, scattering grinds across the table once more. "If I said yes, I doubt it would make a difference since you're already here."

Determined to go about her business and not let him see how he rattled her, she filled the coffeepot with water and sat it on the stove. Drips of water sizzled on the hot iron surface. Behind her, she heard the door close and the scrape of his boots on the wood floor.

Her pulse kicked into a dead gallop. What was he

doing here? Blackmail sprang to mind. That, and other possibilities, had kept her awake the entire night. Rather than stand there and drive herself crazy second-guessing, she swiped her hands down the front of her dress and turned to face him.

"What do you want, Will?"

"To talk," he said.

She threw a glance at the back staircase. "My father will be coming down any minute."

"Then I guess we'd better hurry and say what we gotta say."

Out of habit, he'd removed his hat and held it with both hands in front of him. His eyes looked red-rimmed, as though he hadn't slept either.

Angel crossed to the table, picked up the rag and attacked the spilled grinds again. "After last night, I have nothing more to say to you." She decided on the spot to call his bluff. "If you intend to tell my father you caught me sneaking into the house, then go ahead and do it. There's nothing I can do to stop you."

"I got no intention of runnin' to the old man with what happened last night."

"Huh! I would ask why not, but I'm sure I already know. If you tell on me, there would be nothing to stop me from telling him about your disgusting behavior. And since the 'old man' is my father, there's a slight chance he might be more tolerant of me. You, on the other hand, would be out in the road so fast you wouldn't know what hit you." She flashed him a mocking smile. "Does that sound about right?"

He glanced at the doorway to the stairs. "Keep your voice down."

When he edged closer, she gripped the rag in her hand until her knuckles strained the skin, but didn't give one inch of ground.

"Look," he said, "we've both got a lot to lose here. We've been handed a second chance, and you're about to foul the nest and ruin everything. We both know, no respectable man is gonna come beatin' down your door. I'm all you've got."

"Pity me," she murmured.

Yet, his words battered her because he hit too close to

the truth. They also instilled her with sadness that went bone deep. As hard as she wished to break free, the vicious cycle of her life kept sucking her deeper into a dark hole, and she saw no way out.

"Since you think so little of me and my tainted virtue, why are you so willing to sacrifice yourself?"

When he opened his mouth, she held up her hand.

"Don't answer that. I already know. If you marry me, the Flying C will be yours. You'll become a man of property again, respectable in your own right. You'll be able to spit in the eye of your family, who turned you out without an acre of ground or a dollar in your pocket. So, as it turns out, I'm also all *you've* got—unless you think you can find some other heiress willing to marry the black sheep of the Keegan clan."

His chuckle held no real warmth or mirth. "Smart girl," he said. "At least all that high-flown schoolin' ended up countin' for somethin'."

"So you admit it?"

He shook his head. "I didn't say it. You did."

Her fingers itched to slap the smirk from his face.

His pale gaze flickered over her, lingering on the bodice of her dress. "It won't be all bad." He reached out and stroked a fingertip down her cheek. "I know what it takes to keep a woman happy. I can give you everything you need."

She flinched away from his touch, disgusted by his blatantly sexual insinuation and his foregone conclusion that they were already as good as wed. What did he think she was? She knew, of course. Her confession last night, coupled with years of rumors that pointed to wanton behavior. He believed she tossed up her skirt for nearly every man she encountered.

Only one person knew the truth, the only one that mattered to her—Rane. That he viewed her as nothing more than a willing and convenient dalliance filled her with wretchedness.

A heavy tread on the back stairs announced her father's arrival just before he rounded the doorway, pulling his galluses onto his shoulders. His gray-streaked hair stood stiffly on end. She forced a pleasant expression while flames of guilt burned into her cheeks.

Roy's gray eyes widened when he saw her unexpected visitor, standing there so innocuously with his hat in his hands.

"Mornin', Will. You're makin' your rounds early today. What's up?"

"I just dropped by to tell you some news I heard this mornin'."

Angel had to admit, the man was quick on his feet.

Roy detoured to the stove and touched fingers to the coffeepot, then frowned. "What news?"

"Those renegades we saw in town yesterday escaped last night."

Angel's head came up quickly. Will was looking straight at her. New alarm thrummed with each rapid beat of her heart.

"How?" she asked.

The small, knowing smile that curved Will's lips was just for her. "Some Mex stole the key from the guard and turned them loose."

"Well, that's a hell of a note," Roy injected. "Best keep an eye on the horses. If them skulking devils are still around, we're liable to start missin' a few."

"I don't think there's any danger of that," Will added. "I'd say they're tail to the wind in Mexico by now."

Angel abandoned the men to their small talk, relieved that Wolf and the others had—evidently—gotten away. She resumed her breakfast preparations while hopelessness for her own predicament closed around her tighter and tighter. There would be no reasoning with Will. He'd set his sights on the brass ring—the Flying C—and she knew he'd stop at nothing to possess it. But he could only get the ranch by going through her, and she would never agree to *any* arrangement between them. Never!

So, what were her options? She realized she had none. If she kept refusing him, Will would eventually find a way to force her into the marriage he sought.

Her frantic thoughts turned to Rane. Savage, killer Rane. Feared and reviled by all who didn't know him. But she knew him as a gentle, loyal man. Her heart deflated. If only he loved her as she loved him. If she thought there was even a prayer of a chance, she would willingly defy her father and everyone in the state of Texas to be with him. But he didn't love her. He'd already made that abundantly clear.

Acid tears scalded the backs of Angel's eyes. Rather than let them fall, she turned her face to the searing heat from the stove and flipped strips of bacon with a long-pronged fork.

Damn you, Rane Mantorres! If only I'd never laid eyes on you!

****

Rane hunched his shoulders against the steady drizzle and watched as dismal dawn crept over the mean looking shack squatted on the outskirts of the village. The one-room structure of warped, mismatched planks and crumbly adobe chinking looked in danger of tumbling over in a stiff breeze. The door was missing and a flimsy, sodden blanket—held in place by a couple of nails—hung over the opening.

With the coming of light, he adjusted the brim of his Stetson to cover the back of his neck and waded across the muddy wagon track that served as a road. Quick and silent, he pushed the blanket aside and slipped into the room.

A tallow candle burned in a shallow bowl, surrounded by an assortment of food-encrusted dishes, atop a small, circular table in the center of the room. The fumes of rancid fat hung thick in the dead air, but didn't disguise the smells of dirty clothing and unwashed bodies. A variety of snores sawed through the stillness. Moth-eaten blankets lay over the uneven floor where several bodies sprawled in slumber.

After a quick search to get his bearings, Rane walked to the middle of the room, picked up the fluttering candle, and upended the table with a lift of his fingers. The dishes slid to the floor in a resounding crash meant to wake the dead. The table rolled on its edge until Rane's boot halted it. He reached down and stood it back on its pedestal, then returned the candle dish to its former spot.

Despite the sudden violence, the sleeping transients roused slowly, as lethargic as the denizens of an opium parlor. One by one, they sat up, bleary and blinking as they looked around. The moment they spotted Rane, they scrambled up and scurried out the door like routed rats.

All save one man.

In a corner, Benito Reyes slept on with his crutch cradled to his chest, unfazed by the noise.

Rane paced a slow circle around his quarry while a mixture of disgust and fury roiled inside him. He had imagined this moment and envisioned his vengeance since he learned Benito betrayed him to Lundy's men. He planted a boot against the saggy trousers covering Benito's backside and shoved.

"Get up!"

Benito opened his eyes slowly and blinked. Moving slug-like, he sat upright, lifted the heels of his hands and pressed them to his temples. After a moment, his bloodshot gaze focused on Rane's muddy boots and traveled upward. Recognition, and then shock, leapt to his face. He scrambled to get his feet under him.

Rane wrapped his hand in the front of the little man's shirt and jerked him to the ends of his toes. Snarling, he propelled Benito against the wall and pinned him. The wall shuddered from the impact and gave up several chunks of loose chinking which dropped to the floor.

Reaching down, Rane pulled the knife from the hidden sheath inside his boot. Benito squealed with terror and slammed his eyes shut.

Survival-honed instinct drove Rane. Plunge the blade to its hilt in the cowering bastard's ribcage. Justice, for all the suffering Benito had caused. Yet in that crucial moment, the tattered memory of old friendship, of a woman with smiling dark eyes, stayed Rane's hand. He couldn't kill Benito, but he would instill the fear of the devil's own damnation into his rotten soul.

He leaned in and pressed the blade's razor sharp tip against the traitor's throat. A drop of blood welled on the polished steel.

Benito's eyes flew open. His panicky, stale-whiskey breath blasted Rane's face.

Rane gave the knife a taunting twist. "Prepare to die, *puto*."

"*Por favor*!" Benito cried, then immediately realized the peril the outburst presented to his jutting Adam's apple. Speaking with care, he said, "Please, Señor. Do not kill me. I am nothing but a miserable cripple."

"Your pity act doesn't work on me." Rane applied more pressure, until the expanding drop of blood broke and trailed an erratic course along the flat edge of the tempered steel. "Why did you do it? Why did you betray me?"

"Señor, I never—"

Cutting off the denial, Rane lowered the knife. He jerked Benito forward, and slammed him against the wall again.

"Don't lie to me, *pendejo!*"

The bony knob in Benito's throat bobbed as he swallowed convulsively. "I thought they would kill you!" he blurted. "I wanted you dead."

The confession jolted Rane. For some time, resentment had been brewing between them, but he never would have guessed the little man's bitterness had escalated to the point of murder. Why had he not seen it?

He pinned Benito with a narrow look of loathing. "Why?"

"I may be crippled, but I am not blind!" Benito spat. "Do you think I did not see the way Carmella smiled for you whenever you were there? The way her hips swayed for your eyes?"

Jealousy? Rane had never even suspected. "You dream this," he said.

Benito shook his head. "No. After that night when we crossed the river together and she learns what I tell Lundy's men, Carmella left me. She says she cannot live with what I did to you."

"Drunken fool." Rane released him so abruptly he flinched.

A broken sob escaped Benito's throat. He clapped his hands over his face and slid down the wall like a dismembered puppet, landing in a loose heap at Rane's feet.

Rane stepped back and squatted on his heels to bring himself down to eye-level with the weeping mass of misery before him. As he watched Benito's bony shoulders heave, guilt dug relentless claws into his heart. This was *not* how he imagined the morning would play out. He clasped his hands between his knees and sighed.

"I don't know what to do with you, Benito. You are one *loco borrachón*."

Benito sobbed harder.

"Carmella didn't leave you because of me. You drove her away with your lies and your treachery. I was your *patrón*. Your betrayal dishonored you, took away her dignity. It's this she cannot live with."

"*Basta*!" Benito cried.

Clenching his lips to stop the flow of battering words, Rane sat back on his heels and waited.

Through a hole in the roof, the steady plink of rainwater augmented the strained silence within the shack. Benito sat on the floor with his head hung low, his face hidden in his hands. Rane continued to hunker, waiting him out.

At last, Benito raised his head and expelled a long breath. He lifted his arm and scrubbed a dingy sleeve across his tear-streaked face. "I do not know what to do." His voice still trembled. "To die now would be a relief. I am alone and it is too hard..."

He stretched his emaciated leg upon the floor and banged his fist against his thigh as if the injury he'd suffered was to blame for his misfortune. With each blow an anguished whimper escaped his lips.

Rane watched for several seconds, disgusted, but this wasn't the first time he'd seen Benito vent his anger and frustration on his twisted leg. He clamped a hand around Benito's wrist and stopped him.

"Perhaps it would be better if you beat your head against the floor," he said.

Benito strained against Rane's grip, trying to free his captured arm. "You do not know how it feels. The pain—"

"Is mostly in your mind now, I think. The doctor said your leg would get stronger when you used it. But you didn't try. Instead of throwing away your crutch, you found more to lean on. Whiskey. Carmella."

Benito hung his head once more. "If you are not going to kill me, then go away and leave me alone."

Rane shook his head. "No, I'm not leaving you alone. Where is Carmella?"

Benito shrugged. "I do not know. She hides from me."

In all honesty, Rane couldn't blame her.

"You want her back?"

"*Sí.*"

"Then stop feeling sorry for yourself and do something about it."

Rane released him and stood. Benito cradled his arm against his stomach and massaged his wrist. The man looked as weak as watered down tea.

The cast aside crutch caught Rane's eye. "If you have belongings here, get them."

Benito looked up, wide-eyed with new fear. "Why?"

"You're going with me. Somewhere inside that miserable hide of yours there must be something left of the Benito I once knew. I intend to find him. Then, *he* is going to get your wife back."

****

Angel's hands fell idle in the pan of soapy dishwater. Outside the window above the dry sink, rain, slow and gray, continued to fall. The atmosphere inside the kitchen was dry and overly warm. A safe haven, but she no longer felt secure even here in her father's house. The words Will had spoken earlier that morning clamored repeatedly in her mind.

At least all that high-flown schoolin' ended up countin' for somethin'.

Will couldn't have been more wrong. Sure, she could carry off wearing an elegant gown and stylish coif, but those things were only trappings. Camouflage. Underneath her rebellious nature still thrived and perhaps grown even stronger. A true lady accepted her lot in life with grace. She remained chaste for her wedding night. After two years of intense coaching, she had ultimately failed all the tests. She would go down fighting like a mad harridan before she accepted what Will and her father had in mind for her.

A tap at the back door startled Angel from her guilty woolgathering. She frowned and pulled her hands from the water. Who bothered to knock anymore? Most everyone on the Flying C simply barged in unannounced. Snatching up her drying cloth, she hastily swiped it across her palms.

Angel opened the door and found a woman standing

on the porch. Water dripped from her ankle length skirt and the black *rebozo* draped over her head. Mud caked the *guaraches* on her feet, even to the tan skin showing between the leather straps. Evidently, she'd walked quite a long distance.

When she lifted her dark, soulful gaze, Angel recognized her immediately.

"Carmella!"

"Señorita Clayton." The words sighed out on a breath of relief.

"What are you doing here?" Angel blurted.

"I came to tell you, I am sorry."

"For what?"

"All the bad things that happen to you and Señor Rane."

"None of it was your fault."

"Sí, it is my fault," Carmella insisted. "Benito is my husband. His sins are mine. But no more."

One day, she will leave him.

Angel recalled Rane's prediction spoken with such certainty and remembered her own jealousy at hearing him say those words.

Almost dreading the answer, she asked, "Have you left your husband, Carmella?"

Carmella's chin betrayed a quiver as she forced it higher. "Sí. I honor him no more after what he has done."

Though Carmella tried to appear strong, her expression betrayed too much wretchedness. Belatedly remembering her manners, not to mention common decency, Angel held the door wider and moved aside.

"Please, come in. You're trembling."

Carmella hesitated another moment, then stepped across the threshold. Angel closed the door against the dank weather.

Drawn by the banked heat given off from the cook stove, Carmella crossed the room and crowded close to the warmth. She lifted the sodden *rebozo* from her head, revealing the damp and flattened mass of ravenesque hair hidden beneath.

Angel pulled a chair away from the table and slid it close to the stove. "Please, sit. You must be tired after walking."

With a look of gratitude, Carmella lowered herself to the wooden seat and hugged her arms against her bosom. Spasms of shivers racked her shoulders.

Angel took the discarded scarf from her hands and hung it on a wall peg behind the stove. Turning, she took in the woman's length, the faded dark skirt and too-thin peasant blouse, all soaking wet, and she remembered the kindness Carmella had shown her that night in Rane's adobe across the border. "You need dry clothes. Let's go upstairs—"

"No. I cannot stay."

"Surely you didn't walk all this way in the rain just to apologize."

Carmella ducked her head.

The woman's reticence warned Angel to proceed with caution. Pride was at work here. Or shame. And judging from Carmella's bowed head, Angel guessed the latter. She decided it might be best to take a more circuitous path to try and get at the truth. She paced to the dry sink and propped a hip against the slatted cabinet.

"So where have you been staying since you left Benito?"

After several more seconds hesitation, Carmella lifted her head. "I have some family in the village. An elderly uncle. But I must always hide because Benito looks for me. So I leave now, so I make no trouble for Uncle Tomás."

Angel waited, but Carmella didn't elaborate.

"Is Benito still staying at the adobe?"

"Oh, no." Carmella half turned on the chair to face her. "No one is there. Did you not know?

"Know what?"

"That night you and Señor Rane leave, Lundy's men come soon after. They burn everything."

Burned! Everything? Rane's home. All his possessions. The place where they had made love the first time. Gone. Angel closed her eyes against the sudden ache that filled her heart. He hadn't said a word.

"Now, I have no place left to go," Carmella confessed. "And I need work."

Heat flooded Angel's face. How could she have been so dense? If all of Rane's belongings were gone, it only stood to reason that Carmella had lost everything she owned as well. The adobe had been her home, too.

Angel opened her eyes and pulled in a deep, fortifying breath. She pushed away from the sink. "Well, it just so happens I need help right here with all the housework."

Carmella's eyes widened with hope. "You would let me work for you?"

Before Angel could answer, a heavy tread on the back stairs intruded. "My father," she said.

Carmella started to rise from the chair, but Angel pressed an insistent hand against her shoulder. "It'll be all right."

She looked up and found Roy standing in the doorway, staring at the back of Carmella's head.

"Who've we got here?" he asked.

Angel plastered a bright smile on her face. "This is Carmella Reyes, our new housekeeper."

"Well, it's about time you found somebody to help out around here." He crossed the room and plucked a battered hat from the wall rack beside the door. "Damn rain's settlin' into my bones," he muttered. He plopped the hat over his head and opened the door. When he stepped through and closed it again, Angel released the breath she'd been holding, thankful he'd not interfered for once.

Chapter Nineteen

When Rane heard about the gunfight being waged along the fence line separating the Flying C and the Hacienda, his gut warned him time was running out. He got on his horse and headed out that way. The sun was sinking low in the southwest by the time he picked up the first faint echo of gunfire in the distance. He halted the stallion and listened. The shots came in rapid, sporadic bursts. He was getting close.

He was still a quarter of a mile out when he spotted powder smoke lifting on the wind. He slowed to a walk and proceeded more cautiously. The land here was broken and rocky, treacherous footing. As he moved closer, the scene of the ongoing battle opened before him like a panoramic painting.

To the north, about a dozen or so of Clayton's men were positioned belly-down along the crest of a low bluff. The lay of the land itself provided their only cover. Lundy's men had taken refuge in the thick, tangled brush in the lower lying area to the south, hiding behind the plentiful rock formations the rough terrain provided. The disputed fence separated the two factions, that and the shallow creek that meandered among the lopsided fence posts.

Strangest of all was the sight of a group of spectators clustered just out of bullet range, from a pistol anyway, on an elevated patch of ground to the west. Small time ranchers and homesteaders from the look of them. They stood around talking, some with field glasses getting a bird's eye view of the action. The fact that they'd brought along some of their women and children to watch the hostilities angered Rane.

He left his horse in a sheltering rock formation and continued on foot. From bush to boulder, he ventured as close as he could without risking a bullet, then hunkered down to wait.

Across the creek, Lundy's men kept up a steady stream of gunfire. On top of the bluff, the Flying C men could do little more than keep their heads down and hope they didn't get in the way of a ricochet.

Rane removed his hat and wiped a skim of sweat from his forehead. He pivoted on his heel and looked southward, holding the hat brim at an angle in front of his face so that only the aura from the lowering sun showed along the edge of the black felt Champie. The gauge proved nearly as accurate as a clock.

By his reckoning, thirty minutes had passed and little more than an hour of daylight remained.

Rane turned from the blinding sun and settled the hat back over his head. Keeping low, he peered around the side of the rock. Movement on the south side of the creek caught his attention as several of the Hacienda crew scurried from one spot of cover to the next, working ever closer to the creek.

What were they up to?

As if on cue, many guns on the south side opened fire at once. One man broke from cover and ran willy-nilly toward the fence. The object in his hand was a blur of motion, but Rane had a very bad feeling about it. He eased his Colt from his holster.

The man stopped just short of the creek, drew back his arm as far as he could, and lobbed his payload into the air. Instantly, the guns ceased fire.

In the sudden silence, Rane heard the thing hissing, and it was for damn sure not a snake.

Dynamite.

Reflex kicked in. Rane shifted his pistol to the top of the rock, fired, and missed. The bundled dynamite reached its arc and slowed in mid-air. He fired again.

The airborne blast jerked the air as it hit the face of the bluff. A thick cloud of dirt and small stones flew skyward and rained down on the Flying C crew. All they could do was cover their heads and wait for the dust to settle.

Rane dropped down behind his sheltering rock and quickly replaced his spent cartridges. Those boys up on the bluff were in a bad spot, exposed as it was. Only a few more sticks of dynamite would send them into retreat. Coming darkness would take care of the rest. He needed to buy some time. Where the hell was Clayton with reinforcements?

Following the blast, he heard only the sound of coughing from the top of the ridge. Then, eerie silence settled over the creek.

Rane cupped his hands and yelled, "Let's parley!"

The silence dragged, then someone called out, "Start talking!" The voice came from the south side of the creek.

Rane swallowed, gulped several quick breaths, and wondered what the hell he was supposed to say now. Then, in a clear, white moment of inspiration, an idea took shape. His compressed lips curved in a devious smile. He cleared his throat and proceeded to dangle the bait.

"The way you boys are putting your necks in the noose, Lundy must be paying you a killing wage."

"Ain't none of your damn business what he's payin' us!"

"Did anybody ever collect on the reward he promised for the Clayton girl?" From word of mouth, he was well aware that no money had passed hands on the Hacienda in many weeks.

Rane could practically feel the tension in the stillness that followed. His smile grew broader.

"Bad news, boys," he continued, feeling more confident of his strategy. "There's no reward. No wages. Lundy's out of chips. He's trying to gouge Roy Clayton for money to keep from going under. He's made a lot of promises he can't keep."

Disgruntled murmurs drifted to Rane's ears. He sat back, satisfied. He'd planted a seed. Now it only needed time to grow.

****

The afternoon had started out normal enough. Angel had been helping Carmella take the washing down off the lines. Then in a heartbeat, the tranquility of the day had shattered when one of her father's cowhands rode up to the house on a lathered horse. He reported that a small herd of Flying C cattle had been stampeded over the edge of a dry gorge and plunged to their deaths.

Before the import of the disaster even had time to set

in, another man had ridden in with the news of a gun battle being waged along the deadline down south.

Lundy's men had gone on the offensive. Roy feared it was all diversionary tactics meant to pull him and the rest of the men away from the house, leaving Angel unguarded and free for the taking. He swore not to let her out of his sight.

And that's how Angel found herself riding toward the setting sun with every remaining man her father could muster, including her own Mexican guards.

Riding point, Roy reined in his horse less than a quarter mile north of the creek. He motioned everyone to silence and then cocked his ear southward.

Angel held her breath and listened too. She expected to hear gunshots, but only the soft rustle of the wind moving through the sparse grass came back to her ears.

Roy looked at Will and cleared his throat. "What do you make of it?"

Will shrugged. "Don't know. But I guess we'll find out soon enough."

From the expression on his weathered face, Angel knew that's exactly what her father feared. Finding out. She had a grisly vision of riding onto the scene of a massacre.

Confirming her misgivings, Roy shifted in his saddle and looked back at her.

"Some of you men, stay with Angel and hang back from the rest of us," he instructed.

She knew then, he expected to find the worst.

Angel heard the voices for several minutes before she rode around the base of the bluff. The creek came into view and with it, an unexpected sight.

There were no dead bodies. At a glance, it appeared no one had even sustained serious injury.

Her father's men stood on the north side of the fence. Every one of them looked like they'd been in a howling dust storm that left dirt caked around their eyes and mouths. She could only wonder how they'd gotten in that condition.

Lundy's men had lined up on the opposite side. Only the runs of barbed wire separated the two factions. Most were talking back and forth, while some argued.

Most amazing of all was the sight of women and children milling among the motley crowd as though the fence war had turned into a casual Sunday social. Where had *they* come from?

Angel's heart nearly dropped to the pit of her stomach when she spotted Rane leaning against a fence post. He had positioned himself well away from everyone and stood with his arms crossed over his chest looking detached, but she knew he was taking in everything with avid interest.

Like the opposite pole of a magnet, his dark gaze slid to hers and locked.

Across the distance that separated them, even amid the chaotic voices clamoring to be heard, he spoke to her. Without moving, without words. His very presence allayed her fears. Reassured, she turned, wondering if her father could finally settle the long-running feud between the Flying C and Hacienda outfits.

Wearing a fierce expression, Roy dismounted and faced the crowd. "What the hell's goin' on here!"

Several people spoke at once, some shouting and red-faced.

One of the men on the opposite side of the fence stepped forward. "Mantorres says you're gonna send word down to Laredo and sic the Rangers on us."

Though Angel knew this was news to her father, he didn't blink an eye. She sent a quick glance back at Rane. A small, devious grin sat on the handsome devil's lips.

Her father hesitated a mere beat. "Damn right!" he shouted. He was backing up Rane's bluff. "You can't go around shootin' at people and destroyin' property. Especially *my* property!"

The cacophony of voices started up once more, each clamoring to out-shout the others.

"Shut the hell up!" Roy bellowed. He waited until he had their undivided attention. "Now, I'm here to take names and I wanta know who run some of my cattle over a cliff about two hours ago."

They all got still and found a spot of ground to focus on.

Finally, one man spoke up. "You can't hardly say nothin' about that, not after the way you fenced out Mr.

Lundy's cattle and left 'em to starve. You owe him for that."

All the blood appeared to rush to Roy's face, leaving it mottled with anger. "I don't owe Horace Lundy one goddamned red cent, and any man that says I do is a goddamn liar! This is my land! Horace Lundy's got no claim on it. His herd died of the tick fever."

Even while her father's tirade poured heat into Angel's face, the sight of him taking charge sent a surge of pride through her.

The men continued to argue across the fence. The question of the money Lundy had promised emerged as the main source of discontent.

At last, Roy waved them to silence. "You boys are barkin' up the wrong tree," he said. "Horace Lundy is as broke as last week's eggs. I'm offerin' you another deal right now. Walk away from this, peaceful, and no charges will be brought against you."

"Roy Clayton has always been a man of his word," someone said.

Several others nodded agreement.

"I ain't goin' no-damn-where 'til I get that reward money!"

Roy picked the dissenter out of the crowd with a narrow-eyed glare. "There'll be no bounty money paid out on my daughter! Any man that wants to make an issue of it, step over here, and I'll take it up with you."

No one stepped forward.

"The deal is, you walk away right now, free and clear, and that's it, by God!"

"Yonder comes the bastard now!" someone shouted.

An excited murmur ran through the crowd as everyone shifted and craned their necks to look southward.

From her higher viewpoint atop her horse, Angel was amazed to see Horace Lundy riding toward the hornet's nest at a steady lope on a big bay. Like the others, she watched him come while the restless susurrus around her grew louder. A new fear began to form. All these men were now anxious to hang Horace up on a cross. If they decided to crucify him, who would stop them?

When Horace approached the creek, the disgruntled

young cowhand lifted his gun from his holster and took a shot at him. A woman in the crowd screamed. Angel was forced to take her skittish horse in hand, but not before she saw a startled expression leap to Horace's face and a spot of crimson bloom on his flawless white shirtfront. He slumped forward, over the horn of his saddle. The horse wheeled in a tight arc, nearly unseating him, and set off at a lope in the opposite direction.

The shooter sighted down the gun again, prepared to fire another round. Several of the men standing nearby tackled him to the ground.

All hell seemed to break loose. Across the fence, the shooter wasn't giving up easily and rolled on the ground amid a confusing tangle of legs and arms as he struggled with the men trying to wrest the gun from his hand. The screaming woman continued to let out ear-piercing shrieks. Angel's mare tossed her head and side-stepped dangerously close to the barbed wire fence. Meanwhile, Rane sprinted away from the creek and disappeared among the rocky debris along the base of the bluff.

Angel was still trying to get her horse under control when she heard the hoofbeats of a running horse. Rane appeared astride the black stallion, stretched out in a dead gallop.

The black didn't slow, even though it was headed straight for the fence. Angel held her breath. Surely he didn't intend... Oh, yes, he did! The stallion's powerful muscles bunched in a tremendous leap that sent it skimming the top strand of wire. The horse nearly went down to its haunches on the other side. Following the stumble, it recovered quickly and bounded away with Rane riding low over its neck.

Panic played riot as Angel watched Rane go chasing off after Horace. Did he intend to finish the young cowhand's handiwork and kill Horace? That's exactly what she feared.

Shortening up her reins with a firm grip, Angel wheeled her horse. "Pa! Quick! Cut the fence!" she shouted.

Her father stared at her with his mouth agape. "What do you mean, cut the damn fence!"

"Rane's going after Horace. I'm afraid he'll kill him!"

Cursing a blue streak, Roy stomped to the fence and snatched a pair of wire cutters from a man standing on the other side. With no ado, he snipped through both strands of the barrier his men had risked their lives to protect.

Angel didn't hesitate. She walked her horse through the opening and waded across the creek.

"Hey, you wait up there!" her father called after her.

Up on dry ground, she flicked her reins against the mare's flanks and headed south, onto Hacienda range.

****

The sun had set by the time Angel rode her horse through the outer gate of the Hacienda. Before her, the house's massive front door stood open. She leaped from the saddle and raced up the steps. She heard her father's shout and turned to see him careen through the front gate, hard on her heels, but she didn't wait.

Inside, the cavernous foyer held the utter stillness of a place long deserted. The sconces, hung on brackets along the stone walls, reflected only darkness.

Straight ahead, the open courtyard glowed beneath silver-blue moonlight. She turned and walked along the shadowy portico, her heels clicking loudly on the terra-cotta tiles.

Thin lamplight sliced beneath the door of Horace's office. She placed her hand against the handle, expecting to find it locked. The door swung inward at her touch. She stepped through and then halted with a gasp trapped in her throat.

Horace sat behind his desk with the pallor of death on his skin. Bloody fluid seeped through his fingers where he clutched the wound low in his abdomen. Though sweat glistened on his waxen features, he appeared calm. Too calm. As though he had already accepted the inevitable.

"Come in," he beckoned in a strange, breathless voice. "After all, what good is retribution to a man if there's no one to witness his moment of triumph?"

Angel stared in horrified fascination while the words slipped blithely from his lips. Retribution? Moment of triumph? Had he truly gone mad? She caught a flicker of movement near a window. Cold fear crept through her when Rane stepped from the darkness.

Gone was the cool, self-composed man she knew. Some inner turmoil transformed him, ravaged his handsome features until he looked older than his years. As he walked nearer, his obsidian eyes blazed. Open windows to the violent emotions working at him from within.

"You should not have come, Angel," he said.

When he stepped past her, into the light, Horace lifted his right hand—hidden until that moment behind the desk—and revealed the Colt he'd been hiding. The end of the barrel followed Rane's movements.

The thick, dead air swirled against Angel's exposed skin, disturbed by her father's passage as he silently eased in beside her.

"Put that damn gun away," he ordered with quiet authority.

Horace gave no sign that he heard. "Come in, Roy. The more the merrier. Now I have two of you to bear witness when I shoot this intruder."

The words sent more ice dripping through Angel's veins.

"If you shoot him, I'll swear it was cold-blooded murder," Roy said.

Horace twitched a shoulder as if he meant to shrug and couldn't complete the motion. "It makes no difference. I won't be around to see the consequences."

Rane dared another step toward the desk. "That's right. You're dying, old man. So why not make it easier on yourself and confess your sins."

"Confess my sins? To you?" Horace's chuckle held a brittle edge. "While I'm sure you know much about sin, you're no priest."

A satiric smile twisted Rane's lips. "No, I'm no priest. But only you can say exactly who and what I am."

"Gotten desperate now, haven't you?"

"Confess it," Rane hissed. "This may be the last thing you do, so why not make it an honorable act."

"Easy, boy," Roy cautioned. "Can't you see he's been gut-shot."

A muscle in Rane's jaw bunched. "I only wish it were my bullet in him."

"If you mean that, go ahead and do it now!" Horace

taunted. "Go on. Pull it! You know you can beat me. Put me out of my misery. You'll be doing me a favor."

Rane's hawkish gaze narrowed. "Not yet," he bit out. "You know why I'm here, *viejo*. Before you die, I want to hear you say the words."

Though horrified, Angel hung on every nuance of the exchange with nerve-shattering vigilance. What sort of secret could Horace know that Rane would risk so much to hear him confess it? Was this the "something" he'd tried to extort from Horace when he'd taken her hostage? Had he risked his life, and hers, for nothing more than mere words?

For a long moment, nothing but thick malevolence filled the muffled silence while the two men eyed each other across the few feet of space separating them.

"Say it!" Rane hissed again.

Horace slumped lower in the chair, as if the last vestige of stubborn pride had drained from his body and left him tired and defeated. "Rane Mantorres is my son."

Roy cocked his head as if he hadn't heard correctly. And, truth be told, Angel didn't trust her own ears just then.

"Come again?" Roy blurted.

"I said, this misfit is my son," Horace stated with new strength.

Stunned, Angel's thoughts tumbled into chaos.

"Shit!" Roy exclaimed. "Why the hell didn't you say so before now?"

Horace appeared incredulous. "Claim a bastard, sired on a lowborn peasant as my son! Can you even imagine the repercussions of that?"

"Repercussions," Rane echoed on a caustic note. "In other words, his wife and her family wouldn't have taken the news very well. Francine might have tossed him out of the plush nest she'd paid for here."

He edged closer, the blue vein throbbing at his temple visible even in the poor lighting. He was beyond caution, beyond care. "Tell them the rest of it!" he demanded.

Horace set his jaw at a stubborn angle.

Looking from one to the other, Angel marveled at the similarities between the two men. The aquiline nose, the natural curve that tilted the outer corners of their lips. Easy now to see where Rane had acquired his lordly bearing. He had unconsciously emulated the mannerisms of his father. Why hadn't she noticed these things before?

"From your own lips, you speak of retribution," Rane continued. "So, tell them! Tell them how you got my mother with another of your bastards!"

Angel's father cursed under his breath.

"Don't interfere," she whispered.

While her heart shattered at the sight of the raw pain that ravaged Rane before her eyes, she knew there was still a chance. If he could get it all out in the open, air the past at long last, the terrible scars he carried might yet heal.

"He got her pregnant again," Rane said. His voice had softened to the deceptively mild tones she knew so well. "Only this time, something was wrong. This time, she got sick—so sick she could no longer work. And when the *patron's* wife realized that one of her servants was falling down on the job, she very quickly righted the situation. She ordered my mother off the property." His blazing eyes narrowed to mere slits that burned into Horace. "Do you remember, *patron*?"

The question met with stony silence.

"Damn you, do you remember!"

The unexpected violence in Rane's plea nearly brought Angel out of her skin. She realized, until that moment, she'd never truly heard him raise his voice.

"I came to you, *begged* you on my knees to help her. Do you remember what you said to me? 'Run along, boy. There's nothing I can do.'"

"There *wasn't* anything I could do," Horace said at last. The way his breath heaved faster and the hard dip of his brows betrayed that his son had finally touched a nerve. "I couldn't make special concessions for one insignificant servant. Francine would have questioned it."

"And you couldn't have her asking questions, could you?" Rane retorted. "She might have uncovered your nasty little secret and learned about Maria Mantorres being your mistress all those many years."

Angel had seen Rane in more than one dire predicament, had seen him snuff out life and nearly lose his own. Even in those very desperate circumstances, she had never heard such raw emotion fill his voice. How many years had he lived for this night?

He seemed to run out of steam then, and his dark gaze flickered over each of them before he tilted back his head and released a long, sighing breath. Relief? Sorrow?

"So, what did happen to Maria?" Horace asked. "Since you've accused me of her death, I think I have a right to know."

When Rane looked at Horace again, the brightness shimmering in his eyes shredded Angel's heart.

He swallowed, sending his Adam's apple gliding beneath the skin. "I tried to take her back to Mexico, to her village. She died before we got there. She bled to death on the bank of a creek." His dark, haunted gaze touched on Angel for a brief instant. "That's where I buried her," he concluded.

In her mind's eye, Angel again saw that small grove of cottonwoods near Rane's adobe, and him standing reverently beside a narrow grave with his hat in his hands.

Horace expelled a harsh breath into sudden stillness. "Well, now you've got what you always wanted. I've confessed." Very deliberately, he placed the Colt in his hand on top of the desk. "So, go ahead," he said. "Finish what you came here to do. You've waited for it a long time."

As Rane stared at the old man before him, Angel could almost see him drawing deep within himself, summoning his last shreds of inner strength. Instead of blazing with hatred, his eyes grew cold and impassive.

"No," he said with calm finality. "That would make it easy for you...*Papá*. You'll get no mercy bullet from me. Dying is one thing you'll have to do on your own."

Rane turned and started for the door.

Roy stepped into his path. "Don't leave just yet, Mantorres. This ain't over."

"As far as I'm concerned, it is."

"You just stay put," Roy ordered. He headed for the desk. "Let's have a look at that wound, Horace."

Angel reached out and clutched onto the back of a chair, suddenly feeling as if she might fall without the support. The upheaval of the past thirty minutes was finally taking its toll. She sat quickly and pressed her hands between her knees to try and control their trembling. *Rane was Horace Lundy's son.*

Roy knelt beside Horace's chair and pried his hand away from his stomach. After ripping apart his shirt, Roy examined the wound. When he lifted his head again, grim acceptance carved deeper grooves into his leathery face.

"It don't look good, Horace. Not good atall. There may not be much time, so why not do the right thing?"

Horace's craggy brows peaked. "Surely you don't expect me—"

"I surely do," Roy said. "You ain't got nobody else, so who's it gonna hurt?"

Rane stood leaning against the doorframe, his back turned to the two men, ignoring them, to all appearances. However, Angel was aware that something extraordinary was taking place. Her father pulled paper, pen, and an ink well from a drawer and placed them on the smooth surface in front of Horace.

"Just do it," Roy urged.

Grimacing with pain, Horace leaned forward, picked up the pen and dipped it. After a long moment's hesitation, he started writing. The scratch of the pen moving across the paper grated through the silence for several minutes, then finally stopped. Horace looked up at her father and handed him the quill. "There. If you like, I can sign it in blood."

Ignoring the remark, Roy leaned over the desk and added something to the page Horace had written.

Angel's curiosity nearly pulled her from the chair, but she somehow managed to stay put.

Roy laid the pen aside and straightened. "Mantorres, would you come over here."

Rane turned, his eyes narrowed with suspicion as he walked to the front of the desk.

Horace placed his hand over the sheet of paper and slid it forward. "Here. This is all I can do for you now."

Rane picked up the page and tilted it toward the light. Immediately, his gaze shot to Horace, questioning. "Is this your idea of a joke?"

Horace shook his head. "It's no joke."

"Well, then, you're mistaken," Rane said, "because you just got the last laugh." His lips compressed as he crushed the paper in his fist and let it drop to the floor. Despite her father's protests, he walked out the door and kept going.

Curiosity finally won. Angel stood and walked to the front of the desk. She picked up the wrinkled paper, straightened it, and saw that her father had signed and witnessed Horace's last will and testament.

Chapter Twenty

Warm wind buffeted Angel's face. She leaned into it and goaded her mare to a faster gait. From a distance, the Flying C looked more deserted than the Hacienda. The corrals stood empty, the gates ajar. She slowed to a walk when she reached the compound and listened. Only the chirp of crickets and the muffled plod of the mare's hoofs on the softly churned earth came back to her.

She'd expected to see some of her father's men. The gaping barn door and darkened bunkhouse told her they still hadn't returned from the creek. Perhaps her father had summoned them to the Hacienda.

Will Keegan, along with a couple more of her father's men, had arrived on the scene soon after Rane's departure. Horace had been in a bad way by that time, and getting worse. Her father had sent her from the room to spare her from witnessing the man's death. And she hadn't argued. She walked out of Horace's office and kept on going.

Now, she almost wished she'd stayed.

The sight of the big white house with all its windows darkened filled her with near despair. She had hoped to find a willing ear and solace in Carmella. The small window in the housekeeper's downstairs bedroom stared back at her, as silent and lifeless as the rest of the house. Could the woman possibly have retired without knowing the outcome on such a night? More likely, she'd been afraid to stay alone.

Angel felt her way up the back stairs and crossed the hall to her bedroom. After closing the door, she sighed and leaned into the heavily varnished wood. A long night awaited. Exhaustion pulled at her, but the thoughts churning through her mind allowed no rest.

She crossed the room and dropped her hat onto the seat of a chair. Acrid sulfur filled her nostrils when she struck a match and lit the lamp on her bedside table. Moving to the solitary, south-facing window, she pressed her forehead to a cool glass pane and sent one last yearning look into the dark distance before she drew the curtains together.

The snap of the lock startled her. She whirled, her heart stampeding.

Rane stood just inside the door, watching her.

She clapped a hand to her chest. "You scared the life out of me!"

"It seems to be a habit," he said, his expression as solemn as death.

She lowered her trembling hand, stepped away from the window and blurted the first thing that came to mind. "Did you see Carmella?"

"Yes, I saw her."

"Where is she?"

"I would imagine she's asleep in her room. Why didn't you tell me she was here?"

"I haven't seen you. Until tonight. And you're a fine one to even *try* and suggest I'm the one who's been keeping secrets."

Angel shook her head, frowning. The conversation had gotten off on the wrong track. She didn't want to argue with him. There were other issues more pressing. During the ride home, her thoughts had been consumed with all the different possibilities opened up by Horace's revelation. If only Rane had stayed. After he'd bolted from Horace's office, she'd been wretched with thoughts of him out there somewhere in the night, alone and hurting.

"Why didn't you tell me?" she asked.

"How could I tell you? Besides...would you have believed it?"

At a loss, unable to answer, she turned from him and stood before the dresser.

After a moment, she lifted her eyes and found his reflection in the mirror. He pushed away from the door and moved in close behind her.

"Would you have believed me?" he asked softly.

Her gaze met his in the silvered glass. "You never gave me the chance."

She saw his arm move and felt the brush of his

fingertips against her hair. She closed her eyes as the ticklish sensation wound through her. He moved closer. A touch of warm breath replaced his fingers. He leaned in and pressed a lingering kiss to the nape of her neck.

"I need you tonight, *mi ángela.* Please don't turn away from me."

The rich, dark seduction of his voice, so full of need, stroked more deeply than his hands or his lips ever could.

She turned.

Gently, he cupped her face, his shadowed eyes searching hers, as if he tried to see into her very soul.

"I shouldn't be here," he said. "It's risky."

"I don't want you to go."

She lifted on tiptoe and pressed her mouth to his. For several seconds his lips remained firm, then he softened, and she opened to him, like a budding rose beneath the sun, and offered all she had to give.

The smell of burnt gunpowder clung to his clothing. But the taste of him, the wildly intoxicating essence of him was pure Rane. His tongue glided between her lips to join with hers as he applied gentle suction. A low moan that sounded part pleasure, part protest rumbled in his throat.

She sensed him pulling back from her, even before he ended the kiss. Too quickly, he released her and stepped away, out of reach, putting distance between them once more.

Bewildered, she watched him pace to the far side of the room. He reached up, as though agitated and jabbed his fingers through his hair, already in wind-blown disarray. Then he shuddered. She couldn't even begin to guess at the agonizing memories trapped inside his head. He'd been only fourteen when he watched his mother die and buried her with his own hands. Tonight, he had relived it. Emotions too long held at bay seemed to be clawing to the surface.

"Maybe you shouldn't have left the Hacienda like that."

"You think I should have stayed." The way he said it, flat, emotionless, his voice held neither question nor statement, but both seemed implied.

"He was dying, Rane."

"What did you expect me to do, wait around for it to happen? Why? I was never anything more than dirt beneath his feet."

For a moment, his dark gaze bored into her. He looked away, but not before she saw the telltale tightening of his lips.

"So, tell me. After I left, did he suddenly have a change of heart?"

While he kept his voice emotionless, there was an underlying edge to his words and she knew, although he would never let on, he was hanging on her answer. She fervently wished she could summon the courage to lie.

His heavy-lidded gaze flicked in her direction once more. For an instant, a phantom of his old smile touched his lips. It did nothing to dispel the cold darkness in his eyes. "I didn't think so."

He switched his attention to the carpet and shook his head. An empty chuckle slipped from his lips. "I never truly believed he would admit it. Not even to me. All these years, I've waited. Now that it's done, it's time to move on."

Move on. Panic seized Angel. He was there to say goodbye. Her mind reeled at the prospect.

"But what about the Hacienda?" she clamored, grasping at straws, any reason that might hold him.

"What about it?"

"You're his son, Rane. His only heir." She reached into the pocket of her riding skirt and held up the sheet of paper she'd rescued from the floor of Horace's office. "Look. He put it in writing. He's leaving the Hacienda to you!"

"¡Sangre de Cristo!" He crossed the room with quick strides and snatched the document from her hand. "Don't you understand? This is his idea of a joke. His *own* retribution. He's left me nothing except his debts. Well, no, thank you!" He tossed the will onto the dresser.

"You were born there," she persisted. "It's where you spent your childhood."

"Yes," he agreed, "as an outsider."

Before he could move away again, she reached up and slid her hands inside his collar. Against her fingertips, his skin sizzled, his pulse throbbed wildly at the side of his throat. Somehow, she had to comfort him, alleviate his pain. She wanted to hold him there. With her. Forever.

"What about me?" she demanded, though she feared his answer.

He grew so still, she thought he had stopped breathing.

"Are you just going to ride away from me, too?"

His chest quickly rose and fell. "Aren't you forgetting? You asked for no promises, and I made none."

"To hell with all the things we didn't say! I love you, Rane! Don't you know that by now?"

She could have sworn she saw white-hot flames leap in the depths of his eyes. Just as quickly, they died. Suddenly he reached out, startling her, and clasped her face between his hands. "Don't say it. Don't even think it."

Angel's confession of love sent wild, desperate hope flaring in Rane's heart. Vain longings. Dreams of things that could never be. He dashed them all with vicious, cold reality. She had her world, and he didn't belong there. Gun for hire. Drifter. Even to the mixed blood flowing through his veins, he was all the things her father and his kind despised. His own father had scorned him. Eventually, she would reject him as well. She was meant for better things.

But her eyes, as they looked at that moment, would always haunt him. Blue as sapphires, she watched him through a sheen of tears that swelled and broke, streaking down her cheeks, wetting his thumbs. Heartbreak. His restraint, already tenuous, snapped and he roughly pulled her to him.

She clung, her strength bordering desperation. He brushed her hair with his lips, breathing in her scent. Subtle flowers. Warm female. Her taste, her smell, the feel of her body, all so familiar now. *"Lo siento, mi querida."*

He could have spared them both and headed straight for the border. Impossible. He couldn't go. Not without seeing her one more time.

Tender whispered words of comfort slipped easily from his tongue. He didn't know when their desperate embrace changed, only that it did. With parted lips, he dragged over her skin, igniting heat that dried her tears and had her cleaving to him in a different way. He trailed from her cheek to her ear and felt her shiver.

"Just for tonight, Angel. I don't want to spend this night alone."

She captured his face between her hands and aligned her eyes with his. "Oh, Rane. For tonight, or a million nights, you never have to be alone."

But he would be, his soul cried. After tonight.

He devoured the sweetness she offered with a hunger that only intensified each time they came together. Hands splayed against her back and rounded bottom, he pressed her closer. She shoved her hand between them and found his arousal. He sucked in a breath when she palmed his swollen head and squeezed. Raw pleasure leaped along his nerve endings, and he ached for more.

He melded the lower half of his body to hers and backed her against the dresser. A moan welled in her throat. He covered her mouth with his and smothered the sound, absorbed it with a deep thrust.

While she worked the buttons on his trousers, he opened her blouse, tugged loose the satin ribbons closing her camisole and released her breasts. He stepped back long enough to allow her to drop her split riding skirt to the floor, until she stood before him in only her gaping shirt and undergarments.

He lingered on her heavy breasts, then moved to her face. He wanted to absorb the sight of her. To remember.

The intensity behind Rane's veiled gaze touched Angel's soul with a longing sorrow that went beyond the physical. She swallowed against the teary, burning ache in her throat and reached up, threading her fingers into the silken ebony tangle of his hair. Urging him forward, she pressed a kiss to each side of his sensuous curving mouth.

His kiss scorched her, left her breathless. And then he lowered his head, and his heat seared her as he closed over the peak of one aching breast. He drew her pliant flesh deep inside his mouth. The tugging sensation of his suckling struck a sympathetic throb between her thighs.

He fumbled with the slit in her lace-trimmed drawers until he found what he sought. He sucked in a breath and cupped her, gently kneading. He moved upward and glided back down, parting her moist petals with two fingers. The heel of his hand dragged over her swollen bud with just enough pressure to send her straining against him.

Needing to touch him, to feel his feverish skin beneath her hands, she unbuttoned his shirt and stroked across his rigid muscles. A faint quiver ran through him. She knew he fought for restraint. But just then, she needed him to lose himself. She wanted to possess him. Needed him to take her. Only when he joined his body with hers did they form an unbreakable, perfect bond that made him truly hers.

"Love me, Rane," she urged in a breathless groan. "Now."

"Hold onto me," he said, just as breathless.

Bracing her against the dresser, he lifted her leg and curved it behind his waist, leaving her open and positioned for him. His fiery heat, the hard thickness of him nudged through the opening in her drawers. She swallowed in anticipation and clung harder around his waist.

He filled her, slow and deep. And then deeper still, until his engorged sex nudged her womb and touched off waves of mind-numbing pleasure.

She nearly wept when he started to withdraw, until he surged upward again and set a torturous rhythm meant to drive her mad. As he moved inside her, she knew she would remember the elation, the ecstasy of this moment for the rest of her life. Moisture seeped from her eyes. Only now, her tears were shed in joy.

Her muscles tensed, wound tighter still when he moved harder within her. Faster. She met his thrusts, sending the lotion pots and perfume bottles standing atop the dresser into a jiggly dance.

His breath grated to a ragged pant, his motions grew jerky, out of control, telling her he was almost there. She hovered at the edge of bliss, needing only his hot, rushing release to send her free-falling through the white, blinding heights where he had lifted her.

****

Rane lay flat on his back with Angel draped halfway

across his body and watched the circle of yellow and white lampglow fluctuate on the ceiling. The wavering light played hell with his eyes. Not to mention, he still felt half blinded in the aftermath of his and Angel's last bout of lovemaking.

The first time they'd climaxed together with such intensity it nearly dropped them both to the floor. It wasn't until after when he realized he'd taken her while still wearing his gun and holster.

The second time, they'd moved to her bed. Which proved to be no less strenuous. Or shattering. Now, he felt drained.

He was lost. Doomed by the love of a woman. This woman. Somewhere, somehow, she had breathed life into the cold emptiness of his heart, and he had given it to her.

But how easy it had been to convince himself the attraction went no deeper than physical lust. Angel's fiery nature seemed to thrive on danger, which he amply supplied. Her forbidden beauty had lured him from the very first time he saw her. But it was her rare and caring spirit that finally captured him.

If he left—when he left—his heart would remain here, in Angel's keeping. It was a sacrifice he was willing to make. He had no choice, because he lacked the willpower to stay away from her. With each tryst, they risked discovery, which would surely be her ruin. He'd harmed her too much already.

How much time had passed? He lifted his head. No clock sat on the dresser or anyplace else that he could see. He knew it had to be sometime after midnight. Each moment he lingered now, put them both at risk.

He dropped his head back on the pillow. "I need to go."

She stirred. Her deeply drawn breath molded a bare breast more firmly against his ribs. She lifted her knee beneath the tangled sheet and raked her foot down his shin, turning the movement into a caress. "I don't want you to go."

"What would you do?" he asked. "Hide me here in your bedroom the rest of my life?"

A movement against his chest told him she was smiling. "Mmm. Now there's an idea."

"Seriously. I need to go. Before it's too late."

The sheet rustled, slithered up his legs and carried the earthy scent of their lovemaking to his nostrils. Angel slid to her side next to him, propped her head on her hand, and lay there looking down at him. "Rane, I—"

He pressed a fingertip to her lips. "Don't say it, Angel."

Sorrow smudged her eyes. She reached up and pulled away his hand. "Take me with you."

The impulsive plea stopped him for a moment. "As much as the idea appeals to me, you know it's not possible. Your father would come after us."

"I don't care."

"Yes, you do. You know what it's like to be on the run. It's no kind of life."

"What kind of life do you think I'll have if you leave me?"

"Better than what I could give you."

She shook her head. "No. You're wrong."

The argument would do neither of them any good. "You don't know what you're talking about," he said with finality. He sat up and swung his legs over the side of the bed.

The bed springs creaked. "Fine, then. Just go!"

He stood and dressed, aware of her behind him, watching, and the muffled sounds of her sobs. He dared not look back. He was already dangerously close to doing something even more stupid than sneaking into her room tonight.

When he strapped on his gun, she scrambled up, taking the sheet with her, and came around the bed. Though her lips trembled, she didn't speak. He reached out and caught a tear as it rolled down her cheek. Leaning in, he whispered, "*Está bien, mi querida. Siempre,*" and then placed one last kiss on her tremulous lips.

Though his heart pounded like a war drum in his chest, he walked out of the room without once looking back. It wasn't until he'd gotten clear of the house that he realized there was some kind of extra bulk in his shirt pocket. He reached in and fished out the folded piece of paper he'd tossed onto Angel's dresser. That's where he'd last seen it, and where it should have stayed, but she'd somehow managed to slip Horace's tainted legacy into his pocket when he wasn't looking.

Chapter Twenty-one

Angel could count on one hand the number of times she'd been sick in her life. Once, she'd had a cold that left her with an annoying cough that hung on for more than a month. On her tenth birthday, she'd consumed too much cake and lemonade and suffered a tummy ache that kept her awake an entire night.

Just minor ailments, but this seemed different.

Bent nearly double, she sat on the side of the bed, and clutched her arms tighter around her waist. The few sips of honey-laced tea she'd swallowed threatened to come back up. She sucked in slow, careful breaths, but her nausea persisted.

Thank God for Carmella. For the past thirty minutes, the woman had tended her with all the care and diligence of a concerned mother. Just the thought of trying to drag herself downstairs and rustle up breakfast for her father sent Angel's stomach into another violent heave.

Carmella steadied the bucket, gathered her hair back from her face and held it while she vomited. When it was over, even her ribs felt sore. She sat back and gratefully lifted the cloth Carmella placed in her trembling hands. "I don't know what's wrong with me."

"Maybe something you eat," Carmella suggested.

"No, I don't think so. I ate the same things as you and Pa at supper last night."

Carmella took the cloth from her hands and rinsed it in the basin on the bedside table. After wringing the excess water, she handed it to her again.

Angel applied the cool cloth a second time. She felt better, steadier. She reached for the cup of tea and dared another sip to wash the sour taste from her mouth.

"This is the second time within a week this has happened." And that's what worried her.

The housekeeper stared at her a long moment with

concern etched on her face. “You did not tell me. When was this?”

“The morning of Horace’s funeral. But it wasn’t nearly this bad.” She shrugged. “I figured it was just nerves.”

Yes, nerves. Horace’s burial had turned out to be more of an emotional ordeal than she anticipated. Throughout the small service, she’d held out the hope, had prayed, that Rane would suddenly appear and stand in his rightful place as Horace’s son and heir. When he didn’t, her broken heart had finally splintered into fragments. Everyone assumed she shed tears of grief for their dead neighbor. They had no way of knowing she mourned her own loss. Hope. Love. Rane had taken both the night he walked out of her bedroom.

Carmella carefully took a seat next to her on the side of the bed and slipped a comforting arm across her back.

Despite a few initial misgivings about taking in a woman who was fleeing her marriage, Carmella had proven to be a godsend. During the two short weeks she’d been in the house, a deeper friendship had developed. For the first time in her life, Angel felt a connection with another woman. The close proximity forged mutual confidence, and why not? They knew each other’s secrets.

After a moment of companionable silence, Carmella cleared her throat. “Have you noticed any other...uh...signs lately?”

Angel stopped the rag in mid-swipe and stared at her, puzzled by her obvious reluctance. “Signs? What kind of signs?”

“Swelling. Soreness.”

She started to ask where, specifically, she might have suffered these symptoms when she noticed Carmella looking, and yet trying not to stare, at her chest. She glanced down at the thin lawn nightgown that covered her from neck to toe and saw how it clung to her clammy skin. She’d put on weight. Just a couple of pounds perhaps, but she could definitely see a difference in her bustline when she laced her corset. She lifted a hand and cupped her breast. The feeling of fullness, of deep aching tenderness didn’t surprise her. After several weeks, she’d grown used to the discomfort. Self-consciously, she dropped her hand to her lap.

A faint thrum of warning began at Angel's temples. She pulled in a fortifying breath. "Tell me what you're thinking, Carmella."

Carmella tried to force a smile, but couldn't banish the worry from her eyes. She reached for Angel's hand and clasped it firmly. "I think, perhaps, you may be *encinta*."

Angel frowned. *Encinta*?

Carmella's dark, arching brows eased up her forehead. "You know," she prompted. "A baby?"

Pregnant.

Angel jerked her hand from the woman's grasp and surged to her feet. *Pregnant*. Suddenly, the room felt too close, the air too muggy and suffocating. She rushed to the window and shoved back the curtain. Morning sunlight shot painful needles into her wide, frightened eyes. Just as quickly, she wheeled from the harsh light and pressed her back against the wall to face Carmella once more.

"How can I know for sure?"

Carmella stood. "Think. When was the last time you had your monthly curse?"

Angel's mind flew back over the preceding weeks as she tried to recall, but coherent thought was nearly impossible with panic beating at her temples. Then she remembered because it had occurred at the worst possible time, during the train ride from New York. So long ago. *How could she have been so stupid?*

Misery swamped her, so overpowering she hadn't the strength to stand any longer. Wrapping her arms tightly around her stomach, she sank down the wall to the floor. Dear God, was it possible? Could she really have conceived a baby? *Rane's baby*. She knew the answer was an undeniable *yes*.

****

Angel stepped from the doctor's office and paused on the walk to pull on a pair of black lace gloves. At high noon the streets of El Paso baked under a haze of heat and dust. Underneath her corset, layers of petticoats, and sateen day dress, she was sweating like a pig on a spit. Still, despite her discomfort, she stiffened her spine and held her head high as she angled her steps toward the hotel on the upper end of town.

The brisk walk soon had sweat seeping from her hairline. The oversized hat on her head mostly hid her blond hair, but also held in the withering heat like an oven. In a town mostly populated by dark-skinned, dark-haired Mexicans she stood out like a beacon. And the last thing she wanted was to draw attention to herself after she'd slipped out of her hotel room and ventured across town alone. Her father would have a fit, if he found out.

When Roy had suggested a trip, a much-needed change of scenery for them all, she'd seized the opportunity. It wasn't until later that she learned "them all" included Will Keegan.

She should have known. Her father hadn't given up on the idea of getting her "hitched" to his fair-haired boy. Since their arrival four days ago, she'd been subjected to no less than three candlelit dinners meant to encourage some romance between them. Three nights of imitating civil conversation with Will while trying to force down food had strained her patience to the limits.

If Roy only knew how things really stood between her and his right-hand man. But he hadn't a clue, and she wasn't about to tell him. Not yet, anyway.

Right now, fending off her father's matchmaking attempts and dealing with Will were the least of her worries. The doctor had confirmed her suspicion. She was going to have a baby.

Since the morning Carmella learned of her morning sickness, little else had consumed her thoughts. At times, the idea of having Rane's baby filled her with giddy happiness. The child would be a part of him. She tried to imagine how it might look. Would it have his dark hair and disturbing eyes to constantly remind her of him?

At other times, like now, the reality of what she had done terrified her. All too soon, her condition would become evident. Before that happened, she would have to face her father and tell him the truth. The very prospect was mind-numbing.

Angel reached the hotel not a moment too soon. She was sweating profusely and trembling so, she didn't think she would be able to stand for much longer. She closed the door to her room and leaned against it for support. Fighting tears, she yanked at the smothery hat until the pins pulled free, then flung it onto the bed.

A knock at the door jolted her. She drew herself up, fighting for composure. After smoothing back the wild strands of hair left flying by ripped out pins, she turned and opened the door a crack.

She expected to see a maid in the hallway with an armful of linens. Instead, Will stood with one hand propped against the doorframe. Unsmiling, his pale eyes narrowed on her and traveled downward. She knew he saw the dust coating the hem of her dress, the telltale wetness glistening on her exposed skin.

"What is it?" she asked. She didn't have to force a note of impatience into her voice, it just naturally came out.

A slight shove of his hand away from the doorframe returned him to his full, imposing height. "We need to talk."

She rolled her eyes. "Not now. I'm tired."

"You'll want to hear what I've got to say."

"What's so important it can't wait until later?"

"Your trip to the doctor."

Panic pressed a hard, brawny fist into her stomach. Her heart beat unmercifully against the rigid stays of her corset. *Don't react.* Though her breath heaved past her parted lips in quick gusts, she willed her expression into calm lines. "What were you doing, following me?"

"I saw you leave your room. I thought I'd better track along and make sure you didn't get into any trouble. We're sittin' right on the border, you know, and a lotta things can happen to a woman wanderin' around by herself."

"Why don't you just admit you were spying on me?"

He shrugged. "Does it matter?"

At this point, nothing he did surprised her.

"So, why did you go see the doctor?"

No longer able to withstand his probing gaze, she turned and walked to the dressing table. She knew she'd made another mistake when he stepped into the room and closed the door behind him.

"You shouldn't be in here. It's indecent."

"I think we've gone way past parlor manners," he said.

She knew no protest would dislodge him. Evidently, he had something on his mind. She turned to the mirror.

"So, what did the doctor say?" he persisted.

She forced a chuckle. "Really, Will. There are some things a girl doesn't discuss with a man." If she alluded to some mysterious female malady, she hoped he would behave like a gentleman for once and drop the subject.

Plucking at the fingers of the tight fitting gloves, she pulled them off and tossed them onto the dresser. Leaning in to the mirror, she made a pretense of fussing with her disheveled hair. *Damn it.* She was shaking like a leaf in a high wind. The multiple layers of heavy clothing had grown beyond stifling. If she didn't get some air soon, she feared she would faint.

She gripped the edge of the polished wood with both hands. "Would you, *please*, just go ahead and say whatever it is you came here to say and then leave."

"I know why you went to the doctor." The words resonated anger and disgust.

Angel's breath snagged in her throat.

"You're pregnant."

Her knees threatened to buckle. Still clutching at the dresser for support, she turned. "That's absurd! How dare you!"

"How dare you lie through your teeth!" he countered. "I stopped in and had a little talk with the doctor after you left. He said you and the baby are fine. You and the *baby*, Angel!"

Her mouth fell open on a gasp. She shook her head, disbelieving. "He just came out and told you that?"

"He thought I was your brother. Your very *concerned* brother."

Betrayed. All the grief and pain and terrible fear she'd been holding inside for so long boiled to the surface at once. Scalding tears welled and spilled down her cheeks. She buried her face in her hands.

She reeled on her feet, perilously close to falling, and no longer cared. Until Will's callused fingers closed around her upper arm to steady her. She hadn't the strength or the willpower to pull away from him.

"There's still a way out of this," he said.

What way, her mind clamored. If he thought she would agree to getting rid of her child...the very idea horrified her.

She lifted her head and looked at him. "What do you mean? What way?"

A muscle in his rigid jaw ticked beneath the skin. "I'll say the baby's mine. We'll get married and no one need ever be the wiser."

She stared at him, appalled. "You're insane," she blurted softly. Fury poured much needed strength through her limbs. She wrenched her arm from his grasp and stepped back, out of his reach.

"You would do anything, wouldn't you? *Anything* to get your hands on the Flying C."

Will glared at her. "Yeah, I want the ranch. The way I see it, you're in desperate need of a husband. Pronto. So the answer is staring us right in the face. We get married, just like the old man wants. I get what I want. You get what you need. It's that simple."

"Simple!" she snapped. "You *are* insane!"

"Look," he grated. "I'm willin' to help you clean up your mess."

His blistering gaze narrowed and dropped to her waist. She fought the urge to place a protective hand over her stomach.

"I know there's a chance your baby will look like a Mex," he continued. "But maybe it won't. Hell, you're as blond as a Swede. That might count for somethin'."

Evidently, he'd done some quick thinking during his mad dash back to the hotel.

"Get out of here," she said with steely calm.

"No. There's too much at stake."

She couldn't look at him anymore, couldn't face the damnation in his eyes. She walked to the window and pressed her palms hard against the sill. Beyond the glass, nothing but blurred color swam before her eyes. God help her. She'd made such a mess of her life. What was she going to do?

"Mantorres ain't comin' back, Angel," Will continued behind her. "Even if he did, it wouldn't change things. If you had some idea about it makin' a difference because he's Lundy's son, you can just get that notion right out of your head. Even if his pa was the King of England, he'd still be a stinkin' greaser. Don't be surprised if you hear he's been gunned down in some hole-in-the-wall."

Angel's face convulsed against the glass pane.

"Come to your senses, woman!"

"Just go away, Will," she begged, beyond wretched. "Leave me alone."

For a long moment, she heard nothing but the sound of her own heartbeat slogging through her ears. Then, Will's heavy footsteps crossed the room, retreating. The door opened, and he huffed a weary sounding breath. "I'll be in my room. When you change your mind," he said, his voice a flat rumble.

The door clicked when he shut it. Angel closed her eyes against the streaming sunlight of El Paso at midday and pulled in a long breath. For the moment, she only wanted to be left alone with her misery.

****

Deep detonations of thunder rolled across the land. Behind him, the windowpanes rattled in their frames. The sound roused Rane from the state of oblivion he had worked so hard to achieve. With a muttered curse, he coiled his hand loosely around the neck of the whiskey bottle he'd been nursing and then stood. Weaving an unsteady path to the window, he shoved aside the heavy drape.

Lightning slashed through the night's velvet blackness. He squinted against the sudden brilliance. A heller of a storm was lashing the border country and he'd been oblivious to it.

He let the curtain fall into place and staggered back. The closed-in room felt stuffy, suffocating. On the unmade bed, rumpled linens bore evidence of spilled food and drink. *¡Mierda!* How long had he been holed up here?

The stagnant air threatened to choke him. He felt for the top button on his skirt and yanked, sending it flying, and then the next one. It wasn't enough. Still keeping his hold on the neck of the whiskey bottle, he crossed to the door, wrenched at the handle and lurched through the opening.

Outside, cool dampness washed over his fevered

flesh. Runnels of rainwater poured from the tiles overhanging the edge of the roof. Beyond, rain slanted down at a hard angle and danced against the onslaught of a fretful wind. Rane braced against the rough adobe wall and leaned out. The deluge streamed over his uplifted face, drenching him down to his trousers in a matter of seconds.

Nature's cold dash was a shock, but at least he felt it. He'd lost count of the number of days and nights he'd numbed himself with whiskey and felt nothing at all. Now, the violence of the storm awakened him from his prolonged apathy, stirred to life the dormant wildness in his soul. Like a drunken demon, he threw back his head and laughed, taunting nature's fury.

A spectacular series of forked lightning licked through the blackness, throwing his surroundings into vivid relief. His rented room opened onto the plaza of the tiny border town, the name of which he'd forgotten. Before him yawned the emptiness of a deserted circular road. At its center stood a fountain, a shallow aboveground pool made of mortar and stone. An angel, spectral in the flickering light, her slender arms uplifted to the Heavens, stood to her ankles in the watery basin. The sight startled him.

He braced his back against the wall and waited. The next flash was closer and hung on with a deafening crackle as it ripped through the sky. He had eyes only for the angel. She seemed to mock him with her cold, marble stare. The angel of mercy, her delicate wings glistened with a sheeting cascade of wetness...an angel in the rain.

Rane clutched at the rough wall behind him, feeling the bite of the grainy clay beneath his nails, and surrendered to memory. The winged angel dimmed before his bleary eyes as he envisioned another. His Angel, standing in the pouring rain. His nostrils flared as he again smelled the fire and brimstone of that long ago stormy night. Like a dim echo, he heard her calling his name. An ephemeral sense of her arms around him, the taste of her rain-washed skin, sweeter than creation's finest nectar... he remembered.

God help him, would he never forget!

A strangled sound of raw torment slipped from his

throat. The lightning flashed again with a stuttered cracking that might have been the sound of his own heart ripping from his chest. The angel, remote, unmoving, stared with her indifferent eyes.

Rane shoved away from the wall and staggered into the downpour. *"¡Vaya infierno!"* he shouted at the lifeless statue. He drew back his arm and flung the bottle in his hand with strength bordering on madness. The vessel sailed into darkness and shattered explosively when it struck stone.

He waited, half expecting the wrath of God to strike him down in the mud and streaming water. But there was nothing, only the soft rushing sound of the rain falling around him.

"Why don't you stop feeling sorry for yourself and do something about it."

Slowly, he turned toward the voice. Benito stood in an open doorway, a dark figure silhouetted by wavering lamplight. Rane dashed the water from his eyes and shook his head at the irony of having his own words thrown back at him.

"I can't," he said.

"So, what will you do if you do not try?" Benito asked. He lifted his hand. "It's cold. It's raining. And you are a sorry sight, *amigo*."

When Benito faded back inside his room and closed the door, Rane hung his head. Battering rain pounded the back of his skull and streamed from his face. If only it could run through his burning heart and cleanse his soul with such ease.

He turned and lifted his eyes to the angel once more. *Mercy*, he silently cried. But the lifeless seraph would not be moved to grant him any boons. There was only one living, breathing angel who could help him now. She was far away and tonight he was more undeserving of her than ever.

Being acknowledged by his father hadn't given him the satisfaction he'd thought it would. Instead, it had made him aware that there was something even more vital missing from his life. His own feelings of self-worth, perhaps. He'd wasted so much time chasing after vengeance, he'd lost sight of many other paths where he might have found happiness, or contentment, or at least some sense of peace. Now, he'd strayed so far, he didn't know if he could ever claw his way back again.

What will you do if you do not try?

Too late, he realized he'd turned his back on the one thing that had given his life meaning—Angel's love.

Chapter Twenty-two

The land was ripe and heavy with summer. Tall, slender stalks of yucca stood top-heavy with bushel-sized clusters of opulent white blooms. Vivid splashes of yellow and scarlet dotted scattered clumps of mustard and paintbrush. Strung out over the open range, cattle grazed on tall, waving grass the color of golden ochre beneath a sky so blue and flawless it brought a sweet ache to Angel's heart.

The skies over New York had never been this crisp. The air never so clear and clean. Thoughts of returning to the city, of turning to her Aunt Nelda for help made every moment in this place she loved seem even more precious.

Would she be forced to leave it?

She glanced at her father, relaxed against the worn leather of the carriage seat opposite her. Only his gray gaze moved with a restless sweep as he scanned the lay of the land. Pride softened his weathered face. They were on Flying C range, his domain. She knew he viewed everything around him through the eyes of a cattleman. Grass conditions, soil erosion, even to the number of strays grazing his land. If only he could see her with the same clear vision.

The carriage veered into the lane, tossing up the earthy smell of sun-baked sand from the barren track. In the distance, the two-story white house and its supporting structures stood as a man-made oasis in the midst of some of nature's most unforgiving landscape. Angel sat up straighter. Home at last.

When they neared the house, a woman moved beneath the shadows of the porch roof and stood at the top of the front steps, waiting. Time apart allowed Angel to see the changes that had taken place in Carmella since her arrival at the Flying C. She now wore her thick, lively hair in a coronet at the crown of her head. Her provocative peasant garments had been replaced by a concealing dress of plain calico. She looked every inch the proper matron.

When the carriage rolled to a stop, Carmella hurried down the steps to meet them. A beaming smile wreathed her face.

"Looks like somebody's glad to see us," Roy said as he climbed from the carriage.

"Welcome home, *Patron*," Carmella called.

Roy grinned. "Did you miss us?"

"Very much," Carmella replied. "It is good you are back."

"We had a hell of a trip," Roy told her.

Angel tapped her father on the shoulder, and he turned to hand her down the step. She stood a moment and reacquainted herself with solid ground.

Will descended from the driver's seat and skirted to the rear of the rig. He lifted the cover on the boot, exposing their baggage. Roy walked back to help him.

Still wearing an almost giddy smile on her face, Carmella linked her arm with Angel's and urged her toward the house. "I have much to tell you," she said.

"I have a few things to tell you, too," Angel replied.

On the steps, Carmella looked back at Roy and Will and called out, "I made a cake!"

Upstairs, Angel bustled Carmella into her bedroom, then closed and locked the door.

"What did the doctor say?" the housekeeper asked without preamble.

Angel sighed, relieved to be reunited with her friend and confidante. "He confirmed it. I'm going to have a baby."

"When?"

"Barely more than six months from now."

"And you are feeling all right?"

"Yes, I'm fine." Angel methodically pulled the pins from her hat and tossed them onto the dresser. "He told me to keep soda crackers by my bed for the morning sickness." She removed her hat and laid it atop the pins. Restless, she crossed to the window and looked out. Below, her father and Will still struggled with the baggage. She turned to look at Carmella and crossed her arms beneath her breasts. "But that's not all. Will knows."

Carmella gasped. "How?"

"He followed me and spoke to the doctor. The wretched little man told him everything."

Apprehension clouded Carmella's eyes. She shook her head. "This is very bad."

"Worse than bad," Angel amended. "It's that much more ammunition for his blackmail scheme."

"What do you mean?"

"He still wants me to marry him. He wants to claim the baby as his."

Carmella's eyes widened. "Señor Keegan *es muy loco.*"

"Evidently," Angel agreed.

"What will you do?"

She shrugged and plopped down on the bed. "I wish I knew."

"Someone needs to teach that *hombre* a lesson," Carmella murmured.

"Well, it won't be my father, or any of the men on the Flying C." She knew only one man capable of standing toe to toe with Will Keegan, and he had deserted her.

Carmella took a seat on the bed next to her and captured her hand in a reassuring grip. "Do not give up. There may still be hope." Mischief danced in the woman's dark eyes.

Angel eyed her with suspicion. "Why do I have a feeling there's something you're not telling me?"

Carmella nodded enthusiastically. "*Sí.* I have much to tell you." She sidled closer and lowered her voice to a confidential whisper. "Señor Rane is at the Hacienda. He came back!"

Angel's heart quickened a telling beat.

"I am told Benito is there, too. But why, I do not know, since he is such a worthless *perro.* I figured Señor Rane would kill him, but no, he takes him in and treats him with respect. If he thinks he will help him work, he should know by now—"

"Carmella, please!"

The woman must have realized she was rambling because she instantly ceased. She even managed to look contrite, which gave Angel an awkward moment of guilt for speaking so sharply.

She drew in a deep breath and expelled it slowly. "Now. Tell me exactly what you've heard."

Calmer, Carmella continued. "All I know is, Señor Rane is staying at the Hacienda, and Benito is there, too." Again, she latched onto Angel's hand. "You must tell him about the baby, Señorita. He is strong. He will know what to do."

Angel's jaw clenched. "I'm afraid even Rane doesn't have all the answers. Not this time, anyway. He left me. If he's come back, his return has nothing to do with me."

"You must tell him," Carmella insisted.

Angel shook her head. "No. I won't spring a trap on him when he doesn't wish to be caught."

****

Angel stood on the doorstep of the Hacienda, fighting the anxiety that honed her nerves to a brittle edge. A low rumble of thunder echoed in the distance and the sky threatened rain. The house looked deserted, shrouded in gloom, as if the stone itself had faded to gray the night Horace died.

She shouldn't have come. And she knew no wild impulse was to blame. Since the day she returned from El Paso more than a week ago and learned Rane had returned, she'd been as restless as a doomed prisoner on the eve of execution.

At her touch, the massive door swung inward with a high-pitched whine. She jerked her hand back from the brass handle. After another moment of hesitant uncertainty, she opened the door wider and ventured through.

Her footsteps echoed in the cavernous foyer. She stopped and listened. Unearthly silence sent shivers chasing over her skin. The air felt close and oppressive. A thick film of dust coated the terra-cotta tiles. Footprints, both old and new, trailed in all directions, intersecting like bird tracks at the silty edge of a waterhole.

In the center of the courtyard, now long untended, the marble cherub still hefted its urn, but no water issued forth with a pleasant tinkle. The pool surrounding the cherub's pudgy feet had dried up. A gray mantle of bird droppings covered the statue's head, arms, and wings. Wisteria ran riot and crawled across the stone portico, reaching out from the curved arches with long, unfettered tendrils. The cloying perfume of the lavender pods hung heavy in the still air. The rapid advance of neglect filled her with sadness.

An echoed sound, as though something heavy had been dropped, shattered the stillness. Angel sucked in a sharp breath.

She turned, looking for the origin of the disturbance. The door of Horace's office, the room where he had died, stood open. With her heart beating wildly in her throat, she lifted on tiptoe to keep her heels from clicking on the tiles, and stepped quietly to the door.

Narrow, slanted shafts of weak light filtered between the heavy velvet drapes hanging at the windows. A smoke-like haze and an air of the forbidden pervaded the room. Before one of the floor to ceiling bookcases, a man sat cross-legged on the floor. Thick Turkish carpet muted the clap of the ponderous texts he stacked next to him.

Angel's breath ran shallow, with the anticipation of seeing him again—with the dread that he still didn't need her as she needed him.

"Rane?"

His hands stilled, clutching one gilt-edged volume, and she knew he'd heard her. She stared at his motionless back, at the dark sweep of hair brushing the lower edge of his collar, at broad shoulders that looked capable of bearing any burden. Except hers.

He turned his head and looked at her. She met his disturbing eyes, mesmerized as always by the intensity he projected with just the power of his gaze. An unexpected quiver slid down her spine.

She ventured another step inside the room. "What are you doing here?"

He surged to his feet and moved into the path of wan light coming through the window. "Rearranging the library."

Obviously. To find him sitting in the midst of a pile of books was the last thing she'd expected. And he had sidestepped her question.

Up close, he looked as dangerous and unpredictable

as a starving lobo. The way he watched her... Unease simmered just beneath his calm façade. Did having her in the same room make him uncomfortable?

"Incredible as it may seem, when I was a boy, I read many of the books on these shelves."

She threw a quick glance at the impressive collection of literary works behind him. No wonder he was so well spoken. He'd probably read everything from Chaucer and Shakespeare to "The Cottage Physician" and "DaVinci's Anatomy."

"Don't look so surprised," he said. "I've forgotten most of it."

"Who taught you to read?"

"One of Lundy's hands was an ex-schoolteacher. I guess he thought it only fitting to give the boss's little bastard an education."

She flinched at the emphasis he put on the word "bastard."

"Did Horace know?"

"No. He never would have allowed his precious books into my hands. My mother slipped them in and out of here without his knowledge."

Why was he telling her this now?

They were both behaving as though nothing at all had happened. As though she'd never sworn her love to him. As though he'd never turned his back on her and walked away.

She swallowed. "I don't know what I'm doing here."

He moved to stand behind the desk, and a shadow crossed the upper half of his face. Still, the furrow of his dark brows was evident in the dim light. "Don't you?" he asked. "I know why I came back."

He gripped the backrest of the supple leather chair tucked into the kneehole behind the desk. A memory flashed through her mind. Horace reclining in the chair with his head propped in the same spot Rane's hands now occupied. Suddenly, she knew why she was there. Despite her denial to Carmella, she wanted to tell him about the baby. That's why she had come.

"That night..." She faltered, barely able to force out the words. "You told me you wanted no part of the Hacienda."

"You think I lied."

He shoved the chair farther beneath the desk and stepped around the end of it. Toward her. "I meant what I said that night. I was here for only one reason. Justice."

"And I don't suppose revenge had anything to do with it?"

"Perhaps," he agreed.

A clench of his jaw signaled a swift change. His voice rose an emphatic notch. "Do you think justice was achieved here that night?"

"Horace confessed—"

"He had nothing left to lose. My mother is still dead and buried across the river. Not me." He flung out his hand to indicate their surroundings. "Not any of this. No power this side of Heaven can help her now."

He dropped his hand and pulled in a long breath, visibly striving for the calm that had momentarily eluded him.

"No one can change the past, Rane," she said, "but I'm sure your mother would be happy to know you're finally where you belong."

His chuckle held no warmth. "You think I belong here?"

"Yes."

"Why?"

"By right of your birth."

"Don't you mean the accident of my birth?" Bitterness edged his words.

She thought of the tiny life growing inside her womb. Like father, like son... Would her child be doomed to a life of tragedy because of the accident of its birth?

He turned from her, moved to stand before a shrouded window and raked aside the drapes. Staring out, he shoved his hands inside his trouser pockets and shifted to a hipshot stance. Outside, there was nothing but barren yard. The stone wall surrounding the compound cut off the view at all angles.

"What would you say if I tell you, I've decided to try my hand at ranching?" he asked.

Several emotions warred within her. She was glad he would finally stop roaming from place to place, and yet, she couldn't hold back an overwhelming rush of disappointment. She knew now. The ranch *was* the reason he had returned.

"You're asking my opinion?"

"Yes."

"Well, I think it's wonderful. I have no doubt you can do anything you turn your hand to."

"It won't be easy," he said. "It will take years to pay off the debt my dear old *papá* accumulated on this place."

"But, won't it be worth the effort?" she asked.

He pulled his hands from his pockets and turned to face her. "Yes, I think it will. In fact, I'm betting on it."

The longer he talked, the more cold, dead ashes formed around Angel's heart. She could almost taste them, bitter and burning in her throat. In running to him, she'd made a fool of herself. Again.

He walked closer and crossed his arms tight across his chest, as if he couldn't find anything useful to do with his hands.

"I'm hanging up my gun," he said. "You were right. I've always lived right on the edge of getting myself killed. Never had much reason to care before."

She blinked, trying to will back the prickly sensation that threatened to put tears in her eyes. "I'm glad," she said. "Glad you found a reason."

His disturbing gaze caught hers and held, probing too deep for comfort, touching her soul as only he could, as no one else ever had. Reaching out, he cupped her face between his hands with gentleness and then stepped into the space separating them. She could only stare at him, her self-possession too tenuous, his nearness too devastating.

He stared into her eyes, searching. Always searching, as though he still sought the answer to some yet unsolved puzzle, and she might have the answer locked deep within.

"My reason is you, Angel." A swallow worked his throat. "The night I left, I meant never to come back. I tried to stay away, but I couldn't. You had already become my life."

She frowned into his eyes, certain she mistook his meaning. "My God, Rane. What are you saying?"

The barest hitch of a smile tugged one side of his lips.

"I'm trying to tell you, I love you. With every breath, every waking moment. I am nothing without you."

Through a sheen of tears, she saw his head lower. He kissed her as he never had before. With gentle worship, with tenderness that robbed her of breath and will.

She sighed his name against his mouth, an amen to a prayer.

He lifted his head and pulled her against him, brushing kisses over forehead and hair.

She melted into him and wrapped her arms around his lean, solid waist, absorbing his heat, the familiar woodsy spice scent of his skin. She closed her eyes, content just to let him hold her, to rely on his strength at last. He loved her. In that moment, she forgave him. For deserting her, for breaking her heart so many times she'd begun to think it could never again be whole.

His hot breath fanned the stray hairs at her temple. "There is much to be done," he said. "It might take some time. I will get the house in order, gather a herd. But this house, the land will give me something to offer when I speak to your father."

"I would have gone with you anyway, you know. Without all this." She leaned her head back and looked into his eyes. "So, you intend to do the honorable thing and ask for my hand?"

"Of course," he said, as if it should have been obvious.

"You're much braver than I thought." She spoke the words in jest, but the reality of facing her father filled her with an all too familiar dread.

"I know it won't be easy," he continued, "but eventually even he will accept what he cannot change."

He planned for the future, but time was a luxury that was quickly slipping away from her. She had to tell him. About the baby. About Will's scheme to marry her and claim his child. A nagging doubt held her tongue.

Even if Rane laid down his gun, how long would it last? How long before some wannabe gunslinger, looking to make a fast reputation, challenged him?

She had another precious life to consider now, someone whose needs were more important than his, or her own. Was she willing to risk it, to try and raise a child with a man who might end up dead in the middle of a dusty street on any given day? She couldn't lose him. Not again. Thoughts of her mother flitted through her mind. She'd never known her. How could she wish that same legacy onto her own child, of possibly never knowing his or her father?

She pulled back and ran her fingers into the hair at the nape of his neck, holding him. "Listen to me, Rane. I love you." She pressed a brief kiss to his mouth.

His smile filled her with such warmth her heart ached for what she knew she must say to him.

"But, I'm afraid. Do you really expect to just lay down your gun and walk away? I don't want to lose you. I couldn't stand it if I lose you again."

He stroked her cheeks and pressed his forehead to hers. "You're not going to lose me, *querida*."

"You don't know that. If someone challenges you..."

"I'll be careful," he promised. "After a time, no one will remember me or my reputation."

"Then promise me," she said. "Promise you won't pick up your gun again, no matter how tempted you might be."

He drew back, a slight frown dipping his brows. "You don't trust me to keep my word?"

"Promise me," she insisted. "I have my reasons."

"All right, then. I swear it."

His pledge didn't banish all her misgivings, but she believed he would never willingly go back on his word. She gave him a tense smile and pulled away. Hugging her arms beneath her breasts, she paced to the far side of the room. She couldn't look at him and summon her courage at the same time. "There's something I have to tell you," she said, wondering how he would react to her news.

"What's the hell's goin' on in here?"

Blood roared through Angel's ears. She turned quickly. Will Keegan stood in the open doorway, and he looked furious.

Rane started around the end of the desk. "You're trespassing, Keegan."

Will threw him a withering glare. "And you'd do well to stay out of this, Mantorres. I doubt Roy Clayton will appreciate knowing his daughter's down here without a chaperone. That could get mighty ugly, if you take my meanin'."

Angel stiffened her spine and stepped forward, effectively putting herself between the two angry men. "What are you doing here, Will? Following me again?"

"The old man's lookin' for you."

"Fine. Go tell him you found me. I'll be along in a minute."

"I'm not leavin' you here."

"Still as high-handed as ever, I see," Rane injected.

Will straightened to his full, intimidating height and glared down his nose. "I'll deal with you later, Mantorres. Right now, I'm takin' her home."

Angel wasn't fooled by the smile that curved Rane's mouth. He turned and settled his backside against the desk, then crossed his arms over his chest. He looked relaxed, but fury shot from every tightly leashed muscle in his body.

He lifted his head and looked at her. "Angel?"

He was asking for her signal, how she wished him to proceed. What happened next would depend on her response.

"It's all right," she said. "I'll go."

"Do you want me to ride along and speak to your father?"

"No. Now wouldn't be the best time. We can finish our discussion later."

Trying to appear calm while her heart threatened to beat out of her chest, she started for the door, anxious to put some distance between the two men. Having Rane and Will in the same room was like tossing together fire and kerosene.

Angel stalked out of the house with Will nearly treading on her bootheels. Outside, she gave him no chance to speak. She mounted her horse and wheeled toward the gate, goading the animal into a quick run.

Beyond the wall, he caught up to her and lashed out. Catching one of her reins, he jerked her horse to a halt. The sudden stop nearly unseated her and sent her horse's hind legs dancing sideways.

She expected it, had known when she walked out with him that she would bear the brunt of his anger. At least she'd gotten him away from the house.

He crowded his horse next to hers and latched onto

her arm with a bruising grip. "What the hell did you tell him back there?" He gritted the words through his teeth, so close his angry breath blasted her in the face.

"None of your business!" One shove would send her off the horse. Even realizing her peril, she had to stand her ground with him. Now or never. "Your game's over, Will. You lose. So, go to hell!"

His fingers bit deeper into the soft flesh of her upper arm. "You stupid little bitch! You didn't tell him about the baby. If you had, he wouldn'tve let you walk out of there so easy."

She gritted her teeth against the pain he inflicted. "You willing to bet on that?"

He attempted a smile, but it twisted into something hideous. "Yeah." He nodded. "I'm betting on it. You didn't tell him because if you do, you'll have to tell the old man, too. And you don't have the guts for that, do you?"

His astute reasoning chilled her to the bone.

"So, it ain't over yet, sweetheart. But it soon will be cause that greaser's days are numbered."

Chapter Twenty-three

"I'll have these supplies delivered out to the house first thing."

Angel aimed a gracious smile at the storekeeper. "Thank you, Mr. Dowling."

"Always a pleasure, Miss," he said.

She turned from the counter and walked out of the mercantile with Will Keegan hovering so close to her backside, the hem of her split riding skirt dusted the shanks of his boots.

Four long days had passed since he'd burst in on her and Rane at the Hacienda. Four days during which he stuck to her and her father like a prickly burr. No matter how late she retired at night, he was there keeping her father occupied in the parlor or on the porch. When she came down to the kitchen each morning, he was having his coffee and breakfast at their table, compliments of Carmella.

Always, he watched her, like a snake charming its prey, poised to strike if she made a wrong move. The man had gone beyond annoying and even infuriating. She was beginning to suspect something in his mind had come unhinged.

She thought of running to Rane, but Will saw to it she had no opportunity. Even if she somehow succeeded in slipping away, he would follow. She didn't dare lead him to Rane's doorstep again. He'd already warned her that Rane's days were numbered. She believed, without a doubt, he intended to kill him. Just how and when were the questions that kept her awake at night.

Somehow, she had to warn Rane. Her heart nearly ground to a halt each time she remembered she'd made him promise to never again pick up his gun. Now, he had no idea what awaited him. Her fault. Unwittingly, she'd turned him into a sitting duck for Will's twisted vengeance.

Out on the street, the sun beat down with intense heat, pulling beads of sweat from Angel's forehead and upper lip. A haze shimmered over the dusty ground. The walkways were nearly deserted and her father was nowhere in sight.

She turned and looked at Will. Sweat rings darkened his shirt. The pale, scruffy whiskers on his face looked like they'd sprouted several days ago. His eyes were red-rimmed and bloodshot. She wondered if he'd been staying up at night, watching the house while the rest of them slept. The thought sent a shiver creeping up her spine.

"Why don't you go find Pa and tell him I'm ready to go."

His eyes narrowed. "You'd like that, wouldn't you?" A dubious sound huffed past his lips. "I got a better idea. Let's you and me both go find him."

He wasn't about to let her out of his sight for even a second. She knew she had to do something. Today. Whatever it took, she had to speak to her father. She'd tell him the truth, get it all out in the open. Once exposed for the greedy, conniving bastard he was, Will would hold no more power over her.

Not confiding in her father and laying herself on his mercy from the beginning had been a mistake. Now, she had no choice. This insanity had to stop.

****

Rane halted the stallion when he spotted the rooftops of Clayton Station in the distance. For a long moment, he sat there while he pondered the risks of riding into town unarmed. He promised Angel he wouldn't put on his gun again, which meant he'd have to lay low for a while. Only common sense, if he wanted to go on living. There were plenty of hombres haunting the border settlements who would give their eyeteeth to catch him without his gun.

He hadn't set out to go anywhere near town, but four days had gone by since Angel walked out of the Hacienda with Will Keegan. Since then, there had been no word from her or news of any kind. He couldn't shake the feeling that something had gone terribly wrong.

Had Angel changed her mind?

A visit to the Flying C two hours after sunup did

nothing to allay his suspicions. After informing him Angel and her father had gone to town, Carmella's attempt at polite chitchat had fallen flat. Her smile appeared strained, at best, and her nonstop chatter couldn't mask the anxiety he read in every gesture and facial expression. He knew her too well. She was hiding something from him.

He had to see Angel. If she'd backed out on their plans, all he needed was one look into her eyes. Then he would know.

Rane entered the south end of the settlement and slowed the stallion to a walk. A trickle of sweat escaped his hatband and slid down the side of his face. The twin rows of false-fronted buildings lining the street looked faded beneath the harsh sun.

In front of Dowling's, three horses wearing the Flying C brand stood at the hitching rail. He reined in and dismounted.

Except for the owner, who pored over a ledger behind the counter, the mercantile was deserted. Rane walked into the sunlight once more and started up the street. He made a wary sweep along the empty walks, skimming vacant doorways and windows. The town felt different today. Strange somehow. As if it had drawn in on itself. Nothing stirred, not even a breath of wind. In the utter quiet, he imagined he heard the sun's sizzle frying the moisture from everything around him. Maybe it was just him. Without a gunbelt strapped around his hips, he felt exposed. His heart felt laid open as well. He had to see Angel, if only in passing, and find out where he stood.

He stopped at the end of the walk. Too late, he felt the boards vibrate beneath his feet and heard the jingle of spurs. He started to turn when something latched onto his shirt and hauled him backward. Caught off guard, he slammed against the outside wall of Dowling's. The dizzying impact knocked the breath from his lungs.

Will Keegan, his face red and twisted with fury, crowded his vision. The big man fisted the front of his shirt and wedged it against his Adam's apple, shutting off the little air he had left.

"Got you right where I want you, you sonofabitch!"

Somewhere, a woman screamed.

Keegan smacked him, open-handed. The inside of Rane's jaw tore against his teeth. He tasted blood. If the blow was meant to provoke, it had the desired effect.

He dodged a hoof-sized fist by mere inches. Unable to check his momentum, Keegan's balled knuckles slammed Dowling's wooden wall.

Will recoiled with pain flashing across his face. The fist at Rane's throat fell lax. Seizing the advantage, he shoved with both hands, created an opening, and drove his knee into the soft portion of Will's torso.

A grunt whooped from Will's lips, and his eyes rounded like double eagles. He stumbled back a step, bent, and clutched at his gut.

Rane rammed a fist against the big man's slack mouth. His knuckles met teeth, and he had the satisfaction of seeing blood spurt from Will's split lips.

Like a charging bull, Will slung crimson spittle and lunged.

Rane knew he had to keep his head. Keegan was in a killing rage. He was bigger, had a longer reach. If he made a slip and Keegan latched onto him, the man would simply pound him into the ground and then spit into the gory hole.

He ducked, avoiding a fist, and managed to land another jab into Will's gut. Then he moved out of reach.

"Is that the best you can do, Keegan?" He knew it was stupid to goad the man, but couldn't seem to stop himself.

Will's fist dove in like the head of a striking snake. Rane ducked. Not quickly enough. Rock-hard knuckles raked his cheek and connected with the ridge of his brow. The side of his face numbed instantly. He knew the skin was broken when his vision swam with a red haze.

His sight muddied as they traded punches and Will's relentless fists continued to find a target. The soft inner side of his jaw exploded against his teeth. Again. A white flash of blinding pain flared in his temple. The man nearly knocked him off his feet.

Will charged, snagged him around the waist, and slammed him down to the wooden walk. Blinding white stars exploded before his eyes, followed by the threat of blackness. He blinked, fighting the darkness. Will stood over him, his leg lifting, his knee bent.

Rane hurled himself against the slant-heeled boot descending toward his face, wrapped an arm around Will's ankle and rolled, twisting as he went. He clamped his teeth as a spur rowel sliced into his arm.

The weathered boards splintered into kindling when Will dropped like a two hundred pound boulder.

Rane crawled clear and pushed to his feet. He stood reeling while blood dripped from his fingertips. His head buzzed and throbbed like a swarm of bees with hammers had built a nest inside his skull. He pressed a hand against the wall to steady himself.

Before him, Will Keegan—bloodied and disheveled—kicked and struggled to extricate himself from the hole in the walkway. Wedged rump first, the fancy rig of twin pistols strapped to his hips now pointed straight up at Dowling's awning roof and were the only things keeping him from falling on through to the ground. If Rane hadn't been so furious and out of breath, he might have laughed.

Time to end it.

He shoved away from the wall and swayed on his feet. With measured steps, he circled Will. The big man strained harder to free himself from his wooden trap. Rane dropped to his knees next to him.

"Get away from me! What the hell you doin'!"

Rane spat a mouthful of blood onto the walk. "You've had this coming a long time, *gringo*." He fisted his throbbing fingers and rammed a savage punch into Will's gaping jaw.

Fresh blood slashed across Rane's throat. Nearly hidden behind swollen lids, Will's eyes rolled back in his head. Rane remained as he was, watching the rise and fall of the man's chest. He still breathed, but he didn't move.

Slowly, Rane relaxed his battered fingers. He stood and swiped a torn sleeve across his eyes. A thin stream of crimson oozed from the gash in his arm. He pressed his hand across it to stanch the bleeding.

As the roar in his head subsided, another sound took its place. The sibilant hiss of hushed, whispering voices. He looked up. A crowd had gathered in the street, drawn like a swarm of hungry flies to the sight of blood and violence.

He located his missing hat lying on the walkway. A dusty boot had left a print in the middle of the smashed crown. He picked it up and slapped it against his thigh to pop it back into shape, then gently eased it onto his head.

The curious onlookers parted, stumbling back over their own heels in their haste and gave him plenty of space when he stepped into the street. Though weariness pulled at him, he straightened his shoulders and walked through the midst of them, looking neither right nor left. He knew he'd find no friendly faces.

****

Angel walked out of the hardware store and into the blinding sunlight. She reached up to adjust her hat when Will suddenly muttered a curse and lunged past her, nearly knocking her off balance.

The man hadn't allowed ten feet of distance between them all morning and now, without a word, he hurried away from her so quickly she expected him to start running at any second.

Baffled, she stepped farther onto the walk and watched him go. Too late, she noticed the black stallion standing tied at the hitching rail, next to her own little mare, in front of Dowling's. Rane's horse. Her heart nearly stopped.

Near the end of the walk, Will drew to a halt. Someone else was there. Another man, nearly hidden from view by Will's big frame. Shock leapt through her when Will reached out and grabbed a fistful of the other man's shirt and hurled him against the outside wall of the store.

Rane.

A scream tore from her throat. Reflex sent her running toward them. *Will's going to kill him!* The thought echoed with each beat of her heart. She had to stop him!

Then she remembered.

She halted, pulse pounding. A helpless sob tore from her throat as she splayed a hand over her stomach. She couldn't risk harm to her child.

Only one person could sway Will—her father. She had to find him.

She turned from the dreadful sight of Rane and Will beating each other bloody and raced in the opposite direction. Past door after door she ran, pausing in each one only long enough to ask the same frantic question, "Have you seen my father?"

Tears of frustration and wild panic streaked her face by the time she reached the horse shed at the end of the street. Around back, her father sat on a bale of hay in the shade, palavering with an old-timer who worked the stables.

He looked at her, the words he'd been speaking dying on his lips. "What the hell's the matter?"

Angel gasped for breath. "You've got to come quick, Pa. It's Will. He intends to kill Rane!"

Roy's face crimped. "What the hell?"

"I'll explain later," she said. "Just come on! Please!"

****

Rane walked slowly up the middle of the street with a nagging tingle bothering the middle of his back. Behind him, the crowd continued to talk among themselves, their voices louder now that the spectacle had ended. He flexed his right hand, stiff and achy after the punishment he'd just put it through. He'd always avoided fistfights. The sting in his raw knuckles reminded him of the reasons why.

With each step, the warning chill at the center of his spine grew stronger. He scrubbed his palm over the vacant spot against his thigh where his Colt should have rested. An instant of regret flashed through his mind, followed by acceptance. He'd made his choice.

Abruptly, the crowd fell silent. Dead silent.

Rane stopped walking and waited. Breath moved in and out of his body, slow, measured. The jangling nerves in his back had stopped completely. He knew what to expect. He'd been here before. No sudden movements. He stood as though he'd turned to stone in the middle of the street.

"Mantorres!"

The false-fronted buildings amplified Will Keegan's ragged voice and it echoed along the street like a death knell.

Rane's heart kicked up another beat, yet he felt the

tug against his fingertip as a drop of blood dripped to the street. He pulled in another shallow breath and released it with agonizing slowness.

"Turn around!"

Rane didn't move a muscle.

"I said, turn around, damn you!"

Slow and easy, Rane lifted his hands from his sides and turned. The crowd had scattered. Only Will Keegan, so bruised and bloodied he was barely recognizable, stood in the street. Sunlight skipped along the nickel-plated barrel of the pistol in his right hand. He shifted his thumb to the hammer and levered it back to full cock. From habit, Rane counted the sound of the metallic clicks.

Every nerve in his body thrummed as he looked down the barrel of the loaded gun. Hard as he tried, he couldn't distance himself. Not from the pain. Not from the emotions burning through him like a virulent fever. Most of all, not from the desire to go on living now that he had something worth living for.

Had he changed so much he'd lost his edge?

"Do you plan to shoot me in cold blood, Keegan?" He raised his hands higher. "I'm not wearing a gun."

Keegan spat a mouthful of bloody froth into the dirt. "I aim to kill you any way I can."

"No! Stop it!"

The shout jerked Rane's gaze from the gun in Keegan's hand to the woman running with awkward lunges along the walkway. Angel! She held to her father's arm, practically dragging him with her.

When they drew even with Keegan, Roy pulled her to a stop. He shook off her grasp and stepped into the street. "Put that gun away, Will!"

"No! This is between him and me. Stay out of it!"

Roy didn't budge. "Look at him, man! He ain't even armed!"

Rane dared a glance at Angel. She stood on the walk, her breast heaving, staring at him with fear running wild in her eyes.

"Cold blood, Will," Roy reasoned. "Don't do it!"

Keegan canted his head. His gaze moved restlessly behind swollen eyelids, as though assessing the onlookers crowded close against the buildings on both sides of the street. His upper lip curled back from his clamped teeth. Evidently, he didn't like the size of his audience.

"So I'll even things up," he said. Without losing his aim, dead center of Rane's chest, he palmed the pistol still resting in the holster against his left hip. After a bare second's hesitation, he slung it through the air.

The gun hit the dirt and skidded to a stop little more than two feet in front of Rane.

"There you go, greaser," Keegan yelled. "Now pick it up."

In the dead silence that followed, Rane stared at the revolver. Unconsciously, he curled the fingers of his right hand and then relaxed them again. His palm itched for the familiar feel of it. The smooth grain of the curved butt, the precise balance and weight.

He looked at Keegan, at the barrel of the gun in his hand and detected a slight dip for a fraction of an instant. The man's arm was tiring.

"Pick it up!"

Rane flicked another glance at the gun in front of him, gauging his chances of getting his hand around it, lifting it, aiming and squeezing the trigger. All before Keegan merely clenched a finger. It was suicide. And Keegan would walk away free and clear.

Choices.

In the next heartbeat, Rane made his. He turned and started walking again.

"Damn you! Don't you turn your back on me!" Keegan screamed.

From behind him, Rane heard Keegan's strangled shout of fury. His back muscles tensed.

A gunshot exploded through the hushed town, followed immediately by a howl of pain. Rane jerked to a stop as the sounds reverberated and finally faded beyond the end of the street. Slender arms clutched at him and Angel's face swam in front of his eyes. She was crying. Like a man awakening from a trance, he lifted his arms, even his bloodied one, and settled them around her.

"I thought I'd lost you," she cried.

"I thought you'd lost me, too," he confessed.

She lifted her head from his chest and looked at him, a gasp on her lips. "Your face!"

"Will heal." He tried to smile, but it hurt too much.

"You crazy old bastard! What the hell did you shoot me for!"

"Cause I wasn't about to stand by and watch you shoot an unarmed man in the back!"

"If you knew what that greaser's been doin' with your daughter, you'd let me kill him and thank me after."

Rane turned. Roy Clayton and Will Keegan stood nearly nose to nose on the street. Will cradled his right hand against his stomach and a new trail of blood soaked into the front of his shirt. His gun lay several feet away in the dirt.

Roy, his face mottled with anger, had taken charge. A telltale curl of pale blue smoke lifted from the barrel end of the gun he held on Keegan. "Get on your horse and ride out of here."

Will looked so surprised he managed to open his puffy eyes another crack. "Ride out! What the hell you mean, ride out?"

"You're finished here," Roy declared. "I don't ever want to see you around here again."

"You can't just shoot me and then run me off like I'm some—"

"Shut up!" Roy bellowed. "I said, clear out and stay out! Show your face around here again and I'll be shippin' you back to the K-Bar in a pine box."

Will stumbled back, a befuddled expression on his mauled face. "You're a foolish old bastard," he gritted out. "Now I hope it comes back and bites you right in the ass!" He turned and started for his horse, cursing a blue streak as he went.

Roy holstered his gun, then walked over and retrieved the one he'd shot out of Will's hand. Rane regretted that he hadn't witnessed that piece of work for himself. The old man straightened and suddenly he found himself pinned by a pair of shrewd gray eyes.

"I'm goin' to the house," he said, and there was a grimness about him that told Rane the worst wasn't nearly over yet. "Angel, get on your horse and go home. I expect to see you there shortly, Mantorres. The two of you got a lot of explainin' to do."

The old man turned and walked away. On the walk,

the crowd stepped aside when he neared. But it wasn't fear Rane saw on their faces. On the contrary. They all looked at Roy Clayton with respect. The kind afforded a man who'd worked a lifetime to earn it.

Chapter Twenty-four

The images hung on in Angel's mind. Her father pulling his gun. Will's pistol spinning from his hand. In that moment, her father had shed the blinders from his eyes and seen Will for the blackhearted wretch he truly was.

Even if he disowned her now, she'd always feel proud of him for his brave actions that day. She would remember the moment when he'd cast aside his old prejudices and stepped up in defense of the disreputable gunfighter who held her heart.

If you knew what that greaser's been doin' with your daughter...

What must he have thought when he heard those words, when she threw herself into Rane's arms? She'd seen the look on his face. Shock. Disbelief.

A stray tear slid down her cheek. She swiped at it absently and snuffed back the threat of more. She could no longer afford the luxury of weakness. The time for deception was past. Her father had earned the truth today, and she intended to give it to him.

Angel trotted her mare into the deserted barnyard. Over at the house, her father stood on the porch with both hands braced against the rail, watching. She slid from the saddle and hesitated. A stable hand emerged from the barn. She handed over her reins and allowed him to lead away her horse.

Still, she stood there, her back to the house. She looked down at her clothing and rubbed a fingertip over a smudge of blood on her blouse, delaying. Where was her courage when she truly needed it? She'd imagined this moment a hundred times. In each fantasy she'd been angry, had thrown the truth into her father's face like a weapon. Reality was turning out to be much harder. For two years, she'd tried to live up to the image of her dead mother, and therein lay the problem. The image she aspired to was nothing more than a flat, colorless photograph standing on the mantle. A memorial. A single, frozen second in time from the woman's life. The pattern was incomplete, and Angel had no idea how to fill in the blanks.

She couldn't try any longer. How could she walk in someone else's footsteps, especially when the trail had vanished like dust on the wind? Her own path had been chosen long ago, and she had to follow it, come what may.

Squeezing her eyes shut, she fought to gather in all the straying, ragged edges of her emotions that threatened to tear her to pieces. She had failed to become the lady her father wanted her to be. She'd disappointed him in all things, but amid the muddied chaos of her thoughts, one truth stood out with shining clarity. She liked herself just fine.

Only one question remained. Did her father love her enough to accept her for what she was?

It was time to find out.

Angel opened her eyes and pulled in a deep breath. Over in the corral, a pair of sleek horses stretched their noses through the fence and stared at her. Heat, filled with a fine dust haze hung in the torpid air. Normal, familiar things. A sense of calm filled her. She turned and started for the house.

Her father met her at the top of the steps. The furrows of time plowed deeper into his face. "Let's sit," he said.

In funereal silence, they both took a seat on opposite sides of the top step. Angel sat with her back rigid, her arms looped around her bent knees. Sunlight sliced across the lower half of her dusty riding skirt and scuffed boots, blanching them near colorless.

Her father cleared his throat, and his voice came out in a rusty rumble. "You and Mantorres. I just need you to tell me if it's true."

The air of sadness that clung to him surprised her. She'd expected anger. She dared a glance at his face and found he wasn't looking at her. He sat with his elbows laid atop his knees, his hands dangling between them. His hooded gray eyes were focused on the distant horizon.

Angel heard the sound of her own thick swallow. "I love him, Pa." Having finally spoken the words, her heart galloped, and she felt the vibration clear to her backbone.

Though Roy's head took a slight dip, he still watched the distance. His silence felt more damning than any angry words.

"I—I tried to do what you wanted, but I'm not Mama, and I never could be."

His mustache twitched. "You look like her."

"Maybe," she conceded. "But on the inside, where it really counts, I know we're two very different people." She swallowed back another lump. "Aunt Nelda always said, I might acquire all the polish in the world but underneath it all I'd still be your daughter. I'm sorry, Pa, but I'm afraid she was right."

It may have been wishful thinking, but she would have sworn his craggy old face softened.

He heaved a weighty, deflating sigh and leaned back. Half turning toward her, he tucked one leg in close and wrapped his arm around it, using the newel post as a backrest. "Your Mama wasn't suited to this place," he said. "She hated it." He huffed a humorless laugh. "She never quite cottoned to me either, if you want to know the truth. Back in those days, I was boilin' grease, and she was cool, clear water. We never could manage to mix the two. Near the end, I believe she hated me."

He'd never spoken of her mother before, except to compare their looks or tell her what a fine lady she'd been. To hear him speak of her now in any terms other than respect sent shock racing through Angel.

"Why did the two of you marry?" she blurted.

He leaned back his head and skimmed his gaze along the edge of the porch roof, pursing his lips beneath his brushy mustache, as though trying to remember.

"I was young, and she was even younger, and just so damn pretty it made my heart ache to look at her. She'd come out here from back east with one of the Lundy house parties. That's how we met. And I cut quite a dashin' figure back in them days, even if I do say so myself," he added with a nostalgic smile.

"I guess we both got caught up in the excitement of picnics and long summer evenin's filled with fireworks. It was only after we were married that we ever spent any time alone together. She got a real look at me then, outside the surroundings of Lundy's fancy dinner parties. She saw this place, and me, for what we really were. By the time it sank in on her, it was too late. She was already with child."

Angel blinked back the threat of tears. "Why did you never tell me any of this before?"

He shrugged. "I figured it would hurt you to know."

"It does hurt," she admitted. "Did she even care..." She couldn't bring herself to finish the question.

"About you?" he asked, peering into her eyes.

She nodded.

"You were the one thing she did care about," he said. "Before she died, she made me promise I'd send you back to her folks in New York. She didn't want you growin' up here. And she sure as hell didn't want me to have a hand in your raisin'."

Angel frowned. "But you didn't follow her wishes. Why not?"

"Didn't want to." A sheepish grin briefly compressed his lips. "You were my little girl, and I was proud as hell of you. You thrived here, grew strong. Hell, you could ride a horse before you learned to walk."

He fell silent and absently raked a fingernail over a callus on his thickened hand.

In that moment, he was more exposed than Angel had ever seen him. She never dreamed her heart could break all over again. For her father, no less. But it did. For the first time in her life, she ached to reach out to him.

"I don't even know where the years went," he continued. "They just flew. First thing I knew, you were turning into a woman and people were startin' to talk cause I let you run wild as a Comanche." He dropped his hand to the top of his thigh and shrugged. "I started feelin' guilty. Maybe your mama had the right idea after all. I knew I couldn't hold onto you forever, so I decided to try it her way. I couldn't send you to her folks, of course, since they'd already passed on. So I did the next best thing and sent you to her sister."

Angel sat a long moment with her brows knitted,

trying to sort out all the things he'd told her. There was a message in it somewhere, but she wasn't quite sure she grasped it.

She leaned down and peered into his face. "Let me get this straight. Are you trying to tell me you *liked* me the way I was before?"

He bridled and stared at her as if she'd said something ridiculous. "Course I liked you. Why wouldn't I? While you were gone, I missed the hell out of you. I wanted you home."

"So you sent for me."

"Yeah. And then when I saw you again, it scared the hell out of me."

She shook her head. "That makes no sense."

"You'd changed," he explained. "You looked just like her."

She recalled the first evening she'd dressed in one of her fashionable gowns and styled her hair. He'd walked into the room and looked like he'd seen a ghost.

"Not only that, you talk all proper now and have to have everything in the house just so-so. I didn't figure you'd want to be here anymore. After what happened, I was afraid all the talk would start up again. I was afraid you'd want to leave. So I got the idea of gettin' you hitched up with Will."

At the mention of the man's name, she rolled her eyes. "Pa, Will only had one thing on his mind. Getting his hands on the Flying C. And he didn't care who he had to hurt to accomplish it."

"Well, he won't be throwin' his weight around here anymore."

"No. Not after today," she agreed.

He sighed and turned his tired looking eyes on her. "I don't know, Angel. Everything's gotten into such a tangle. Do you think we'll ever be able to get it all straightened out again?"

She scooted closer and was surprised when he slipped his arm across her back.

"I think we will, Pa. For the first time, I truly think we will."

He sighed again and closed his hand around her upper arm, coming as close to hugging her as she could ever remember. She laid her head against his shoulder and closed her eyes. He smelled of tobacco and sun-drenched cotton, with an underlying earthiness of honest male sweat. She smiled, filled with a sense of peace. At last—at long, long last—she'd finally come home.

Far too soon Angel felt her father stiffen as he sat up straighter. "Rider comin'," he murmured. He pulled his arm from behind her back and stood.

The harmonious moment dissolved like vapor when she climbed to her feet next to him. Out on the lane, the hoofbeats of a cantering horse broke the stillness. She shaded her eyes. It was the black stallion, Pago, with Rane seated tall and resolute in the saddle.

"Are there any final words you need to say before I talk to this man?"

She dropped her hand and stared at her father, aghast. Had the past thirty minutes never happened? "I told you, Pa. I love him. I have no idea what you've heard, but he's a good, decent man."

He started down the steps. "I'll try to remember that."

Rane walked the big horse the final distance, then halted and sat there, waiting. Somewhere, he'd changed into a fresh shirt and washed the blood from his face. His dark gaze turned in her direction for a mere instant, and she offered a tenuous smile. Then he focused on her father with a familiar wariness in his eyes.

"Climb down and cool your heels," her father said.

Without turning his back, Rane levered his right leg over the cantle and dropped to the ground. He released his reins and stepped forward, until he stood face to face with her father.

Roy stared at him a long moment, as though taking his measure. "Last time I saw you, you looked like you'd been drug through a slaughterhouse behind a rank horse."

Angel pressed a hand to her mouth, heartened to hear a teasing note in his voice.

Rane still looked uncertain of his welcome. "I... What you did in town earlier. I'm beholden." He thrust out his hand.

Slowly, Roy shoved his own hand forward and they

shook. "I can't help wonderin' what possessed you to go into town without your gun."

"That was my fault," she injected. "I made him promise not to wear it anymore."

Roy brows crowded his hairline. "And you listened to her?"

Angel's knees still turned weak when she thought about how close he'd come to dying that day, all because she'd asked him not to wear his gun. She would never make that mistake again.

Confusion flickered in Rane's eyes. "You asked me here for an explanation about what happened in town."

"I *ordered* you here to find out exactly what your intentions are regarding my daughter," Roy amended.

"My intentions."

"Yeah."

Still looking like he expected a fist between the eyes at any second, Rane said, "I had planned to do this differently. But since you ask about my intentions then I'll tell you they are honorable. I want to marry your daughter."

"Why do you want to marry her?" Roy fired back.

"Why," Rane repeated. His brows beetled. He opened his mouth once and then closed it again. He was getting so flustered, Angel hoped her father would take pity on him soon.

"Because I love her," he blurted at last.

Angel's heart welled until it was impossible to stop the tears that spilled from her eyes. Rane was too busy glaring at her father to notice.

"Don't worry," he continued. "I have no plans to snatch her from your home and set her down in the middle of hardship. I'm trying to build a herd. I know it will take some time, but I believe I can bring the Hacienda back and turn it into a profitable operation, like the one you have here. This is what I planned, and I think it will be worth waiting for. I only want the best for Angel. I want to make her happy."

"And you think she will be?" Roy asked. "With you?"

"Yes," Rane replied with conviction.

Angel's heart stampeded. It was now or never. She lifted her hand and called out, "Excuse me."

Both men swiveled on their heels to look at her.

Having the full strength of their combined, undivided attention trained on her threatened to strip her courage. She pulled in a fortifying breath. "I hate to put a hitch in your negotiations, but I don't think this plan is going to work."

Now they both looked puzzled. She ventured to the bottom of the steps. "It's your time frame that concerns me."

"What's wrong with wantin' to get on his feet before marriage?" her father demanded.

Angel only had eyes for Rane. With her heart beating to near bursting, she walked to him and laid her hands against his chest. "I meant to tell you the other day at the Hacienda. If you're going to make an honest woman of me, you need to do it soon."

He lifted his hands and covered the backs of hers, pressing her palms more firmly against his muscled flesh. His heat penetrated, along with the wild staccato beat of his heart pounding in rhythm to her own. "Why, Angel?" he asked softly.

She tried to smile, but the tremor in her lower lip made it impossible. "Because," she said, "in less than six months you're going to be a papa."

****

Rane walked out the door and found Angel standing at the porch railing. On the horizon, the sinking sun flared with otherworldly brilliance across the sky. Instead of watching the sunset, her eyes were closed.

With light steps, he moved in behind her and slid his arms around her waist. Her familiar warmth and softness beckoned him closer. Sighing with pure contentment, he settled his hips against her sweet, rounded bottom.

She relaxed into him and pillowed the back of her head on his chest. "Mmm," she murmured. "I can tell you've missed me."

His hands tightened at her waist, gathering her closer still. It had been too long since he'd touched her. Loved her. The instinct to move upward and cup her full breasts in his hands nearly overpowered him. Instead, he turned his hands downward and splayed his fingers over the barely detectable bulge of her stomach.

A baby. *His* baby. Each time he thought of this miracle he wanted to shout to the heavens.

He nestled his nose into Angel's upswept hair and breathed her, the subtle floral scent that had long haunted his dreams. Was he dreaming still? How had he gotten so lucky?

"Your father is taking it very well," he said.

"He and I had a talk before you got here."

"Is that why you told me..."

The whine of the screen door and a soft gasp halted him in mid-sentence. He turned, taking Angel with him. He didn't dare step from behind the cloak of her skirt just then and risk exposing his aching state of arousal.

Carmella stood with one hand holding to the screened door and a cheesecloth wrapped parcel in the other. A startled expression froze on her face.

Just as quickly, she bit her lip and dropped her gaze to the floor. "*Perdone me, por favor*. I saw Señor Rane leave the house and hoped to catch him before he rides away. I did not mean to interrupt."

"It's all right, Carmella. We were just talking," Angel said.

"Why did you wish to see me?" he asked.

If anything, the question put Carmella even more ill at ease. "I... There was too much pie left from today. I thought you could take some with you when you go." She held up the parcel. "For you...and Benito."

"Ahh. I see." And he did see. Very clearly. The pie was, evidently, a peace offering for her estranged husband. He sucked in his cheek to keep from laughing out loud with satisfaction. "Give it to me, and I'll see that he gets it."

"The pie is for you," she insisted.

"Yes, I know. Me, and Benito."

She nodded. "*Sí*." She crossed the porch and placed the cheesecloth into his outstretched hand. "Be sure to tell him I make it," she added with a twinkle in her eyes.

"I will," he assured her.

Before she left, she stretched up on tiptoe and kissed them both on the cheek. "I am so happy for you," she whispered and her dark eyes danced with the proof of her words.

Quietly, Carmella slipped back inside the house, leaving Rane and Angel to settle into their former spot. The sun had slipped lower and dusk quickly stole over the land, shrouding them in the intimacy of shadows. He feathered a kiss against her ear. "In all my dreams, I never thought I'd stand here on your father's porch and hold you in my arms."

She sighed, a contented sound. "It is rather like a dream, isn't it?"

"And the best part is, we don't have to wake up."

There would be time later to plan, to build, to think back over the incredible events that had led him to this night. For now, he simply needed to feel Angel in his arms, next to his heart. He desired nothing more. For the first time in his life, he felt complete.

Epilogue

Nearly Six Months Later

The old man shoved his foot against the wood burning in the parlor grate, collapsing a teepee of logs. A brilliant shower of orange and blue sparks shot up the chimney. Earlier, Carmella had witnessed him using his boot in place of the poker and lectured him about tracking soot onto the carpet. For all the good it had done.

Roy continued to poke at the fire until he had a roaring blaze going. Then he turned his backside to the inferno and thrust his rear end dangerously close to the flames.

Though the temperature had dipped drastically since sundown, Rane didn't feel the chill. As he had countless times that evening, he paced the length of the parlor and back, then out into the hallway, pausing a moment to stare up the stairwell at the closed door of Angel's old bedroom.

What the hell was taking so long?

Behind him, the front door opened. Benito entered with another armload of firewood, stomping his boots on the threshold to rid them of mud. He looked at Rane and gave an exaggerated shudder inside his wool jacket. "Ees too cold for my thin blood."

"Just close the door and keep your voice down," Rane snapped.

Benito took another step into the entry and nudged the door together with his heel. Despite his impatience, Rane noted Benito's sure strides when he walked into the parlor and dropped the load of wood into the box on the hearth. During the past several weeks, he'd improved so much his limp was barely noticeable.

"Sit down," Roy called. "You're wearin' a rut in the carpet."

"I'm only rubbing in the soot you keep tracking through," Rane retorted. "And if you tell me to sit down one more time, I swear, old man, I'm going to find a gun and shoot you."

The amused look exchanged between Roy and Benito didn't escape Rane. He gritted his teeth and stomped to a window. His own watery reflection stared back at him from the sweating pane.

He turned, his attention snagged by the whiskey bottle standing on the bar. The last time he'd looked, it had been half full. Now, it was nearly empty. Small wonder the old man appeared so calm. He'd consumed enough alcohol to pickle a barrel of beets.

"I should be up there," he said.

"It ain't seemly," Roy replied. "What you need to do is relax. Babies are born everyday."

"Not my baby," Rane reminded him. He couldn't stand the thought of Angel up there laboring. How many hours now? If anything happened to her...

Out in the hall, the big Regulator emitted a loud click and began to chime the hour. Rane counted ten gongs.

The last chime faded into stillness and he heard another sound. A weak mewling howl drifted down from the upper floor. As one, Roy and Benito started for the hallway. Rane shoved past them and took the stairs two at a time to reach the second floor landing. He stared at the closed-up bedroom while on the other side the cry grew steadily louder. Unseemly or not, he raised his fist and pounded on the door.

"*Uno momento*!" Carmella demanded. She sounded out of breath.

Roy gained the landing with Benito only a step behind him.

The cry continued unabated. And then, suddenly, it stopped. Rane's heart nearly stopped as well.

Several more agonizing minutes passed before the door opened and Carmella appeared with a smile on her face.

"How's Angel?"

"How's the baby?"

"Is it a boy or a girl?"

Carmella held up her hands to halt the barrage of

questions. "I'm not telling. You have to go in and see for yourself." She threw Rane a pointed look. "*Papá* first."

Rane eased the door wider and paused on the threshold. Heat smacked him in the face, along with a raw, earthy smell he couldn't identify. A bucket of soiled, bloody linens sat on the floor just inside the door.

Angel lay in the center of the bed with her arm curved protectively around the bundle lying next to her. Beneath the covers, her stomach had lost the bulging roundness he'd grown accustomed to and appeared almost flat. Her damp hair was as limp as tangled ropes against the pillows. Purple shadows of exhaustion smudged the soft skin beneath her eyes.

"Don't just stand there," she said. "Come see your daughter." Her voice sounded weak and drowsy.

"It's a girl!" Roy exclaimed joyfully from the doorway.

A daughter. Rane's chest expanded with pride. Unlike most men, he hadn't wished for a son as his firstborn. He'd wanted a daughter. A healthy, happy, beautiful little girl with her mother's spirit. Even in this, Angel had given him his heart's desire.

Moving with care, he perched on the edge of the bed and felt for Angel's hand among the tangled covers. When he found it, she held onto him and he returned her gentle pressure.

"Aren't you going to say anything?" Angel asked. The gorgeous, rumpled man sitting on the edge of her bed—the same man who'd faced death more times than she could count—actually looked frightened. She pulled her hand from his and lifted fingertips to his dear face. "I'm all right, Rane. And the baby's fine. Take a look."

She watched in awe while he leaned over and peeled back a corner of the blanket and revealed the precious bundle beside her.

"Her hair is dark," he said.

"Just like yours," she told him.

He touched a fingertip to the cap of damp curls and sucked in a breath. The baby's face reddened and her tiny, translucent lips puckered into an O. His face alight with wonder, he traced down and stroked a velvety cheek. His smile slowly grew. More confident, he slipped a hand beneath her tiny body and lifted her.

Roy crowded the other side of the bed and craned his neck to get a peek at his granddaughter. "She sure is a beauty."

"Yes," Rane concurred. "Just like her mother."

"A little angel," Roy added.

"Oh, Pa, don't start calling her that," Angel scolded. "You'll jinx her."

"Well, what am I supposed to call her? Have you decided on a name?"

Rane brows lifted expectantly. His gaze slid to hers, silently questioning.

"Go ahead and tell him," she said.

He carried the baby the rest of the way to his broad chest and cradled her with such tenderness Angel's breath hitched. "We're going to call her Ilsa Maria," he announced in a strong voice.

Her father nodded and Angel would have sworn she saw tears gather in his gray eyes. "I'm sure both your mamas would be proud of that."

Still standing in the doorway, Carmella nudged Benito farther into the room. Soon, they all had gathered around to marvel and touch a doll-like finger or tiny toe.

Smiling faces blurred before Angel's drowsy eyes. Their hushed voices blended to a soothing hum that surrounded her like a warm blanket of security. She smothered a yawn. "Rane?"

She blinked and found him hovering above her.

"Yes, my love. I'm right here," whispered the voice of her husband, her love. Her life. "Always."

Always. The sweetest promise this side of Heaven, and he'd shown her many times over that he was a man of his word.

A word about the author...

From my earliest memories, I've been fascinated with all things western. My first cases of hero worship were aimed at Audie Murphy and John Wayne, and I never did get past them. As a young woman, I traveled much of the southwest and saw the breathtaking vistas that had inspired such awe in the old western movies from my childhood. Though Texas claimed me for several years, I now live in the picturesque foothills of the Appalachian Mountains with my husband and two children. My passion for the west and those dashing sagebrush heroes remains as strong as ever. I write about those characters and their times because I can't imagine doing anything else. I hope you enjoy reading about my heroes and heroines of the old west as much as I loved writing about them.

Contact Devon at devon@devonmatthews.com

Visit Devon's website at www.devonmatthews.com

Printed in the United States
101673LV00001B/9/A

9 781601 540454